Y0-ABH-733

love
is
war

love is war

George
Stade

is

war

Turtle Point Press

NEW YORK

ISBN 1-885586-47-7
LCCN 2005926846

Cover design by Jeff Clark and
interior design and composition by Tag Savage
at Wilsted & Taylor Publishing Services

Printed in Canada

love
is
war

one

Quod superium, sicut inferius.
[HERMES TRISMEGISTUS] ❡ *Hair on the rims of the ears is an
exclusively male trait.* [CAROL ANN RINZLER, Why Eve Doesn't
Have an Adam's Apple] ❡ *Males not hereditarily equipped
to combat with other males have been excluded from sex,
and their traits have thus been discarded by natural selection.*
[ROBERT WRIGHT, The Moral Animal: Why We Are the Way We Are:
The New Science of Evolutionary Psychology] ❡ *Anyone who sees
humans as animals, driven by sexual and other coarse
impulses, can't be all bad.* [ROBERT WRIGHT, The Moral
Animal: Why We Are the Way We Are: The New
Science of Evolutionary Psychology]

WE MIGHT AS WELL BEGIN with Charles Craig Lockhart's walk to work. He walked fast, did our Chuck, in
part because his legs were long, but also because there was
a chronic impatience about the man, as though if he didn't get moving he would miss out on something. In fact, as you might expect, he
often missed out on the bounty of the present moment in his hurry
toward the next.

I can see him now, striding west toward Broadway along the
south side of 110th Street, his sports jacket billowing out behind
him. There was a bounce to his step, as if he were keeping time to
Red Mitchell's bass solo on "Blues Going Up." The curve of his bil-

1

lowing jacket was congruent to the curve of his back. Chuck Lockhart, you see, leaned forward a bit, especially when he was moving. He leaned forward because of the way he drew in his already concave belly: the drawing in of his belly also resulted in a compensatory tuck forward of his pelvis, so that there was a single unbroken curve from his first cervical vertebra, called "the Atlas," to his coccyx. Another unbroken curve crossed his back from armpit to armpit, for Lockhart had long ago discovered, while trying on a dark olive Harris tweed sports jacket (to go with his new black shirt, present from a pair of satirical coeds), before a triptych of mirrors in Brooks Brothers, that a small rounding inward of his shoulders showed off his stingray *latissimus dorsi* to their best advantage. Stepping back a little, I see Lockhart as a man walking into a stiffish wind that no one else can feel.

A psychosomatics of human posture, man—that's what we need. How a man stands, the way a woman walks, says something, don't ask me what. Chuck Lockhart's hips were abnormally narrow, his butt unnaturally flat, an egregious flaw that the fool emphasized by wearing surplus officer's pants (which come without back pockets). Just the same, the front or back view was undeniably impressive, the view from either side less so, for if Lockhart was wide, he was not deep.

There he goes, nimble and limber for a fifty-year-old, his eyes darting this way and that, hyperaware of his relations to everything around him, as though he were on patrol in territory held by an enemy notorious for booby traps. He crossed 110th Street against the light, for he had more faith in his ability to dodge cars than in the willingness of New York drivers to stop at the red. He hopped onto the sidewalk giving the finger to a honking muscle car that drove by close enough to have sliced a washer off his butt had there been more of it.

He juked his way uptown through heavy pedestrian traffic, sidestepping at the last minute a frozen-faced battle-ax who was not going to change her course for *him*, zigzagged between a pair of oldsters with canes, did an end run around three immense women walking slow side by side but talking fast ("I tole him, I said, you stay home tonight or you stay away for good"), swivel-hipped through a gang of construction workers with tools that could kill you hanging from their work belts, slip-slid past students in short pants, past dog walkers, past sheepish smokers in doorways, past two cops who for some reason stared at him, past faculty wives out for a cappuccino and croissant, all the while studying the faces of women he passed in search of kissable lips, not that he expected to kiss anyone, but he did like to look, for Lockhart thought of himself as sexually deprived. He caught up to a pair of students, her left hand on his right shoulder, his right hand in the right rear pocket of her cut-off jeans: this ordinary tableau broke Lockhart's rhythm, flattened his bounce, extracted a sigh.

Lockhart pulled up before one of those conveyer affairs, you know, the kind that looks like a horizontal ladder with rollers instead of rungs. One end of it disappeared into the dark and cavernous maw of a parked truck. The other end was supported on legs a yard or so from the ope'd and ponderous jaws of a cellar. A man would appear in the dark bay of the truck and throw a carton of, say, canned artichokes onto the conveyer; at the other end another man would catch the carton and throw it down a slide that carried it into the darkness of the cellar under Poppa's Minimart. Timing themselves so as not to collide with cartons of, say, Erivan Acidophilus Yoghurt, pedestrians were walking single file through the gap between the conveyer and the cellar. On the other side of the gap, Lockhart bent over to see if he could see what was the fate of the cartons.

Did they simply crash into the cellar floor, thus jeopardizing the goods preserved in jars rather than cans? Did a third man catch them so that he could stack them neatly, the goods that were to be sold first placed closest to the dumbwaiter? Did the cartons whiz off the slide and onto another conveyer that carried them past stations and curves and switches, over bridges, through tunnels, and onto sidings at the farthest recesses of the cellar? Lockhart was never to know, for as soon as he had bent over to look, sticking his can out, someone bumped into it, not gently either.

Lockhart whirled around, waxing wroth. Moving away from him was a man about his own height, a blond ponytail hanging out from under his cap and onto a navy blue jacket too heavy for early September. On his feet were sandals, an offense that further infuriated Lockhart. The man, without breaking his stride, turned and threw a smile toward Lockhart, but whether it was a smile of apology, or derision, or of an absurd and existential delight in the unearned gift of life Lockhart could not tell. This man looked like a burlier and plumper Jon Voigt, a face Lockhart hated, for the butcher's son, Henny Kramer, over there on 85th and Lex, who was three years older, used to kick the shit out of little Chuckie Lockhart regularly and for no reason but an absurd and gratuitous dislike.

Lockhart took a step after him—to do what, he couldn't have said. He was restrained not by his usual circumspection, but by a big hand around his bicep.

"Easy now, Professor, you're a man of words, not deeds," said the voice of Core or Corrie, short for "Hardcore," a panhandler with whom Lockhart sometimes shot the breeze. "Besides, he's got to have, what? thirty pounds on you."

"I've got this theory that every time you swallow someone else's shit, you shorten your life," said Lockhart.

"If that's so, no black man get by his fifteenth birthday," said Core.

"I've missed your guidance," said Lockhart. "Where've you been?"

"The judge say 'Pay the fine or do the time,' and where am I gonna get two hundred dollars?" said Core.

"What was the crime?" Lockhart said.

"I did 'wrongfully urinate against a public building,'" he said. "One way or another, it's always my dick gets me in trouble. By the way, you don't happen—"

But Lockhart was already pulling out his folding money. He

placed two dollars in Core's outstretched hand, not because he was rich, for he was not, and not because he was openhanded, though he was, but because he liked to be liked, even by panhandlers.

He brushed by Core, who in effect stood guard over the entrance to the building behind him, Gwinnett Hall, a dormitory at the southwest corner of the campus. If you looked like the kind of person who would tip, Core would open the door for you. But Lockhart got there first, walked decisively into the foyer, walked down two flights of steps to the sub-basement, strode across the landing to a steel door, flung it open, and stepped boldly into the labyrinth of tunnels, storage areas, and power centers that sustained the visible university aboveground. For some reason, even on a nice day, Lockhart liked to walk to his office, over two blocks away, through this underworld —the guts of the university, he liked to pretend, or better yet, its subconscious. For one thing, down there he felt a connection to powers that other people would not acknowledge, the beasts in our basements. The ambience encouraged in him fantasies of violent subversion.

Energy and information pulsed through cables that writhed on the ceiling or clung to walls; cooling air gusted through the old galvanized ducts and the newer plastic; water coursed through dripping pipes; thicker pipes evacuated sewage. Some of the passageways, the oldest of them, were of brick, the ceilings arched; others were of rough plaster hairy with dust; still others, the newest, were of gray cement block. There were indeed graffiti, not much of it, more on the cement block, some of it (on the brick) over a hundred years old, most of it, in Lockhart's opinion (and he was a connoisseur) of a decidedly superior quality. He nodded at a favorite— OEDIPUS WAS A MOTHERFUCKER—for his own sense of humor had its undergraduate side. Beat and bounce were returning to his gait, no matter that one passageway might end in two or three steps down and another might end in three or four steps up, in neither case for any discernible reason. In this dim light, a man less alert to his surroundings could wind up with a busted head.

5

He did not shorten his stride through this dark stretch of brick tunnel, three overhead bulbs in a row burned out behind their wire cages. But whoa, something he saw in the fading flicker of the next bulb, a new graffito, brought him up short:

THE JEWS
KILLED JESUS

It could put you in a mood, dammit—not that Lockhart had any feeling for or against the Jews in general. What got to him about other people were their personal or human dimensions, not the historical or social or national or local dimensions, all accidental in Lockhart's eyes, and tedious to boot. As for himself, he preferred to believe that he was the product of his own choices, on the one hand, and of millions of years of evolution, on the other, rather than of two hundred years of capitalism. No, Lockhart was miffed because he did not like to see this subterranean space (over which he thought of himself as presiding like some Hermes Psychopompos) contaminated by politics or religion. The psychopathy he could live with so long as it was sexual. He slipped out of his shirt pocket the marker pen he carried for just such occasions, and under the offending words wrote this:

YEAH, BUT WHAT HAVE THEY
ACCOMPLISHED SINCE THEN?

Energized by this small feat of naughtiness, by this concession to his browbeaten Imp, by—and it's time to get just a little bit scientific here—a saving in the expenditure of psychic energy needed to maintain repression, Lockhart burst through another steel door into the sub-basement of Hancock Hall and ran up the six flights to his office. On the bench outside his office was a woman whose face would have taken his breath away, if he had had any left. Sitting there, face down, reading, showing only the right side of her face, she looked (as poor Willie Yeats said about one of the women he

6

mooned over) like a profile of Demeter on an old Greek coin. He pulled his eyes away from her, opened the door to his office, strode in, turned on the air conditioner, for he could feel sweat trickle over his sternum, and collapsed into his swivelly desk chair, as though he had already done a day's work.

two

Nothing captures our attention like a human face, and nothing rivals the face in communicative power. [NANCY ETCOFF, Survival of the Prettiest: The Science of Beauty] ❡ *Whosoever looketh on a woman to lust after her hath committed adultery with her already in his heart.* [ST. MATTHEW] ❡ *In the somatosensory cortex, the part of the brain linked to the genital area is larger than any other.* [DEAN HAMER AND PETER COPELAND, Living with Our Genes: Why They Matter More Than You Think] ❡ *The sexual principle lies at the heart of all behavior as well as history.* [W. B. YEATS]

PROFESSOR LOCKHART?" said a voice that goosed him out of his reverie and made him drop the book he was pretending to read. A face topped with curly red hair, and there was something . . . looked in at him from around the doorway. What was this anyhow—a refugee from Mardi Gras, a shaman, a half-painted woman, a burn victim? He could see now that it was the woman with the profile, but the two sides of her face would not align. And then he saw that the left side of her face was decorated with a delicate pink birthmark, the color, say, of a blonde's areolae.

"Could you spare me a minute?" she said, stepping into the office before Lockhart could say a word. The birthmark was shaped something like Africa—Somalia near the wing of her nose, Senegal near

8

the delicate tragus of her ear, the Cape of Good Hope near the corner of her very kissable mouth.

"I don't want to be a bother," she said, "but I've been sitting out there trying to jump-start my courage." Her shoulders were broad and full under the white tee shirt, on which, Lockhart was glad to see, there was no logo or slogan.

"I need to ask you a favor," she said. From the small expanse of thigh revealed by her shorty overalls, Lockhart was confident that there was no cottage cheese farther up.

"Spit it out," he said. Just the same, thought Lockhart as she sat down, there was something unformed, immature, about her legs, as though they were younger than the rest of her, thirteen-year-old legs under a . . . well, let's say thirty-year-old torso and face.

"Can you let me into your Yeats seminar?" she said.

"I've already admitted seventeen, two too many," he said.

"Are any of these too, too many, poets?" she said.

"They are graduate students," he said, "and therefore undergoing an immunization to the poetry in poems."

"The poetry in poems," she said, "that's my bag." She smiled brilliantly, but crookedly: the birthmarked side of her face, so it appeared, was less mobile. The mark, as Lockhart now saw it, seemed not so much in her skin as under it, faintly showing through. As the smile faded, her lip snagged on the eyetooth on the left side of her face, which, unlike the eyetooth on the right side of her face, was prominent.

He passed her the book he had been pretending to read, still open to the page he had been pretending to read, his finger by a poem entitled "The Lover Mourns for the Loss of Love," and said, "Ever read it?"

"No," she said.

"I can't say I've spent much time on it myself," he said. "There's not much there."

"Well, there's—" she said.

9

"Go ahead, read it aloud," he said. "Read it as though you had written it."

Here's what she read, and you'll have to take my word for it—the woman had an impeccable sense of rhythm:

> Pale brows, still hands and dim hair,
> I had a beautiful friend
> And dreamed that the old despair
> Would end in love in the end:
> She looked in my heart one day
> And saw your image was there;
> She has gone weeping away.

"All right!" he said: "now what do you see as the poetry in that poem?"

"Well, let's see," she said. "One, two . . . seven lines, rhyming, yes, ABABCAC. The first four lines make up a quatrain, the ur-stanza. The next three lines . . . well, you could say they are a frustrated quatrain, completion denied."

"That's a good one," he said.

"Yes, the first four lines arouse an expectation that the last three won't satisfy—and unsatisfied desire is what the poem is about."

"Very ingenious," he said.

"You notice, I suppose, that there are seven syllables in each line, so that each line replicates the whole?" she said.

"What's that you say?" he said. He rose out of his chair and circled the desk to her side of it so that he could look over her shoulder, observing along the way how the strap of her overalls cut into her trapezius. "That has to take some doing—and how many readers would bother to count?"

"It's what poets do," she said.

"All right," he said. "You're in; you can sign up for the course."

"I just noticed," she said: "each line is striving for four beats, but falls a syllable short," she said, "as the whole poem falls a line short, another aroused desire denied."

"Enough," he said.

"And every other line ends in an anapest," she said, "except for the eighth, which is withheld, a ghost that is there and not there, like the image in the poet's heart."

"Ye gods!" he said.

"What I particularly like," she said, "is that the middle line looks both ways: 'end in love in the end' is practically a palindrome, with love in the middle of the middle."

"In the end, for poor Willie, love ends in despair or hate and murder," he said. "Has he got it right?"

"If the lover's a woman, you would have to add suicide," she said. "Think of Dido, Anna Karenina, Emma Bovary."

"I've been coming to the conclusion that lust is the reality," he said, "that love is a mere epiphenomenon."

"You mean like consciousness?" she said. "You believe in that, don't you?"

Damn the woman. He stood up. "Well, it will be useful to have a formalist in the class."

"I think maybe what I am is a moralist about form," she said.

"I've spent so much time figuring out what poems say that I've neglected how they say it," he said.

"How can you tell the dancer from the dance?" she said, walking out, getting the last word. Her shorty overalls were too loose for Lockhart to tell whether or not she had a nice ass.

three

Scratch a lover and find a foe. [DOROTHY PARKER] ❡ *I have never known love but as a kiss / In the mid-battle, and a difficult truce / Of oil and water, candles and dark night, / Hillside and hollow, the hot-footed sun / And the cold, sliding, slippery-footed moon— / A brief forgiveness between opposites / That have been hatreds...* [W. B. YEATS] ❡ *The degree and kind of a person's sexuality penetrates every corner of his being.* [NIETZSCHE] ❡ *The gradual synonymy of sex and sin in Christendom is surely based on the fact that sex often leads to trouble rather than that there is anything inherently sinful about sex.* [MATT RIDLEY, The Red Queen: Sex and the Evolution of Human Nature]

LOCKHART ALSO SPENT PSYCHIC ENERGY to suppress his craving for cigarettes. Kicking his two-pack-a-day habit this past summer made him wonder if he didn't have some willpower after all. In his own eyes it was the most difficult thing he had ever done (except for living with his wife). There was this shrink used to brag how through hypnosis he had transferred the tremor in a trumpet player's lip to his big toe, thus saving this bebopper's career. Well, Lockhart transferred his addiction from cigarettes to coffee. So he took up his tall stainless insulated cup, made by Nissan, man, and carried it into the departmental office, for the secretary who made coffee made coffee as Lockhart liked it: strong to begin with and harshened up with espresso, almost as good as a Pall Mall.

In general, Lockhart entered an occupied room as a secret agent enters enemy headquarters: there was this fear of exposure—but exposure of what is not so clear. It may be that he suspected, not quite consciously, that people could read his thoughts in his posture, gestures, and expressions—for Lockhart, you see, the body is a signifier. It is sure that he feared and in part hoped that to other people his thoughts and, even more, his fantasies would seem monstrous. Then there was his secret disdain: the sad fact is that Lockhart was an undeclared body snob, another kind of moralist about form, let's say. With a few exceptions he looked down on people with fat or otherwise unshaped bodies, to whom he was therefore especially considerate, kindly. Such was his peculiar psychology. In the nook—a converted closet, actually—that served as the department's kitchenette was one of those exceptions, his colleague Tony Felder, who was plump and rumpled, his hair dandruffy.

From the looks on their faces, Felder had been teasing Simone Song, the secretary who made coffee the way Lockhart liked it. They turned to him with their different smiles, which grew.

"Is it yourself?" said Felder, the Irishism an allusion to Lockhart's interest in the literature of the bloody old Emerald Isle.

"Tony," said Lockhart.

"Hi, Chuckie," said Simone Song a touch satirically, for normally, in front of other people, at least, she called him "Professor Lockhart." Suddenly, she gave him a hug. Like Lockhart, she was flat and hard. Like him, she was compulsive about working out. Let her miss one day and she became impossible, better watch your step. But right now there was a sweet little blush on her tan Korean face. "Coffee's just about ready."

"I was telling Simone here we ought to rebound into each other's arms," said Felder. "Men with a little flesh on them are a comfort on cold nights."

"It's eighty-five degrees out there," said Ms. Song.

"Rebound from what?" said Lockhart.

"Being dumped," said Felder.

Then Lockhart, who knew nothing about music but knew he liked the blues and in any case had to discharge whatever it was that had built up inside him during his interview with the redhead, without warning sang this:

> If autumn comes, can cold be far behind? (Woo, ooo)
> If autumn comes, can cold be far behind?
> My baby dumped me,
> Gave me frostbite of the mind (oh woe).

"Brain fever is more common," said Felder.

Then Simone Song, who was at ease with these two as with no one else, sang this:

> If Felder comes, can a line be far behind?
> If Lockhart comes, can the blues be far behind?
> If Simone Song sings,
> You know her lover's not kind (never mind).

"I have long believed that you two should be singing duets, birds of a feather," said Felder.

"You forget that Professor Lockhart is a married man," said Song.

"Henpecked to boot," said Felder. "Or is it pussy-whipped you are?—the preferable condition, if you think about it." This Felder character married young, soon discovered that, though he liked his wife, he disliked marriage, divorced. Now, though neither young, nor handsome, nor rich, nor stylish, nor (as he admits) an artful lover, nor a feminist, he always seems to be dating some well-turned-out young thing, a publisher, or editor, or writer, or agent, or flack. He was neither ostentatious nor secretive about his many amours. Lockhart often wondered what Felder had that he himself so sadly lacked. He also wondered about the perpetual air of melancholy that hung over the man.

14

Lockhart also very much admired the book Felder was writing. This book argued that literature was an adaptation, in the biologist's sense. No known human society was without a "literature," even if it amounted to no more than sayings, tall tales, war chants, and etiological myths. That made literature a species-specific behavioral trait. Literature, in short, so the bulk of the book argued in detail, was equipment for living, like opposable thumbs, which allow us to grasp things, and rounded buttocks, which keep us upright.

"Maybe Chuck's just principled," said good old Simone, pouring Chuck's cup full.

Or chickenshit, thought Lockhart, like Simone herself—with this difference: whereas Simone was afraid of sex, Lockhart was afraid of women. "Thanks," he said, meaning for the coffee and for coming to his defense.

"God save it's not principled he is," said Felder, "or I'd have to drop him like a hot potato," and he accepted coffee from Song with a nod.

"Is that how Karen dropped you?" said Lockhart.

"She had the choice of staying in New York and getting downsized or transferring to Austin and getting promoted."

"Did you ever think of going with her?" said Song.

"No," said Felder.

"But you would have expected her to go with you?" said Song.

"The world believes that you love 'em and leave 'em," said Lockhart to Felder.

"Gross calumny," said Felder. "What happens is that after a while my lady friends discover that I don't have what they need."

"What's that?" said Song.

"I haven't a clue," said Felder.

"He asked me out to dinner," said Song with a nod toward Felder. "Should I go?"

"Yes," said Lockhart.

"No," said a voice from the doorway, which none of them had been facing. "Don't you dare!" Oh God, it was Betty Blondell, pro-

15

fessor of medieval literature. She aimed her steel-blue eyes at Lockhart and said, "We know what Tony is. But that doesn't mean you have to pimp for him."

This Betty Blondell was a pisser, man. She was prurient and she was puritanical. She saw sex everywhere and she didn't like what she saw.

"What am I, then?" said Felder.

"You're a sinner, is what you are," said Blondell. Then she looked at Lockhart: "Go ahead, laugh."

"Whatever was it that connected sin to sexuality?" said Lockhart. "If you stand back a little, the connection is by no means self-evident."

"Classical civilization's failure of nerve," said Felder. "The Christians prohibited sexual pleasure because the flashy empires around them revered it, just as the Jews who spawned them made pork taboo because everyone around them loved spare ribs. It's how pipsqueaks assert themselves, right up to martyrdom."

"God made the connection," said Blondell. She picked a piece of lint off Lockhart's jacket. She was always doing things like that, straightening your tie, brushing dandruff off your shoulder, taking out a hanky, wetting it with the tip of her tongue, wiping a smudge off your cheek. I'll say this, though: her tongue was very clean.

"I've got to get back to work," said Song.

"Yes," said Felder, "God is the all-time leading conversation stopper."

"But *why* did he make the connection?" said Lockhart.

"I don't presume to know God's motives," said Blondell. And turning, she said this (with some vehemence) to Tony Felder's back, for he was following Simone Song out the door; "and Christians aren't the only ones who make the connection. It's universal."

"Fewer and fewer people make the connection, Betty," said Lockhart. "That's why you believers are so uptight. Ever listen to talk radio?"

16

"Look around you at the people we both know," she said. "What is the biggest single cause of their unhappiness?"

"Thwarted vanity," he said.

"It's sex," she said, "and you know it."

"It's an insufficiency of sex, if anything," he said, "or of the right kind," and he gently put his hand on her back and brought her with him as they walked out the door, side by side. As the two of them moved out of earshot, you could hear Blondell saying, "But he's twenty years older. It's practically pedophilia."

four

… men's preferences in a mate remain entirely mysterious. [DAVID M. BUSS, The Evolution of Desire: Strategies of Human Mating] ❡ *… among all peoples sexual intercourse is understood to be a service or favor that females render males.* [DONALD SYMONS, The Evolution of Human Sexuality] ❡ *No woman needs intercourse; few women escape it.* [ANDREA DWORKIN] ❡ *For once you must try not / to shirk the facts: / Man is kept alive / by bestial acts.* [BERTOLT BRECHT]

YOU MAY NOT BELIEVE IT, but those few damp squibs of conversation lit Lockhart's fire. He sat down at his desk and began to write. He began to write an article on love among the modernists that he had long ago proposed to *Procrustes Review.* He had proposed the article to *Procrustes Review* rather than to, say, the *Francophile Review* or *Rictus,* because it retained an old-fashioned interest in the modernists. The article was overdue because Lockhart was a procrastinator. Here is what he wrote:

> The first generation of literary modernists, those giants on whose shoulders we stand (the better to dump on them), were doubtful, even scornful, about romantic love. Their reasons were various, of course, sometimes merely sour grapes, but in the main they were out to smash the icons of their immediate predecessors. The most solemn of these icons was love, the last resort "of the last century, the eunuch century, the century of the mealy-mouthed lie, the century that tried to de-

18

stroy humanity, the nineteenth century," in the words of that moderate man D. H. Lawrence. In the classics of high modernist literature, love has become a swindle, the rhetorical glue holding all the received hypocrisies together, puritanism's other face, or backside, the ideological bustle standing between us and the real thing, the rallying cry of frontmen for a creeping, weeping Jesus.

Yes, yes, I know. But you have to cut the man some slack. Lockhart's wiseass style was a screen behind which he hid his diffidence. It was his substitute for that note of sincerity within reach only of people who deceive themselves entirely. Lockhart, however, knew that he did not know whether he believed what he wrote. Without the wiseassisms he could not have written criticism at all. As it is, that paltry little paragraph cost him three hours of exacting labor. When he came out of his writerly fugue, his untrusty Timex told him it was one o'clock, an hour past the time at which he normally began his weekday workouts. He hurried through the tunnels to the university gym, on the way passing Hardcore, who was taking a siesta in one of those alcoves, the original function of which is unknowable.

There he was, legs spread, knees locked, palms flat on the floor, warming up, when a voice, a female voice, from behind him said, "There you are." Lockhart did not pause to wonder what woman would recognize him from behind, bent over like that: he straightened up and turned around. It was the tall redhead with the profile (and birthmark). She was wearing a heavy black sweatshirt, black tights, and over them loose, gray sweatshorts. What was the woman hiding?

"I need your signature on this form from the School of the Arts or they won't give me credit for your course," she said.

"School of the Arts?" he said.

"I'm in the writing program," she said.

"Where's the form?" he said.

"In my locker," she said.

"Do you want to get it now or after we work out?" he said.

"After," she said.

"Are you a runner or a lifter?" he said.

"Both," she said.

"Then let's boogie," he said, guiding her by the elbow to the track.

So they ran three miles together and lifted free weights together and took their saunas separately and, at Lockhart's invitation, had a late lunch together and, at her suggestion, had a second beer after lunch and, at his urging, had a third beer and he signed her form and they talked about poetry and talked about Yeats in love and laughed and talked some more until the corset of anxiety Lockhart wore around his chest fell away and he felt able to leap tall buildings at a single bound, for there is nothing, not anything, equal to the sympathetic attentions of a congenial woman for making a normal man feel that the world is his oyster. Claire McCoy was her name, and she had a husband, about whom, her tone implied, the less said, the better.

They were sitting in the bar of the Other End, in the smoking section, that is, though neither of them smoked anymore. But when Tony Felder and two pals, all three members of the Smokers' Club, professors of English who still smoked in defiance of something or another, arrived for their late afternoon liquid offerings to Pentheus, the tutelary spirit of academe, then Lockhart knew it was time to go home, for his wife would be waiting, and his wife was not someone you kept waiting with impunity.

"You're late" is how Jane Lockhart greeted her husband.

"Tony Felder and them were having a few to welcome each other back," he said, for he had a superstitious fear of telling her an outright lie.

"Your breath reeks of beer," she said.

"I'll go brush my teeth," he said.

"It never occurred to you that I might like to be welcomed back, too?" she said.

"Come on, Jane, you impressed on me this morning how busy you'd be all day," he said.

It was not that Jane had a job or spent much time keeping house (she had a cleaning woman, named Bettina, who did the heavy stuff) —it was that at age fifty-one she was a student again. She had already dropped out of the school of journalism because the ambience was mendacious; she had dropped out of law school because the other students were litigious; she had dropped out of business school because the whole scene was avaricious; and she gave up her job at a high-toned private school because the spoiled brats were know-it-alls. As for her goat farm in the Catskills, the does produced enough milk to make enough cheese to sell for enough money to pay her factotum, but the bucks, which dropped from the placental paradise into this vale as frequently as the does, and which tenderhearted Jane would not slaughter or sell for meat, ate her into bankruptcy. These ventures, among others, such as her dog-grooming salon and her line of hand-painted neckties, had left the Lockharts without any savings whatsoever. Jane was now taking courses at the School of Social Work. Her goal was to counsel battered wives or unwed mothers, maybe both, although faintly, as at a distance, she was beginning to hear herself on talk radio giving advice, telling callers how to straighten up and fly right.

"I hope you didn't expect me to have dinner waiting for you," she said.

"I guess not," he said; "I'll throw something together," for Lockhart would rather slam pots and pans around than talk to his wife. He poured her half a glass of red wine—red, because Jane had switched when she heard (from an anchorperson) that red wine prevented myasthenia gravis; half a glass because alcohol did not make Jane verbose or morose or grandiose, not jocose or lachrymose, not even, alas, comatose, but bellicose.

Let's see, yes, there were chicken breasts in the freezer, for Jane eschewed red meat. Lockhart dropped them into hot water right out of the faucet, to thaw. There were (canned) onions and a single potato, but a big one; there was the hot curry powder he had bought himself. That's all he needed. And as luck would have it, there was a half box of rice, for Jane was on a high-carbohydrate diet. She had never liked vegetables, anyhow, nor fruit either. Poultry and fish she could take or leave. So she fed mainly on potatoes, pasta, rice, and bread (and cake when no one was looking), for Jane belonged to the school that held you could lose weight by eating something rather than by not eating it. A look at her neck, shoulders, arms, and chest, which were scrawny, could make you wonder why she wanted to lose weight. But her belly had the size, shape, and hardness of a ripe watermelon. That and her hunched-over posture and her long chin made for an interesting silhouette, very wasp-like.

During supper, Jane, instead of engaging in conversation, which is said to aid digestion, turned over the pages of a book large enough to serve as a tombstone, her lips pursed. Jane had a small mouth, but a widening face from the cheekbones down, so that there were large expanses of pale flesh from the corners of her mouth to the corners of her jaw.

"Interesting?" said Lockhart, for whom silence implied negation, smacked of the void, sensitive soul that he was.

"It better be," Jane said. "It cost eighty bucks." She stood it on end so that Lockhart could see the title: *Social Subjects: An Introduction to Social Psychology.* "It's all about the social construction of the self."

"Bah," he said.

"You could encourage me for once," she said, "instead of always belittling whatever I do."

Lockhart could not remember ever openly disparaging any of Jane's projects; but he knew that in the unlit corridors of his mind he had come to disdain all of them. Therefore he was contrite. "Maybe you'll be able to tell me who jerry-built this ramshackle self I occupy."

"You worry too much about your precious self," she said, "that's what made it ramshackle."

No doubt about it: every now and then Jane scored big. Lockhart carried the dirty dishes to the sink, put a flame under this morning's coffee for himself, put water on for Jane's tea (she did have one cup of coffee, with a cigarette, first thing every morning, to activate peristalsis, for Jane's physical being was sluggish), and, as he walked to the refrigerator, looked down at the irregular part through Jane's dusty-black hair, which part, for some reason, tugged at his heart.

He put his hands on her shoulders, kissed a crook in her part, spoke in her ear, and in a low, husky, and he hoped sexy tone said, "Suppose I clean up and we fall into bed together for some, uh . . . marital bliss? I'll bring a nice glass of Kahlua," icky stuff and not much of a disinhibitor, but Jane liked it.

This request for sex, for that is what it was, brought to Jane, as it always did, a certain confusion. On the one hand, her mother had brought her up to believe that it is the wife's duty to give the old man a touch of honey now and then. On the other hand, her father, former pastor of a sect he had invented way up there in northern New York, had taught her to believe that sex is dirty (although he did not himself abstain). On the third hand, for in this story three hands are possible, a browse through her husband's books on evolutionary anthropology—books recommended by Tony Felder —had introduced her to the idea that sex was invented by genes to perpetuate themselves, but she was past the age of passing on genes, which happy fact made sex (for her) supererogatory. Her own feelings, were she to consult them, would tell her that sex, if not dirty, was messy and a bother, her practice of faking orgasm subtly demoralizing.

She pressed her cheek up against his lips prettily. "How about tomorrow?" she said. "I had planned to get the basic concepts under my belt before bedtime," and she tapped her finger on *Social Subjects*, Lockhart censoring the thought that she had too much under her belt already. Aside from everything else, Jane was not good at handling sudden changes of plans, whereas Lockhart relished them, perhaps because he seldom had anything planned that he expected to be fun. And in any case, experience had led him to believe that tomorrow never comes.

So it was that Jane spent the evening leafing through the pages of *Social Subjects*, sipping wine, rehearsing the phrases she would use to fix the broken lives of her future clients. And Lockhart spent the evening reading *Loveguage: The Coevolution of Language and Sex*, sipping bourbon, the set on (to *Court TV*) for company. Later on, lying next to a twitchy Jane, he put himself to sleep with a fantasy of civilization at an end, New York City in ruins, himself prowling through it, a solitary predator, everything permitted.

five

... kissing—a biological mystery if there ever was one—functions as a kind of genetic test. [DEBORAH BLUM, Sex on the Brain: The Biological Differences between Men and Women] ❧ *Stolen waters are sweet, and bread eaten in secret is pleasant.* [PROVERBS] ❧ *Behind every successful man is a woman. Behind her is his wife.* [GROUCHO MARX]

TWO OR THREE TIMES A WEEK Claire McCoy joined Chuck Lockhart for his midday run. It turned out that they were both comfortable doing three miles in twenty-one minutes. They both sweat copiously ("Sweat is good," said McCoy). One of Lockhart's crackpot ideas had it that anxious types sweat a lot, whereas depressed types become spiritually damp, whatever that means. After the run, on days when neither had an early-afternoon class, they would meet in Lockhart's office for lunch. If he knew there would be something worth eating for supper (because he had shopped for it, because he would cook it), he ate a light lunch: an apple, an egg roll, a fried chicken leg. On days when Jane was scheduled to cook, he ate a large New York sandwich: pastrami or corned beef or brisket or hot sausage or roast pork or barbecued beef or a gyro, good stuff like that. He always bought a large sandwich for Claire, who would eat half and then wrap up the other half to take home for supper, for she was poor. They both liked half-sour pickles.

Just the same, they did not eat in Lockhart's office to save money. The idea was to stay out of sight. Claire especially did not want them

25

to be seen walking together across the campus or eating together in a restaurant, although their relationship was chaste. Her husband was neurotically jealous, said McCoy; she herself was neurotically self-conscious. In fact, a hostile witness might say they both had a touch of paranoia. But even the most hostile of witnesses would have to admit that the English department was a gossip manufactory. Further, McCoy and Lockhart believed that they were the kind of people that other people noticed—because of her height and birthmark and bosom, McCoy supposed, because of his height and his bushy eyebrows that almost met in a straight line over his nose, Lockhart supposed.

One day Lockhart decided to show McCoy . . . It's about time we got on a first-name basis here. One day Chuck decided to show Claire how to get from the gym to his office without being seen. He got out of his workout togs, in and out of the shower, and into his workday duds double-quick, surprised her outside of the women's locker room, took her down three flights of stairs to the swimming pool level of the gym, and led her through a heavy steel door into that subterranean complex of tunnels, his hidden world of chthonic energies. As they walked through one of the oldest sections (red brick, arched ceilings), Claire said, "I've been here before—in dreams," evidence to him that they were soul mates. He took her hand, which was large and shapely and kissable, the better to guide her through the reddish shadows of that section of tunnel with three defunct light bulbs, and wouldn't you know it—there was another graffito, not three feet from the one about Jews and Jesus.

"Fuck this," said Chuck, who seldom used bad language in the hearing of others, although he often cursed under his breath. The new graffito read as follows:

THE WAGES

OF SIN

IS DEATH

He took out his marker pen and wrote,

THE WAGES OF

VIRTUE IS

LIVING DEATH

Claire slipped the pen out of his hand and wrote,

THE WAGES

OF LIVING

IS DEATH

Evidence that if he could be tough, she could be tougher. She made a quarter-turn and looked up at him (for if she was tall, he was taller) with a complicit little smile on her face. That is when he put his arms around her, pulled her up against him, and kissed her smack on the lips, her breasts a chestful. He couldn't have surprised himself more if in an eyeblink he had turned into the Minotaur, but Claire absorbed this assault with equanimity, with only a slight widening of the eyes maybe.

In silence and confusion Chuck led Claire to his office, where she sat at his desk reading Christopher Smart while he went out for sandwiches—which they ate pretty much without the usual chatter, subdued by their own audacity.

Without any lead-in, while they were still sipping the bitter dregs of coffee left in their containers, Claire in something like a trance began to speak of her husband, Ivan Tervakalio. She had met him shortly after college, during her "bohemian" phase, there among the "lowlife" on the fringes of Greenwich Village. But Ivan was by no means a lowlife. He was a folksinger, not the kind, however, whom anyone paid to play: he would appear with his guitar, for free, at picket lines, street fairs, demonstrations of almost any kind, marches for this or that, for "open mike" at Hoboken taverns, at school board meetings, tenant mobilization meetings, block association meetings, Take Back the Night rallies, Mothers Against Drunk Driving vigils, Gay and Lesbian Liberation Front parades, People for the Ethical Treatment of Animals street theater, gatherings before an execution, high school reunions, and on any occasion when people chained themselves to something. In his willingness to put aside his own convenience, in the man's endearing lack of acquisitiveness, he reminded Claire of her parents, part of his initial attraction, she guessed. Even now he spent hours every week working for Greenspace.

> I'll sing you one, O
> Red fly the banners, O
> What is your one, O
> One is workers' unity
> And ever more shall be so.

The downside was that he had never, in any one of his thirty-two years, earned more than eleven thousand dollars a year. His work as handyman and janitor of the three-story building in which they lived took care of their rent, but nothing else. Claire, of course, was a woman of her time: she couldn't expect her husband to support her. Therefore she worked for a big law firm on Fridays, Saturdays, and Sundays, no big deal. The big thing, in fact, was what with work, school, and keeping house (Ivan was incompletely housebroken), there was little time left over for her writing. She hadn't completed a new poem in three months. She hadn't sold one in five months ("sell" was her hard-bitten term for publication, although she was seldom paid anything). She had sent her completed volume of poems to every contest she'd heard of, the usual prize being publication. Then in a wondering kind of voice she said she owed it to Ivan that she was a poet at all. When they were first going together, she helped him with the lyrics of his songs and at last wrote them entirely, for Ivan was not good with words. Then, with an abrupt change in the tone of her voice along with a sharp glance, she asked if he, Chuck Lockhart, would like to read her poems, and she stood up, as though to leave. He'd love to, he said.

"You're a good kisser, Pops," she said over her shoulder, just before opening the door and passing through it.

Wouldn't you know it? Not a minute after Claire strode out the door, Simone Song sidled in, a paper cupful of coffee in each hand. She placed the cups on Chuck's desk, collapsed into the visitor's chair still fragrant with Claire's body (as Chuck allowed himself to think), sprawled, put an elbow on the armrest and her head on a hand, and smiled brilliantly.

"Who's the carrottop you've been running with?" she said. "You don't often see a woman that buff with big tits."

"Shush," he said, looking toward the doorway. "Not a word. Do you understand me? *Not a fucking word*, not to anyone."

"Jesus," she said.

"You have no idea what Jane . . . ," he said. "She would make it her life's work to destroy me, even if she had to destroy herself in the process. She's been looking for a career—ruining me in every way would be it."

"Simmer down," she said. "I won't say anything. I don't know anything."

"There's nothing to know," he said, pouring coffee from the paper cup into his steel mug.

"I do know the rules," she said. "You can be my father confessor, but I can't be your *ficelle*." (Simone was a degenerate reader of Henry James.) "It's not fair."

"How do you know she has big tits?"

"I saw her changing in the locker room," she said, "not that she was showing off or anything. She was sort of hidden in a corner and hurrying into her sports bra."

"The usual thing is, if you got it, you flaunt it," he said.

"I would," she said. "Don't men size each other up in locker rooms?"

"A quick glance down at the one thing," he said. "Speaking of that, how are you and Tony getting on?"

"Very funny," she said. "If he's a seducer, he's a patient one. It wasn't until just the other day that he asked me—well, his exact words were 'I wonder if I might have the honor of kissing you good night?'"

"What did you say?" said Chuck, looking at Simone's shapely lips and perfect teeth.

"Ever kiss someone while you're still laughing?" she said. "It's not very romantic. But if Tony minded, he didn't let on."

"Tony's manners are excellent," he said.

"I've grown to like him a lot," she said. "He's a great listener. He's interested in everything because he believes in nothing. And I believe he really likes me."

"Tony is a fervent believer in disbelief," he said. Then he leaned forward and lowered his voice: "How come you and I never became lovers? Is it because I'm too timid or because you're too moral?"

"It's because we're friends," she said.

"I see," he said, though he didn't, for in certain areas of experience Simone's wisdom was greater than his own.

Why men marry poses a puzzle.
[DAVID M. BUSS, The Evolution of Desire:
Strategies of Human Mating] ❡ *If women didn't exist, all the money
in the world would have no meaning.* [ARISTOTLE ONASSIS] ❡
There is no reason to think of design or purpose or directedness.
[RICHARD DAWKINS, The Selfish Gene]

i
T WAS EARLY EVENING and Chuck was still muzzy-minded
from too much bourbon before supper and too much meat loaf
(his own recipe) during it. Jane had eaten two baked potatoes
with sour cream, a single spear of asparagus, for roughage, and a
forkful of meat loaf, with a nod to the cook, who didn't give a shit
what she ate. Now Chuck was in his study, organizing the scraps of
paper, no two the same size, on which he had written notes for his
essay on love among the modernists, when Jane, saying "May I come
in?" walked through the door, an unusual occurrence, for what he
did there brought him the small local regard that she nevertheless
resented, and sat down. "What are you doing?" she said.

"Trying to write," he said.

"About what?" she said.

"Modernism," he said.

"I was under the impression that modernism has already been
written about," she said.

"What's up?" he said.

"Daddy called," she said.

"I'm sorry to hear it," he said.

"He misses his little girl," she said.

In accordance with the maxim that had so far preserved his marriage ("Not everything has to be said"), Chuck said nothing. But his view of Jane's father was not favorable. In fact, Chuck saw the eighty-eight-year-old Reverend Luke Hartung as a big baby, not one who had entered his second childhood but one who had never left his first. He was an I WANT made flesh. He wanted this and he wanted that and above all he wanted all the attention he could get. He wanted unqualified love and everlasting devotion. He wanted praise and he wanted sympathy. He wanted to talk about himself and he wanted to be remembered. He wanted to live forever and he wanted to be cradled in the arms of Jesus or, better yet, Mary. (Chuck believed, on insufficient evidence, that a religious calling unleashes the normally choke-collared lechery of men.) Sure, he had all on his own founded and established the First Church of Christ, Avenger, and yes, he had made lots of money selling insurance, mostly to parishioners, but he was not content. He was dissatisfied with God, Who had not restored his eyesight, in bad shape from macular degeneration, Who had not cured his diabetes (nor his sweet tooth either), Who had put cancer in his prostate and taken the starch out of his penis. He was not happy with his asshole, which sometimes betrayed him. He grumbled about his hip replacements, which were wearing out. He complained about his round-the-clock attendants, redneck women sent by the Sacandaga Homecare Service, who would rather watch the soaps on television than listen to him talk about himself, and he complained about the woman who came in once a week to clean up but would never sneak in more than a single magnum of cheap brandy at a time for him, and he complained about the ex-parishioner who came in once a week to pay his bills and deposit his checks and do his paperwork in general but would not give him a blow job. For all that, the Reverend Hartung exemplified Chuck's crackpot theorem #89: "If you act as though the world owes you, the world tends to pay up."

"He says he has no one to talk to," Jane said.

"You'd think he had talked himself out by now," Chuck said, skating on thin ice.

"He fell down last week and the woman taking care of him was too weak to lift him, so she dialed 911," she said.

Chuck was careful not to smile, let alone guffaw, but he did allow himself a vision of the EMS guys rushing in, struggling to lift the big, bulky, old baby, keeling over from brandy fumes, and Tammy June, or whatever her name was, dialing 911 again, new EMS guys rushing in, struggling, keeling over, Terry Lynn or whatever her name was running to the phone, Pastor Hartung calling down lightning to strike them all dead if they didn't get him the fuck up... "Yes, old age is a drag," said Chuck.

"I think I'd better drive up there and spend a few days with him," she said. "Up there" was Sacandaga, New York, two hundred miles away, site of the First Church of Christ, Avenger, which, since Pastor Hartung's retirement, has evolved into the cheerier First Church of Christ, Provider, although the women still wear shapeless long dresses and the men wear dour expressions that are somehow also superior, all in envy of a local clutch of Amish.

"How about your classes?" said Chuck, who was infuriatingly responsible.

"If you ever listened to anything I say, you'd know that I arranged a schedule leaving my Fridays and Mondays free," said Jane. "I'll drive up Thursday after class and get back late Monday."

"I'll get a couple of knishes for you to eat on the way up," he said.

"No, I'll stop at McDonald's for fries and Nathan's for onion rings," she said. "Someone else can cook and clean up for a change. Do you think you can fend for yourself for a few days?"

"I'll manage," he said, for Chuck's friendship with Claire had given him the courage to lie.

"I don't want to come back and find crumbs in the toaster oven and coffee dust in the grinder," she said.

"Yes, ma'am," he said.

"There must be something in the male genome that prevents men from cleaning up after themselves," she said.

Later, his mind gradually clearing, C. C. Lockhart (as he signed his publications) over the next four hours continued his essay on love among the modernists with these winged words:

> Consider Hemingway's "Soldier's Home," for example. Harold Krebs has just come home from World War I, and he likes the look of American girls. He would like to bed down with one, but "it would not be worth the trouble. . . . He would not go through all the talking," in particular, the obligatory protestations of love. Then, over breakfast, his sister starts in on him. "Do you love me?" she asks. "Uh huh," he answers. "Will you love me always?" she says. "Sure," he says. But when he equivocates about going to watch her play baseball, she says, "You don't love me. If you loved me you'd want to come over and watch me play."
>
> The sister leaves and Krebs's mother takes over. She tells him how she prays for him ("all day long"), worries over him, wants him to get married ("I know the temptations . . . I know how weak men are"), to get a job. "God has work for everyone to do," she says; "there are no idle hands in his kingdom." Says Krebs: "I'm not in his kingdom." But she goes on, and at length. He remains unresponsive. She plays her her trump card: "Don't you love your mother, dear boy?" Krebs, before he can stop himself, simply says "No." She cries, of course; he has to eat his words: "I didn't mean I didn't love you." He begs her to believe him; she resists; but by now he is ready to promise her anything. "I'll try and be a good boy for you." She relents, asks him to kneel and pray with her. He kneels, but he cannot or will not pray, so she does it for him. In the last few sentences of the story, Krebs thinks of how, through various avoidances, he had gotten his life to run smoothly; but "that was all over now, anyway." And in the last sentence, he gives into his sister's moral bullying, as he had to his mother's: "He would go over to the school yard and watch Helen play indoor baseball."
>
> In half a dozen pages, Hemingway exposes Krebs to sexual, soro-

ral, maternal, and Christian love. In his thoughts and feelings, Krebs backs off; in his actions he goes along, a split that makes the pure line, grace under pressure, difficult to maintain. Too much of the social and domestic realms is organized by love for Krebs to resist its importunities, which unman and infantilize him. Therefore the lure of the woods, the trout stream, la corrida, the battlefield. Hemingway's exposure of hidden motives behind the promoters of love has its own ulterior motives—his misogyny, his need to cut the apron strings, his no-holds-barred battle with the woman within him. For all that, the heroes of all his major novels yearn above all for requited love.

Muzzy-minded again, Chuck put himself to bed, put himself to sleep with the early episodes of an epic fantasy of a worldwide cataclysm from which he would rescue Claire McCoy—who, as though in gratitude, appeared in his office the next morning with two containers of coffee and two apple Danish. Clearly, in spite of her poverty, Claire had visited a hairdresser, for her hair was straightened and combed to one side (over her birthmark), as on that actress—what's her name? Veronica Lake was her name. But Claire's hair was not exactly straight; it descended in fetching ripples, incipient curls, butterfly kisses against your face. A couple of inches down, her eyes seemed less hazel, more a bright and lecherous green, tiny glittering flecks in them, could put a serious scare into you. And here I thought the purpose of contact lenses was to make you see better, not to make you look badder. This was a big woman, five-ten or five-nine anyway, broad shoulders, big arms, sumptuous bosom, but wearing a black jumper over a white blouse, coming on like a schoolgirl.

In her repertoire of smiles Claire had a lopsided one that was ironic in general, rather than at anyone's expense (or maybe it just looked that way, the left side of her face was less mobile than the right). She showed it to Chuck, who understood it to mean that he should neither praise too much nor criticize at all her new look.

It took a while for him to come up with it, but finally he said, "The more I see of your infinite variety, the more I like it," for what is the good of a literary education if you can't get a line out of it?

35

Never before had Chuck seen Claire blush. "You still want to read my poems?" she said.

"Yes, I do," he said.

Out of her backpack she pulled seventy or eighty pages held together by a black binder. On a white label stuck onto the front cover were these words:

ON THE WAY
By Claire Siobhan McCoy

"The first section was written second, the second first, and the third I'm still working on," she said.

"What are you doing tomorrow night?" he said.

She cocked an eyebrow.

"My wife's traveling north for a long weekend," he said.

"Ivan's going south to play his guitar in D.C.," she said.

> I'll sing you two, O
> Red fly the banners, O
> What is your two, O
> Two, two, a man's own hands
> Working for his living, O
> One is workers' unity
> And ever more shall be so.

"Why D.C.?" he said.

"Native Americans are demonstrating or holding a vigil or something," she said. "They want the Washington Redskins and the Atlanta Braves and the Jeep Cherokees to change their names."

"Well, how would you feel about a team called the Secaucus Micks?" he said.

"Yes, yes, I know," she said. "No doubt my husband is a saint. Someday I'm going to kill him. Let the noble Native American fight his own battles."

Claire's sentences were seldom so paratactic. Chuck interpreted the space between them as evidence that something was being left

36

out, repressed, in fact. Good for her: Chuck had a phobia of strong feelings, especially when vented by a woman.

But she was wearing her ironic smile again. "You asking me for a date?"

"I'm asking whether you want to eat dinner together."

"I'll have to be home by eight," she said. "Ivan will call the moment he hits D.C."

"Shall we meet here?" he said.

"At five fifteen, when the main office is closed," she said.

Chuck sat back in a glow of satisfaction: he had just arranged his first assignation, for his premarital meetings with Jane could hardly be called "assignations." They had been more like tutorials. He was full of half-baked ideas and she was hungry for any idea about anything, so long as it was uncontaminated by the egotism of her father on earth and the menace of her father in heaven.

Claire stood up abruptly, some transaction concluded, said "Later," and went off to prep for the famous Yeats seminar, sipping at her container of coffee. A jumble of heaving emotions was scratching around inside Chuck like a half-dozen cats tied together by their tails. He was proud, but just a bit ashamed of himself. He was elated, but he was anxious. He was turned on by Claire, but put off by her manner. He was determined to finish his article, but one thing he was not, was able to sit at his desk and work on it.

He jumped up, took out his keys, opened the door, fetched his mug of coffee, and walked out the door and down six flights of stairs to his subterranean haven. Risk-taking is like sin, in that one moment's daring leads to the next. Chuck was in a mood to trespass on novel terrain. He therefore took a turn to the left where normally he went straight ahead. After about fifty yards—and was he hallucinating, or was he on a path that sloped just the tiniest bit downhill?—he came to a narrowing of the passageway, the bricks wet, as though sweating. He stopped, put his hand on the wall, and sure enough, it was warmer than the ambient air. And now that he was no longer clumping along, he could separate out a sound that had been like an echo of his footsteps. Yup, there it was, a kind of raspy, throbby panting, as though some big animal, a rhinoceros maybe, was either in the throes of passion or breathing its last, for the little death often sounds like the big one.

"Gotta get a grip" would have been the verbal equivalent of the impulse that made Chuck turn and continue on his way (almost perceptibly) downward, swinging left one more time, until he came to a dead end. On the steel door that blocked his way, churlish red letters proclaimed the following:

RESTRICTED

KEEP OUT

Across the door was a steel bar with slots cut on either side. But there were no padlocks in the loops, no padlocks, a curious omission. Chuck pulled the bar off the loops and placed it on the floor by the door, which he opened. If there was a light switch, he couldn't find it. He stood there, looking into the darkness, not like some conquistador upon a peak in Darien, but like an ungulate that's caught a whiff of cheetah. By stages too gradual for the eye to catch, a portion of the darkness gathered itself into a darker shade of black, a rectangular mass about the size of a one-car suburban garage, a squat ponderosity more felt than seen. Two faint glims of reflected light looked back at him. Fuck this shit! Abruptly, Chuck shut the door and affixed the bar.

He quick-stepped back to where he had first strayed left and returned to the straight and narrow, heading for the gym. It was a half-hour early for his weekday run, but Chuck felt a need to be among other people, for your cowed ungulate returns to the herd. He was arrested by a new graffito:

GOD IS LOVE

Chuck stood there, looking at this dubious sentiment, fishing around in his mind for a rejoinder, reaching for his marker pen.

"That you, Professor?" said a voice, Hardcore's voice, from behind him. Chuck turned. "Some bitch been writing on the walls. You see him?" said Core.

"You're the first person I ever ran into down here," said Chuck.

"It's a shame what he been writing," said Core. "You got some change you don't need?" Chuck gave him a dollar.

Chuck was on his third lap (on his way to thirty), running easily, when Claire stepped out of the warm-up area and onto the track and fell in behind him. Well, he led her around the track one lap's worth, nice and easy, prickles on his face, prelude to a sweat. But as they passed the warm-up area Claire sped up until they were neck and neck, side by side, stride for stride, for if the truth be known, Claire's legs were also too long. Then she passed him by, falling in line before him, picking up speed, her haunches bunching and relaxing, this side, then the other. He picked up some speed himself, man, hot on her heels. One lap of that and he passed her by, fell in line before her, cleaving the wind. Another go-around and Claire took over. And so they went, round and round, taking turns, changing places, faster and faster, until after a dozen laps or so they were neck and neck, sprinting for the finish—which Claire crossed first.

Well, you can imagine—we're talking about a guy fifty years old here; bent over, gasping, rubbery-legged, he made it over to the wall around the track, leaned back against it, and slid down, bum on heels, in a squat one thinks of as peculiar to Third Worlders.

Claire came over, took him by the hand, pulled him to his feet. "Come on," she said, "Walk it off." And that's what he did.

After, Claire went for the free weights and Chuck went for the sauna. When he came out of the locker room, showered and shaved and red-faced and feeling clean, Claire was talking to some guy. Chuck did not like his looks, which were familiar: he looked like the older brothers of the schoolyard toughs who used to beat him up in junior high over there in Yorkville, a burlier, plumper Jon Voigt, as tall as Chuck, standing back on his heels, confident of his right to exist. He was not at this moment wearing that feral smile, prelude to a flurry of punches that Chuck remembered all too well. At the mere thought of it, Chuck could feel the flight-or-fight response coming over him. In fact, the look on this guy's face and his gestures (hands shoulder high, fingers spread) were apologetic. He was wearing a dark blue wool coat, vaguely nautical, but not quite a pea jacket. Somewhere there's a picture of Jack London wearing a coat like that. On his head, pushed back, emitting a blond ponytail, was one of those caps—what is this they are called; is it a "Greek sailor's cap"?—you know, black or navy blue, patent leather visor, braided band, flat top, couldn't keep you warm, good for nothing but ornamentation. There are pictures of Lenin wearing a cap something like that.

He kissed Claire lightly on the lips and took off. When he was out of sight, Chuck walked over. "That was my husband," she said.

"So I gathered," Chuck said.

"He's going to Washington a day early, right now, in fact," she said. "There's going to be some kind of pre-demonstration jamboree."

Chuck, who was as resolutely apolitical (he was a Democrat) as he was irreligious, wondered what kind of man would rather participate in a demonstration than stay with Claire.

> I'll sing you three, O
> Red fly the banners, O
> What is your three, O
> Three, three, the rights of man
> Two, two, a man's own hands
> Working for his living, O
> One is workers' unity
> And ever more shall be so.

seven

Reason is, and ought only to be, the slave of the passions; and can never pretend to any other office than to serve and obey them. [DAVID HUME] ❡ *Facts are stupid things.* [RONALD REAGAN] ❡ *... emotions are things that happen to us rather than things we will to occur.* [JOSEPH LEDOUX, The Emotional Brain: The Mysterious Underpinnings of Emotional Life] ❡ *In psychic life the intellect is how, the emotions why.* [DONALD SYMONS, The Evolution of Human Sexuality] ❡ *Much learning doth make thee mad.* [ACTS]

O N HIS WAY TO THE DOOR to his apartment—and the seminar went well, Claire demonstrating how often Yeats's poems were about themselves—Chuck Lockhart heard the voice of Dr. Lena Pitts in a diatribe against the ALA. "Dr. Lena" (as she called herself—she had a Ph.D. in communications from Pepperdine) was having a fit over the American Library Association's refusal to install devices that would prevent adolescent boys from calling up "smut" on library computers. She was the host of a call-in radio show that was broadcast from nine to noon in New York and rebroadcast from three to six out of New Jersey.

"How'd it go today?" said Chuck to Jane, who was in the kitchen, peeling potatoes. She held a finger up to her lips to signify that she was listening to the radio and that Chuck, therefore, should shut his yap.

"As Robert Bork long ago proved," Dr. Lena said, "the First Amendment is used to justify all forms of degeneracy."

"She offends your liberal pieties, does she?" said Jane, observing the look on Chuck's face.

Dr. Lena: We have time for one more caller: Claudia, from Tempe, are you there?

Chuck: They're not pieties, more like preferences. I thought they were your preferences, too.

Caller: Thanks for taking my call, Dr. Lena. My question is, am I morally obligated to . . .

Jane: I'm beginning to realize that I was wrong to let you and your liberal friends brainwash me all these years. No more.

Dr. Lena: Yes, you must excommunicate the relationship . . .

Chuck: Not all my friends are liberal. Some are radical. And I happen to think that the harm in a thirteen-year-old looking at dirty pictures is nowhere near the harm in censorship.

Caller: But I felt . . .

Jane: You would. Dr. Lena is right: everybody is oversexed nowadays.

Dr. Lena: Don't talk to me about feelings. Feelings don't have rationale. They don't have an I.Q. They lack common sense.

Chuck: It's only because courageous pioneers brought us within sight, but only within sight, of the Promised Land. Our patron saint is Tantalus.

Caller: Yes, but—

Chuck: What's for dinner?

Dr. Lena: The Ten Commandments are not feelings. They are absolute rules for governing our behavior. Period. End of sentence.

Jane: Potatoes au gratin. [Chuck felt his heart or, rather, his stomach sink, for he had skipped lunch.] If you want meat you'll have to cook it yourself. Period. End of sentence.

After supper—and it turned out that potatoes au gratin tasted pretty good if over them you spooned a can of chili enhanced by jalapeños (Chuck always kept a jar of them at the back of the lowest shelf of the refrig)—Jane was leafing through Durkheim's *Suicide* by way of preparation for her Thursday class; there was no professional football game on TV; reading Claire's poems seemed like too much of a chore; therefore Chuck worked on his essay:

> In these respects he is like D. H. Lawrence.
>
> Throughout *Women in Love*, Ursula works Rupert Birkin, Lawrence's spokesman and stand-in, to say that he loves her. His objections, delivered in a series of diatribes, are various. "Love includes everything," she says. "Sentimental cant," he says. "Love isn't the main thing; it is just one thing after many others." "Love isn't a desideratum—it's like an emotion you feel or don't feel, according to circumstances." Further in the sensuous deeps and sanctified highs where men and women truly come together, love doesn't exist. "Ultimately there is no love." Penultimately, love is a form of bullying. "Love is a process of subservience with you," says Birkin to Ursula, "and with everyone. I hate it." In any case, the word "love" and the concept are tied to an obsolete morality; on top of that, they have been here diluted and there wrenched out of shape. "We hate love because we have vulgarized it. It ought to be proscribed, taboo from utterance, for many years, til we get a better idea." Birkin does not change his mind, but his emotions take over. "Yes—my love, yes—my love," says Birkin, hugging and kissing Ursula. "Let love be enough then, I love you then. I'm bored by the rest." When the fit is on you, we conclude, love may be awful, but it is also everything—all in accordance with one of modernism's operative assumptions, which is that knowledge, reason, the fruits of experience haven't a chance against emotion.

Enough, more than enough! These damn literary critics can't just let you enjoy a good read without worrying it to death. Chuck was surprised to see that the time was half past one. Obedient to the call of his least-considered habit, he put himself to bed, although he was not sleepy. He lay there next to Jane, planning tomorrow's assignation with Claire. Yes! That was the solution: his office rather than some restaurant downtown where they were unlikely to be seen by anyone who knew them—hide right under their noses, as in that story by E. A. Poe.

How about a boom box, a little Charlie Parker with strings? A woman with Claire's artistic acumen would appreciate Charlie Parker, no? If not, he would never speak to her again. Like fun he wouldn't. O.K., no boom box. First, clear off the desk, give it a good rub with Jane's Lemon Pledge. Buy a couple of wine glasses, a bottle of Merlot, for Chuck took it as a point of honor not to know much about wine. Appetizer? Why not?—two cellophane containers of sushi, six to the container (and don't forget to buy a bottle of soy sauce), something to keep the first glass of wine company. (Chuck did not much like sushi but assumed all women did.) And did he not see, in a supermarket cooler, ready-made chicken cordon bleu that you can heat in the departmental microwave? There would have to be a green, if only to offset the tan and white of the other stuff. Don't talk to me about your packages of dried-out ready-mix "mesclun" minisalad, comes with a little foil package of sugary salad dressing, not a chance. But how about a can of gourmet asparagus? That's settled—the only question was whether to go for a small jar of mayo or small bottles of oil and vinegar. The latter, he thought, for French bread dipped in olive oil tastes as good as French bread smeared with butter—and that would take care of the carbohydrate. Chuck could not interest himself in the question of dessert. He preferred to picture them, bellies filled, sipping a liqueur, Courvoisier, say, clinking glasses, hooking arms to drink, gazing into each other's eyes, but that was no reason to rule out a small, select box of chocolates, yes, the kind they call truffles.

Anything else? How about one of those picnic packages of salt and pepper, a white plastic shaker and a black? And how about paper plates, dummy, or were you planning to eat right off the Lemon Pledge? All right, paper plates then, he supposed, no, not paper plates, better those plastic plates good for playing Frisbee, for who wants to eat on a blotter—red for the sushi, black for the chicken, add a note of decadence, napkins to match. No candles, candles were out. Chuck had a feeling that with Claire it was best not to lay it on too thick. Garnish? Jesus Christ and crackers, what was this he was turning himself into, worrying about garnish?—"Mother Lockhart," they'd call him.

Supper settled, Chuck turned his mind to his fantasy epic in progress. New York lay smoking in ruins behind them, for the dying, in their rage to live before they died, had become destructive. Less than ten percent of the population, epidemiologists believed, was immune to the blue flu. There was no vaccine. Chuck and Claire had escaped New York (after their spouses died) by swimming the Harlem River. They were hiking north, following cover, having many adventures on the way. At least they were fully equipped with the best camping gear, about which Chuck had suddenly become expert, except that they only owned a single sleeping bag, which therefore they shared, for while outside the slarming boog was weem, inside the beeping sarm was womb. . . .

When, next morning, Chuck made it to the kitchen, later than usual, Jane was dawdling over her cup of black coffee with four spoonsful of sugar, already listening to Dr. Lena. The latter was praising a Floridian high school principal who forbade (*forbaid* is how she pronounced it) the girls' track team to work out wearing nothing over their sports bras. To show that she was evenhanded, the principal a few days later forbaid the boys' track team to work out shirtless. Dr. Lena was going to send this paragon a tee shirt with the legend DR. LENA'S LEGIONS stenciled on it, front and back.

"Well, hail to the sleeping beauty," said Jane.

"Mumf," he said and began to make coffee, grinding the beans, adding a tablespoonful of espresso.

Caller: Hi, Dr. Lena, I'm so glad you took my call, 'cause I listen to you every day, 'cause I don't know what I'd do without you, 'cause like the announcer says, you're "the conscience of America."

45

Dr. Lena: What's your question for me?

Caller: My question for you is . . . am I morally obligated to let my brother take my daughter to Disneyland?

Dr. Lena: Is your brother a pedophile?

Caller: Gosh, no, what made you think that?

Dr. Lena: How old are you?

Caller: Thirty-four.

Dr. Lena: Your daughter?

Caller: Fifteen.

Dr. Lena: Your brother?

Caller: Thirty-seven.

Dr. Lena: What color are his eyes?

Caller: What does that have—

Dr. Lena: Just answer the question.

Jane: You still pals with whatshisface, the dean of the school of journalism?

Chuck: We're on a couple of committees together.

Caller: Brown.

Jane: I want you to speak to him.

Dr. Lena: What's wrong with your brother that you don't want him—

Caller: He plans to bring his girlfriend.

Chuck: What do you want me to say?

Dr. Lena: If you interrupt me once more, I'll cut you off.

Caller: Sorry.

Jane: I've been thinking of going back to journalism school.

Dr. Lena: Is the girlfriend a pedophile?

Chuck: It's the director of admissions I should speak to.

Caller: No, no, they're both very well educated. It's just that they're living together and—

Dr. Lena: Aha! They're shacking up!

Jane: Whatever. If one old boy says to the other old boy, "Let the bitch in," the bitch gets in.

Caller: Well, I guess you could put it—

Dr. Lena: Absolutely not.

Caller: Absolutely not what?

Chuck: In fact, it may be the dean of students I should see. Maybe I can convince her you only meant to be on a leave of absence all along.

Dr. Lena: Don't let them take your daughter anywhere. A fine pair of role models they are. Do you want your daughter to think it's all right to spread her legs for some stud she hasn't married?

Jane: Use your charm on her, flex a muscle or two.

Caller: I was afraid you'd say that. The thing is, they're a good influence on my daughter, ever since that time she ran away. They take her to museums and when she sleeps over Sharon teaches her how to make foreign dishes like Canadian bacon or burritos. They play Scrabble with her to improve—

Chuck: That's not how it works.

Jane: I can see now that the mistake I made was to think in terms of print journalism. Newspapers, books, reading, they're all on the verge of obsolescence.

Dr. Lena: Wolves in sheep's clothing! Your daughter's not mature [pronounced *mahtoor*] enough to see the degeneracy behind the disguise. But you should be.

Chuck: I hope not, or I won't have the salary to pay your tuition.

Caller: There's my dilemma. I don't want to hurt my brother's feelings, even if he is immoral.

Dr. Lena: You have to stand up for principle. If that means you have to alienate from him, do it. Period. End of sentence.

Caller: Yes, Dr. Lena. Thank you, Dr. Lena.

eight

Ye must know that women have dominion over you: do you not labour and toil, and give and bring all to the woman? [1 ESDRAS] ❡ *Love's like the measles — all the worse when it comes late in life.* [DOUGLAS JERROLD] ❡ *Then, said I, Lord, how long?* [ISAIAH] ❡ *Sex is the last refuge of the miserable.* [QUENTIN CRISP]

BY FOUR FORTY-FIVE Chuck's desk was neatly set for two. The red and black plates, the white plastic knives and forks, looked good against the dark Lemon-Pledged brown of the desktop, for things that are discordant in theory are often harmonious in practice. As much could be said about Chuck's deeply considered ensemble, an olive corduroy sports jacket, a button-down denim shirt, an abstract-expressionist tie with brown and blue in it, Levi's. It can be truly said that at no time since his dissertation defense had the butterflies in his stomach been so active. No writer worth reading neglects affairs of the heart, and Chuck knew a lot of writers, in the flesh or through their words, but as he now recognized, when it comes to affairs of the heart, for all his reading, he was an innocent, a booby, a case of arrested development. He tried to kill the time until five fifteen, when Claire was due, by alphabetizing the books on his shelves. At five sixteen, and he checked his watch every twenty seconds or so, Claire had still not arrived.

At five thirty Chuck gargled some of the mouthwash he had

48

bought for the occasion and spit it into his wastebasket. A sudden, near irresistible urge to do some push-ups came over him, but he restrained himself, for some women (Jane, for example) are repelled by the smell of male perspiration. At five forty-five he poured himself a glass of wine. He did not call Claire to remind her of their date, because after the one time he had called her, she lit into him. The problem was, you could never know when Ivan would be home. And if you called and then hung up when he answered, he would dial star 69 to get your number. So calling her was strictly verboten. At six o'clock he started on the sushi, not that he knew what he was doing. Five minutes later he was surprised to see that the container was empty.

From six to six thirty Chuck stood by his window, unconsciously posing, looking out over the campus from his aerie. He did not distinctly see much of what was there, but the harder he looked, the more he could see of a ghostly Claire hurrying toward him, flushed, flustered, out of breath, afraid he had gone off in a mood, cursing Ivan, who had gotten himself arrested and . . . and fuck this.

In a kind of recoil Chuck backed away from himself to where he could see himself, nor did he entirely like what he saw. But then it was Chuck's way to look himself over through the eyes of his favorite authors. Right now, for example, he saw himself not whole but in shreds and flashes of phrase and image—he saw himself, that is, in the boy who narrates Jimmie Joyce's "Araby." This boy, you will remember, who has a desperate and exalting crush on Mangan's sister, hurries to a bazaar, looking to bring her back a present. But he doesn't get there until closing time, gets himself dissed by a salesgirl flirting with two guys, and, as the lights go out and he gazes around at the dark and empty booths, sees himself as a creature "driven and derided by vanity," his eyes burning "with anguish and anger."

And in flitters and glimmers of image and phrase Chuck saw himself as Gabriel Conway of "The Dead." He is alone in a hotel room with his wife after a necrotic party, away for once from the kids, when a great feeling for his wife comes over him. He is literally "trembling with desire"—but she has been thinking how when she was a girl a "delicate" boy had sung to her in the rain and died of it. Gabriel is too nice a guy to break into her mood with sexual overtures; instead, "A shameful self-consciousness of his own person assailed him. He saw himself as a ludicrous figure . . . a nervous well-meaning sentimentalist, orating to vulgarians and idealizing his own clownish lusts, the pitiable fatuous fellow he had caught a glimpse of in the mirror."

Poor Gabriel . . . and poor Chuck. Still, why does he have to be such a wuss? If you are going to see yourself reflected from fictions, why not choose Sam Spade or Tarzan or Vito Corleone or the Count of Monte Cristo, Joyce's choice, and act accordingly. There in his office, instead of cursing Claire for making him look ridiculous in his own eyes, Lemon Pledge and plastic plates, he had a sudden vision of his fist landing alongside Jane's jaw, breaking it, for let me tell you, Chuck knew how to throw a punch. Back there in his thirties, you see, when he first decided to build himself a body, he did time learning how to beat up punching bags. With sparring partners he was less formidable. But he took a certain satisfaction from getting tagged. For the time being, he packed up with misplaced vehemence. What the hell—if he moved fast he would be able to watch *Jeopardy* while eating the cordon bleu. A timid knock on the door made him jump, and he dropped the can of asparagus. He hurried to the door, behind which stood Simone Song.

"I had a beer with the guys and came back for a book and saw that your light . . . what's wrong?" she said, alluding to the expression on his face.

He jerked his head to signify that she should come in, picked the can of asparagus off the floor, began to set the desk for two. "Here, you're handy with the microwave," he said, plumping down the two containers of chicken. "But first—" and he poured them each a glass of wine. They clinked glasses and drank.

Simone went to the dark departmental office (she had a key) with the chicken while Chuck stood there, can of asparagus in hand, remembering that he forgot to bring the can opener. He went into the kitchenette and stood behind Simone, who was standing in front of the microwave. "Have we got a can—?" he said, and damn if Simone didn't tilt backward until she was leaning against him. He was not surprised, either because he had more vanity or because he had more understanding than we have been giving him credit for. He put his arms lightly around Simone and rested his chin lightly on her head. They began to sway, just perceptibly, from side to side. In a minute he could feel that she was crying. A medium-large feeling came over him, not specifically for Simone, or even particularly for himself, even if it is always Margaret you mourn for.

While they ate and drank, and drank, good-hearted Simone, her antennae attuned to Chuck's mood, carried the conversation —"Have you ever read 'The Beast in the Jungle'? I've just been rereading it, and you know, James is right, it's not so much the unexamined life you have to look out for, it's the unlived life, or are they the same?"

Chuck felt his shame drain. A slow anger seeped in to fill the vacated space, anger not so much at himself, even less at Claire, but mostly at things in general. "If Henry had come out of the closet when he was young," Chuck said, "he would not have had to write all those stories of the unlived life."

"You're the polarized opposite of our American puritans," she said. "You put too much faith in the power of sex to do good."

"Well, Henry's loss is our gain," he said. "Fuck him, too."

And so they maundered. Simone did not ask why Chuck had a shopping bagful of dinner for two, and Chuck did not allude to Simone's tears, though God knows, by the time they got to the Courvoisier both were talking a mile a minute.

The two of them ran out of words at the same time. There was a moment of silence, during which they simply looked at each other. Then Simone jumped to her feet and said, "I'd better go." Chuck, whose manners were old-fashioned, also stood. She went over to him, gave him a hug. When he held on a count too long, she whirled him away in a waltz, around and around the office, maintaining a space between them, humming "Love Makes the World Go Round," Chuck finally joining in an octave lower.

At home Chuck was surprised to discover that he missed...well, not Jane, exactly, but her presence. He was in no mood to read the poems of a woman who had just stood him up; nor was there a game of professional football on television; so he returned to his essay:

> Virginia Woolf, who championed the woman within her and waged war with the man in men, is like Lawrence and Hemingway in depicting love as awful, but unlike them in attributing the emotion and its ulterior motives mainly to men. Her heroines tend to renounce love for something preferable—for art in *To the Lighthouse*, for a room of one's own in *Mrs. Dalloway*, for death in *The Voyage Out*. "From the dawn of time odes have been sung to love," observes Lily Briscoe; "wreaths heaped and roses; and if you asked nine people out of ten they would say they wanted nothing but this—love; while the women, judging from her own experience, would all the time be feeling, This is not what we want; there is nothing more tedious, puerile, and inhumane than this...." But then, thinking of the Ramsays, she concedes that "it is also beautiful and necessary," although not for her.
>
> "Horrible passion!" thinks Clarissa Dalloway; "Degrading passion! a destroyer: everything that was true went." Pairing love with religion, Clarissa pictures them as "clumsy, hot, domineering, hypocritical, eavesdropping, jealous, infinitely cruel and unscrupulous...." Unlike Krebs and Birkin, Virginia Woolf's heroines do not give in. Clarissa loves her husband pretty much as Virginia loved hers, as a comfort, as a crutch that you resent to the extent that you need it, that you despise to the extent it lets itself be used. Her notion of love as a power exploited by men to subdue women has since become widespread.

nine

My fight has been against depression, repression, and suppression. [MAE WEST] ❡ *... forcible violation of women is the essence of sex.* [CATHARINE MACKINNON, Toward a Feminist Theory of the State] ❡ *There is nothing safe about sex. There never will be.* [NORMAN MAILER] ❡ *Is Sex Necessary?* [JAMES THURBER AND E. B. WHITE]

CHUCK GOT UP LATE and then did what he had long day-dreamed about doing, about doing every day once he hit the lottery for thirty million. (It would be worth giving Jane fifteen million just to get rid of her.) He took possession of a sidewalk table outside the Other End, ordered coffee, toast, and grapefruit juice, and read the *Times* with one eye, magisterially surveying the passing scene with the other. He just sat there, drinking cup after cup, until time for his midday run. If you had asked him, he would have said that he owed himself the indulgence as recompense for yesterday's disappointment.

Right from the start, before he had completed a lap, Chuck had that sinister feel of being followed. Either someone was hot on his heels or the slap of his sneakers on the track was producing a quick echo, SLAP slap. He cast a glance over his right shoulder but saw no one. He was about to risk a look over his left shoulder when Claire ran by it. She then eased over in line before him. After a lap he passed her by, eased into line, neither of them quickening the pace, neither of them sprinting to the finish, which they crossed side by side, Chuck holding out his palm, Claire slapping it, right on, Bro. They walked around the track two laps' worth until Chuck's breathing smoothed out. Then he turned to face her, arms akimbo, a question on his face.

"Don't ask," she said.

Well, if she had better wind, he had bigger muscles, as he demonstrated by working out with a hundred-pound barbell while she did her thing with two fifteen-pound dumbbells. Her thing was enough to redden the rest of her face to the color of her birthmark, which got even redder, as though out of some need to remain conspicuous. She was still flushed when he met her outside the women's locker room, a surplus M-65 field jacket over a Mother Hubbard that fell down to her sandals, as though the year were 1968, and led her to those mazy passageways underground, where she took his arm, a first.

They walked along in silence, Chuck tensing his arm under Claire's hand to show off his bicep, until they came to the stretch of tunnel with three burned-out bulbs, a fourth flickering like a migraine. Sure enough, there was some new graffiti. Claire read it aloud:

ABSTAIN FROM FLESHLY LUSTS
WHICH WAR AGAINST THE SOUL
—1 Peter 2:11

TOUCH NOT; TASTE NOT; HANDLE NOT
—Colossians 2:21

FOR THE IMAGINATION OF MAN'S HEART
IS EVIL FROM HIS YOUTH
—Gene

The tail end of the last attribution was smeared into unintelligibility.

They stood there for a moment or two, but neither came up with a rejoinder, maybe because Chuck was thinking of something else. Then there was one of those eerie occurrences when thinking something seems to make it happen. Claire swung him around by his bicep, pulled his head down, brought their lips together, and man, they leaned into each other. Then she abruptly jerked her head back. "Someone's coming," she said.

Chuck didn't hear anything, but he took her by the hand and pulled her quick-foot down the path he had first trod himself just the other day. He slowed down when he came to the narrowing of the passageway, the crumbling brick, the green mold, the damp, and put a hand on the wall. "Feel," he said.

She put a hand on the wall. "Feel what?" she said.

"It's all hot and sweaty," he said.

She took him by the wrist and held up his hand where he could look at it, giving him one of her crooked, ironic smiles.

"All right, then listen," he said, putting his ear to the wall.

She put her own ear to the wall.

"Listen to what?" she said.

"That sound like hoarse breathing," he said.

"'Projection' is what it's called," she said. "Come on, that was probably campus security I heard."

"There's no law against us being here," he said, but he led her by the hand to

RESTRICTED

KEEP OUT

From his gym bag Chuck extracted the slender little flashlight he had brought along for just this purpose, pulled the bar off the loops welded to the frame, and placed it on the floor by the door, which he opened. The feeble beam from the flashlight was largely swallowed up by the darkness before it reached the blacker shade of black at the center of our explorers' field of view. Chuck pulled Claire in after him and let the door close behind them.

It was a couple of moments before the two of them realized that they were looking at a squat old coal furnace, big enough to house a family of rednecks. It was then that Claire saw the light switch, by the door but higher than usual. Claire threw the switch. A single flickering fluorescent bulb came on.

By way of containment or domestication or even gentrification, the furnace had been immured in whitewashed bricks. But you could see the streaked and rusty cast iron where grout had crumbled and bricks had fallen out. The furnace was set in a recess maybe four feet below floor level, so whoever was responsible for the damned thing could walk around and fiddle with dials and gauges, now inscrutable with grime. Pipes bristled out of the brick and ended in midair. On them were little brass wheels you turned to let water in or steam out, so Chuck surmised. Steps led down to an area before the unbricked fire doors. There was plenty of space for some muscular, sweaty guy to shovel coal into the maw.

Hand in hand, they walked carefully down those steps and onto that space. Across the bottom of the furnace was a door wide and thin as a schoolmaster's mouth. It was out of this door, surely, that ashes were drawn. And indeed, leaning against the furnace was a black iron, long-handled, hoe-like implement. For some reason the back end of it came to a point. Above that door were two others of the kind that swung out from the center to either side. Chuck swung them open, and can you believe it? What came out was a cold draft that somehow smelled hot, ashy, and mephitic. He slammed the doors closed, turned, and bumped up against Claire, who had been standing right behind him.

They stood there, touching, chest to breasts, pelvis, thighs, just looking at each other. Then Claire said, "I knew it would come to this," and reached down for the zipper of his fly.

Taking short steps, for his pants were around his ankles, Chuck rotated 180 degrees, taking Claire with him, until her back was against the furnace. She dropped her panties and hiked up her Mother Hubbard, draped a knee over his hip bone. He slid in easily, for she was well lubricated, nor did it take them long to get the old reciprocating machine going, until Chuck slipped out. Have you ever noticed that sex is funny, except, of course, when you're doing it? She helped him back in, the two of them on tiptoes, panting, pelvises tucked under and working like woodpeckers, until he slipped out again. "Mary, Mother of Jesus," she said. She tried to slide him in again, but he had gone limp. "Never mind," she said, and she pulled her panties off her left ankle, spread them on the floor, kneeled on them, took Chuck's dangle in her mouth. It is a character in John Updike, is it not, who says that to fuck is human; to be blown, divine?

Claire, her work done, rested her head against Chuck's thigh. "Now you'll think less of me," she said. You would have to work at it to get further from the truth, for Chuck was that figure of fun, a grateful lover. He bent over, pulled her to her feet, and hugged and hugged and hugged. Then he slid down his right hand, copped her mons, and inserted a finger where it might do the most good.

"Don't," she said. He started to sink knees first toward the panties, saying, "Let me do you," but she said, "No, I can't, you can owe me one." The last of the fluorescent bulbs went out.

They walked back past the sweaty brick slowly, nonchalanting it, holding hands and swinging them forward and back, Claire no longer uptight and anxious—perhaps because she had just performed on Chuck what in the hidden recesses of her psyche was an act of expiation, perhaps because she had magically stolen the male member's mana, perhaps because she had just had some sexual pleasure, if of the kind that left her depths undisturbed, perhaps because she was the kind of person who got pleasure by giving it, and if so, long may she flourish.

When they came to the turn to Chuck's office Claire said, "Wait a minute" and pulled him toward the gym. And when they came to the place of graffiti, she said, "Lend me your marker pen." Then, underneath the other quotations from the good book, she wrote

BLESSED BE HE THAT COMETH
IN THE NAME OF THE LORD
—Psalms

ten

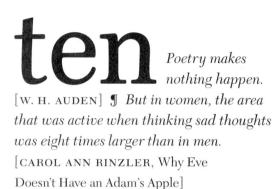

Poetry makes nothing happen.
[W. H. AUDEN] ❡ *But in women, the area that was active when thinking sad thoughts was eight times larger than in men.*
[CAROL ANN RINZLER, Why Eve Doesn't Have an Adam's Apple]

CHUCK WAS FRESH OUT of papers to grade; he was already ready to teach next week's classes; there was no Friday night football this week; so he sat down to read Claire's poems—it was the least he could do by way of showing his gratitude.

Now this volume of poems—like Gaul, like, in fact, *Ulysses*, like, come to think of it, other books he taught each year, like *Nostromo*, like *Passage to India*, like *To the Lighthouse*—was divided into three, a good sign, he thought, for Chuck was also capable of magical thinking. The severe, cool style of the first section was also a good sign, Chuck decided, skimming. I mean these poems were chaste and pure in diction, triple distilled, a prophylaxis against sentimentality, maybe, against that form of narcissism we call self-pity, most like— so Chuck began to feel as he got into them, for this unfree verse had a story that could get to you. The subject was Claire's girlhood.

The poems are not in chronological order, so we are halfway through them before we learn, in an aside, that her parents were radicalized by the events of 1968. One consequence was that they dropped out of graduate school. Another was the birth, one year later, of Claire Siobhan McCoy. There are poetic snapshots of mother and father carrying her like a papoose, through marches, rallies, riots. In 1974 mother and father married, placed Claire "with the nuns" (in a foster home?), devoted themselves full-time to the Cause. Cumulatively, from poem to poem, the word "nun" comes to signify everything that oppresses and depresses. For a while, apparently, Mom and Dad went underground, but they resurfaced when it became clear that no one was after them.

Claire seems to have been of junior high school age by the time the three of them were living together again, Mom and Dad selling pottery they made themselves in the garage attached to their downscale suburban cottage, for money from home had run out. One day, in a drunken rage, Mom broke the lid of a clay casserole pot over Dad's head, told him to get lost. He went. Within days she tracked him down to the local chapter of the Progressive Labor Party, where he was sleeping on a desk, and tried to coax him home, but she had made the mistake of giving him an excuse to do what he had long wanted to do, get lost.

In one poem we read (in parentheses) of Father's new "chubby child bride with fur on her legs." Mother, we gather, took over the pottery business, for the child-support checks were not forthcoming. Mother also became a binge drinker. Claire would come home from school to find her mother naked and comatose in the backyard, or asleep in the tub, or throwing clumps of clay at the walls, or taking a sickle to the neck of the plastic flamingo on the lawn of her neighbor on the left or arranging the tulips she lifted from the garden of her neighbor on the right. From time to time mother would push daughter out of the house, lock and chain the door, draw the shades, refuse to answer the bell or the door. Poor Claire would have to phone the police, for there was no one else, father having moved to El Paso, where he hustled Indian jewelry and congratulated himself on never having sold out, though no one had ever tried to buy him. Mother would be put away to dry out. Claire would have to take over, run the household, make out the checks, cook and clean up, talk sense into her mother.

None of these poems offer an unrefracted perspective on Claire, not on her looks or on what's doing within her. But from our peripheral vision we gradually make her out to be quiet, obedient, watchful, anxious, lonely, a good girl, the best of students, neat, even prim, containing the terror, counterbalancing her mother's abandon, could break your heart. We come to see her as self-conscious about her birthmark, then about her height, then about her flourishing bosom, all occasions for schoolyard teasing. She clearly hated, loved, and identified with her mother, whose craziness sometimes looks like a form of integrity. She darkly hated, loved, and longed for her dashing father, the hurt over his desertion forever unabated. She did not have a date until her sophomore year in college. She did not lose her cherry until her junior year. During her senior year she cut loose entirely.

Didn't Claire say that the poems in Section II were written first, although the events in them occurred second? Yes, she did. She is out of college and living in what Bobbie Graves described as "dyspeptic bohemian squalor" among the "lowlife" (Claire's word) down there on the fringes of Greenwich Village. The earliest poems (they seem to be arranged in order of composition) are less evolved than those in Section I, less worked over, as though written quickly, before the critical, or maybe censoring, intellect can intervene. The diction is hip, jazzy, and jokey. Here's a poem as though written to her parents about their utopianism:

ANIMAL FARM

You cat-callers beware.
Lay low, or the golden
Goose will get you.

That barnyard wherein
The birds cluck tutti,
And no orders pick or peck,

And the fox eats grapes,
And the goats reek incense,
And the lambs are armed to the teeth,

Who wants it? Not you.
You thrive on gravel in the crop.
When the fields are golden with corn,

It takes hairier types than you
To play with foxfire.
If you dream your world into flesh

Just what will you have left to hatch?

There were years of poets, painters, and pot, of pill-popping parties, of what seems to have been a lesbian experiment with an actress, men being such bastards, of, in general, sex, drugs, and rock and roll. But writing lyrics for Ivan Tervakalio gradually made her realize that she had a vocation. She decided to move uptown and take Ivan with her. She resolved to get her shit together, get a real job, get married, get squared away, write.

The poems in Section III spiral out of Claire's personality to circle around such impersonalities as manners, morals, metaphysics, religion. There's a longish poem in heroic couplets, for example, entitled "In Search of Zeus" (God of Things as They Are). There's a gorgeous and chilling double sestina in which every question put to the universe evokes only the same six ambiguous responses. There's a sonnet sequence in which astronauts are finally sucked into a black hole. Poor Claire: apparently, she started out under the delusion she would find meaning, oh my. She then decided that you could create it yourself and still believe in it, ah woe. Then she decided you could do without it, oi vey. What she finally wound up with, for the time being, anyhow, is an attitude, nothing you could go so far as to call a belief. Here's a poem marking that stage of her journey:

TROGLODYTE MANIFESTO

No vampire regrets the light of day.
Even the sun at dawn can burn.
Vampires hang head down in a cave.

Though a windy star draws praise
From this teem and that swarm
No vampire regrets the light of day.

If chirpers build higher than shade
Where penetration cracks to the worm
Vampires hang head down in a cave.

The tanned arm peels in time of plague.
Sudden rain rusts the summer corn.
No vampire regrets the light of day.

The augured conflagration can rage,
Can raze the crust. Within, out of harm,
Vampires hang head down in a cave.

After the siege falls bloody rain.
Suckers pillage the hollowed cairn.
Then songbirds hang head down in a cave.
Then vampires refract the light of day.

Well, Chuck was sort of overwhelmed, if you know what I mean. He was getting all choked up again while rereading that first section, the self-controlled little girl and the uncontrollable mother, when the phone rang. It was his wife, on whom he was cheating in thought and deed. "So you're there," she said. One of Chuck's regrettable habits was to break into song apropos of nothing, except stress. He now belted out the opening lines of "Ain't Misbehavin' " but stopped short of "Saving my love for you."

"Just you and your radio," she said. "Do you good to listen to Dr. Lena."

"I agree that it's important to know the enemy," Chuck said.

"Poor Papa, that's all he has strength for, to listen to the radio," she said. "He's failing, Chuck. He won't eat anything but sweets."

"He always had a sweet tooth," he said.

"And he's giving away things," she said: "his chain saw, his snow-shoes, his hunting jacket, silverware, the Spode and Lalique, a rug. He wants me to take the guns."

"That old Parker must be worth thousands," said Chuck.

"He said—" and here Jane's voice broke, "he's getting ready to vacate the premises."

"Jane—" he said.

"He said he knows he's dying because he no longer has to wrestle with his lust," Jane said.

"Why not?" Chuck said, alarmed.

"Because he doesn't have any anymore," she said.

"That's the saddest thing I've ever heard," he said.

"You don't have to joke about it," she said, but Chuck was not joking.

"Maybe it's time to think of moving him into a home," he said. "There are lots of homes for the aged upstate. It's the only growth industry."

"The only home I'll move him into is ours," she said. "Hear?"

Chuck did not say "Over my dead body," but he did picture himself lifting the Reverend's five-inch-thick *Peake's Commentary on the Bible* at arm's length over his own head and bringing it down WUMP on the old man's crown, to the detriment of the vertebrae underneath. What he actually said was "I mean, could he stand, well . . . being beholden?"

"You leave that to me," she said. "Tomorrow I'll take him with me to church so as to show these hicks around here that God is not dead.

Monday morning we'll listen to Dr. Lena together. Then I'll drive back. You can take care of supper. Why don't you take a stroll down to Citarella's and pick up some of their homemade gnocchi?"

Nor did Chuck say "Drop dead." He did say, as Jane slammed down the receiver, "We'll see," meaning he would get the gnocchi for Jane, but he would also get a rack of spare ribs for himself.

Chuck had not yet let go of the receiver when the phone rang again. Man, he jerked his hand back as though the infernal thing had grown fangs. Better answer it, just the same. "Forget something?" he said.

"How are you?" said Claire.

"Claire!" he said.

"Herself," she said. "The reason I didn't meet you for supper is I was under surveillance. Ivan asked his sister to come over and keep me company while he was away. I could kill him. She's such a snoop! It's 'What are you writing—can I see?' or 'Why do you spend so much time in the gym?' *So I won't become a fat slug like you, you creep.* You'll have to bear with me. I'm all wound up."

"Unwind, let go, cut loose, don't hold back, so long as I'm there to pick up the pieces," Chuck said.

"She keeps leaning on me to write for FIN, the Finnish Information Network, of which she is co-founder. It's all about how wonderful Finland is, its friendly and industrious people, how clean they are, its state-of-the-art manufacturing (a wonderful opportunity for investors), its spectacular scenery and unspoiled countryside (a wonderful opportunity for outdoorspeople), its fishing and golf, its colorful and scrofulous Laplanders freezing their asses off up north because no one will let them come south, its saunas and birching (a wonderful opportunity for perverts)...," and by now they were both laughing.

"Let's run off to Finland together," he said.

"Oh, Lord," she said. "If your parents are would-be IRA types like mine, full of 'the old country,' you grow to hate all ethnic chauvinisms."

"Or strive to outdo them," he said.

"The road not taken," she said.

"Where's your sister-in-law now?" he said.

"She's out on Broadway looking to buy some pastry for a snack," Claire said. "Already I can see the cannoli cream hanging from her mustache."

These words flashed an improper image across the screen of Chuck's mind. At her next words the screen whited out. "How'd you like to spend Sunday afternoon with me at the Wanhope Hotel?"

"Claire . . ." he said, in a kind of whimper.

"The Wanhope is where that law firm I work for puts up expert witnesses from out of town," she said. "Nothing fancy."

"Oh, Claire," he said.

"I've got a reservation for one o'clock, unless you have something better to do," she said.

"Claire, oh Claire," he said, fairly inadequate for a man who lived by the word.

"What you do is you call the hotel at one thirty from across the street and ask them to connect you to the room held by Gleason, Carson, and Wang," she said. "I'll be there and I'll tell you the room number so you won't have to stop at the desk. Wear a suit, carry a briefcase, walk to the elevator like you owned it."

These prosaic details, with their aspect of something in a story-book for boys, helped Chuck recover. But this oaf, instead of telling her what he felt about her, how no one else had ever, etc., he went on about her poetry, with examples. But it seems he bumbled into saying the right thing. No one had ever, not her husband, not her parents or best friend, had known how to praise her poetry. Oh yeah, one teacher had said that some of the poems in Section I were "lovely" and another had said they were "gut-wrenching," as you might hand someone a consolation prize. Chuck came to realize that nothing he could say about Claire herself would mean as much to her as praise for her poetry.

Chuck put himself to sleep by reimagining the early episodes of his fantasy epic. Nine months into the blue flu epidemic, New York was smoldering. Smoke hid the sun. No birds sang. The streets were empty of people, except for corpses and marauding gangs. Chuck and Claire were foraging through the streets between Manhattan Avenue and Central Park West. He carried a slide-action shotgun; she carried a customized Ruger 10/22—both once the property of the Reverend Hartung. Sometimes in an overlooked basement apartment, especially if the emanating stench of decaying flesh did the work of a barrier, you could find a cache of canned goods, a bag of dried beans, a box of Uncle Ben's converted rice. As for Jane and Ivan, they...

eleven

Unto you is paradise opened. [1 ESDRAS] ❡ *Nakedness in a woman is always a pose.* [LOUISE GLÜCK] ❡ *Sex is like money. Only too much is enough.* [JOHN UPDIKE]

THE WANHOPE HOTEL, there on 8th Avenue in the 50s, a block uptown from the venerable offices of Gleason, Carson, and Wang, reminded Chuck of his father's sister, the older one, that is, Aunt Harriet. She was widowed young by a husband who disdained insurance. But Harriet was too genteel to work, so although she was neat and clean, her severely respectable clothes, after fifty years of use, could be fairly described as threadbare. Members of the family took turns inviting her for dinner on holidays (Chuck's father said that she invented the doggy bag). No one much minded that she would palm a dollar or two out of the collection basket, but when one Sunday she deposited a neatly wrapped turd (still warm) in the basket and then went out to beat a flamboyant streetwalker with her umbrella (never opened, for the fabric was in flitters), the Presbyterian Synod found her what Chuck considered an idyllic rustic retreat to rail and rave in, though Harried herself claimed that this old castle on the Hudson, bequeathed to the church by an exuberantly sinful old Calvinist, was haunted, that her husband, now an incubus, pestered her nightly with his sexual importunities. That's how the Wanhope looked: genteel, neat, threadbare, haunted. And wasn't that Elisha Cook sitting there in one of the lobby's two stuffed leather chairs?

The door to room 1133 was an inch or two ajar: Chuck boldly pushed his way in, and there she was, face flushed, birthmark prominent. Claire's plenary smile was distinctive in this: her lips formed an isosceles triangle, the long side on top. You could then see that her teeth were remarkably white and even, except for her left eyetooth, which had not entirely descended. As her smile closed down, as Chuck crossed the room to her, her lip snagged on this tooth, nor did that hint of a snarl put a hitch in his stride. No doubt you have noticed that a kiss is like a tomato in this: when it is good, it is unsurpassable. They disengaged, looking stunned. Claire, recovering first, reached behind her for a bottle in a form-fitting silver bag adorned with a big red ribbon tied in a bow. She held it up to Chuck, who loosened the drawstring and removed the bottle: champagne, no less. Could it be true that women like Claire did after all exist outside one's fantasy life?

They drank to each other out of stemmed plastic glasses. Chuck led her to the bed, sat on it, fumbled with the fasteners on her slacks, for Claire was wearing a businesswoman's pants suit (which, given her shoulders and bosom and height, made her look linebackerish, an effect that Chuck found attractive), dropped the slacks, kissed her in the navel, on her belly, at the juncture of trunk and thigh, and began to lick her lower lips, at a right angle to her upper lips, for he had not forgotten that he owed her one. Her exudate exuded. Her breathing became audible. Then she pulled back, put a hand on his shoulder, said, "What's the hurry?" So he desisted.

She did allow him to undress her, and since turnabout is fair play, she undressed him. Then she threw back the bedclothes, climbed into bed, pulled the top sheet over her, held the other side of it up invitingly. Chuck joined her. "Let's talk," she said. So they talked and laughed and drank champagne and kissed and hugged and stroked and probed until Chuck found himself on an unprecedented high, which got higher and higher when she went down on him. Then, because turnabout is fair play, he went down on her, he lying on his right side, she also on her right side, her thighs with a firm grip around his ears, thereby shutting out the rest of the world, and who needs it? Well, she came first, for one of the consolations of male senescence is that you don't come so quick. You will be interested to hear that the subsequent talk was even better than the precedent ditto, none of that *post coitum tristis* stuff for these two.

We can date the inauguration of their affair to that Sunday afternoon at the Wanhope Hotel, the rest mere foreplay. As though Mother Nature herself were one more moralist, no love affair, so it seems, can sustain itself on fleshly pleasures alone. The chastening fact is that such pleasures get their staying power from mental enhancement, the meaning we invest in them. Certainly Chuck became heavily invested. He allowed himself an inward swagger each time she came to him, to him, a young, smart, talented, good-looking woman like that, and don't ask what good is a trophy you can't display. Are you kidding? It was not in his relation to the world but in his relation to himself that Chuck sometimes felt he was a loser. Then there was that interesting frisson that comes from transgression, defiance, sin, not to mention the less interesting satisfaction of getting back at his wife, never mind the adrenaline released by the risk of getting caught. He could feel himself coming back to life, knocking over his gravestone, but there was more: through Claire, such was his theory, he was recuperating a life of deprivation and loss. To look at him you would not think he was deprived, nor was he, on the material plane. It was on the immaterial plane that his slogan had been "I Can't Get No Satisfaction." We can sum it up by saying that Chuck was finally having his adventure.

What I mean is that after a month or so he began to see that she was his grail and he had found it. It took him two months to realize that it was better than that. He then saw her as a gift that had bestowed itself upon him, for free. The best part was that he did not have to do anything to earn her, for the best prizes are gratuitous, unearned, untaxed, free. There were times when Chuck saw Claire as a one-woman refutation of American puritanism, which operates on the principle that all pleasures have to cost, or else. There was even a moment when Chuck saw Claire's generosity as a synecdoche for a benevolent universe, but he soon recovered.

And Claire? Clearly she liked Chuck, liked him all the more because he liked her poetry, but there has to be more to it than that. No doubt there were times when she considered the possibility that through Chuck she was reclaiming the father who had deserted her, for Claire had once read a lot of psychoanalysis in an attempt to cure herself. And she too was far from immune to the low pleasures of dissing an uncongenial spouse, of committing a sin, of committing a sin because it was a sin, of courting danger. She too saw the affair as a compensation, even as revenge, for numerous deprivations. But there was something above knowable reasons that drove Claire to Chuck. Some may call it "love," but neither in the case of Claire nor of Chuck can we rule out the possibility of an unconscious drive to self-destruction. Such things do exist, you know.

For all they meant to each other, I can't pretend that the course of their love always went smoothly. There were material obstacles in the way, after all, mainly their spouses. Finding someplace where they could be alone together was a problem. The Wanhope, at a hundred dollars a pop, was more than either of them could often afford. Oh, Chuck could have pried loose a hundred every other week without going under, but it was a tradition for him to sit down with Jane on the fifth and twentieth of every month to pay bills, make out deposit slips, take stock—Jane would have noticed unusual expenditures. One morning in early December, as the term was winding down, Claire called Chuck in his office and told him to meet her at RESTRICTED KEEP OUT—and to bring his flashlight.

When Chuck arrived, there she was, red hair ablaze in the overhead light and curling around her pale face, hip-shot in her field jacket over a checked shirt, jeans, and work boots, by her side a duffel bag and a length of two-by-four. They kissed. Once inside the furnace room, Claire jammed one end of the two-by-four under the doorknob and the other end against the floor, kicking it in tight. She then led him by the hand down the steps into the well before the furnace door, opened the duffel, removed an inflatable mattress, inflated it, removed a sleeping bag, spread it on the mattress. (The puritans, as usual, are wrong: it is not necessity but desire that is the mother of invention.) She then gave him her fullest isosceles smile, which nevertheless looked just a little bit sinister in the beam of the flashlight shining on it from below.

Humming "Night Train," she then fell into a surprisingly skilled striptease, under the checked shirt a lacy bra, which she hung on a defunct gauge, under the jeans frilly panties, which she hung on a pipe that led nowhere, while Chuck held his flash on her as though it was a spotlight, saying "Take it off, take it off." Her red-gold pubic hair sparked. He could see that she had recently trimmed it into a tight, nappy little triangle. When, sitting on the sleeping bag, he put his arms out and around to grip her firm and fine nether hemispheres so that he could pull her toward him, he could tell that her delta was perfumed, gilding the lily. He pushed his tongue into her, moved it around, said, "What did I do to deserve this?"

With a lofty disregard for logic, she said, "It's my birthday" (for Claire was a Sagittarian), and Chuck understood: in his eyes it was like Claire that on her birthday she should be the one who was doing the giving. He had nothing of near value with him to give her in return, but by a prodigious piece of luck, for sometimes the universe does seem benevolent, the better to disarm us, he had just that morning, apropos of nothing, bought her a box of chocolate truffles. They ate the truffles in the sleeping bag, wrapped up in each other, feeding each other, Claire going on about the effect Dylan Thomas achieved with the four symmetrical spondees in "If my head hurt a hair's foot, pack back the downed bone," Chuck explaining that packing was an old method of abortion and that "downed" referred to both the down on the fetus's head and its position, while "hair's foot" referred—and Claire said, "I want to have your baby." Oops.

In the weeks that followed, as the term careened to a close and

Claire received a well-earned grade of A+ for her work in the Yeats seminar, our two amorists furnished their hideaway with a few amenities. Chuck brought a battery-powered lantern and then a kerosene lamp, a portable radio, three chairs, one good for a table in that its back was broken off (all of them scrounged from a subterranean room in which damaged or outdated office furniture was discarded), enameled metal cups, blue with white speckles, and a mirror, so that Claire before she went out to face the world again could repair the damage. But there never was any damage, for curly hair tends to be even more curly after, than before, lovemaking, and Claire's lips did not need lipstick, least of all after Chuck had been massaging them with his own for hours. Claire brought a broom, a plastic washbasin, a washcloth, a towel, and water (in two surplus canteens she carried in her knapsack). They surprised each other with consumable or inconspicuous presents, invisible to suspicious spouses: chocolate truffles, liquors, a thick anthology of poems by American women, a pair of exercise grips, for Claire wanted to develop her forearms, a Western-style belt with a big silver buckle for Chuck to wear with his jeans, a watchband to match, sexy underwear, a fountain pen, sushi, a neat little memo book in which Claire could record phrases that came to her out of nowhere, like one of Cupid's arrows, an up-to-date thesaurus arranged alphabetically, a black and purple necktie to go with Chuck's black shirt, an olive drab wool scarf to go with Claire's field jacket, Chap Stick. Once every couple of weeks Chuck stuffed the sleeping bag into Claire's duffel and took it to a laundromat that Jane never used, for the Lockharts had a washing machine in their apartment. A time would come when Claire and Chuck looked back on this period as the golden age of their relationship.

Aside from the material impediments to a smooth course for their affair, there were those interior traps, those damned emotions, dropouts from reason, rocks in a brook. In Claire's case it was mainly guilt that ruffled the flow. "Go to school with the nuns, matriculate in guilt." Sporadically it made her moody, paranoid, snappish. "Suppose you and I were married and I was screwing Ivan, how would you feel?" She began to hate Ivan for what she was doing to him. She wanted Chuck to be the Perseus that released her from guilt, and got furious with him for only increasing it. She began to despise herself for the sneaking around that had once seemed adventurous. She began to feel that all anyone had to do to know what was going on was to see them together. They no longer jogged side by side.

In Chuck's case it was mainly possessiveness that troubled their currents. He wanted Claire to be with him always. He grew to hate weekends, during which she had to work while he chafed at the end of Jane's short leash. And there were times when the mere thought of Ivan Tervakalio (that lurching hulk) embracing Claire made his heart shake and his mind go black. He had to sit down or risk falling.

On the six-month anniversary of their first get-together at the Wanhope, they were together again, at the Wanhope again, in room 1133 again, in bed again, once more enjoying a postcoital gab fest. Each had thought to surprise the other by bringing a bottle of champagne, so neither was entirely sober.

"Would you marry me if I divorced my wife?" said Chuck.

"Would you marry me if I killed my husband?" said Claire.

"Let's kill them both—and anybody else who gets in the way," he said.

"He gets me so mad sometimes," she said. "When I bitch at him he just stands there with his face hanging out, with this look, I don't know, of hurt and flabbergasted innocence. Then I really get mad. Did you catch that hendiadys?"

"Why do you bitch at him in the first place?" Chuck said.

"Because he's so holy," she said. "He's so selfless, you know. He'll hitchhike to Ohio to protest the cutting down of a hundred-year-old tree, but he'd never think just once of washing the windows or cleaning up after supper or not leaving a ring around the tub. Once I made cabbage and potatoes for supper five days in a row. He never noticed. I pointed out that we were too broke to buy meat. He said that we were still eating better than most people in the world. You can imagine what I said to that."

"Does he ever strike back?" said Chuck.

"He's inarticulate to begin with," she said, "but when you get in his face, words desert him totally. Instead, you can see the veins on his forehead swell and his hands curl into fists. Someday he's going to hit me. Then I'll truly kill him."

"I'm still trying to figure out why I married Jane," he said. "Why did you marry Ivan?"

"Out of pity," she said. "You know what he said to me, just the other day? I'm his proof to the world that he's not a complete loser."

"Ow!" Chuck said.

"I don't need that kind of burden," Claire said.

> I'll sing you four, O
> Red fly the banners, O
> What is your four, O
> Four for the years it took them
> Three, three, the rights of man
> Two, two, a man's own hands
> Working for his living, O
> One is workers' unity
> And ever more shall be so.

"How would you do it?" Chuck said, kissing her.

"Do what?" Claire said, returning the kiss.

"Kill Ivan," he said, pulling Claire on top of him.

"Ha, ha," she said. "I'd kill him with whatever is nearest to hand, a potato peeler, my cast-iron pan, a Brillo pad, a beer bottle, a dumbbell—we're not talking premeditation here," and she flutter-kissed his sinewy neck.

"The idea would be to get away with it," he said, stroking her firm butt, probing its cleft.

"What would you use, smart guy?" she said, moving south, kissing his nipples.

"There are poisons that are hard to detect," he said, inserting a finger.

"A woman's weapon," she said, raising gooseflesh with big sucking kisses on the sensitive skin of his belly. She rotated on her knees until her body was at a right angle to his, so that he could more comfortably reach into her treasure trove, which he did.

"It's an interesting problem," he said, stroking her G-spot.

Claire did not at first answer, for her mouth was full. But after a bit she raised her head to say "Two problems."

"Yes," he said, "... Ivan and Jane ... two fatal accidents waiting to happen ... accidents ... that's the way to go."

"Um," she said. And so they went at it, daydreaming of murder.

twelve

Whatever makes any bad action familiar to the mind renders its performance by so much the easier. [ROBERT WRIGHT, The Moral Animal: Why We Are the Way We Are: The New Science of Evolutionary Psychology] ❡ *If we consider sex to be as dangerous as a loaded Kalishnikov rifle, it is because it is the source of all immorality.* [ALHAJ MAULAVI QLALMUDDIN of the General Department for the Preservation of Virtue in Afghanistan] ❡ *Throughout history, adultery has had few rivals as a cause of murder and human misery.* [JARED DIAMOND, The Third Chimpanzee: The Evolution and Future of the Human Animal]

THIS SHRINK I KNOW, the one who saved a bebopper's chops by transferring the tremor on his lip to a big toe, was telling me about a patient with a fixed idea, a case of obsession, you might say. The patient was dumped by his girlfriend, knocked him for a loop. He was consoling himself with fantasies of revenge when out of the blue, nothing leading up to it, so he swears, the idea of suicide struck him. That would show her. But the idea of suicide lacked glamour: suicide was for sissies. On the whole, he enjoyed life. Hell, he was young enough to find another woman. There were even times when he was glad to be rid of the baggage, always dragging him to operas and foreign films. And what about his parents? They would be devastated. But he could not shake off the idea. Whenever his mind went slack it would begin to dally with methods of doing away with himself. Pictures of himself taking a swan dive off the George Washington Bridge or shooting himself so that his shattered and bloody head fell forward onto his desk, on which were spread photos of his ex-girlfriend, kept him awake at night. Thoughts of suffocating himself in a plastic bag interfered with his attempt to masturbate himself into tranquility. Finally he duct-taped a nine-by-five photo, suitable for framing, of his heartless beloved on the tile wall beyond the foot of his bathtub, swallowed a handful of sleeping pills, prescribed by my shrink friend, filled the tub with hot water so that the whole room was steamy, climbed in, and with a single-edged razor held in his right hand cut surprisingly deep through the flesh, tendons, and blood vessels of his left wrist, lay back, slowly died.

That's pretty much how it went with Chuck, except that his fixed idea was murder. It was on his mind as he put down one hundred dollars plus tax for their afternoon at the Wanhope, gave Claire a twenty for cab fare home, took the subway to 110th Street, laid a dollar bill on Hardcore's outstretched hand (which gesture left him with $1.68 in walking-around money), made his way through the tunnels to his office. He was so absorbed in tabulating means of murder that he did not hear the click of her perdurable high heels as Betty Blondell with a firm tread walked along a passageway that intersected Chuck's and turned the corner, CRASH, right into the man. She said, "Chuck! Whatever are you doing down here?" just as he said, "Betty! What brings *you* down here?" though it must be said that he had the greater claim to surprise, for if there was anything chthonic about Betty Blondell, he had never seen it.

"I'm on my way to the radio station," she said.

"I didn't know KWAP was down here," he said.

"By the swimming pool," she said.

"You about to thunder at some student announcer for mentioning sex?" he said.

"For your information, studies show that married Christian couples have sex more often than their secular counterparts," she said. "How like you that, big boy?" and she poked him in the chest.

"That's because the women have been browbeaten into believing they must 'graciously comply' with their husbands' demands," he said.

"Don't you ever speak to your wife?" she said. Then she plucked at his eyebrow.

"Ouch," he said.

She held up between forefinger and thumb something that Chuck could not quite make out, for his eyes were fifty years old.

"Strawberry blonde and frizzy," she said: "where've you been putting your face?"

"What do you mean by that crack about my not talking to Jane?" he said.

"Not only am I on the KWAP Board of Faculty Directors," she said, "I also have my own weekly radio show: 'Religions of the World.'"

"What has that got to do with Jane?" he said.

"Jane and I are working up an interview for my show about the church her father founded," she said.

"The First Church of Christ, Avenger," he said.

"God takes offenses against his commandments personally," she said.

"He would," Chuck said.

"I suppose you know that Jane wants a call-in show of her own?" she said.

"I know she needs something to keep her occupied," he said.

She straightened out the knot in his tie. "Sometimes," she said, "I can see through a chink in that armor you wear that you're not a happy man. I can help."

Chuck was quiet for a moment as he took this in. If you were to construct a consensual American beauty, she might look very much like Betty Blondell. Certainly the proportions were right, that swell of calf and thigh. Just the same, there was something... well, she looked as though the flesh under her skin was pulled too tight across, encasing her in her own substance. And she looked as though if you tried to carry her over a threshold she would be hard and heavy as a life-sized bronze statue of Artemis. Chuck put his hands on her arm, which was humanly pliant, ready to say thanks, maybe even to kiss her on the forehead, when she said, "Let me bring you to Christ. It's the only consolation that never lets you down."

That tore it, though Chuck did actually kiss her on the forehead, for he felt that there was more than religion in her offer. "Let's have lunch next week," he said, patting her arm, taking off, thinking (unjustly) when was the last time Jane had shown him sympathetic concern or even run-of-the-mill affection, for God's sake.

As he picked up his briefcase at the office and started home, his legs a bit wobbly, for it was more than twenty years since he had made it with a woman twice in one day, he thought

gun
knife
blunt instrument
garrote
an undetectable poison
a plugged-in radio thrown into a tub full of water and Jane

Jane was sitting at the kitchen table, wearing a white blouse and a black skirt. Her hair was neatly combed, and she was actually wearing lipstick—with nail polish to match, a first. On the radio Dr. Lena Pitts was praising a warden who, according to the *Los Angeles Times*, had confiscated all his inmates' nudie magazines. She was going to send him a tee shirt.

Jane: I'm studying Dr. Lena. The secret of her success is that she radiates authority.

Caller: Am I morally obligated to ask my father to my wedding?

Chuck: The secret of her success is that people listen in to laugh at the simple souls who call her.

Dr. Lena: The Bible tells us to honor our fathers.

Jane: See? The whole country is hungry for obedience.

Caller: Even if he's having an affair?

Jane: Yearns for discipline.

Dr. Lena: How tall is he?

Jane: Craves control, direction, regulation.

Chuck: [*groans*]

Caller: Six feet.

Jane: Wants to be told what to do.

Dr. Lena: How about your mother? Is she spreading her legs for some stud?

Chuck: The woman's a lunatic!

Caller: Well, she's been confined to a wheelchair for years. But lately she's beginning to lose it mentally.

Jane: Must have religion, can't do without it.

Dr. Lena: Your father's a degenerate. You don't owe him anything.

Chuck: The woman's a moral imbecile! [*Jane puts a finger to her lips, signifying that Chuck should button his.*]

Caller: There's one side of me that feels that because my mother—

Dr. Lena: Don't talk to me about feelings. I'm not a feelings person. I'm a behavior person. You've got to resist the emotionality of today's sex-crazed culture.

Caller: I always thought it's the way you feel that makes you do things.

Dr. Lena: I don't care what you thought. Something wrong with your hearing? I told you I was behavior orientated.

Caller: I felt, I mean I thought, that is, I understood the Bible to mean you've got to, you know, understand another person's feeling before—

Dr. Lena: Understanding is irrelevant. Listen to me very carefully. Sex is a gift that a wife gives her husband when they have entered the covenant of marriage. Sex outside marriage is for animals. Period. End of sentence.

Caller: I feel so wishy-washy compared to you.

Dr. Lena: It's childish. You've got to learn to assert assurity and matoority.

Caller: I won't invite my father, then.

Dr. Lena: That's between you and he. I'm not interested in the details. I gave you the philosophic basis for a decision. The rest is up to you.

Caller: But—

Dr. Lena: But me no buts. Whenever I hear the word "but" I know I'm in for a dose of waffling.

Caller: Yes, Dr. Lena. Thank you, Dr. Lena.

Chuck grabbed handfuls of his hair with both hands and pretended to be pulling it out, his teeth clenched, his eyes wild.

"You're not so matoor either," Jane said. "You're like these liberals who find excuses even for child molesters: 'His mother was mean to him,' blah, blah, blah."

"Listen to me very carefully," said Chuck. "I'm driving down a suburban street. A kid runs out from between two cars on the right. I swerve sharply to the left and run over a dog. Got it? O.K., I'm driving down a suburban street. Up ahead I see a dog trotting along the street on the left. I accelerate, swerve sharply to the left, and run over the dog. The same act but two very different degrees of wrongdoing."

"It wasn't the same act," said Jane. "In one case you swerved away from the kid. In the other case you swerved toward the dog."

"Objectively considered, in the eye of a camera, let's say, the two swerves were the same," said Chuck. "Both times I swerved toward the dog or I wouldn't have hit it. Period. End of sentence."

"Professor's skimble-skamble," said Jane. "Just because you get more practice using words. If you want to know, being a housewife is a lonely occupation."

"I don't remember ever trying to dissuade you from getting a job," Chuck said.

"What I meant to say was that a real man lives by a strict moral code," she said. "So does a nation that's not going into decline like the Roman Empire. We're sinking into permissiveness and relativity and entropy—into sensationalism and sensuality and sin—look at television."

"And I'm telling you that strict morality is always immoral," said Chuck, "that every moral truth is in some ways and at some times false, that every lasting emotion is mixed, that every conviction worth fighting about is suspended over the void."

"You think I don't know what this is all about?" she said. "You want to commit adultery, but you haven't the courage. You're trying to talk yourself into justification. If my father had wanted to commit adultery, no one could have stopped him."

"She *is* a witch" is what Chuck thought. But he said, "What's for dinner?"

"Pizza," Jane said, "whenever you want to call for it to be delivered."

While he sipped bourbon and ate pizza, his half with pepperoni, Jane's half without, he thought

a car bomb
a push out the window
a hitman (Hardcore?)
a cement block accurately dropped from a roof
find a rabid bat near her father's place; put its blood in her soup
feed her bourbon until she passes out; press a pillow to her face

"I'm sorry about what I said before," Jane said. "I didn't mean it. It's just you goaded me into striking back. I remember how you put yourself between that cop and Leonard Sistrunk during the demonstration against . . ." and Chuck was thinking how his physical courage had not truly been tested since he was ten years old, when he didn't have any. "Fifteen years later and you still have a lump on your head from that mick's nightstick. . ." and Chuck was thinking how they had moved to East 84th Street so his father could be near Hans Jaeger's, where he was maitre d', and Henny Kramer and his pals punched him around daily. ". . . the way you bearded the adminis-

tration over stipends for graduate students . . . practically led a revo-
lution . . . Vice President Whatsherface, that bitch, gave you only a
one percent raise for five years after by way of getting back at you
until she became president of Bennington . . ." and Chuck remembered how he had gone to his father and his father had said if Chuck
couldn't or wouldn't fight back he would have to learn either how to
run or talk fast and that's what he had been doing ever since. "The
real problem is that after all these years of marriage, you still don't
understand what my needs are," Jane said.

"'Understanding is irrelevant,'" said Chuck, who had hardened
his heart, but he did not say it loud enough for anyone to hear.

> bow and arrow
> a push off a cliff
> a push into the lions' lair at the Bronx Zoo
> feed her bourbon until she passes out; blow out the pilot light;
> > turn on the gas; leave a candle burning
> a poisonous icicle propelled through a plastic tube
> > by a puff of air

"Are you giving me the silent treatment?" said Jane.

"No, no, I'm just thinking about what you said," he said. "What is
courage?"

"Everybody knows that," she said. "Don't be such a professor.
It's whatever it takes to face up to danger. It's carrying something
through against intimidating odds. There!"

"Courage is fear," he said, "fear of other people's opinion or of
your own superego: do the deed or go down in dishonor."

"That's what professors do: they make the obvious obtuse,"
she said.

"You mean 'abstruse,'" he said. "Or courage is simply a berserker
rage that burns out all thought of consequences; or it can be mere
stupidity or overriding greed or a desire to impress . . . or madness."

"Yada, yada, yada," she said.

"But," he said, his face stern and flushed, pointing a finger, "but it takes the most courageous courage of all to fight through a phobia. It's not the actual pad of steel wool or dripping faucet or earmuffs you fear but the meaning you've invested in them. To you the other guy's fists are more than flesh and blood: they are haunted . . . so you slink away. Only if—"

"What's got into you?" she said. "You know what? You scare me sometimes," and she stood up, walked around the table, sat on his lap, snuggled her head under his chin, and said, "Does my big, brave Daddy want to have a glass of Kahlua and then take his little girl to bed?"

"How about tomorrow?" he said.

thir-
teen

Common chimps already carried out planned killings, extermination of neighboring bands, wars of territorial conquest, and abduction of young nubile females. [JARED DIAMOND, The Third Chimpanzee: The Evolution and Future of the Human Animal] ¶ *There is nothing especially odd about the Yanomamo. All studies of preliterate societies done before national governments were able to impose their laws upon them revealed routinely high levels of violence. One study estimated that one-quarter of all men were killed in such societies by other men. As for the motives, sex is dominant.* [MATT RIDLEY, The Red Queen: Sex and the Evolution of Human Nature] ¶ *In his study of Eskimo life, Rasmussen (1931) reports that he never met a grown man who had not been involved in a killing.* [DONALD SYMONS, The Evolution of Human Sexuality] ¶ *Indeed men who have demonstrated their prowess through killing other men (unoka) have more wives and more children than same-aged non-unoka men.* [DAVID M. BUSS, The Evolution of Desire: Strategies of Human Mating] ¶ *Overall, homicide is the tenth leading cause of death in the United States.* [CAROL ANN RINZLER, Why Eve Doesn't Have an Adam's Apple]

CHUCK'S HEAD WAS SPINNING just a wee bit from bourbon when he went to bed that night and lay down next to Jane, who was in a wee bit of a coma from red wine. Before his closed eyes Chuck and Claire were trekking north, making for the Reverend Hartung's house, which had long been prepared for some glorious apocalypse, wood stoves, gravity-fed water, a cupboard full of kerosene lamps, drums of kerosene and gas in an outbuilding, crosscut saws that the Reverend had made Chuck learn how to sharpen. They moved easily under their knapsacks and on the two-hundred-dollar hiking shoes they had liberated from a sports shop in a strip mall outside Suffern, skirting built-up areas, keeping to woods when they could find them, following a line parallel to the Thruway but at least a couple of hundred yards west of it, hunting knives on hips, sidearms in holsters, long arms in hand, for there were bands of desperadoes (but fewer every day) who would like nothing better than to loot their gear and rape Claire.

At dusk they settled in for the night under a conifer, who knows what kind?—this is a city boy talking to you. The point is that there were low, thick, spreading branches, shield against a chill wind and hostile eyes. They had a cocktail of bourbon and water before dinner, which consisted of canned chili fortified with strips of beef jerky, their dessert the last of a jar of maraschino cherries (including the juice), for Chuck, even as a fantasist, knew that the good Lord was in the details. After dinner, Claire went out of the circle of light cast by the fire for a quick pee, brushed her teeth, kissed Chuck good night, and by no means perfunctorily, crawled into the sleeping bag, promptly fell asleep. Chuck sat there looking into the fire, listening to Claire's regular breathing, which bespoke confidence in his ability to protect her, sipping bourbon and water, thinking how the next night they would have to camp near water so they could wash up, chilly or not, and have some sex, when he heard the crack of a snapping branch not far down slope.

He slunk to his right, crouched over, silent as a pard, knife on hip, Colt 1911 in shoulder holster, Winchester Model 12 in hand, toward an outcrop fifty yards away, from which the whole slope would lie exposed to his gaze. There, under a bright and crazy moon, ragged clouds blown across it by a high wind, he saw brush agitated by a low wind, three men moving through it toward where Claire was sleeping, her back to the fire. The angles were such that the three men would get to Claire before Chuck, barring a berserker's charge, a paralyzing war cry. He slunk his way back slowly, silent as a pard.

"On your knees, bitch." The speaker was tall, blond, wide across the cheekbones, a pony tail sneaking out from under a ridiculous cap. In his hand was what looked like a big old Colt SA Army. His fly was unzipped, his dangle unnaturally long, but limp. To his right, not far from where Chuck lurked in the dark, stood a man holding one of those dumb Israeli-made machine pistols, you'd be lucky to hit a garage door at arm's length with it. To his left stood a skinny redneck type holding a lever action carbine, looked like a Marlin. Claire, shivering in her red long johns, knelt before Blondie. As he said, "Come on, bitch, let's see you gobble—" Chuck stepped into the flickering light of the fire.

"Freeze, motherfuckers," he said. The joker to the blond's right, to Chuck's left, started to raise his pistol. Chuck destroyed his chest with a round of double-O shot, fifteen .32-caliber pellets to the round. As the big blond swung his revolver toward Chuck, Claire, her athlete's reflexes kicking in, reached up and grabbed it with both hands. Blondie was trying to get Claire to let go with a flurry of left hooks when Chuck's first shot at him removed his jaw. He had not even started to fall when Chuck's second shot, in a nimbus of blood, pretty much removed what was left of his face, for you can shoot a pump gun just about as fast as a semi-automatic. The third bad guy stood still, pale and swaying, his prominent Adam's apple going up and down, his rifle at port arms. He closed his eyes when Chuck pointed the shotgun at him.

Claire made the potentially fatal mistake of moving between them to pull the rifle out of this loser's hands. She worked the lever once to make sure there was a round in the chamber. A round flew out of the ejection port, catching the firelight. "Drop your knapsack, shithead," she said, and he did it. "Put your hands on your head, asshole," she said, and he did it. "Turn around, numbnuts," she said, and she patted him down. "You listen to me, rat turd, you start walking, and you walk fast, and you don't stop until you've gone a mile, at least, and if we ever see you again, you're dead."

"Can I have my knapsack?" he said.

"You can have three seconds to get moving," she said. So he got moving. When he had taken six steps she shot him just about midway between the shoulder blades. At close range the slow, fat, bluntnosed Marlin .444 is a very destructive round. "We don't want to be looking over our shoulders all the time," she said.

The knapsack was full of money, packs of twenties, fifties, hundreds, thous... might never be worth anything again, but then... Claire looked up at Chuck from where she was squatting by the... and her lips never looked more kissable, in spite, or because, of the swelling on the right side where... drops of blood on her forehead, in her hair...

Chuck kissed Claire on the lips and sat down, for they were just hanging out (grumpy Claire being a day into her period) in their underground hideaway, for the world was too much with them.

"Do you really want to have a baby?" he said.

"Course I do," she said. "A poet has to experience everything. But it's got to be with a real man, someone who can provide."

Chuck did not mention his own theory, which is that poets tend to experience relatively little—except in their imaginations. "Every time I suggested to Jane that we start a family," he said, "she would accuse me of trying to hold her back."

"From what?" Claire said.

"Her career," he said.

"Which is what?" she said.

"Looking for a career," he said.

They were quiet for a moment. Then Chuck leaned over and took Claire's hand in his own. "You leave Ivan; I leave Jane; we move in together, file for divorce."

"Ivan would never give me a divorce," she said. "He'd fight me every step of the way. He'd drag out the process forever. And he'd have lots of help from that awful sister of his, who's a lawyer. She hates me."

"There's one more thing we have in common—the kind of person we married," he said.

"And even afterward he'd always be hanging around, that big lugubrious face of his hanging out, calling up at all hours on some pretext, stalking me, in fact," she said. "I'd never be rid of him."

"I could probably get a job in California," he said. "Jane hates California, though she's never been there."

"Ivan loves California, though he's never been there either," she said.

Chuck got out of his chair and pulled Claire to her feet so he could hold her to him, from knee to neck. "If we had a child, she would become a great athlete," he said. "I see her winning a gold medal in the decathlon."

"If we had a child, we'd teach him how to make money, if only someone would teach us first," she said.

They squeezed each other until it hurt, then sat down.

"Well, we'll have to kill them, that's all," said Chuck.

"There have been times . . . ," she said.

"The question is whether we have a greater right to be happy than they have to live," he said.

"Mother of God," she said.

"On the other hand, you have a right to stop someone who's trying to steal your happiness," he said. "The only way to stop Jane and Ivan is to kill them."

"Q.E.D.," she said. "Twaddle about the rights and wrongs of something is always foreplay to a swindle."

"Speaking of which," he said, sliding his chair up against hers, sliding his hand under her sweater, under her bra, kissing her and kissing her.

She pushed him away. "Now tell me true: could you really do it?" she said. "Just curious."

"Could I kill my wife?" he said. "Yes, I could. I never hated her that much until I met you. But now I could kill her, yes, I could."

"Taking another person's life . . . ," she said. "Think how much you value your own."

"You couldn't do it, then?" he said.

"I couldn't kill Ivan, not in cold blood, much as he infuriates me sometimes," she said. "I'd find it hard to kill anybody up close and personal. But if it was a matter of those religious reactionaries, those puritan pipsqueaks, those chrome-plated Cromwells, those totalitarian creeps who are trying to take over the country and gaining ground every day . . ." For Claire, when you came down to it, was her parents' daughter, even though she was laughing at her own vehemence.

"My wife is turning herself into a disciple of Dr. Lena," he said, releasing both breasts from Claire's bra.

"Poor Chuckie," she said, kissing him on the forehead. "Well, the only way to go is you kill Ivan; I kill Jane."

Chuck, who had been mouthing a nipple, sat back and up. He was stunned and he was flabbergasted. What an idea! Leave it to Claire. . .

"That way your . . . let's say *history* with the victim doesn't inform on you," she said. "Besides, the police always look to the spouse first."

Chuck pictured himself sending first a right cross and then a left hook into Ivan's fleshy face, and a big but unnameable emotion filled his chest. He relaxed and slid down into his chair to accommodate Claire, who was trying to unzip his fly. "Just for the fun of it," he said, "how would you go about it?"

"Let's see," she said, lazily stroking his quasi-hard member. "Start with the goal of making murder look like an accident. In that category I include those maniacs who bean perfect strangers with a brick or push them under a subway."

"Don't stop," he said, for now he was altogether hard.

"O.K.," she said. "So you stalk your victim. You find out everything about his routines. The fatal accident has to look like a mere glitch in his daily rounds. You will agree, I believe, that the monstrous always emerges from a chink in the quotidian."

"Expelled from the nookie of the world's body," he said.

"Chuckie dear," she said, "I have to tell you that metaphor is not your métier. The first stage, then, is information-gathering. Hunters thrive on intimate knowledge of their prey."

"In that respect they are like lovers," he said.

She pinched his corolla.

"Yipe," he said.

"You've got to be finely tuned to all the particulars of the scene," she said. "There's no telling in advance which will be critical. Overlook anything and you could wind up in the hot seat."

He slid a hand inside her panties, which were under her tights, which were under her miniskirt, and placed his finger on her rosebud. "'Tis a consummation devoutly to be wished," he said.

"It's no use forcing the weapon of your choice on the situation," she said. "You've got to use what is there, so it can't be traced back to you."

"What's your weapon of choice?" he said.

"Bludgeon," she said, waggling his. "What's yours?"

"Ideally speaking...I'd have to say *bare hands*," he said. "Using a weapon on an unarmed adversary would be too much like cheating."

"Save the chivalry," she said.

"For what?" he said.

"For literature," she said. "Ivan is very strong."

"In all modesty," he said, "How about me?"

But she said no more, for her mouth was otherwise engaged.

It's a good thing they were not walking hand in hand, as they often did, for not twenty feet away, arm in arm, walking briskly, Betty Blondell and Jane Lockhart swung around a corner right into their path.

"Betty, Jane, I'd like you to meet my student, Callie Pigeous," Chuck said. "Miss Pigeous, meet Professor Betty Blondell and my wife, Jane Lockhart."

"Hello," Claire said tonelessly.

"Ms. Pigeous," said Betty, giving her a look that you would have to call penetrating.

"Yeah, hi," said Jane, pretty much ignoring Claire. "What are *you* doing down here?" Jane said to Chuck.

"Taking a shortcut to my office," he said.

"Do you want to watch us do the show on Daddy's church?" she said.

"Can't: office hours," he said.

"A couple of students are going to tape the show," Betty said. "You can watch it on videotape."

"We're off," said Jane.

"Break a leg," said Chuck.

When the two women were out of earshot, Claire said, "Poor Chuckie."

"Lucky Chuckie, whose lover is Claire McCoy," he said, ever the gentleman. He kissed her.

Further along, they came upon a new graffito:

SET YOUR AFFECTIONS ON THINGS ABOVE
NOT ON THINGS ON THE EARTH
—Colossians

Claire stood in the middle of the corridor looking at this advice to live in delusion. "Come along, Claire," Chuck said. "The poor in spirit always have ye with you."

"Wait," she said. "It's coming. . . . Got it!" She pulled the marker pen out of Chuck's pocket and wrote this:

DEEP CALLETH UNTO DEEP
—Psalms

"How come your head is all full of that stuff?" said Chuck.

"I guess I never told you that I once wanted to become a nun," she said. "I studied the Bible every day. Then I began to grow boobs."

"And you became callipygous," he said.

"Damn straight," she said.

four-teen

Who is this that darkeneth counsel by words without knowledge? [JOB 38:2] ❡ *A scarecrow in a garden of cucumbers keepeth nothing.* [BARUCH 6:70] ❡ *Love covereth all sins.* [PROVERBS 10:12]

SECULAR LOVE DOES NOT WORK OUT WELL in that exemplary modernist poet, T. S. Eliot—*Oed' und leer das Meer.* Neither does Christian love, a straining after something unobtainable. Such was secular love to W. B. Yeats, arguably the greatest love poet of this century. His poems celebrating his marriage to George are thankful for sex and many small comforts; romantic love is hardly an issue. As for Christian love, "Rihb Considers Christian Love Insufficient" is the title of one of those poems in which Yeats says through a "cracked" persona what he normally kept behind his other masks. "Why should I seek for love or study it?" asks Rihb, a good question, especially for a poet who had once admired past lovers who "would sigh and quote with learned looks / Precedents out of beautiful old books." Rihb, rather, studies "hatred with great diligence" to free his soul from "terror and deception," from "that trash and tinsel." Yeats's Crazy Jane, who gave all for love, squelches the Bishop by pointing out that "Love has pitched his mansion in the place of excrement"—good news or bad, depending on what irons out your kinks, but closer to the facts than precedents from Castiglione. Similarly, Wallace Stevens, in "Le Monocle de Mon Oncle," opposes a middle-aged and modernist lust to the romantic love of the young and of his poetic predecessors. "A deep up-pouring from some saltier well bursts their radiant bubble." Lust is the real amphibian in imaginary gardens:

94

Last night, we sat beside a pool of pink,
Clippered with lilies scudding the bright chromes,
Keen to the point of starlight, while a frog
Boomed from his very belly odious chords.

Chuck was far from satisfied with this paragraph. It lacked some-thing—verve, bite, arresting details, above all, point. Yes, it lacked point: why was he writing it? Chuck's unprofessional bias was to-ward writing that relieved or released something, like longing or spleen, that decreased pain or increased pleasure. But the expected yield of pleasure was not forthcoming. Maybe the problem lay in Chuck's refusal to admit, even to himself, that he was writing the article to get back at Jane, who was a great believer in love, but only on the verbal, rather than on the material, plane. To admit that would be to admit that as paybacks go, this article was small potatoes, especially when set against what Chuck now considered twenty-five years of deprivation.

forty whacks with an ax
hanta virus in her rice
a rattler in the bed in the room in Sacandaga that her
    father always keeps ready for her
get Jane to look in the trunk of their car; rev the engine;
    shift into reverse

Chuck reined in his runaway imagination right there. You see how dangerous a habit of thought can become? If it's murder that Chuck was going to play at, it wouldn't be Jane's. No, the time had come to track down Ivan Tervakalio. At the thought, a surge of energy coursed through his body, leaving a tingle in his legs. Easy now, hold back a little, for when young, Chuck, like so many of us, had been a premature ejaculator, first things first, first scout out the where and when of how the man spent his days, work up to the con-summatory act gradually. Then look for that chink in the quotidian out of which the monstrous can be delivered. Then—and at that point Chuck heard the front door open and slam shut, for it was not Jane's style to close doors quietly.

"Helloooo," she said.

"In here," he said.

She walked into his study and threw herself into the big brown stuffed leather chair that Chuck had bought for six dollars in a thrift shop in Sacandaga twenty years ago. Chuck loved that chair. She looked at him. He looked back, knowing that something was expected of him but not knowing what. Her face was flushed, lit up, full, the angles softened, and Chuck was reminded of how she looked when his sister, whom he has never forgiven, first introduced them: naïve, eager, young for her years. "Aren't you going to ask me how the interview went?" she said.

"How'd it go?" he said.

"It went well," she said, but then she couldn't hold it in any longer: "Oh, Chuck, it was wonderful," and she leaned forward to squeeze his arm—"finally I was doing what I was meant to do. I was a hit, I know it, Betty said so herself. You know that the last half hour of her show is given over to calls from listeners?" ("No," he said.) "Well, I fielded every question without a flub—you wouldn't believe how many students, even here, are still religious. There was just one dicey moment: some kid with a lisp, if you know what I mean, asked what my father thought about gay marriage or civil unions or legal recognition of blah, blah, blah. Well, I never heard Daddy mention the subject. If you're gay up in Sacandaga, you keep it to yourself. So I simply said you can't get around the fact that the Bible is against sodomy. Period. End of sentence. And this little snot nose says, 'I know what the Bible is against, but what about you? If you've never been buggered, you're missing something. Give me a call—' That's when Betty cut him off. But I put the little prick in his place anyhow. I said that God or nature or what have you formed men and women to fit each other, that homosexuality is an abnormality, like, for instance, Tourette's syndrome. That comparison is Dr. Lena's."

"Or like perfect pitch," Chuck said, " or like an I.Q. of two hundred."

"Before I could really get going, Betty put on another caller," Jane said. "She later told me that GLAD—that's The Gay and Lesbian Action Directive—is very militant."

"I can see why," Chuck said.

"After, Betty and another faculty advisor took me out for a drink," she said. "We talked about the possibility of me having a show of my own," she said.

"Well, this calls for a celebration," said Chuck. "Let's have a drink and then go out to eat."

"Let's," she said. "Let's have pasta—oh, and I've got to talk to you about something. Whatshisface, the other advisor, thought maybe I should get a degree in psychiatric social work or counseling or whatever. Who should I see about that? It's funny that I never thought of psychiatry before. I think I'd be a natural. You'd have to call me 'Dr. Jane.'"

"I'll look into it," Chuck said as the phone rang. It was Lana Faye Sammis, one of the Reverend Luke Hartung's keepers. Chuck handed the phone over to Jane and watched her as she listened, the color draining out of her face, her knees weakening so that she had to sit down. She missed the cradle with the phone when it came time to hang up.

"Daddy's had a psychotic break or something," she said. "When no one was looking he slipped out of the house and walked down the street waving his arms and yelling 'Help, help, they're trying to kill me.' Lana Faye says he tried to stay awake the last forty-eight hours for fear the women who take care of him would castrate him once he fell asleep. He wouldn't eat for fear they put a sleeping potion in his food." Her face twisted in the way that precedes a good cry.

In spite of all, Chuck had the decency to walk over to Jane and put his arms around her. "He'll be O.K.," said Chuck; "you know how strong he is. They just need to adjust his meds."

"Someday he'll never be O.K. again," she said. "I can't bear it. It's like someone let the air out of the universe."

"Give him a call," Chuck said. "Reassure him. If he trusts anyone, it's you."

"He's in the hospital," she said. "Lana Faye says they've got him tied to the rails of this stainless-steel crib they put him in."

"Maybe you ought to go up there," he said.

"You could offer to drive me," she said.

"Can't," he said: "I've got a dissertation defense tomorrow."

"You've always got something when I need you," she said.

"Take the train," he said; "enjoy that Hudson Valley scenery. Take a cab from the station. If you need to get around in Sacandaga, use the good Reverend's pickup."

"I know you never liked poor Daddy," she said. "He always liked you. He just wanted you to act more manly. That's why he made you learn how to use guns and the splitting maul."

"I always showed him the greatest courtesy and respect," he said.

"Wasn't it you who told me courtesy was a way of keeping people at a distance?" she said. Suddenly she broke away and dramatically shook her fist at the ceiling and said, "Oh, God, why did you do this to me today, of all days, after I finally got on the radio?"

Why indeed?

In such wisdom is much grief: and he that

fifteen

increaseth knowledge increaseth sorrow. [ECCLESIASTES 1:18] ❡ *The entire evolution of man from the earliest populations of* Homo erectus *to existing races took place during the period in which man was a hunter.* [S. L. WASHBURN AND C. S. LANCASTER, "The Evolution of Hunting"] ❡ *Hunting and gathering was the context in which humans evolved, with our impressive intellectual, psychological, and physical endowments — as well as our limitations.* [S. BOYD EATON, MARJORIE SHASTOK, AND MELVIN KONNER, The Paleolithic Prescription: A Program of Diet and Exercise and a Design for Living]

ARLY THE NEXT MORNING Chuck went with Jane by cab to Penn Station, waited with her for the train to come in, helped her on with her suitcase, gave her a hug that made her spine creak. "Oof," she said. For the exercise and because spring was in the air, he walked the four miles or so uptown and positioned himself across the street from the doorway to the house in which Claire McCoy and Ivan Tervakalio lived.

At 9:36 Ivan carried out a half-dozen big clear plastic bags, of newspapers and magazines, of bottles and cans, all for recycling, for Ivan earned his rent by working as the building's janitor. At 9:48 he carried out four big black bags of garbage. He arranged these bags artfully around the doomed ginkgo tree in front of his house. By

10:10 he was sweeping the entranceway to his house and the street in front of it. By 10:21 he was polishing the brass mailbox doors, the brass plate around the bell buttons, the knob and push plate on the front door, the hinges, and doing a good job of it, too. His movements had a jerky, lunging quality about them, as though he were putting more energy in them than he could control. When he stepped forward, he plopped his feet, like a man trying to save himself from a fall on his face. He whistled while he worked.

A barber from the shop next to Ivan's house stepped out of the door, holding two small paper cups, and I say "Ivan's house," although the house was not, of course, Ivan's—he just worked there as the janitor. And he lived there. He lived there with Claire McCoy, for which crime he was going to die. The barber, who looked something like Caesar Romero, walked over to Ivan and placed one of the paper cups in his hand. They saluted each other, but did not clink cups, for you cannot make paper clink. They drank the contents of the cups in a single glunk, but whether what they drank was espresso or a nice little brandy such as Philippe Secundo, Chuck could not tell, and it was unreasonable for him to be miffed that they hadn't offered him a cupful. The barber held Ivan by the elbow and began to tell him something, laughing between words, and you could see the smile widening on Ivan's face. A waitress from the Spanish restaurant on the other side of Ivan's house joined them. She was short, beautiful posture, lots of black hair that tumbled down to her shoulders and beyond, a vigorous behind. She carried a medium-sized paper cup from which she filled the small cups held by the men. They saluted each other and drank. The barber continued his story, the other two smiling, then laughing. The waitress began to poke Ivan about the sternum with an index finger, on her face a look of mock severity. The three of them collapsed in laughter. For some reason this innocuous tableau held Chuck's fascinated attention.

Ivan took the small cup from the barber, who went back into the barbershop, and the larger cup from the waitress, who went into the restaurant, and walked over to the recycling bags under the doomed ginkgo. He untied the knot that held together the mouth of one of the bags, pushed in the three paper cups, for Ivan was conscientious about not littering, retied the knot, went into his house. Chuck crossed the street and looked through the clear plastic of the recycling bag to see that the three cups had held espresso, or maybe hot chocolate, but not brandy. He did not even try to explain to himself his feeling of disappointment. Nor was Ivan's apparent popularity with his neighbors consistent with the view Chuck wanted to have of him.

Chuck recrossed the street to his old vantage point and waited, trying to stifle his habitual impatience, for hunters are paragons of patience, wished he had a cigarette, rerecrossed the street, bought a container of coffee (dark, no sugar) from the short waitress with the long hair, rererecrossed the street, waited. Some of the people walking by looked at him suspiciously. He walked to the corner and deposited his empty coffee container in a trash basket, for if Ivan could be conscientious, so could Chuck. At 12:10 Ivan emerged from his house, wearing his nautical coat and cap, walked uptown to 110th Street, walked crosstown, right past Chuck's house that was not really Chuck's, to Broadway, Chuck, like Eliot Ness, following at a safe distance.

Ivan bought a tabloid newspaper from the stand at 110th and Broadway, exchanging badinage with the Arab proprietor, clumped down the steps into the subway, read the back pages, the sports pages, while waiting for the downtown local, which he ultimately boarded —and from which he disembarked at Houston Street, never once so much as looking in Chuck's direction. He plodded some blocks down West Broadway and then some blocks east, never mind how many, for Chuck neglected to count, he was so busy digging the local people, and why were they all so young? Ivan walked without a glance left or right, like an implacable force brooding over an inscrutable intention, as Joseph Conrad put it. He took a wide turn, like a truck going too fast, into a door beside a large storefront window.

Chuck stopped, considered, arranged the hood of his parka into a kind of high collar all around, scrunched down so as to hide even more of his face, moved into a casual stroll, looking this way and that, like someone from Indiana, say. As he walked slowly by, he peered through the large storefront window. He saw a large room, a large table in the center of it, strewn with papers, two desks standing out at right angles from the left-hand wall, a man sitting behind one of them, people standing all around, a number of them holding bottles of the kind of water you have to buy, a stocky woman with bangs and a prominent bosom giving Ivan a big hug. Chuck kept on walking, crossed the street half a block away, walked half a block back, assumed a position across the street from the regional headquarters of Greenspace, shifting his weight from foot to foot, for he had to take a pee something awful.

By and by, Ivan emerged, trailing six neo-hippies. Chuck followed them two blocks east, to where they boarded a minivan and took off. Chuck then walked two blocks west, six blocks north, entered the McDonald's, found the john, used it, and, thus refreshed, walked six blocks south to the regional headquarters of Greenspace, and it seems to me I've mislaid a few blocks somewhere along the line. He entered and walked up to the first desk, behind which sat the stocky woman with bangs. She did not look up from the letter she was reading, though she had to know that Chuck was standing there. Remember, he told himself, hunters know how to be patient. Finally she looked up, said, "And who might you be?"

"Orion Hunter," he said.

"A likely story," she said.

"I sometimes write for *The West Side Watch*," he said, "and—"

"The West Side Whatsit?" she said.

"*The West Side Watch*," he said.

"Just what is it you watch?" she said.

"We watch over the West Side from 59th to 125th," he said.

"You don't like those dark folks above 125th?" she said.

"We have more dark folks working for and with us than you seem to have," he said, looking around the room at all those drinkers of bottled water. "We liaise with Harlem newspapers all the time. Charlie Rangel is one of our subscribers. I bet that's more than you can say."

She made a weary gesture, rested her elbow and her boobs on the desk, her head on her hand. "Look, Bud, I already subscribe to more periodicals than I can read." It wasn't until then that Chuck noted what was unusual about her manner of speech. She spoke with her teeth gritted together. It was a feat that Chuck had never before witnessed.

"I'm not here for subscriptions, but for a story," he said. "You've probably got more supporters per acre on the Upper West Side than anywhere else on earth. They want to hear what's doing."

"Ronald Blemp is getting a clearance to build a casino on the Palisades just north of the George Washington Bridge," she said. "We're calling out the troops for a world-class demonstration. How's that for a story?"

"I want to build up to it by starting with the activities of a single Greenspace worker," he said. "Take, for example, that big guy with the ponytail who just went out with six acolytes."

"I'm surprised you didn't recognize him," she said. "That was Ivan Tervakalio, the folksinger and activist."

"I knew I'd seen him someplace before," Chuck said.

"He's a wonderful man," she said, a touch starry-eyed.

"Yes . . . ," he said.

"We're awfully lucky to have him with us," she said.

"Just what does he do, exactly?" he said.

"He's a regional manager," she said. "The 'acolytes,' as you called them, are canvassers. They drive to some neighborhood where we have evidence of support and go door-to-door for contributions. It takes capital to muzzle capitalism, you know."

"I know," he said. "Do you think I can tag along one time?"

"Ask him," she said. "He gets down here twelve thirty or one most Tuesdays, Thursdays, and Saturdays."

"Thank you," said Chuck, starting to turn away. But he checked himself and said, "Does he get paid?"

"He gets a percentage of the take," she said, her jaw muscles showing. "When the pickings are slim, he doesn't keep any for himself. Ivan's a real mensch."

"What percentage?" he said.

"None of your business," she said.

"Thank you and good-bye," he said, turned, and walked out. So ended Chuck's first whack at a surveillance of Ivan Tervakalio, folksinger and activist.

> I'll sing you five, O
> Red fly the banners, O
> What is your five, O
> Five for the years of the Five-Year Plan
> Four for the years it took them
> Three, three, the rights of man
> Two, two, a man's own hands
> Working for his living, O
> One is workers' unity
> And ever more shall be so.

He did not walk back to his home grounds, as he would have preferred, for he had a lecture course from two thirty to four. He took the subway. As usual when he was uninspired or had his mind on other things, his class was thick with information rather than insight, thus leaving no space for any back-and-forth with students, the best part of teaching, but also the most demanding. Claire was waiting for him when he came out the classroom door.

"Professor Lockhart, have you got a moment?" she said, students swirling around her.

"Ms. McCoy," he said, walking on. "What's up?" She fell in beside him.

"I was wondering if you have time to read this thing I've written," she said.

"If it's not too long," he said, but by then they had walked away from the students clustered around the elevator and the stairwell.

"Could you go for a drink?" she said. "Ivan's off to a meeting of the Greenspace steering committee. They're going to make the world safe for nuns."

"Meet you at the Other End in twenty minutes," he said, for Claire did not like them to be seen walking together across the campus. It was early enough for Chuck to choose his booth. He chose one in back, where few could see them and no one could hear them. If anything, Claire was early, bless her, for Chuck hated to be kept waiting. The woman was a treasure. On top of everything else she had asked him out for a drink, rather than the usual other way around. It was a character in John Steinbeck, was it not, who noted that for taste nothing can equal the day's first mouthful of beer. Chuck felt coming over him the sense of earned well-being that can make one fatuous, or at least unguarded.

"I put Ivan under surveillance this morning," he said.

"You did *what*?" she said.

"I watched him perform his janitorial duties and then followed him down to Greenspace," he said.

"Why? What for?" she said.

"You know," he said, leaning forward, lowering his voice.

She looked at him, steady-eyed and serious. "You don't want to play games with Ivan," she said. "He's usually very easygoing. You have to work at it to get him mad. But when you do, look out. He's uncontrollable. I thought he was going to kill me last night."

"What's this you say?" he said.

"I'm invited to this poetry festival in Middlebury weekend after next," she said, "seminars, workshops, and I've been asked to read, so I'll hear what other poets have to say about my poems. There'll be editors and agents and people who can get you published. Naturally I expected Ivan to drive me."

"I didn't know you had a car," he said.

"We don't," she said. "But if we give them enough notice, Ivan can usually borrow one from Greenspace. But the point is, he's got to be at this dopey demonstration. So I lit into him. I really let him have it. I was in a rotten mood. This time I went too far."

"I wish I had been there to see it," he said.

"No, you don't," she said. "It wasn't pretty. When I goad him like that, he gets red and swollen and begins to splutter because he can't get the words out to defend himself. He was actually shaking with frustration and rage."

"What did you do?" he said.

"I began to feel sorry for him," she said.

Chuck groaned.

"That was after I ducked into the bathroom and locked the door," she said.

"I can't believe this," he said, for he came from a family in which people did not hit each other or hold shouting matches or even slam doors. In some ways Chuck had a sheltered upbringing; it left him unprepared to deal with strong emotion, either in himself or in others.

"You've got to understand," she said. "You and me, we're word-people: we can get our rocks off with words. Ivan's a kinesthesiac: he's got to do something, preferably with his hands. Have you ever looked at them? They're big and hard, and amazingly skillful—he can fix anything. But I'd hate to be around if he decides to use them in anger."

"This can't go on," Chuck said.

"You don't have to worry," she said. "The word is mightier than the fist. I began to talk him down the minute I got behind the door, before he got it into his head to break it in. Pretty soon he was apologizing. There were tears in his eyes when I came out of the john. I made it up to him by helping him with the words to a couple of songs he was writing especially for this demonstration. I wrote one of them with you in mind: it's a blues."

"Could you go for another?" Chuck said, pointing to Claire's glass.

"Don't you have to get home?" she said.

"Jane went north to attend her father," he said.

"How is the old coot?" she said.

"You know how some people"—and here he signaled to the waitress that she bring them two more—"wind up becoming what they've been pretending to be?" he said.

"Then maybe I'll be a poet someday," she said.

"You *are* a poet," he said. "Well, the Reverend Hartung has pretended to be at death's door for so long that he's gotten there."

"I just wrote a poem that's in part about becoming the role you play," she said. "Want to see?"

"You know I do," he said.

Claire unsnapped a breast pocket on her field jacket, pulled out a folded sheet of paper, unfolded it, gave it to Chuck, said, "I got the idea from this old Steve Reeves movie Ivan and I watched last night after we made up." Here is what Chuck read:

TO AN ACTOR IN
A PERIOD EXTRAVAGANZA

Though mirrored heat forced out the gloss
that sweat is yours. Your real beard curls
though curled. The chemical scar seeps
through real blood to stain the marrow.
The crass sword fits your perfect grip.

Was it for this
you stretched the sun up
and ran through the morning?
(steak, eggs, peppermint tea),
and hefted dumbbells
til the lumps became you?
(squats, jerks, tape on your knee).
For chi-chi girls with low ambitions?
For crazy boys with paltry sorrows?

107

For cozy men with soft fingers?
If so, it was worth it,
if not for you, for us.

The technicolor sky
the democratic mob
the cardboard arena
unfocus:
                    You stand clear.

From downcast sockets, the opaque eyes stare:
The antique slant, the hip-shot slouch
Define our posture:
                        We stand clear.

Though soon you will break off
to half-nelson the lion
skin, or rescue extras,
for now the gesture is all.

Great Dioscuri, smile on him still.

"Is this supposed to be me?" said Chuck, that chucklehead.

"It's supposed to be a poem," she said in the coldest of voices and with a look that could give you frostbite. She reached across the table for the poem; he withdrew it; she reached for it again, leaning forward; he held it over his head, thus attracting the waitress.

"Another round?" she said.

"Yes," Chuck said, and she moved off. Then to Claire: "I just thought—"

"If you don't mind, for the hours I worked on this poem I was able to tear my mind away from you," she said. "I can do that sometimes."

"What I meant—" he said.

"It's a poem about the authentic body, about the humanity in humans, not only surviving the kitschifying roles it has to play, but even revealing itself, better yet achieving itself, through them," she said. "I can't believe I said that."

"Yes," he said, rereading, "now I see. It's a great poem, a grand theme."

"Don't try to soft-soap me," she said.

"No, no, I mean it," he said, and he went on about local beauties, such as the lion / skin enjambement and about the idea of hefting weights until the lumps became you with the lovely pun on "became," until in fact he began to see how much the poem could be made to mean, though at the heart of it he still saw a wry metaphor for his own lack of authenticity, his purely cosmetic muscle, until Claire began to relent, to accept his appeasements, until like a woman who has been told that she looks beautiful but says she's not sure that her new lipstick isn't too dark, Claire said she wasn't sure she liked "opaque eyes" but "blank eyes" wouldn't give her the rhythm she wanted or anticipate "antique," and she wasn't sure she liked "chi-chi girls" but she wanted "chi-chi girls" to go with "crazy boys" and "cozy men" and what did Chuck think? as the waitress brought the beers.

Well, Chuck thought that "opaque" and "chi-chi" were fine but didn't know what an antique slant was and she explained something about statuary and let her hand touch his and he went on about what a triumph of rhythm the first stanza was and he put his hand on hers and said that their tutelary spirit was Hermes, not either of the Dioscuri, and she said that the Egyptian version of Hermes was Thoth, god of writing and the underworld, and she squeezed his knee under the table and he asked if she would like to see his apartment and she said she would have to go home in a minute because Ivan promised or threatened to call at six and Chuck said "Fuck," though he seldom cursed out loud in the presence of ladies.

They drank in silence. "Let me keep the poem and read it over," he said.

"Sure," she said. "See if you can think of something better than 'chi-chi,'" she said.

"How about 'party'?" he said.

"Chuckie, my love, you've got a prose sensibility," she said. "In a

109

poem the sound is as important as, maybe more important than, the sense." She stood up. "I've got to get going."

With the obsolete courtesy handed down by his head-waiter father, he stood up too. With the discretion pounded into him by Claire, he did not kiss her or hug her or even shake her hand. Nor did he shout after her, "How about 'cozened'?"

He sat there finishing his beer, thinking that "costly" didn't quite do it. He began on what was left of Claire's beer, smiling at himself as the words *kissing*, *chastened*, *castaway*, *costive*, flit across his brain, when Simone Song and Tony Felder, materializing out of nothing, slid into the booth.

"Is it McChuck O'Lockhart?" said Tony.

"We didn't want to intrude," said Simone.

"But we need to borrow your car," said Tony.

"We're setting up housekeeping together," she said.

"She's moving in with me under the influence of a rescue fantasy," Tony said.

"He hadn't balanced his checkbook in twenty years," she said.

"I thought I did once, but I was off by a zero," Tony said.

"He's been sending money to cold callers from bucket shops," she said.

"You had to hear these guys," Tony said.

"He had thirty thousand in stock from companies that have been losing money since a week after they went public," she said.

"My advisors counseled patience," he said.

"He hadn't paid off his credit cards—seven of them!—in months," she said. "Just imagine the interest!"

"Enough," he said.

"And then there's the way he eats," she said. "Used to eat."

"She drags me to the gym three times a week," Tony said. "The things you'll do for love."

"He's worth it," she said and grabbed him by the arm with a smile that Chuck thought was a touch complacent.

"I was talking about the things *I* do," Tony said.

In the silence that followed Chuck said, "I'm very happy for you both," though in fact he was down, for their chipper chatter, an oblique advertisement for their affair, had exposed to him the sad hugger-mugger of his own affair. He wanted to bask in the pleasure others would take in the open pleasure he and Claire would take in each other, if only... "Here's the car key and here's the key to the parking lot," said Chuck. "It's at—"

"I remember the beast and its lair very well," said Tony, for during the summer Jane, Tony, and Chuck regularly drove to Jones Beach, for Jane liked to sunbathe, Chuck liked to ride the waves, and Tony liked to look at the girls.

"Give me a call if you need help lugging stuff," said Chuck, standing.

"Simone travels light," said Tony.

"I've got to go," said Chuck.

"What's wrong?" said Simone, looking at his face.

"Got to go" is all he said, walking out. He crossed Broadway. He slapped a dollar bill into Hardcore's hand as he passed by him into Gwinnett Hall. He descended into the catacombs and walked by, without reading, a new graffito:

WIDE IS THE GATE

AND BROAD IS THE WAY

THAT LEADETH TO DESTRUCTION

He ran up the seven flights to his office, grabbed his teaching copy of *To the Lighthouse*, trucked on home, poured himself too much bourbon, fell into a chair, clicked on the TV, out of which an anchorperson spoke to him of "a deadly, sometimes fatal strain of *e. coli*," whereupon Chuck fugued it.

six-teen

A huge majority—980 of the 1,154 past or present societies for which anthropologists have data—have permitted men to have more than one wife. [ROBERT WRIGHT, The Moral Animal: Why We Are the Way We Are: The New Science of Evolutionary Psychology] ❡ *We're left with having to explain the facts that* both *the institution of marriage and the occurrence of extramarital sex have been reported from all human societies.* [JARED DIAMOND, The Third Chimpanzee: The Evolution and Future of the Human Animal] ❡ *For men, the optimal strategy to preserve the species is to have as much sex with as many different partners as possible.* [DEAN HAMER AND PETER COPELAND, Living with Our Genes: Why They Matter More Than You Think] ❡ *The male desire for sexual variety may make the number of available partners always seem insufficient and male "discomfort" inevitable.* [DONALD SYMONS, The Evolution of Human Sexuality] ❡ *Love is the fulfilling of the law.* [ROMANS 13:10]

WHEN CHUCK CAME BACK TO HIMSELF, the New Jersey correspondent was going on about St. Ursula's, there on the Palisades, formerly a convent, now a retirement home for the Sisters of St. Sebastian of Solace, which convent Ronald Blemp was trying to buy. The Church, apparently, was willing to sell, other ex-convents becoming available now that novitiates were harder to come by. But Blemp, so it seems, had not yet been able quite to buy off all the politicians responsible for zoning—for if you look west from the banks of the Hudson on the New York side you will see that the Jersey shore is all built up, but only south of the George Wash-

ington Bridge; along the cliffs north of the bridge there is only nature and St. Ursula's and the tops of a few buildings inland. The correspondent assured his listeners that the view from the cliffs, at least
ten stories high, was awesome. But this correspondent, who was under the delusion that he had a sense of humor, also noted that the
cliffs were awfully convenient to a gambler who had lost everything,
should Ronald Blemp get his casino. As the weatherperson said, "In
terms of temperature, tomorrow we're going to bring in a cooling
trend," Chuck, sipping bourbon, fell into a reverie.

Claire wanted to keep the six-shooter, but Chuck insisted they
take nothing that could be tied to the three dead men sprawled
around the campfire. All night long they hiked north, silent as pards,
pausing to listen when the wind let up, keeping to shadows cast
by the glaring moon that followed them behind leafless branches,
ragged clouds scudding across its face. At sunup they breakfasted:
cold squirrel meat cooked yesterday until it fell off the bone, mixed
with a thimbleful of beechnuts, all the damn greedy deer had left for
them, flavored with salt, pepper, and thyme, for you couldn't expect
them to schlepp a whole spice rack around with them. Then they
moved out, dragging ass, especially Chuck, reminding each other
to be quiet, for they kept forgetting, Claire observing, with a touch
of delirium, that though tall stands of conifers were wonderfully
quiet underfoot, they offered inferior cover, it being one of the un-
expungeable facts of human life that there are no unmixed blessings,
Chuck saying "Amen." They split a can of Dinty Moore's beef stew
for supper. As Chuck spread out the sleeping bag, Claire said, "Can
you let me have some toilet paper?" for the kind of food they ate often left them irregular. But Chuck had used up the last of his roll
that morning. Claire was soon to discover that as an ass-wipe fallen
leaves are grossly overrated. Still, the day ended well, as did all
his days nowadays, in a sleeping bag, that is, snuggled up to Claire.
His last thoughts were that tomorrow they would have to break
into a house and stock up on food, soap, and toilet pape . . . and the
phone rang.

It was Jane, calling from the house in actuality to which he and Claire had just been hiking in his imagination. I make the distinction for the sake of those who think there is one and that it is stable. In Chuck's mind, at least, there was a continuous process of one gestating and consuming the other until it became it.

"You there?" said Jane.

"Not entirely," said Chuck.

"I would think that you'd ask me about Daddy," she said.

"How's your father?" he said.

"Coming around, I think," she said. "He said just my being there was the best treatment he could get."

"Yes, a loving child must be a potent consolation," he said.

"I do what I can," she said.

"I know you do," he said.

"He still gets these queer notions, in spite of the new meds," she said.

"Well, now Jane—" he said.

"Don't say it," she said. "I was sitting there reading this magazine, an article about a mother and daughter who have the same boyfriend, while he was resting, I thought, when he let out this unearthly screech. Then he started to shout, 'They're biting me all over.'"

"Did you ask him who 'they' were?" he said.

"Well, I went over to calm him down, you know, and I stroked his hand, and can you believe that it's just as hard and calloused as ever?"

"Yes," he said.

"So he squeezed my hand real hard, pulled me close to him, and gave me this evil look that made me go all over goose pimples," she said. "Then he said, 'I don't want to die without ever having fucked some woman up the ass.'"

Chuck had to admit that it was possible to sympathize with the Reverend Luke Hartung, after all. But he didn't say so. "What did you do?" he said.

"I pried my hand loose and went out to tell a nurse," she said. "What did you think I did?"

"What did the nurse do?" he said.

"She said she was sorry but she belonged to the school that believes in keeping a tight asshole," she said. "Have you noticed how rude uneducated people are nowadays?"

"What's the prognosis?" Chuck said.

"Well, they're worried about this touch of pneumonia he has— they say that is why he sounds like Louis Armstrong," she said.

"He's going to outlive us both," he said. "When are you coming home?"

"You'll have to do without me for a few days at least," she said.

"I'll do my best," he said.

"You should come on up here," she said. "You know how you can feel a sneeze coming? That's how it is when you go outside: you can feel spring coming just that way."

"The way you feel when you're about to come?" he said.

"What is it about men?" she said.

It's that they don't get enough sex, he thought. The implacable force that through the green fuse drives the flower drives them on and on, over the edge. Has any man, even one with harems of a thousand, ever been satisfied?

The call over, Chuck prowled the apartment, down the hall into the living room, from the living room into the dining room, from the dining room into the kitchen, from the kitchen back into the hall, at the other end of which was the master bedroom. After fifteen minutes of this, he changed into jeans, sneakers, and a tee shirt, turned on *Court TV*: microscopic examination of hairs and fibers extracted from the scene of the crime led to the conviction of a woman who killed her husband in the (mistaken) belief that her rich boyfriend would marry her. While watching, Chuck alternated sit-ups and push-ups for another fifteen minutes, until he jumped suddenly to his feet, as though someone had pushed a button on a remote control that governed his actions. He threw on a sweatshirt and his parka and ran out, not even turning off the TV.

He walked his long-legged way west along 110th Street, slightly bent forward, like the eager prow of a ship, ducked into the subway, paced the platform until a train came, got off at Houston Street, walked downtown and east until he stood across the street from the regional headquarters of Greenspace.

Even from across the street he could see eight or ten people seated around the big table, plastic bottles of water, containers that held their latte grande or whatever it's called, bottles of wine, papers strewn everywhichway, and Ivan Tervakalio, sitting sideways to the table, feet up on a second chair, a glass of wine to his lips. Sitting next to him was Bangs with the clenched teeth, pouring herself another. Never mind the wine, the gathering was different from the faculty meetings of Chuck's experience in this: no one looked pissed-off. A guy sitting across from Ivan, short, defiantly unathletic, glasses, too much frizzy hair, ripped the top off a large bag of nacho chips, passed them to his left, ripped the top off a large bag of Cheese Doodles, reached in for a handful, passed them to his right, began to talk. Chuck knew that this twerp had the soul of a commissar because even as he talked and chewed his face was utterly without expression. Although Chuck classified such crunchy munchies with breakfast cereals as leading to mental and moral degeneracy, they did remind him that he was hungry. Concluding that the Greenspacers were just getting under way and that, moreover, they were given to talking at length, he walked back to West Broadway and north to McDonald's. The mentally challenged teenager who took his order (a double quarter-pounder with cheese and coffee to go) belied the notion that McDonald's was a source of fast food. Chuck decided not to eat supper until he had made it back to his lookout. As he neared his goal he was pleased to see that all the stores were closed or closing, except for an upscale Army and Navy store that displayed in its window an amazing assortment of knives. Yes, and the streets were emptying, except for the area in front of Greenspace, which was discharging its steering committee.

Some of them dashed right off, to their healthy suppers of tofu and kohlrabi, poor dears. Others stood in clusters of two or three, among them Ivan and Bangs, rehashing tactics—not much nourishment there either. He was tall and she was short, and he leaned over her in an attitude that Chuck described to himself as solicitous as she vehemently made her point, karate chopping the air. He raised his hands ear-high and tipped his head to the side in the appeasement gesture Chuck had seen him use on Claire way back there in the gym. Then they hugged, for an unseemly length of time, in Chuck's opinion, reluctantly released, said their good-byes. Ivan sauntered off in the other direction; Bangs, looking back over her shoulder, in her quick, determined step, walked a diagonal across the street, right toward where Chuck was standing. He turned and practically ran to the Army and Navy store, ducked in.

The security guy at the door, a nervous, wispy Hispanic kid, confiscated his bag of McDonald's. The saleslady, who was petite and Asian, clearly wanted him out in a hurry. But—and not only to break her chops—he bought himself a fatigue jacket, size tall extra large (for Chuck was wide), a liner, which he buttoned in, a red bandanna, and an evil-looking pocket knife, black plastic handle, blade shaped like the head of a pterodactyl, a knob where the eye would be, so you could open the knife quickly with your thumb, using only one hand, in case the other arm was engaged, wrapped around the other guy's neck, say. He paid and walked out but forgot to retrieve his supper from the Hispanic kid, who, as he watched Chuck walk out, said nothing. Whether he wanted the McDonald's for himself or was punishing Chuck for keeping the store open past closing time is not known. The saleslady was already turning off the lights.

Chuck ambled over toward West Broadway, thinking about his piece on love and the modernists. He'd have to get cooking on it this weekend. He had never yet failed to hand in a promised article. He turned the corner to walk north. Yes, the street was deserted—no, not quite: there on the corner, a block away, a shape was leaning against a building. A point of light floated up, glowed more brightly, descended—must be a cigarette. The headlights of a car going cross-town revealed the shape to be Bangs, for Pete's sake. It was not a good idea to let her see too much of him: he was about to turn and walk down to the subway on Canal Street when Ivan lurched around the corner a block uptown, spotted Bangs, went over to her.

They hugged, and damn if this time they didn't also kiss. She closed her hand around his bicep and led him uptown. They went into McDonald's and came out, Bangs holding a bag twice the size of the one Chuck just now remembered he had forgotten. They walked two blocks farther north, Chuck following at a safe distance, silent as a pard, until they went into a building, two floors of lofts above a store that sold stuff designed by Calvin Klein, Ralph Lauren, Tommy Hilfiger, and their ilk. Chuck waited five minutes and then sidled up to the lobby, which was empty. Inside, there were four bells with name tags next to them: Toby Fairly, Eve Able and Caitlin Eden, Amoranti Productions, and Mavis Mills, whom Chuck was willing to bet had bangs, clenched teeth, and big tits.

He walked across the street, leaned against a building, looked up just as bright lights went on behind the windows one flight up, to the left. Ivan came to a window, opened it as though he lived there (and Chuck was not surprised that Ivan was a fresh-air fiend, for it was by no means warm out), seemed to look right at Chuck (but Chuck was in deep shadow), pulled the window down until it was open no more than six inches, pulled down the shade. The unnaturally bright lights behind Ivan projected his silhouette onto the shade. Something about the angle of the lights made the silhouette larger than life, as when you dredge up a memory of a child's-eye view of Papa in a rage. Mavis appeared beside him, in profile, her bust prominent. They clinched. They disengaged, then walked away from the window, his arm around her shoulders, getting smaller and smaller, until they disappeared below the sill.

Chuck was astounded and he was aghast. He was flabbergasted and he was furious. What kind of moral and aesthetic imbecile would cheat on Claire McCoy? From observation and experience he knew enough about the vagaries of male desire; he well knew that he was himself an adulterer. But although he believed in equality under the law, he did not believe that everyone was equal *existentially*, let us say. Being unfaithful to Jane was not the same as being unfaithful to Claire, as striking a match on a hydrant was not the same as slashing a Renoir. Think of her red hair, curly and damp after lovemaking. Think of her arms and shoulders, strong and perfectly formed. Think of her perfectly formed thighs and her unformed lower legs, tugged at your heart, never mind her sweet bottom and sanctified bust, never mind her intelligence and creative fire, her isosceles smile. Oh man, who could want more? In Chuck's opinion there *was* no more, no, no, there was none.

He pulled his new knife out of its box, out of its plastic envelope, stuffed the wrappings into his left-side parka pocket, and tried to open the knife inside his right-side parka pocket, but there was not enough space. He slipped out of the parka, rolled it into a ball, pulled out his field jacket, pushed his parka into the big plastic shopping bag, slipped on the field jacket, zipped it up, and yes, there was room for the knife to open inside the pocket if you held it at an angle, heel of the knife at the top back corner of the pocket, point opening into the low front corner. He practiced until he could slide his hand into the pocket and open the knife in one quick motion, ever careful not to stab his privates.

He walked downtown to McDonald's. When Chuck gave his order, the kid whom he had thought of as mentally challenged said, "Why don't you have some fries? That way you won't be hungry again so fast." "I was just reading," said Chuck, "how carbohydrates little by little can shrink your joint to the size of a McNugget."

"Not," said the kid.

"Can so," said Chuck.

"Can't not," said the kid.

"Little by little," said Chuck, paying up, shaking his head sadly, walking off with his bag of semi-fast food.

He was standing at his post, munching on the first of his double quarter-pounders with cheese, when the brightly lit shade across the way flew up. Ivan opened the window as far as it would go and leaned out, his hands on the sill, his arms straight, and took a series of deep breaths. He was not wearing a shirt. When he breathed in he opened his mouth wide and bared his teeth (some piece of Oriental hocus-pocus, no doubt), so that in Chuck's jaundiced eyes he looked like a gargoyle. When he began to sing in a deep, powerful voice, Chuck jerked in surprise, nearly dropping his supper. In low-down, funky, bluesy blues accents that Chuck could not have imagined were in his emotional range, Ivan sang this:

> Ronald Blemp came to the mountain
> He saw that it was high
> Ooooeeee Ronald Blemp came to the mountain
> Saw that it was high
> Took out his checkbook (yeah)
> Said this is something I got to buy
>
> Now Ronald Blemp said to the Sister—

Ivan flew backward into the room, for Mavis Mills, wearing only her brassiere, had grabbed him, probably by the back of his belt, and jerked him in. He turned and bowed formally; she curtsied and moved into his arms; they waltzed. Around and around each other and around the room they went, framed for an instant in the window by Chuck's camera eye each time they whirled by, Chuck delighting in the show of animal energy, forgetting for the moment who was who and why he was there. They whirled by the window one last time and whirled toward the back of the room, out of sight, never to return, never, never to return.

Chuck sipped at his coffee. Mavis, wearing a white blouse with a high neck, appeared at the window, looked out in all directions but gave no indication of seeing Chuck. He pulled out his second double quarter-pounder, unwrapped it, pushed the wrapper into his left-side pocket, bit in. Mavis pulled down the window, pulled down the shade. Chuck washed down his mouthful, which was on the dry side, with coffee. The light behind the shade dimmed. Chuck put his container of coffee on the ground, his burger into his left hand, and reached into the McDonald's bag, which he had been holding between his knees, for two packages of salt and three of pepper, which he dumped onto what was left of his burger, under the bun, retrieved his coffee, stood up. Shadows moved in the foyer across the street. Chuck put his back against the wall. The door opened and was held open by Mavis so Ivan could step out. Ivan gave Mavis a big, theatrical hug and kiss, as though for an audience, and as she went in, letting the door shut behind her, he turned, tugged at the bill of his cap, and started across the street, on a direct line for Chuck.

Well, Chuck had enough time to place the remnants of burger between his teeth (there was too much left for him to swallow as though it were a pill, for the coffee was now in his left hand) and to place his right hand into his right-side fatigue jacket pocket, where he kept his pterodactyl, before Ivan was in his face.

"Who you?" said Ivan.

Chuck opened the knife.

"I seen you before," said Ivan.

Chuck started to draw his knife as Burt Lancaster (whom he slightly resembled) drew his gun in *The Gunfight at O.K. Corral*, but the knife sliced through the pocket and snagged at the top, where the fabric was doubled over. Ivan, who was looking Chuck in the eye, seemed not to notice. Chuck turned his left side toward Ivan so that the three inches of blade sticking through his pocket was out of the man's field of view.

"*Linguam Angliam loquoi non possum,*" Chuck said in his iffy Latin.

"Fucking Bulgarians," Ivan said, and stalked off.

Finishing the second of his double quarter-pounders with

cheese, pulling his knife back into his pocket and folding it, sipping coffee, Chuck watched Ivan lurch uptown, getting smaller and smaller, finally winking out of sight.

> I'll sing you six, O
> Red fly the banners, O
> What is your six, O
> Six for the Tolpuddle Martyrs
> Five for the years of the Five-Year Plan
> Four for the years it took them
> Three, three, the rights of man
> Two, two, a man's own hands
> Working for his living, O
> One is workers' unity
> And ever more shall be so.

seven-
teen

Of making many books there is no end; and much study is a weariness of the flesh. [ECCLESIASTES] ¶ *From birth to death, love is not just the focus of human experience but the life force of the mind, determining our moods, stabilizing our bodily rhythms, and changing the structure of our brains. The body's physiology ensures that relationships determine and fix our identities. Love makes us who we are and who we can become.* [THOMAS LEWIS, FARI AMINI, AND RICHARD LANNON, A General Theory of Love] ¶ *He that loveth not knoweth not God; for God is love.* [1 JOHN 4:8]

UT THE MODERNIST OF MODERNISTS, [Chuck wrote with a sinking heart] the standard by which the others are meas-ured, is James Joyce, whose attitude toward the claims of love was accordingly severe. Nora Joyce had as much trou-ble getting Joyce to say he loved her as Ursula had with Birkin, al-though Joyce volunteered many admiring phrases about Nora's body.

And in a climactic moment of *Ulysses* the apparition of Stephen Daedelus's dead mother appears before him to press her claims. She is wearing *"lepergrey,"* is noseless, toothless, eyeless, green with grave-mold, *"a green rill of bile trickling from a side of her mouth."* She speaks with *"the subtle smile of death's madness,"* and as she speaks *"a choir of virgins and confessors sing noiselessly."* She appears, that is, pretty much as Mrs. Krebs would have appeared if in Hemingway's story interior states had taken perceptible form. Mrs. Daedelus im-mediately begins to work on her son's guilt. "You sang that song to me.

123

Love's bitter mystery." Stephen at first tries to be a good boy for her. "Tell me the word, mother, if you know now. The word known to all men." Hans Gabler has discovered that in a passage Joyce dropped from an earlier episode Stephen had said to himself, "Do you know what you are talking about. Love, yes. Word known to all men"—a piece of information that explains nothing. In what Joyce retained, Mrs. Daedelus goes on like Mrs. Krebs: "Prayer is powerful.... Repent, Stephen." Instead, he exclaims, "The ghoul! Hyena!" When she says "Years and years I loved you. O, my son, my firstborn," Stephen's response is "The corpse chewer!" And when she says "Beware God's hand," Stephen recovers himself enough to assert his old motto, *"non serviam!"* and to smash the chandelier with his walking stick, thus exorcising her ghost. It's the kind of gesture poor Hemingway could never get his heroes to bring off, although he never stopped trying to exorcise the ghost of his mother. Some critics, incomprehensibly, have cited this passage from *Ulysses* as a ringing endorsement of love.

Such critics point to another of the muffled climaxes in *Ulysses*—

And the phone rang.

"Yes," said Chuck.

"Is that you?" said Jane.

"How's your father?' said Chuck.

"I'd think you would first ask me how *I* was," Jane said.

"How are you?" Chuck said.

"Not good," she said.

"I'm sorry," he said.

"When I visited him this morning Daddy said, 'An angel, an angel!' in this awful gargly voice he has," said she.

"Credit given where credit is due," said he.

"Then he started shouting, 'Not yet, not yet,' until he couldn't anymore because he was coughing too much," she said. "That rude nurse with the tight asshole came running in and gave me such a look. As though I would hurt my own father! The thing is, he thought I was a real angel coming to take him away," said Jane.

"What, he was afraid he was going to hell?" said Chuck.

"You mean because I look like some horrible demon?" Jane said.

"I mean because of his sins of the flesh," Chuck said.

"My father's God is not some wimp, you know," she said. "He likes manly men."

"I see," he said.

"I was going through his papers to see if there were bills that had to be paid when I came across his will," she said. "He's leaving everything to me."

"I should think so," he said.

"Guess how much he's worth?" she said.

Chuck withheld the impulse to say "79 cents." "Well, I know he was very frugal," remembering how he never helped them out when they were getting started, remembering the Christmas presents of an old porringer or an antique set of little plates to hold pats of butter.

"Eight hundred thousand," she said. "With that I wouldn't have to be beholden to you for tuition and such."

"Have I ever—?" he said.

"And then there's the house and a lot of land," she said.

"I know you're in no hurry to be an heiress," he said.

"Of course not," she said. "But he's getting this yellowish tinge all over. Besides the pneumonia and diabetes, he's got liver problems."

"They're no match for his rage to live," he said.

"Bet on it," she said. "I'll be home when I get there and I don't want to see any dishes in the sink or crumbs on the table."

"You won't," he said, hanging up.

It's his own fault, Chuck thought. He had neglected to confront Jane with her own disagreeable traits, so she could amend them, from the beginning. He was just not a confrontational person, hated confrontations, hated open conflicts of any kind, had hated them from childhood on, and not only because he was most often the one who backed down. Besides, what's the cure for stupidity? There is none, not for his own, either. Somehow he had failed Jane, though not as much as in his own eyes she had failed him. Still, he felt *something*, and it was suspiciously like guilt. Chuck had never been able to fellow-travel with the partisans of guilt: it softened your courage, weakened your resolve, sapped your will to live. The usual recourse was anger at whoever inspired the guilt. That's right: get rid of Jane and you get rid of the guilt. Then you feel guilt for getting rid of Jane. Fuck that. Oh, sure, one of Jane's manly men would have established a deference order with the male breadwinner on top. Probably such a man would not only keep her in line, but also keep her happy. Well, if the Reverend Hartung's God did not approve of Chuck, to pretend for a moment that He existed, Chuck did not approve of Him. The real question is this: was he going to kill Ivan Tervakalio out of weakness or out of strength?

A question not to be asked, or the native hue of resolution would be sicklied o'er. Enough of that. This time he would act first and think later. But for all the ferocity of his imaginings, Charles Craig Lockhart was essentially a good boy—so he had to finish his article before the deadline:

Such critics point to another of the muffled climaxes in *Ulysses.* The chauvinistic and anti-Semitic loungers in Barney Kiernan's pub have been giving Leopold Bloom a hard time. At first he stands up for himself and his co-religionists, but then he suddenly crumples:

—But it's no use, says he. Force, hatred, history, all that. That's not life for men and women, insult and hatred. And everybody knows that it's the very opposite of that that is really life.
—What? says Alf.
—Love, says Bloom. I mean the opposite of hatred.

No doubt Bloom sounds pretty good, compared to his company. But critics who have understood his rejoinder to be the novel's last word on the subject did not read a half-dozen lines farther down the page:

Love loves to love love. Nurse loves the new chemist. Constable 14A loves Mary Kelly. . . . Jumbo, the elephant, loves Alice,

126

the elephant. Old Mr. Verschoyle with the ear trumpet loves old Mrs. Verschoyle with the turnedin eye. The man in the brown macintosh loves a lady who is dead. His Majesty the King loves Her Majesty the Queen. Mrs. Norman W. Tupper loves officer Taylor. You love a certain person. And this person loves that other person because everybody loves somebody but God loves everybody.

In Conrad love kills; in Waugh it makes nothing happen; in Faulkner it is psychopathic; in Fitzgerald—

Chuck's train of thought was derailed by a vision of Claire, inspired by what, he could not have said. She stood in the doorway to his office, hip-shot, field jacket open over a blue plaid flannel shirt, Levi's, work boots, her birthmark lurid, her smile wry. He actually rose from his chair and stretched out his arms to her, like Eurydice or someone. She faded away, of course. Just what did you expect?

Chuck fell back in his chair, faint from an attack of fulminant yearning, a condition compared to which the deepest depression and the acutest anxiety are as a haircut is to a beheading. He staggered to the kitchen, poured himself three fingers of brandy, stumbled back to his study, sat, sipped away, his mind blank, his eyes stinging. He stood up suddenly, picturing his subterranean love nest, but a warm blackness rushed to his head and he keeled over. He came to immediately, flat on his back, staring at the ceiling but seeing his subterranean love nest. He got off the floor carefully, put on jeans, and yes, he had a blue plaid shirt, though it wasn't flannel, put on his Timberland hikers, for he lacked work boots, eschewed his parka, and put on his field jacket. He followed his legs out of the apartment and into the dusking air.

He followed them to Gwinnett Hall, where Hardcore guarded the entrance.

"The door's locked on Sundays, Professor," said Hardcore. "I thought you knew that."

127

Chuck reached into his pants pocket, where he kept not his knife but his folding money.

"Course, I managed to get a key," said Hardcore. "It helps to have friends in Maintenance."

"It helps to have friends in general," Chuck said, slipping a fiver into Hardcore's hand, who then unlocked the door.

"There's something going on with the hot-air system," said Hardcore. "There's this moaning growl, man, can make your poop go all runny, but it's just air."

Chuck followed his legs down and around (and around) until he came to the place of graffiti, where he read

THOU SHALT NOT ADULT COMMITTERY

but did not take it in. He moved on, to the swinging beat of Miles Davis's "Walking," never asking himself where he was going, but visualizing the hideaway, where he would crawl into the sleeping bag and sniff in Claire's natural fragrance, for she did not use perfume, cologne, underarm deodorant, mousse, gel, pussy powders, depilatories, emollients, or smelly soap. But dammit, someone was breaking his rhythm, as when you're listening to Count Basie swing the blues and some fool in the next room turns on Lawrence Welk. Chuck spun around, and there was Betty Blondell walking toward him, her heels going clickity clack click on the stone floor.

"I was tracking you to your lair," she said. "Just what is it you're doing down here, anyhow?"

"Looking for you," he said.

"You look dazed," she said; "are you on something?"

"I've been writing," he said.

She hooked her arm in his, pulled him back the way he had come. "It's cocktail time," she said; "looks to me like you need a drink." As they passed THOU SHALT NOT ADULT COMMITTERY a horrible sound washed over them—imagine hyenas closing in on a mortally wounded elephant. Betty threw herself into Chuck's arms. "Help," she said, and in the faintest of voices. Well, it was practically a reflex to hug her back, but he kept on hugging her beyond propriety, for the pressure of her body against his made him feel as though he was seeping back into himself from some other dimension. "What was that?" she said, finally pushing him off.

"Hardcore says it's just air," he said.

"Who?" she said.

"The guardian at the gate," he said.

"I have no idea what you're talking about," she said. "Let's get that drink."

Hardcore was not at the gate; he was leaning against a car, drinking from a Starbucks container; he winked at Chuck as the latter walked by, arm in arm with Betty Blondell.

"There he is," said Chuck.

"Where?" said Betty, looking back over the wrong shoulder.

In the Other End Betty went straight for the booth he and Claire had been at just the other day, but it was occupied by undergraduates. They settled for a nearby table. Betty took Chuck's field jacket from his hand as he was about to hang it on a hook, sat, spread the jacket across her knees, pulled a sewing kit not much bigger than a pack of cigarettes out of her handbag, threaded a biggish needle with thick black thread, and, as Chuck ordered drinks, began to sew up the slash in the right-hand pocket of his field jacket. "I've long thought we should get to know each other better," she said.

"With me being married and all . . . ," he said.

"What's this?" she said, holding up his pterodactyl.

"Jane once informed me that from her earliest memories of dear old dad she assumed a proper man always carried a pocket knife," he said.

"A proper man . . . ," she said, looking him in the eye. Then she shook her head once. "You know, I suppose, that I've taken Jane on as an assistant until she's ready to do her own show."

"You're a saint," he said.

"You know what my father used to say?" Betty said. "He said a woman who lets herself go thereby abrogates the marriage contract."

"What about a man who lets himself go?" said Chuck.

"He said that a man abrogates his marriage contract when he stops bringing home the bacon," she said.

"There were giants in the earth in those days," he said.

"I guess I used to think I was some kind of saint myself," she said. "Not consciously, of course."

"What changed your mind?" he said, telling the waitress to fill 'em up again.

"You did," she said. "You asked why there should be a connection between sin and sexuality. I began to chew the matter over. I couldn't get no satisfaction. I know some of the theology, of course. But theology is for people who have been made gullible by too much time among abstractions. Who cares what Augustine said? The question is why so many other Christians bought it. And the Garden of Eden—you have to squeeze that poor little fable pretty hard to get more out of it than injunctions against disobeying God or seeking knowledge. The Church Fathers! Bah! No good reason is given anywhere for a necessary connection between sex and sin. Amazing! The connection is just there, taken for granted, irrefutable, not that anybody tries to refute it."

"You can't refute it any more than you can refute the Incarnation," Chuck said. "You ever meet a believer who gave a shit about evidence or logic? It's enough simply to deny it."

"The point is this: think how many lives have been blighted," she said. "Think of all the needless renunciations," and she placed her hand on his.

At this auspicious point in their tête-à-tête, Simone Song slipped into the chair on Chuck's right and Tony Felder plopped into the chair on Chuck's left. "The two of you make so handsome a couple, we had to come over," said Simone.

"So we could bathe in your luster," said Tony.

"Tony and me, we're callitropic," Simone said. Either she was wearing falsies, or she used to bind her breasts but did no longer, or she was growing a pair. And she was wearing lipstick, a first. She had also done something to her eyebrows. And wasn't Tony's hair neatly combed, sans dandruff, his face leaner?

"We're having a serious discussion here," said Betty. "No kidding around. Why is sex sinful?"

"I thought it's because God said so, and ours is not to reason why," said Tony.

"I take it as a first principle that what God said was put into his mouth by humans," said Chuck.

"It must be that the reasons began as practical," said Simone: "the man wants to be sure that his wife's children are his own; the wife doesn't want to lose her meal ticket to some hussy."

"That doesn't explain the sinfulness of premarital sex," said Tony.

"Or sodomy," said Chuck.

"Experience showed that you turned out best if you were brought up by two parents, one male, one female, the same ones from birth to adulthood," said Simone. "Gradually any kind of sex that didn't lead that way became taboo."

"Too rational by half," said Tony. "We're dealing with human beings here."

"And then there's violence," Simone said. "Jealousy and cuckoldry are great destabilizers. Think of the Trojan War."

"But Simone, none of that explains the feeling tone that goes along with sinning," said Chuck, signaling for another round.

"Yes," said Betty, "that feeling tone: it's because of *that*, rather than in spite of it, that some people sin."

"That feeling tone is socially constructed," said Simone. "In some societies you can get it from stumbling into a sacred grove; in others, from looking your mother-in-law in the face; in still others, from seething a kid in its mother's milk."

"If all that's true, then there is no sexual sinning," said Betty, "only violations of ossified customs and conditioned responses."

Well, Ms. Worldly Wise and the two Misters were not immediately ready to go quite *that* far.

"So be it," Chuck finally said.

"Certain relationships imply fidelity," said Simone; "infidelity becomes a violation of trust, a secular sin."

"That's what I was afraid of," said Betty. "Without sin, I mean real sin, everything becomes sort of lightweight, without gravity—but a real sin disturbs the universe."

"There you have it," said Tony. "Sex *does* disturb the universe, so far as the universe is man-made. Libertinism is the only form of revolt that doesn't propose an alternate form of tyranny. Sex knots two people together but loosens up everything else. That's why Big Brother, like der fuehrer, is always a puritan. But so far, at least, the perennial totalitarian type has not been able to control sex entirely. Confine sex here and it breaks out there in craziness and cruelty. Where's the waitress? All this talk is making me dry."

"Yes," said Betty, "we've all read *Civilization and Its Discontents*."

"But have you ever felt that discontent?" said Tony. "Have you ever felt an irresistible urge to violate every boundary, to fart in church, to shit on a wedding cake, to piss in Her Majesty's teacup, to hiss at a Veterans' Day parade, to slap your grandmother, to rape a nun, to kill! kill! kill! Where's that waitress?"

"As a matter of fact," said Betty in the meekest of voices, "I have."

"You want to rape a nun?" said Chuck.

Simone stood up. "I'm off to the Ladies'," she said.

"Wait for me," said Betty, starting to rise, but tipping over on her high heels into Simone, for Betty had little experience with alcohol. Chuck got to his feet, for his father had taught him to rise when women came to the table or left it. The ladies linked arms, departed.

"Seems to me that Betty is about to become interesting," said Tony. He told the waitress, white shirt, black leather pants that squeaked, to bring more of the same all around. "Don't you think?"

Chuck vaguely felt that merely to talk about how Betty was becoming interesting would be disloyal to Claire, such was his delicacy, but his delicacy did not stop him from observing that the waitress was callipygous. "By the way, are you finished with the car?" he said.

"We didn't need your brawn—you can't imagine how strong Simone is," Tony said.

"You might as well let me have the keys, while we're thinking of it," Chuck said, for sooner or later he was going to have to drive to Sacandaga.

"Simone wants me to drive her to this place on City Island where they really know how to cook fish—though the difference between fish that is well prepared and fish that is ill served has so far escaped me. O.K. if I bring the keys around tomorrow?"

The drinks arrived. Chuck and Tony drank. By and by, the girls arrived, arm in arm, giggling.

"We better get a move on," said Simone to Tony, who stood, gave Betty a real kiss on the cheek. Chuck stood, gave Simone a hug, and damn if those new breasts under her old Left Bank black turtleneck sweater didn't feel real. Betty plopped down into her chair.

"Whew," she said. "I'm just a little bit woozy here."

"How about something to eat?" said Chuck, who signaled the long-suffering waitress even before Betty said, "Good idea."

"I guess I knew I was in a state of crisis," she said, "when I found myself before the TV watching professional wrestling for the third night in a row. Those guys are something."

"They're not your type, Betty," Chuck said.

"You're my type," Betty said. Can you imagine! This fifty-year-old man and this thirty-something woman blushed.

They ate in silence for a while, she her individual pizza, he his roast pork. "You don't know what it's like to live alone, Chuck," she said. "You feel like a ghost."

"I always thought of you as completely self-sufficient," he said.

"To have someone give and get pleasure by touching you," she said. "What better evidence that you exist?"

"There have been influential people who said—there are still influential people who say—that only the spirit is real, that the flesh is an illusion or snare," said Chuck, who was a bit out of his depth.

133

"Suppose you were to kick one of these influential persons in the balls?" she said.

"He'd bend over gasping, clutch his crotch, and say that pain is also an illusion," said Chuck. "One way to become a superior being is to deny your experience and suffer the consequences."

"Don't drink any more," said Betty, "you're getting obscure."

Manners, and not just manners, required that Chuck offer to walk Betty home. When they arrived at the doorway to the building in which Betty had her apartment she turned to him with an expectant look, just as Chuck had hoped and feared. Come on, what harm can there be in kissing a mouth as clean-looking as hers? Well, old Betty held him by the biceps, pulled him toward her, slid a thigh between his legs, and gave him a kiss, man, that made him glow all over. Manners, and not just manners, required that Chuck enter into the spirit of the thing, so he did. Her response, to Chuck's surprise, was to back off. "Consternation"—that's the word for the look on her face as they disengaged, until it modulated into an appeasement smile.

"Let's have lunch sometime," she said.

"I'll give you a call," he said, pecking her on the forehead and walking off. He would have bet that just a minute ago she was ready to ask him up for a nightcap. What he wanted to know about himself is this: did he feel more relief or more regret that she had not? He decided that what he felt more of was relief. How do you like that? It could only mean he was really in love with Claire. Wait a minute! Him, Charles Craig Lockhart, in love? But he didn't believe in love. Could it be, could it be that he was one of these people who assume a vantage point of superiority by denying their own experience? The question was answered by a wave of yearning for Claire that washed over him and buckled his knees.

eighteen

A last luminous power of the limbic domain: love alters the structure of our brains. [THOMAS LEWIS, FARI AMINI, AND RICHARD LANNON, A General Theory of Love] ❡ *What is the nature of aching loss and the desperate urge for reunion with those we love? / What makes passion savage and inexorable?* [THOMAS LEWIS, et al.] ❡ *Whoso findeth a wife findeth a good thing.* [PROVERBS]

CHUCK SPENT MONDAY AND TUESDAY taking care of business: teaching, preparing classes, reading student prose, writing letters, clearing his desk, for stalking Ivan had lost some of its romance. On Monday morning Claire called. She was under the weather, looked like a reptile, would have to take a bye on their usual Monday run followed by lunch. Chuck, who if he lived long enough might yet learn how to deal with women, did not try to talk her out of it, though a wavelet of that black, warm tingle passed through his head. On Monday evening Jane called. Despite wearing an oxygen mask full-time, her father had somehow managed to get himself a girlfriend, a woman three rooms down the hall who was waiting for a spare heart. He visited her constantly, and they sat on either side of her bed eating off their trays of food, talking about God's mysterious ways, making plans for a future when they were well.

On Tuesday morning Claire called again. She still felt and looked like death warmed over. She was really sorry, she wanted to see him, too: this was the longest they had been apart since that first time at the Wanhope. On Tuesday evening Jane called again. Neither Jane nor the girlfriend nor the two of them together could get Daddy out of bed for his morning and afternoon strolls down the corridor or even to sit up and wouldn't you know just as he was beginning to seem a little like his old self. Late Tuesday evening Betty Blondell called. She wanted to know why she hadn't heard from him. Weren't they supposed to have lunch together? She had been waiting for his call. Then her tone changed, became girlish. She knew she had been a fraidy-cat on Sunday. But Chuck was an experienced man. He should understand such things. Were they on for lunch tomorrow? Twelve o'clock? Good. A little before midnight Claire called. She had to see him. Could they have sandwiches together in their hideaway? At twelve? Good. It was a little, very little, past midnight when Chuck called Betty. Something had come up. Could they reschedule for Thursday? If he didn't want to get together, he should just say so, she said. He does, he does, he said. Well, if he was sure, let's make it Thursday at twelve at the Other End. He was looking forward to it, he said. Better yet, let's make it her place, she said. But . . . he said. Now who's a fraidy-cat? she said.

Just before twelve on Wednesday Chuck stood before RESTRICTED KEEP OUT, a bag with lunch for two in his hand. The bar and locks were off the door, yet Chuck did not just turn the knob and walk in. He knocked, a stupid thing to do, for who can say that someone—Betty, for example—might not have heard and come over to see what was going on, their little secret a secret no more. When no one answered, he turned the knob and walked in. Claire was standing as far from the door as possible, in the shadows on the other side of the well, leaning against the coal bin where the horizontal one-by-six slats that held back the coal were at the apogee of their bulge. Dim as the light was, Claire sported a pair of sunglasses.

"That coal bin makes me nervous," said Chuck: "someday it's going to burst like a dam and bury us in tons of coal."

"Poetic justice," she said, walking toward him around the well.

She had resorted to the hairstyle that covered one side of her face, sunglasses, birthmark, and all. Apropos of nothing she hugged him, leaned into him, snuggled her head under his chin. He patted her on the back with one hand, the other occupied by the bag of lunch. She lifted her head so that he could kiss her, which he did. He kissed her mouth, exploring the corners with his tongue, kissed the wings of her nose, her cheeks all over, her neck, and wouldn't you know it?—her eyes being covered by glasses, that's where he wanted to kiss her next. He removed the glasses and saw two things at once: that a tear was brimming over the lower lid of her right eye, that the area surrounding her left eye was black, blue, green, yellow, red, and swollen. There was a spot of blood on the white of her left eye. There was a short gash through her left eyebrow that could have used a couple of stitches when it was fresh. Chuck kissed it. He put an arm behind her legs, lifted, carried her over to the stairs and down them into their "living room," and said, "what does the other guy look like?" He sat in an ancient desk chair, Claire on his lap, and kissed her eye, to make it better.

"Unmarked, the bastard," she said.

It was a peculiarity of Chuck's that he felt rage mainly in his face, and wrists, which seemed to swell. "I'll kill the motherfucker," he said.

"This time I went too far," she said.

"So did he," Chuck said. "I want the details."

She was working on a new poem, she said, in the "In Memoriam" stanza, which she wanted the reader to recognize, except she was rhyming it ABBA BCCB CDDC and so on, the last stanza to rhyme AAAA, a kind of *quattro rima*, except none of the rhymes were exact, because she wanted an air of dissonance. For example, she rhymed "barn" and "burn" to create a subliminal suggestion of barn burning and "both" and "bed" to suggest lovers, somewhere below consciousness, though the stanzas were overtly about something else.

"Holy moly!" he said.

Anyhow, she was really getting into it, thinking of making it the title poem of the volume "On the Way" when Ivan came over to the corner of the bedroom in which she had her "study." He wanted her to help him, right then and there, with the words to a new song he was composing especially for the demonstration on Saturday. "Later," she said. The thing is, he said, the demonstration was in just a couple of days, and she was going to have to get the melody in her head before she could come up with the words, and can you believe this asshole, he started to hum this nowhere tune in that nasal voice he uses when he's in his folk-singing mode and Claire just blew up, couldn't help herself. How come his lousy songs always took priority over her poems? He didn't respect her poetry, he didn't respect her, she was just his cook, housekeeper, sperm depository, and thesaurus. At first, he retreated, but when she pressed the assault, he counterattacked: at least he wrote his songs to make the world a better place, but when she wrote poetry she was just playing with herself. Well, that was a low blow and it hurt all the more because what was left in her of her parents raised the suspicion that he might be right. Oh yeah, she said, and what were all these do-gooders doing if not stroking their already tumescent self-importance? Just what did his songs ever make happen? And what is he doing with them if not fucking himself up the ass? It was at this point that Ivan socked her. He must have held back because Claire was still standing. He already had his hands up to his shoulders and was putting on that shit-eating grin when she spat in his face. This time he didn't hold back.

Claire went down, but not out. She wanted Chuck to know that at no point did she lose consciousness. Ivan reached down to lift her, hands under her armpits, already sniveling about how sorry her was, but she shrugged him off. She got on her hands and knees, then tipped over onto her side, still groggy. She pulled herself up by her desk chair, tottered to the john, leaned on the sink, studied her face. She smiled, for the damage, the pain, made her feel good, feel, you know, relieved somehow.

"Poets are different from other people," said Chuck.

Claire washed the gash through her eyebrow and with cuticle scissors cut the hair on either side. She then cut some adhesive tape into thin little strips, while Ivan knocked on the door, asked if she was all right. She pressed an end of a strip of tape on, say, the right side of the gash and pulled it tight across. Then she pressed the end of a strip of tape on, say, the left side of the gash and under the first strip and pulled it tight across, and so forth, ersatz stitches. She walked out of the john, her intention to continue walking, right out of the apartment, but being weak in the knees, she only made it as far as their one easy chair, into which she sedately lowered herself, careful to reveal nothing. Nor did she speak, for she knew that the only thing to upset Ivan more than her barbed tongue was the silent treatment. So she sat there with a distant look in her eye. And Ivan? That big baby fell to his knees, put his head in her lap, wrapped his arms around her thighs, and blubbered on about how he loved, loved, loved her, which is why he lost it when she put him down so hard. Poor baby, she now told Chuck, the minute Ivan hit her he lost the battle. This is the part Chuck won't believe, she said: when she came to herself, her hand was in Ivan's hair, ruffling it, fit subject for a Victorian narrative painting.

Chuck stood up, still holding Claire, carried her over to the sleeping bag, slid her into it, slid in beside her, and pulled her on top of him, so she could rest her face on his chest, for his crackpot theorem #318 held that the regular beat of a lover's or mother's heart had healing properties. Claire slept, while Chuck, supine, watched over her—until it was time for him to meet his class.

The phone was ringing when Chuck walked through the door to his apartment, in his hand a bag containing four thick-cut shoulder pork chops, for neither he nor Claire got to eat lunch, for while the cat's away the mouse ate what he damn well pleased. He picked up the phone in the kitchen, said "Hello" into it, wedged it between jaw and shoulder, unwrapped the chops.

"Hi, um, Chuckie, it's, ah, Betty," she said.

"Hi," he said.

"How you doing?" she said.

"I'm doing good," he said.

"What're you up to?" she said.

"The usual," he said, for Chuck, no disrespect meant to Betty, had his mind elsewhere. He dropped three of the chops into his big black cast iron frying pan.

"How's Jane?" Betty said.

"Still up north tending her father," he said, thinking how he would fortify himself with pork chops, travel downtown to a certain loft, and he emptied a can of sauerkraut into a saucepan.

"How is he?" she said.

"Up and down," he said, thinking how he would take out Ivan Tervakalio and Mavis Mills with his pterodactyl, and he sliced a large onion and half a small apple into the sauerkraut, sprinkling in caraway seeds, adding a can of water, putting a flame under it.

"About lunch tomorrow?" she said.

"I haven't forgotten," he said, trying out in his mind the alternatives of slitting their throats and stabbing them in the heart, and he started trimming the ends off some brussels sprouts.

"I'm, um, going to need a rain check," she said.

"Sure," he said, thinking that the real problem was how to do the job without getting blood all over him, and he decided to cook up the whole batch of sprouts, for he liked them the next day, cold, with mayonnaise, salt, and pepper.

"It's just that I'm, um, well . . . something came up," she said.

"No problem," he said, thinking that the answer was to travel north and filch one of the Reverend Hartung's handguns, except guns were so noisy, and he poured cold water on the sprouts, not enough to cover them.

"What are you doing for supper?" she said. "I don't mean at my place."

"I've already got something on the fire," he said. "Why don't you come over here?" thinking that there were books that told you how to make a silencer, and he turned down the fire on the sauerkraut, for it was simmering.

"I just . . . can't," she said, "know what I mean?"

"You bet," he said; "I'll call Monday, see when we're both free for lunch."

"I hope by then you'll be a little more forthcoming," she said, and hung up.

Whereupon he realized that he had failed Betty. All right then, he would call her back, after he put some oil in the pan with the chops, for he liked his pork chops fried in olive oil, encourage her by indirection to talk, for some people found it easier to open up over the phone than face-to-face. The phone rang.

"Hi, Betty listen—" he said.

"This is your wife," said Jane.

"How are *you*?" he said, "and how's your father?"

"Do you really care?"

"What's the matter now?" he said.

"What's the matter!" she said. "My father's dying. That's what's the matter. You could show a little sympathy."

"We're all dying, Jane," he said. "Your father lived the life he wanted to live. And he lived it for a long time. You can't do better than that."

"You don't know what it takes out of you to have to watch your father fade out of existence," she said.

"I was holding onto my father's hand when he died," said Chuck.

"You father smoked and drank himself to death," she said. "My father always took care of himself. And still he's falling apart."

"That's the way his God arranged things," said Chuck. "Why don't you send *Him* a letter of complaint? See how much sympathy you get."

"He keeps slipping in and out of consciousness," she said, "and when he's awake he's perfectly lucid. He knows exactly what's happening to him. It's so sad," and now she was crying.

"I'm sorry, Jane, really I am," he said. "You know I always had a perverse liking, even admiration, for the old goat. He's like a natural force."

"Just to show you: I was sitting by his bedside this morning with my hand around his forearm—it's bigger than yours, you know—so I could feel the life surging through him," Jane said. "Then he opened his eyes, gripped my forearm, and pulled me close to him. 'Send Debbie June over to see me,' he said—that's the ex-parishioner who stops by a couple of times a week to take care of little things. So I said 'What for?' And he says, 'For one last blow job.' I burst into tears. That a lust for life like his—"

"I hope you brought Debbie June over," he said, "by force, if necessary."

"Do you know that sometimes you're disgusting," she said. "I prayed for him instead. I'm learning how to pray all over again. And I'm shedding that chi-chi cloak of atheism you hung on me."

"As I recall, you were in a muck-sweat to try it on," he said.

"You were a serpent!" she said. "You seduced my body and you seduced my mind. No more! I spoke to Daddy's lawyer today, whatshisface. There's no doubt about it—I'm going to be an heiress big time. A million dollars' worth, at least, counting everything. And soon I'll be on the radio. Then you won't be able to lord it over me anymore."

What Chuck was thinking was that he'd sentence her to death, if he hadn't already done so, but he held his tongue.

"You should drive up here, to show respect," she said.

"This weekend," he said, just then remembering that Tony Felder had not dropped off the car keys.

"Make sure you clean up after yourself," she said. "Don't leave it all for Bettina."

"Yassuh," he said. He hung up and turned on a fire under the chops, for he liked them cooked covered and over a low heat for thirty minutes. He was deciding whether to pour himself a drink or do some push-ups right there on the kitchen floor when the phone rang.

"Hello," he said.

"Hi, Chuck, it's Claire," she said. "I just had to call to tell you how sweet you were this afternoon."

If flesh could melt, Chuck would have been a puddle.

"Those two hours on your chest were the best sleep I've had in days," she said.

A wave of warm blackness washed over his mind and receded, leaving behind a soft ringing in his ears.

"After you ran off to class, I ate both sandwiches, my first meal since I got bopped," she said.

He was too choked up to speak.

"You're as good for my body as for my soul," she said. "How can our relationship be bad?"

"It can't," he said in a croak. "It raised me from the walking dead."

"I'm not an ubermensch," she said. "I can't just throw off a lifetime of indoctrination or the whole weight of public opinion."

"You can do it," he said, "do a kind of St. Ignatius, a spiritual exercise, like resolving to be nice to your Aunt Katherine, or revving yourself up for a gold medal performance, or disciplining yourself to sit down every morning to write."

"Sitting down every morning to write . . . ," she said. "That's not discipline—that would be deliverance."

"How's the big poem going?" he said.

"I can't write in a charged atmosphere," she said. "I feel like my head's vibrating."

"He's not going to hit you again, is he?" Chuck said.

"Oh, no," Claire said. "He's all solicitous and groveling. He's upstairs right now cooking dinner, instead of going to one of his eternal steering committee meetings. What he's doing, in fact, is frying up some bratwurst. He's got a jar of herring in sour cream for appetizer and a container of potato salad to go with the wurst. That's it."

"I've eaten worse," Chuck said.

"But I can feel the hostility building up inside him," she said. "He's pissed that I'm going to this poetry festival I've been invited to instead of standing by his side at the demonstration this Saturday. He thinks I'm competing with him."

"He's a pipsqueak," said Chuck.

"I'm downstairs in this little place next door, sells cigarettes and papers and Snapple," Claire said, "which reminds me, I better put another quarter in this pay phone here or we'll get cut off. I just had to talk to you," and Chuck felt another wave of blackness crash on his overloaded brain. It left behind not only a ringing but a mild headache as well. He put a hand on the wall to steady himself. What was he doing with the vapors anyhow?

"How about you and I spend Friday afternoon at the Wanhope?" said Chuck.

"You always say the right thing," she said.

"Use venery for health, said Our Father Ben Franklin," he said.

"I feel better already," she said.

One of the many things Chuck did not know about himself was why he hadn't told Claire about Ivan's using venery with Mavis Mills. He did know he felt impelled to make up for the tricks life had played on Claire—her parents, her husband, her birthmark, her poverty. Therefore he carried with him to the Wanhope on Friday a forty-dollar box of Godiva chocolates, a thirty-dollar bottle of wine, the most he had ever spent for the stuff, and a delicate onyx necklace, though Claire's neck needed no adornment. Instead of just pouncing on her in the usual male way, he tried to create a mellow, romantic atmosphere with wine, endearments, butterfly kisses, and the four cigarettes, two apiece, that he had bummed from a departmental secretary. Then he undressed her slowly, kissing each patch of flesh as it became bare. Then he went down on her. She writhed, swung her head from side to side in tempo, twitched, let out a long deep shuddering sigh, and came prettily. She started to reciprocate, for Claire hated to owe anybody anything, but Chuck said no, this

144

is lady's day. Then he fetched two glasses of wine, offered Claire a chocolate, got into bed, pulled her close to him, pulled the sheet over them, and started to talk, for Chuck suspected that what Claire like best about their get-togethers was the postcoital talk.

Through a chain of associative links Chuck could not follow, the conversation moved around to Ivan, who was, understandably, on Claire's mind. She had met him through her mother, whose protégé he had been, a working stiff with aspirations. He was working for a landscaper in Long Island, and in Claire's opinion Ivan would be a better and happier man if he had stayed close to the soil. But he got a job with the Parks Department in New York City to be close to Claire. It was Claire's mother who encouraged his guitar-playing, his singing, taught him protest songs and that species of folk song written on the east side of Manhattan. Claire moved in with Ivan because as an educated middle-class woman she was in debt to any working-class boofhead. It was a matter of reparations, of her parents' political program transposed to the private sphere, but also, Chuck surmised, of nunnish self-sacrifice. In any case, her motives for marrying Ivan were impure. Claire was less in love with Ivan than with the idealized image she had of herself for marrying him. Once married, they moved to Greenwich Village and became déclassé bohemians together.

Claire said that for the first time she understood Coleridge's "Ancient Mariner" from the inside: she too had enticed a wild thing out of its element, turned it into a homebody, cast it away, and was now wearing it around her neck. Ivan didn't consciously know about her affair; awareness was not his strong suit. But on some level he knew, without knowing how he knew, or even that he knew, that Claire was moving out of his orbit, that at the very least she was unfaithful in spirit.

Chuck poured out the last of the wine, paused, said, "You know, Claire, to blame yourself for everything is also a sneaky way of taking credit for everything." But then he was less likely to idealize the laboring classes, having been beaten up regularly by Henny Kramer,

Walter Kastner, and Willi Schwock, whose fathers were, respectively, a moving man, a truck driver (for a beer distributor), and a stevedore.

"Maybe Ivan's right—maybe poets *are* narcissists," she said. "I can live with that. Can you?" and she ate a candy that was in six layers, one of them green.

"All I know is, that if you were me, I'd be in love with myself," he said.

"Yeah, but could you give yourself blow jobs?" she said.

And so they nattered on, until Chuck had to go home, in case Jane called.

And so she did. Daddy was about the same, except his breathing was more labored, and he never truly woke up all day, though once when she squeezed his hand, he squeezed back. That rude nurse had suddenly turned kind and wheeled in a cot, so Jane could sleep in the same room with her father. But the doctors kept chasing her out, so they could do this or that, they wouldn't say what. There was this spooky monitor with a yellow electronic line zigzagging across it, except when it went crazy and made all these spikes like stalacwhat-doyoucallums and was she boring him? No, no, he was hanging on to every word.

As he was falling asleep, he and Claire, trudging through one of those heavy early spring snowstorms, arrived at what had been the Reverend Hartung's house. Smoke drifted out of the chimney. Icicles hung from the porch roof. He approached the entrance, Claire crouching behind a rusting pickup truck, rifle pointing at the door, and knocked. The door was opened by a tall blond man, wide cheekbones, beard, long hair tied into a ponytail by a strip of red bandanna.

"We don't have any to spare," he said.

"This is my house," said Chuck.

"Was, maybe," said the man.

"I got a deed in my knapsack to prove it," said Chuck.

146

"Maybe you haven't noticed," he said. "Things is changed. Possession is now ten-tenths of the law."

"The whole mudroom is full of preserves, canned food, dried beans, and the like," said Chuck.

"Yes, that canned woodchuck, when you simmer it in a salt pork gravy, can taste pretty good, if you're hungry enough" is what this cracker said. "But as I say, we don't have any to spare."

"I've got my wife with me," Chuck said, for that's how he thought of Claire. "I don't mean to see her starve."

"There you are," the man said. "That's how I feel about these two women I got to keep me warm on cold nights." Behind his shoulder Chuck saw a woman with bangs and a prominent bust. Was that a woman with the silhouette of a wasp farther back in the shadows? "There's a fellow up the road about five miles I hear got himself a nice doe the other day. Maybe he'll let you have a piece of neck meat. He's a little soft in the head." As Chuck turned, to come back another day, the cracker said, "And if I see you around here again I'll just assume you aim to make a pest of yourself. Understood?" Chuck was hoping that Claire would shoot this loser, who was as good as dead, anyway, but her sweet face floated up into his field of view, blotting out everything else, snow falling on her birthmark.

nine-teen

Among the Yanomamo tribe, a boy does not achieve full status as a man until he has killed another man. [DAVID M. BUSS, The Evolution of Desire: Strategies of Human Mating] ❡ *It will lead you into criminal activity if you're too powerfully in love with someone.* [AILEEN WOURMOS] ❡ *All fixed, fast-frozen relations, with their train of ancient and venerable prejudices and opinions are swept away, all new-formed ones become antiquated before they can ossify. All that is solid melts into air, all that is holy is profaned, and man is at last compelled to face with sober senses, his real conditions of life, and his relations with his kind.* [KARL MARX AND FRIEDRICH ENGELS, The Communist Manifesto]

SEVEN HOURS LATER Chuck awakened from a dream of desperately seeking Claire through a howling blizzard. Was she playing hide-and-seek or was he deceived by a swirl of snow into thinking he saw glimpses of her now here now there? How many times had he reached out to an apparition of Claire only to feel his arms close through an empty whorl of air and big, fat snow-flakes? But her life depended on his finding her, and—the bedroom he awoke into was cold and sunny.

A brisk wind whistled through the fire escape and through the near window, which was open three inches; it blew across Chuck's body, for he had kicked off the covers while desperately seeking Claire. Shivering, he found on the bottom of his gymwear drawer a pair of black long underwear pants, size tall 32, and a black long underwear top, size tall extra large, neither worn more than twice before. He rushed into the bathroom, closed the door, and turned on the shower, full steam ahead, get a little warmth in there. Ahhhh, between the long johns and the steam he began to warm up. He wiped some steam off the mirror and looked at himself. Yes indeed: he needed a shave, as he needed one every morning. But today he was just not going to shave, so there. Today was a day for playing hooky. No classes today, no meetings, his wife was way north, his girlfriend farther north yet, "Love and Modernism" would have to wait, and besides, he had no idea how to end it.

He came out of the bathroom into a bedroom that had suddenly become gloomy. He looked out the window, which faced south. Ragged clouds raced across the sky, alternately shedding sun and gloom on the rooftops. Sun suddenly burst through the window and poured through him, so it felt. In his hooky-playing mood, he put on a pair of 501 Levi's, his blue plaid shirt, his fatigue jacket, his new Gore-Tex work boots, made him feel young again. Into his back pocket, instead of a handkerchief, he stuffed his new red bandanna. He slapped his pockets: wallet, folding money, pterodactyl, sunglasses: all set. Man, he walked out the door with a spring in his step, whistling "Bea's Flat."

He walked past the newsstand on Broadway, where he bought a copy of the *Times*, walked uptown on the west side of Broadway, the sunny side, until he came to the Other End, where two waitresses in leather pants and white blouses were putting out chairs and little tables for the first time that year. Sun slanted down across the roofs of the houses across the street and shone on leather pants thin and flexible enough to mould themselves around the young bottoms of the waitresses. What better way to play a day (the rhyme a sign of a lax mind) of hooky than to sit in the sun, read the *Times*, have breakfast served by a handsome woman in tight pants, for Chuck usually found breakfast too costly to eat out and too much trouble first thing in the morning to cook and clean up after at home, for Chuck eschewed breakfast cereals. As he sat down and opened the *Times*, a cloud got between him and the sun. There on the bottom of the first page of the *Times* was an article on the demonstration organized by Green-space against Ronald Blemp's plan to build a gambling casino on the site of a retirement home run by and for the Sisters of St. Sebastian of Solace, the demonstration to take place starting at twelve noon that very day across the river right there outside downtown Engle-wood Cliffs on the Palisades.

Chuck sprang to his feet as though an invisible puppeteer had pulled his strings. He left the *Times* and too much money on the table and started to walk uptown, taking alternate bites out of the strip of bacon he held in one hand and the slice of toast he held in the other. It was not until he was standing on 122nd Street, reach-ing into his pocket for the key to the lock on the gate to the entrance to the parking lot, that Chuck remembered who had both the gate key and the car keys, that irresponsible bastard, Tony Felder. There was a pay phone two blocks away. Chuck used it to call Tony, whose recorded voice said that he could not get to the phone right now, but if you wanted you could leave a message after the beep. The core of Chuck's message, sans embellishment, was that Tony should put the fucking keys in Chuck's office box instanter. Instead of his car, Chuck took the subway to 181st Street, from which he made it to the walk-way across the George Washington Bridge.

Once over the water he paused to lean on the railing to take in the view. This view upriver, man, unless you had the shrunken soul of a congressman on the Republican right, was commensurate to anyone's capacity for wonder, and the Palisades were a large part of it. Perched on top of them was the gothic pile that housed the retired Sisters of St. Sebastian of Solace. But the wind was some-thing, shadows of the clouds sailing across the rippled gray river. Once again Chuck paused to admire the construction of his field jacket, which was keeping him warm from mid-thigh to neck.

He turned to give his fellow pilgrims a once-over. On the whole they were less flamboyant than the demonstrators of his youth, no colorful patches on the jeans, not a Mother Hubbard in sight. The style this year among the young was for black nylon windbreakers from The Gap or Banana Republic or leather from China over poly-ester fleece from everywhere. There were guys from the 'hood in their black, puffy, North Face parkas. There were guys his age with lots of face hair looking over the chicks, some of the latter wearing retro bell bottoms. There were women his age or older with shorn gray hair and a stern look; these were not your permed and blue-rinsed old dears. There were guys at the low end of middle age adorned with gold-rimmed glasses and those ascetic Irish faces you used to see in seminaries. There were women of the same age and look who would rather drown the Indian subcontinent than allow a scientist to experiment on a guppy. And then there were the blessed young, golden girls and the boys of summer, out to have a party, but willing to be crucified. Only a few had hair dyed fuchsia or char-treuse. Chuck joined them on their way, taking out and folding his bandanna, tying it around his forehead like Cochise or someone, slipping on his sunglasses, out to join the party.

Traffic was moving slowly, slow enough for Chuck to keep pace with a Greenspace minivan in which Ivan Tervakalio, Mavis Mills, and the frozen-faced would-be commissar with the big puff of frizzy hair were all looking straight ahead. A ramp off the bridge fed into Palisades Parkway, where northward traffic came to a full stop. Ivan et al. disembarked, headed north on the grassy median, left the mini-van with the Greenspace logo in the care of its driver, a young woman who looked flustered, frightened, and furious. Chuck walked over to the driver's side window. "Need help?" he said. "Fuck off," she said. Chuck stepped onto the median and followed Ivan and company. Other cars were turning onto the median or the grassy shoulder, the occupants disembarking, locking up, joining the march northward.

Chuck did not believe that anyone had expected this big a turn-out. From time to time there was a glimpse of Route 9W, which was also jammed. Pedestrians were not allowed on the Palisades Park-way, but the notorious New Jersey state police were nowhere to be seen. Suddenly, and with a start, Chuck became aware that someone was walking beside him, there to his left, keeping pace, step for step. When Chuck looked at him, this guy said, "How ya bin?" He was nearly as tall as Chuck, clearly thin inside his field jacket, blondish hair, blue eyes, long face, three-day stubble, a blue bandanna around his bony forehead, a slouching attitude.

"As usual," Chuck said. "You?"

"The same," he said. "It's been a long time." He had no teeth top right from the eyetooth back. A cloud came between them and the sun. In the new lighting this character's face turned a lighter shade of pale.

"Forever," Chuck said.

"Slow down," said the other. "Walk that fast, you don't see nothing."

"What's to see?" said Chuck, slowing down.

"The nuns don't know which way to go," he said. "Naturally they don't want to lose their flop, but they're sworn to obedience. If the Church says 'Sell!' they got to go along with it. I don't want to see them hurt—unnerstand?" and he gripped Chuck around the bicep, brought them both to a halt, gave him a look.

"Understood," Chuck said, pulling his arm loose. "Don't bruise the material."

"Nice jacket," said this pest, probably a madman. "These protesters? Most of them are environmentalists. That's O.K."

"What else would they be?" said Chuck.

Once again this clown brought Chuck to a halt, hand around his bicep. "It's a good thing you're staying in shape," he said, dropping his hand. He leaned forward, lowered his voice. "You know who they are. They're revolutionaries. They're out to destabilize Church and State any way they can. They don't know the meaning of the word *restraint.*"

"There's a wild bunch on the other side, too," Chuck said. He did not like the way his companion smirked, black hole where his teeth were missing, winked, patted Chuck on the chest.

"Better get moving," said the other, pulling Chuck forward. They could soon see how maybe 150 yards ahead, cars and pedestrians were turning off the parkway onto a road that looped back toward the bridge. "Come on, I'll show you a shortcut," said Chuck's guide, crossing the parkway between cars barely moving, pulling Chuck into the woods between the parkway and the Palisades, down a slope and onto a road clogged with traffic, across the road, down another slope, onto another road, the access road, as it turned out, to the compound run by the Sisters of St. Sebastian of Solace but owned by the Church, for the time being. Cars were parked bumper to bumper on both sides of the road. The road itself was jammed with demonstrators, now walking faster, their destination in sight.

The inland side of the compound was surrounded by a low stone wall, only knee high but nicely made, the stones fitted snugly together, holding their positions without mortar in the baddest of weather. The entrance to the compound was a two-lane gap in this wall, a continuation of the access road, a stone pillar on either side. Inside the compound, the cobblestone access road turned into a broad cement walkway that ran straight ahead about halfway to the main building, St. Michael's Fortress. From there it curved out on either side and then in again to form a circle in front of St. Michael's, so that if you were to look down on it from inside a helicopter it would be shaped like an old-fashioned magnifying glass. Inside the circle was a big lawn, already greening. St. Michael's was a rectangle reclining on its long side, five stories high, gray stone, a nun looking out of every window, gothic arches over every window, bars across every first-floor window, a turret on each corner, gargoyles along the roof, a seagull shifting its shoulders on top of the bell tower.

It didn't look as though any visitor would get to examine St. Michael's more closely, not if New Jersey's Finest had anything to say about it, for they were lined up shoulder to shoulder across the entrance, three deep, nightsticks at the ready. But way to his right, Chuck, who was taller than most folks, saw a young guy, college age about, step over the wall and run to the center of the magnifying glass and dance in place, arms over his head, like Rocky. The madman who had attached himself to Chuck gave him an elbow in the ribs. Four cops peeled off the line and corralled Rocky, who did not resist or try to escape. "Come on," said the Madman as he pulled Chuck by the sleeve onto the wall for a better view. As the cops were bringing Rocky to the entrance for expulsion, two guys who had been standing with him stepped over the wall and ran onto the mall. Cops peeled off the line to run them down. Now a guy on the left stepped over the wall and ran out, then another guy from the right side, then a girl from the right, a girl from the left, a middle-aged couple through a gap in the line across the entrance where cops had deserted their posts to reinforce another part of the line, for demonstrators, pressured from behind by new arrivals, were mobbing up against the cops. Their line bulged inward like the slats in the subterranean hideaway holding back the coal.

Standing on the stone wall, Chuck could see how in the distance one of Rocky's friends was having some fun dodging the two cops who were trying to take him down. He juked, sidestepped, spun away, slowed down to give a pursuer hope, then, as an arm reached for his shoulder, burned rubber. One cop, no longer young, pulled up to puff and pant, heartattacksville. The other cop, right behind the Artful Dodger, looked ready, given his posture, to have a go at a flying tackle, when the Dodger, looking back over his shoulder, suddenly buttonhooked left—right into a third cop, who was standing over a young woman he had just handcuffed; this cop began to massage the Dodger with his club. "See that?" said the Madman.

"Come on," he said to Chuck, jumping off the wall. He ran two steps, turned, waved Chuck onward, turned, ran to the melee. Chuck stayed put. The cop who had been massaging the Dodger greeted the Madman with the end of his nightstick to the gut, as though thrusting with a javelin. The Madman doubled over. The cop who had been chasing the Dodger whacked the Madman across the backs of his thighs. The Madman went down. Two more cops came over, so that from where Chuck was standing you could see only the bent-over backs of four cops, their nightsticks rising and falling, a mistake, Chuck thought, for the Madman (and the poor guy had done nothing to earn that label) seemed to be on their side. A groan escaped from the would-be demonstrators crowded along the wall and across the entranceway.

As though organized by an emerging group mind, the crowd suddenly surged forward, flowed over the wall, burst through the barrier of cops, engulfing them, pooled in the top central part of the mall, in front of the entrance to St. Michael's Fortress. Four cops were dragging Chuck's former companion, who was in handcuffs, to the left side of the circular walkway, where an ambulance and a paddy wagon were parked. The woman in handcuffs walked behind them, unescorted, under her own steam, head held high. A phalanx of cops was using nightsticks to pry their way through the crowd to the right side curve of walkway, where three patrol cars were parked, lights flashing. Demonstrators continued to flow into the central lawn enclosed by the walkway. They moved to the top half of the magnifying glass. A cohort of demonstrators marched in chanting "God yes, Mammon no!" Reinforcements arrived, transport wagons, cops with plastic shields jumping down, spreading out to take positions between the police vehicles, patrol cars, paddy wagons, transport wagons, now evenly spaced on both sides of the walkway. Demonstrators in the northeast quadrant of the magnifying glass began to chant, "Hee hee, ho ho, we want Blemp to blow." Chuck's eyes swept the field of action before him. Here and there skirmishes broke out between demonstrators and a cop or two who had not yet made it to the haven of the walk that circled in front of St. Michael's to enclose a mall equal in area to a football field.

A group pretty much in the center of the mall, younger and more varied of costume than the others, began to chant, shaking their fists in tempo. Their chant went like this:

What do we want? A clean stream.
When do we want it? Forever
What do we want? Clean cliffs.
When do we want them? Forever
What do we want? Naked nature.
When do we want her? Now and forever

There was a horrible electronic howl. Chuck was surprised to see that while he was watching the crowd someone had set up amplifying equipment at the top of the steps leading into St. Michael's. The guy with the frizzy hair was fiddling with the mike. He made the mike howl again and he made shushing gestures, palms forward, hands pushing forward and down. He ticked the mike with his fingernail, could puncture an eardrum. Then he put the mike up to his mouth, and as the babble from the crowd continued he began to speak in a conversational voice: "Simmer down, now, simmer down, yes, it feels good to make yourself heard, feels good to make yourself visible, nice to be surrounded by like-minded friends, nice to let it all hang out, but we've got work to do, we've got to WILL YOU SHUT THE FUCK UP?" and that did it.

As more and more of the crowd, amid shushing noises from the others, shut the fuck up, he just stood there holding the mike, no expression on his face, except for maybe that smileless smile you see on archaic statuary, counting the house. To his right stood Ivan and Mavis. "Listen up," he said. "We're expecting Senator Azcan and Representative Badalamente any minute. But first we have a treat, to put us in the mood. Standing to my right is the man you've been waiting to hear, the Bard of the Movement, Ivan Tervakalio," and he nodded to the bard. "Ivan," he said.

Amid a few cheers, Ivan positioned himself in front of the mike and let loose with a sequence of gloriously dirty chords that talked back and forth to each other, and once again Chuck marveled at his feeling for the blues. The sun came out from behind a cloud. Then

Ivan sang how Ronald Blemp came to the mountain. Far as Chuck could tell, the crowd was getting into it. After another sequence of deep funkery he sang:

> Ronald Blemp said to the Sister
> God's just one more CEO
> Wooooee Ronald Blemp said to the Sister
> You know God's just the biggest CEO
> If he wants to keep his Church producing
> He got to have that dough
>   That dough

The audience seemed a little divided about that one. The "What do we want" bunch cheered raucously, but there were mutters from the "God yes, Mammon no" contingent. And wasn't that a single long, loud boo? Just as Ivan hit a high wailing note and began to come down from it in minor thirds and sevenths and flatted fifths, Frizzy put a hand on his arm, restraining him, whispered something in his ear. Ivan rolled his eyes up, pulled his arm away, and, as Frizzy began to speak into the mike, walked off, in a snit is how it looked. He charged down the steps and turned to his right, onto a walk that ran along the front of St. Michael's and on a tangent to the circular walkway. Ivan was heading north, and so was Chuck, walking on top of the stone wall, watching his step, but keeping an eye on Ivan.

The wall came to its end against an outbuilding, its back to the world. On the other side of the outbuilding was a driveway, on the other side of the driveway another outbuilding, a big shed full of clean-up gear, blowers, ride-in lawn mowers, a jeep with snowplow attached, a wood shredder, stuff like that. Chuck walked along the driveway between these buildings toward the river, toward Ivan. He came out from between the buildings onto a lawn. Up ahead the lawn sloped up into a hemispherical mound.

Around the mound was a stone wall such as the one Chuck had just walked along. On top of the mound was a structure of matching stone made into the shape of a scallop shell two stories high. Chuck followed the wall to the other side of the shell, the concave side, to see what was there. There was a break in the wall, steps leading up to a statue of Mary, Mother of God, who, rather than surfing on the shell, like Venus, had her back against it. She was in a prayerful attitude, palms pressed together. Encircling her head was a halo on which was written, in gold, against a black background, "I am the immaculate conception." At her feet was a child kneeling in prayer. The child was disproportionately small. But Mary wasn't looking at it anyhow. She was looking out over the Hudson, looking over the head of Ivan Tervakalio, who was standing near the cliff edge.

There was no protective railing along the cliff edge. Instead, maybe eight or ten feet back, was a line of boulders ranging in size from a Volkswagen beetle to an easy chair. There was plenty of space between them, four or five feet, so that anyone who wanted a running start to his dive off the cliff had plenty of room to run between two of the boulders, like a fullback between guard and center. Leaning against one of these rocks that was, say, chest-high was Ivan, looking across the Hudson toward New York, his arms folded along the top, his chin on his hands, his back to Chuck, his guitar beside him—an evocative tableau, but Chuck was in no mood to be evoked. Silent as a pard, he pussyfooted down the slope from Mary on the half shell toward Ivan.

Chuck had not halved the distance when Ivan turned to face him. He leaned back against the boulder as a gunslinger leans back against a bar, while Chuck had time to wonder whether Ivan had turned because his senses were so acute by way of compensation for the bluntness of his intellect or whether his turning was a mere accident, uncaused, free—though normally Chuck had grave doubts as to whether any event was, strictly speaking, an accident rather than the outcome of confluent causes so numerous and tangled as to be beyond any human intelligence to unravel—as, for example, in the case of his coming face-to-face with Ivan on this partly cloudy Saturday.

"What the fuck do *you* want?" said Ivan, straightening up, taking a step toward Chuck.

"You," said Chuck, taking a step toward Ivan.

"What are you?" said Ivan. "FBI? One of Blemp's goons?"

"I'm a music critic," said Chuck.

"Now just a minute, now," Ivan said. He bent over and picked up a stone about the size of a checker. "It's not my fault if those mackerel-snappers are too dumb to realize that I wasn't making fun of their precious God." He turned and skimmed the stone through the air between two of the boulders and out over the Hudson. "I didn't even write those lines about God being a CEO. My wife did." This was too much for Chuck: he rushed forward, arms outstretched before him, meaning to push Ivan over the cliff.

But as his hands made contact Ivan simply twisted his torso to the side so that Chuck slipped off him and fell forward onto his hands and knees, head hanging over the precipice. The way down to the gray wrinkled water was unobstructed by ledge or outcrop or tree. "Why you do that?" said Ivan, who grabbed the collar of Chuck's field jacket and flipped him over on his back. "You crazy?"

Chuck scrambled to his feet and put up his dukes, began his long-practiced Ali shuffle, circling to the left. He could tell from the way Ivan held himself that Ivan was no boxer. Ivan threw a roundhouse right that missed by half a foot. Chuck answered with a straight left jab over Ivan's right to his mouth. That backed him out of his crouch. "You sonabitch," he said, blood covering his lips as evenly as though he had applied Maybelline with a steady hand. He charged Chuck, swinging wildly, a right that missed, a left that missed, a right to Chuck's shoulder, a teeth rattler. Then, instead of crowding Chuck, his only chance, he backed off and just stood there, blowing, already out of breath.

Chuck shuffled forward, feinted with his left, let loose with a right that had a lot behind it: Henny Kramer's bullying, Jane's unamiability, doubts about his own masculinity, hours in the gym, his crazed love of Claire, if that's what it was, his lunatic jealousy of Ivan.

The punch landed on the rear corner of Ivan's jaw, right under his cowboy-length sideburns. He fell forward.

He fell forward onto his hands and knees. His Greek sailor's cap rolled off over his forehead. Chuck was outraged, for some reason, to see that Ivan was balding from the crown outward: thus the perdurable hat. At another time Chuck would have felt an incapacitating pity. But not now. A string of bloody saliva hung from Ivan's mouth. He lowered his forehead to the grass, rested it there. Chuck got behind Ivan, grabbed his nautical jacket by the collar with both hands, flipped Ivan over on his back, tit for tat, pulled him to the edge of the cliff, Ivan's bald spot pointing to New York. He walked around to Ivan's feet, took one foot in each hand, and began to push, leaning into it. Ivan's legs folded at the knee so that Chuck lost his leverage. All right, then—Chuck swung Ivan's legs to the side so that he was lying parallel to the cliff edge, about a foot in. Chuck put one hand on Ivan's hip, the other on his shoulder, in the position of a man about to roll a log. Ivan lifted his head, looked at Chuck, his eyes out of focus, and said "Don't" just as Chuck rolled him over the cliff edge. If he screamed on the way down, Chuck didn't hear him.

Chuck took off his bandanna, wrapped it around his right hand, careful to cover his fingers, noticing that he had a cut on his left index finger, just below the knuckle, where it had connected with Ivan's teeth. He picked up Ivan's cap, bandanna over his fingers, and Frisbeed it out over the water. He picked up Ivan's guitar by its neck, swung it around in a circle a couple of times, like a discus thrower, and sailed the guitar after the cap. He looked around, saw nothing out of the way, grass springing back through his footprints. He crawled up to the edge of the cliff, so as not to be silhouetted against the sky, and looked down, but he saw no sign of Ivan or his hat or his guitar, not even concentric circles radiating out from a point of impact. He backed away, stood up. Something crunched underfoot: his sunglasses, one lens of which was now cracked neatly across. He put them into his pocket, with the unused pterodactyl.

He walked back past Mary, past the equipment shed, to the stone wall. He walked along the wall toward the access road, the sun directly overhead and as bright as lightning on a dark night.

Soon he was in earshot of Frizzy's voice. "You don't have to assume a conspiracy," he was saying. "You don't have to picture cigar smoke, fat cats in black three-piece suits around a polished table. What we're dealing with here is an anonymous unplanned inexorable process driven by the insatiable greed of corporate capitalism. It has gobbled up our political institutions and the pols that serve them. It has gobbled up our arts and crafts and leisure and skills of all kinds. It has gobbled up our farms and downtown shopping centers and mom-and-pop everythings. It is gobbling up our schools, where Coke machines and golden arches preside over the lunch rooms. It is even gobbling up our prisons, where convicts manufacture consumer kitsch under conditions that make sweatshops look like eleemosynary institutions by comparison. It has long been devouring our habitat. Now it is openly feeding on our churches. That is why we are here. . . ."

Chuck walked along the access road away from the compound, past stragglers going the other way, wrapping the bandanna around his cut index finger, his mind a whirligig of pictures and words. Finally a thought precipitated itself as out of wind-driven snow: there were powerful forces at work here, Church and State and Business and the counterculture. And Chuck? What did he stand for? He stood for Eros, the mightiest force of them all. And with Ivan out of the way he was nearing his desire.

I'll sing you seven, O
Red fly the banners, O
What is your seven, O
Seven for the hours of the working day
Six for the Tolpuddle Martyrs
Five for the years of the Five-Year Plan
Four for the years it took them

Love Is War

Three, three, the rights of man
Two, two, a man's own hands
Working for his living, O
One is workers' unity
And ever more shall be so.

twenty

Do we not yet smell the divine putrescence? —for even gods putrefy. God is dead! God remains dead! And we have killed him! How shall we console ourselves, the most murderous of all murderers? [FRIEDRICH NIETZSCHE, Joyful Wisdom] ❡ *Whatever is done for love is always beyond good and evil.* [FRIEDRICH NIETZSCHE, Beyond Good and Evil]

CHUCK STEPPED OUT across the George Washington Bridge as he had stepped out on his way to work that morning when he first met Claire; he stepped out to the beat of Red Mitchell's opening bass solo on "Blues Going Up." But his mind was like a water strider skittering around on the surface of things. Splinters of sunlight flashing off the Hudson dazzled him. He reached for his sunglasses, only to rediscover the cracked lens. Well, better that than to have left them behind, where someone looking into the death of Ivan Tervakalio might get ideas. His finding them when he didn't know he had lost them was evidence that the Gods, in Whom he did not believe, were on his side. He chose to think of the sun as smiling on him, for there was not a cloud in the sky. He nodded to straggling demonstrators going the other way as they passed by. One carried a placard that read U.S. OUT OF NORTH AMERICA. That's the spirit, politics as Dada, the best kind—for Chuck's crackpot theorem #117 was that a strong interest in American politics is an infallible symptom of baffled sex, but then, what wasn't.

He rode the subway to 116th Street and walked a couple of blocks down to the Other End, picking up a copy of *Newsday* on the way. There were the outdoor tables; there was the waitress with the tight leather pants. He sat, and since he was going to hell with himself anyhow, he ordered a pastrami sandwich on rye with cole slaw and hot mustard, and he ordered a glass of beer. The first bite of the sandwich, which was two inches thick and succulent with fat, tasted good enough to make Chuck feel slightly faint. In his eyes having a drink with lunch was not much less decadent than going to the movies in the afternoon—but he did it and he was glad. Just for the hell of it, he tipped Hardcore five bucks at the entrance to his world beneath the world.

Sure enough, there was a new graffito:

VENGEANCE IS MINE
SAITH THE LORD

But Chuck's brain was too out of focus to locate a rejoinder. He had to make do with muttering an uninspired "Fuck you." Believe it or not, there were the keys to the car in his office mailbox, another good sign. In the office a blinking light told him that someone had called and left a message. He picked up the receiver, punched in his code, and listened for Claire's rough-edged contralto. Instead, he got Jane's serrated soprano: "Where are you? You're never there when I need you. My Daddy's dead and you're off somewhere. I want you up here right away. I think the lawyer, Billy Whatshisface, is trying to cheat me. These north-country rednecks and good old boys are used to women who are doormats. Well, not me. I want you to sit down with him and tell him what's what. Hear?"

Chuck dialed the number of the Reverend Luke Hartung's residence in Sacandaga, New York. Without preliminaries, Jane's voice said, "Leave a message, I'll get back to you," but not in a tone that inspired confidence, for Jane believed that politeness lowered you in the eyes of the person to whom you were polite. After the signal, Chuck said, "I'm on my way." Chuck hurried home, packed a bag, walked to the parking lot at 122th Street, retrieved his old Caravan, drove to his apartment, retrieved his bag, set off on his four-hour drive north. His usual route was across the George Washington Bridge, up the Palisades Parkway, and onto the New York Thruway, but not today. He did not want to be anywhere near a certain demonstration. Instead, he headed north along the Sawmill River and onto the Taconic, which in any case was more scenic.

To distract himself from the vision of Ivan on his hands and knees that kept rising before his inner eye, Chuck, as he crossed from the Taconic to the Thruway via the Rip Van Winkle Bridge, turned on the radio. He found the rebroadcast from New Jersey of Dr. Lena Pitts's morning show.

Caller: I need some advice.

Dr. Lena: I don't give advice. I'm an authority on right and wrong. That's my calling.

Caller: Well, the thing is, I don't know the right thing to do about my son.

Dr. Lena: What's his IQ?

Caller: A hundred and something, I don't know. The point is, my sister and me moved in with my father, to take care of him, you know, because he's losing it, you know?

Dr. Lena: That's between you and she.

Caller: Well, the other day my sister was going through my father's checkbook and that.

Dr. Lena: Did she have his permission?

Caller: He gets, you know, confused sometimes, and we wanted to know why the rent check bounced.

Dr. Lena: Does your father have false teeth?

Caller: It turns out my son was forging checks—for walking-around money, he says.

Dr. Lena: Did you call the police?

Caller: Well, no.

Dr. Lena: Why not?

Caller: Well, I felt that...

Dr. Lena: I don't want to hear about your feelings. I'm not a feelings person. I'm a behavior person.

Caller: Well, he *is* my son, and he's only nineteen.

Dr. Lena: Listen to me very carefully. The Ten Commandments don't tell you how to feel—they tell you how to behave.

Caller: Then what should we do?

Dr. Lena: Call the police, send him to jail.

Caller: Then he'll never get a good job.

Dr. Lena: He doesn't want a job, or he'd have one.

Caller: My sister and me, we were thinking of making him join up.

Dr. Lena: Don't you dare! Those are nice boys in the military. They're defending America against atheistical communism and other evildoers. Don't foist off a bum like your son on the military. Send him to jail.

Caller: The thing is, once you get a record...

Dr. Lena: Don't you ever listen? I said send him to jail. *Send him to jail.* Period. End of sentence.

Caller: Yes, Dr. Lena. Thank you, Dr. Lena.

If it were not for the other cons, jail might have its attractions. In that respect, jail was like the monastery. Or so Chuck allowed himself to think, for he was muzzy-minded from the beer, the big lunch, the monotonous drive, the day's excitements. And then there was the nunnery, and he imagined himself hiding out in a nunnery, in the communal shower where nuns had to wear chemises but a chemise when wet and sticking to the body left little to the imagination so that he could see and he was awakened by the right-side tires of his car going over the rumble strip that divided the Thruway proper from the soft shoulder. He jerked the car back on course, and that sharp pang in his chest was surely no more than the effect of a sudden spurt of adrenaline. It was a relief finally to exit the Thruway at Amsterdam, gateway to the Adirondacks, a relief to have something besides trees to look at, like strip malls and houses that had seen better days and, after a while, deep country, the Great Sacandaga Lake on the right, downtown Sacandaga, a dozen stores and a post office on Main Street, and in the hills ten miles outside of town the residence of the late Reverend Luke Hartung, founder of the First Church of Christ, Avenger.

Jane was inside, waiting for him.

"I've been waiting for you," she said.

"I'm so sorry about your dad," he said.

"I hope you brought along some decent clothes," she said. "People will be stopping by. This isn't New York, you know." Jane herself was dressed in a splendid black skirt suit, white blouse, dark panty hose, black suede heels. Someone had to have helped her select that suit. Someone had to have put that curl in her hair for her. She saw him looking her over. "When yesterday morning the doctor said that Daddy was fading fast, I drove over to Saratoga Springs to get some decent clothes, so as to show respect, you know."

"When did he die?" Chuck said.

"Around noon," she said. "Apparently he just stopped breathing. I was eating lunch in the cafeteria, so I didn't see it happen."

"Do I smell coffee?" he said.

"Yes—why don't you bring us each a cup to drink out on the porch?" she said.

So that's what he did. "I've been going through Daddy's dressers and closets and the attic," she said.

"That must be interesting," he said.

"I've come across twenty-three pocketknives so far," she said.

"I suppose when you get older it's harder to keep track—" he said.

"One of them is from the World's Fair of 1939; it's only an inch long," she said.

"Might be worth some—" he said.

"Another one has a clear plastic handle," she said. "On each side, under the plastic, is a photo of a naked woman."

"Oh, well, probably someone put it in the collection basket," he said.

167

"I also came across his pornography collection—two cartons' worth in the attic," she said.

"I see," he said.

"I never knew my father was a pig," she said.

"These manly men have strong sex drives," he said. "It's better to look at pornography and jerk off than to rape someone."

"And you're another," she said.

"I try," he said.

She just gave him a long, speculative look, but a woman was coming toward them up the walk, middle-aged, thick, flowered dress, pigeon-toed, needed practice on those high heels. "Sally Mae, meet my husband, Charles; Charles, meet Sally Mae Vanderveer. Charles, be a dear and get Sally Mae a cup of coffee and the plate of cookies on the kitchen table." So that's what he did. Other women arrived, and Chuck went off to look for the pornography collection. The idea was to rescue a memento or two from the anticipated auto-da-fé.

He was removing the cover from a fine old cedar blanket chest when a voice behind him said, "What you're looking for is in the closet under the staircase. It's locked." This was Billy Vandamm, one time lawyer of the Reverend Luke Hartung, now Jane's. He took Chuck by the elbow and led him into the study, sat him down, poured them each a glass of brandy. He then explained the complications of the Reverend's estate, the work involved in transferring it to Jane, the infamous provisions of the estate tax, the justified but delicate maneuvers, not to be attempted by the inexperienced, to evade them, all in the manner of a man among men who understood, forgave, and knew how to circumvent the vagaries of women. Chuck assured Billy Van, as he was familiarly known, that he couldn't imagine the Reverend's old friend doing anything but his best for the Reverend's only daughter. Just think what effect the mere hint of a rumor to the contrary would have on a tight-knit community such as this one, full of the Reverend's old parishioners. That got him a long look, a nod, and finally another dose of brandy, whereupon Chuck promised to say as much to Jane, it being understood that this discussion was not billable. Billy Van assured Chuck that his visit was purely social.

That night, when Chuck slid into bed, he was dreaming while still awake how he would plot with Claire to oust the redneck who had usurped his house, once the property of a man of the cloth, when Jane reached over to yank his chain. "Here, Piggy, Piggy," she said. He jumped as though someone had shoved an icicle up his bum. Man, he was flabbergasted. "Oink, oink," she said with a giggle. What could he do but respond, for he was churlish only within limits. But Jane had another surprise in store for him: after some fairly aggressive loveplay, she pushed him onto his back, straddled him, and rode him like a cowgirl until she came, just before he did. Well, he lay there, stunned and depleted and sweating, while Jane used the john, went off somewhere, came back with a brandy for him and a liqueur for herself. She sat cross-legged on the bed. "According to Billy Whatshisface," she said, "after expenses, like for the funeral, and fees and taxes and blah, blah, blah, I'll still be nearly a millionaire. That means I'll be twenty times richer than you."

Chuck was lying on his back, eyes closed, blips and squiggles of neon floating across the black behind his lids. "Umph," he said.

Jane tickled his ribs on both sides, digging in her fingertips, usually enough to fold him up like a jackknife, but not this time, for Chuck was numb all over. "You know what?" she said. "Money is an aphrodisiac."

"Sex is an aphrodisiac" is what Chuck said, but in a mumble.

Jane looked at him for a moment and then began to laugh and then laugh some more and harder. Chuck joined in, weakly at first, but when she said, "That's a good one," they both began to roar, Jane pounding him on the chest, Chuck kicking his heels against the mattress, tears running out of their eyes. When they subsided, Jane said, "Don't go away," and moved, still naked, toward the kitchen.

Amid the pinwheels and pyrotechnic blossoms under his eyelids, Chuck was trying to picture the front of the very house he was in, snow falling, smoke rising from the chimney, next to the rusting pickup truck an old cast iron bathtub with bait fish swimming around in it. He was circling around through the woods to get a view of the back of the house when Jane returned, in her hand a plate heaped with the steak fries she had brought back in a doggy bag from the Lakeside Lounge, where the Lockharts had eaten dinner. She sat tailor fashion on the bed; and as Chuck confirmed what he had expected, that the chopping block and pile of unsplit wood was behind the house, she pushed a steak fry into his mouth, burning his lips, for she had reheated the fries in her father's immense microwave.

The trouble was that the back porch was jammed full of firewood from floor to rafter, for the winters around here are long and cold, and the days of oil heat were just a memory: therefore you couldn't see the back door. You wouldn't know that anybody had come out that door until he or she had walked through a tunnel of wood as long as the porch was wide. Jane had thoughtfully put lots of salt and pepper on half the fries, for that's how Chuck liked them, for that's how Chuck liked all such things as rice and pasta, and couscous, for that matter, well salted and peppered. Jane, her mouth full, was going on about this mother-and-daughter team that specialized in selling off the contents of houses; they would come by and label everything, advertise in the local papers, conduct the actual sale themselves, keep only twenty percent of the take. Billy Van said they were tight with dealers in antiques and collectible kitsch, for it was mainly dealers who came to these sales. But Chuck was watching a woman who emerged from the tunnel of firewood, walked halfway down the steps off the porch, put her hands on her hips, and looked skyward, like a person wondering if this fucking snow would ever end.

She was skimpy above the waist, but rotund of abdomen, long of chin, small of mouth, and with the beginning of a dowager's hump, so that her back was curved not like an S but like a C. In profile she looked like a wasp or hornet or anyhow one of those insects that sting. Chuck raised the rifle to his shoulder and put the sights on her sternum, but he couldn't pull the trigger. The idea was to get rid of the redneck, after all, not to kill his women. He was lowering the rifle when Jane said, "Hear? You haven't listened to a word I've said. It's the old story. He has his way with her, then rolls off her without a word to dream of other women."

"Um," he said.

twenty one

The only cure for love is mar-riage. [SCOTTISH SAYING] ⁊ *If the king male is gone, the largest female goby changes into a male.* [DEBORAH BLUM, Sex on the Brain: The Biological Differences between Men and Women] ⁊ *The story is that Coolidge and his wife were inspecting a government farm. While the President was off somewhere, Mrs. Coolidge observed a rooster mating with a hen in the chicken coop. "How often does he do that?" she asked. "Dozens of times a day," said the guide. "Please mention this fact to the President," said Mrs. Coolidge. Later, when the President passed the chicken coop, he was told of the rooster's prowess. "Always with the same hen?" the President asked. "Oh no, a different one each time," said the guide. The President said, "Please tell* that *to Mrs. Coolidge."* [DEAN HAMER AND PETER COPELAND, Living with Our Genes: Why They Matter More Than You Think] ⁊ *Feminism encourages women to leave their husbands, kill their children, practice witchcraft, destroy capitalism, and become lesbian.* [PAT ROBERTSON] ⁊ *Let's go get stoned.* [RAY CHARLES]

EHIND THE HOUSE AND TO ONE SIDE, the Reverend had kept a steel drum in which he got rid of burnable trash. Six inches up from the bottom was a ring of holes (for ventilation). Up six inches further a refrigerator shelf was set across the inside of the drum (for a grate). Upon this grate Chuck placed a thick layer of kindling (which he had made by sawing a splintery one-by-eight into six-inch lengths and then splitting them into pieces about thrice the thickness of a pencil). He then soaked the kindling with kerosene. He then neatly folded his field jacket and placed it on the kindling. He then soaked his field jacket with kerosene. He then lit a twist of newspaper with a match and dropped the paper onto his jacket. There was no whump and ball of fire, for we're dealing with kerosene here, not gasoline, but there was soon plenty of flame, too much black smoke, and a satisfying crackle of the kindling. Then Chuck threw in the bandanna.

Burning his jacket gave him a feeling, which one he couldn't have said—something mixed with regret, maybe. It was associated, after all, with the only extraordinary thing he had ever done. He might have felt that he was diminishing the experience by destroying the evidence. He stirred the remnants of jacket with a pitchfork, for he wanted every bit of it burnt, except for the zipper, which he intended to bury. His eyes drifted toward the porch, which he saw in a series of gestalt shifts: 1) a woman stepping out of a tunnel of firewood to stand on the porch steps, place her hands on her hips, look up at the snowy sky; 2) a porch three-quarters empty of wood looking gray in the weak early spring sun. The door opened and Jane, once again wearing her new black suit, stepped onto the porch.

What is this that has been happening to him lately: a weakness in the legs, a tightness and tingle in the head, a momentary blackout? He leaned on the pitchfork for support. "Now what are you doing?" said Jane.

"Tidying up," Chuck said—"just to have something to do."

"You're not burning Daddy's clothes, are you?" she said. " 'Cause we get a tax write-off if we give them to the Salvation Army. A quarter, I thought I'd say his underwear pants were worth, but a half dollar for his tee shirts, and up from there. You think I could claim a dollar for the tee shirts?"

"No," he said.

"There must be three dozen plaid shirts," she said, "some of them wool. You can have one if you like."

"My arms are too long," he said, stirring the ashes.

173

"Well, I'm off to see about the memorial service," she said. "I'm going to be one of the speakers."

"Good for you," he said.

"I want you to be there for moral support," she said. "I've never spoken in public before."

"You'll wow them," he said. "Talk about his pornography collection."

"You know, sometimes I think you're jealous of my father," she said.

"Do you think he could have killed a rival who was seriously in his way?" he said.

"In a minute," she said. "But don't forget, my Daddy's God was an avenger."

Now what did she mean by saying that?

"And you ought to do something about that finger. It's beginning to look regusting," she said, turning to go back into the house—and out through the front door and into her Daddy's pickup and over to the First Church of Christ, Provider and into Pastor Verplank's office. Chuck had to admit that his left index finger, which he had cut on Ivan's teeth, was looking nasty. There were no newfangled antibiotics in the Reverend Hartung's medicine cabinet, but there was an old bottle of iodine. That damn finger began to throb, now that he was paying attention to it, and it was already pretty much the color of iodine, but Chuck painted it anyhow.

In the mudroom was a doorless closet in which the Reverend had kept a couple of work jackets, a hooded sweatshirt, a slicker, rubber boots, and a badminton racket (for swatting the occasional bat that somehow got in the house). Hanging on a nail on the back wall of this closet was a ring of keys. One of these keys opened the gun cabinet, from which Chuck removed the Ruger Bearcat. This is a .22 caliber revolver that is in the style of the famous old Colt Single-Action Army, but much reduced in size. Chuck wanted a revolver, rather than a semi-automatic, because revolvers do not eject cases where the police can find them and give them to ballistic experts who can then match them to the gun that fired them. And he wanted this re-volver in particular because he remembered Jane's father telling him how a recent widow (now dead) had given her pastor the Bearcat as a memento of her husband, who had gotten it from a hunter up from New Jersey in return for a nice little four-pointer he (the hus-band) had just shot. It would not be easy to trace this gun back to the Reverend Hartung and thence to Chuck. He also withdrew from the cabinet a box of .22-caliber bullets, forty-grain high-velocity roundnoses—which, he believed, would do a lot of damage when fired at close range into a human skull, for though a hollow-point ex-pands more quickly, perhaps too quickly in the case of a .22 hit-ting a head bone, a roundnose is more likely to penetrate and then bounce around, once inside.

Lawyer Billy Van was right about the location of the Reverend's pornography collection, for another key on the ring fit the lock on the door to the closet under the stairs, where there were two cartons of videos, photos, magazines, pamphlets, and playing cards. But it did not take Chuck long to lose interest in the collection, for among the common perversions, buggery was low on his hit parade.

In back of the house, to the side opposite the incinerator drum, was a chopping block and a pile of hardwood rounds a foot long wait-ing to be split up into stove wood. In the tool shed was a collection of axes and mauls head down in a barrel. Chuck selected a ten-pound maul and got to work on the woodpile. The wood, cut from straight-grained tops and limbs (the gnarled and knotty stuff was saved for the fireplace, the bole for lumber), split neatly; further, Chuck had unconsciously internalized his parents' myth that work was redeem-ing; and finally, muscular people like to use their muscles—so be-fore long he was feeling good. Chopping wood is a well-known rem-edy for tension, anxiety, perturbation, anger, runaway testosterone, and guilt, should you have any. He removed his sweater and his blue checked shirt and soon sweated through his undershirt. Instead of replenishing the porch, he decided to build a stack the size of a face cord, one by four by eight. He was careful to make sure that the ends of wood facing the house were all exactly flush, the idea being that the stack should look as through a giant had cut it through with a single stroke of his giant axe.

He was standing there, admiring his handiwork, half-consciously striking a pose, one hand on a hip, when the door opened and Jane stepped out onto the porch.

"Hi there, goodlooking," she said. "You look like whatshisface in *Brute Force.*"

"How'd it go?" he said.

"Pastor Verplank is a sweetheart," she said. "Then I stopped by Billy Van's—he was still in his pajamas and the kind of bathrobe Hugh Hefner always wears. But he didn't try any funny business. He was very helpful, now that I'm an heiress. I needed him to fix things so I can right away start withdrawing money from Daddy's accounts. Do you think if I donated money to KWAP for new equipment, they would give me my own radio show?"

"They'd be fools not to," he said.

"Do you mean it?" she said.

"I was waiting for you to come back before driving to the city, in case you wanted to come along," he said, and he started up the steps to the porch.

She met him halfway and crushed herself against him, her black suit against his sweaty undershirt, like someone in the movies. Then she gave him a big kiss on the lips, a real smerp. Then she pushed him back. "I've got too much to do up here," she said. "See if you can stay out of trouble without me being there to watch over you."

Jane held the door open with one hand, and she bowed with mock deference, but as Chuck walked through the door she goosed him vigorously. No, he did not kill her right then and there, but he thought about it, and the thought came along with that tingle in his head, that darkening of vision, that weakness in the legs. Nevertheless, he kept on walking without a word, though he waddled for a stride or two.

"Oh, don't be such a party poop," said Jane.

There is a substance with a long name beginning "succ" used by veterinarians as an anesthetic; an adequate dose paralyzes all the muscles in the body, pertinently those of the heart and lungs; suffocation follows. This substance breaks down into naturally occurring chemicals in the body and is therefore hard to detect.

The Reverend Hartung's tractor is relatively small and light-weight but heavy enough to crush you to death should you fall or be pushed under it.

One night Beverly Jane Batease loaded her father's shotgun and stepped out of her house and onto the back porch, looking to get the pesky raccoon that kept on raiding her garbage, but she tripped on a piece of firewood and blew away a good portion of her head.

Propane bottles have been known to explode.

The Reverend Hartung's kitchen stove does not have a pilot light; if a person were to be knocked out by a blow across the back of the head, with, say, a stick of firewood, and then laid on the floor as though she had received the injury in a fall; and if you were to turn on the gas, but not ignite it, and then carefully close the door to the dining room as you left, the person on the floor would asphyxiate.

Even very careful people sometimes inadvertently leave a live round in an "unloaded" gun.

So Chuck maundered as he drove back to the city. He had taken the scenic route, through the Catskills, for like many city boys, he felt the allure of the wild, but at a safe distance. There, to his right, was the slope on which Claire had shot the marauder. After, they had trekked north at top speed for twelve hours until they were sure no one was following them, washed in a stream, eaten, crawled into the sleeping bag together, and Chuck could feel Claire under his hands though they were on the steering wheel, his left index finger throbbing. Such desire erupted within him that he had to stop the car, get out, walk to a big rock, sit down on it, and pant. Coming out of it, he asked himself where was this that he was. Ah, yes, he was outside Durham, in the Irish Alps. He wanted to call Claire, but she was at a poetry festival, or returning from it. He got back into his car and started driving, far too fast, pissed at any car or traffic light that slowed him down, for in Chuck's case frustrated yearning turned not into depression but anger, the healthier emotion for him who experiences it, however unhealthy it may turn out for others.

He began to castigate himself. Wasn't he a certified intellectual? Hadn't he published in *Procrustes Review*? Well, then, if thirty-something percent of the murders committed in the United States go unsolved, in spite of the fact that most murderers are dimwits, he ought to be able to find a way of getting rid of Jane without getting caught. Nothing too fancy, that was the first rule. Ingenuity invited accident and left traces. It would be a great mistake and an act of hubris to underestimate the police. Collectively, the police are smart, no matter how smart or stupid the individual cop. Another rule: nothing that would cause pain for more than an instant. He did not want Jane to suffer; he just wanted her gone. Nor did he want to see her body mangled, for Chuck had a superstitious horror of mutilation, concealed organs obscenely exposed. Third, he must have an unassailable alibi—he must be far away from the scene of Jane's demise, somewhere in the presence of witnesses and at a designated time, for the police understandably look to the spouse first. Come to think of it, what better alibi than to be in a classroom standing before a class?

As a replacement for his field jacket, Chuck was wearing the former Reverend Hartung's barn jacket from Banana Republic, for an extra-large barn jacket from Banana Republic, bless them, is also extra-long. In the right hand side pocket of this jacket was the Ruger Bearcat; in the left-hand pocket was his pet pterodactyl. But the deployment of these required that you be on the scene. Chuck did not know how to get poison without leaving a paper trail. He did not know how to make a bomb. In some respects his education was sadly deficient. To push Jane over a cliff would be to invite comparison with another recent murder—besides, how could you push someone off a cliff at a distance? You could give her a push while she was washing a window or watering a window box, but Jane didn't wash windows or grow plants. During the rush hour you could maybe push someone onto the tracks just as the train was coming into the station and get away with it, say, if you wore a disguise. Enough of this push-and-shove stuff! Chuck liked the idea of throwing a plugged-in hair dryer into her bath water, but Jane didn't have a hair dryer, nor did she listen to the radio while bathing. Now a car—there was a potential weapon for you. How many people died each year in car accidents? Yeah, but faking a fatal accident isn't so easy. Another thing Chuck did not know how to do is hot-wire a car; still another is how to sabotage the brakes. Damn, this being a murderer required a lot of out-of-the-way know-how.

As he passed through the Harriman tollgate, Chuck turned on an all-news station to catch the traffic report, for there was more than one way to get to the city from where he was. The New Jersey correspondent was blathering on about yesterday's demonstration in a tone of world-weary disapproval. Forty-three demonstrators, including two nuns, had been arrested. One cop was in a hospital, trying to recover from a heart attack. Things had gotten out of hand when a dozen cops stormed the portico to St. Michael's Fortress and attempted to arrest Mavis Mills, Saul Green, founder of Greenspace, Representative Badalamente (who, so Chuck remembered, was a Democrat, as the cops, most likely, were not), and the sound tekkies. Hotheads from the crowd rushed the cops. Cops on the circular walkway rushed the crowd, nightsticks flailing. The cop putting handcuffs on Mavis keeled over. Two nuns emerged from St. Michael's. One tended the fallen cop; the other picked up the microphone and pleaded for peace; both were handcuffed. The crowd everywhere broke through the police cordon and began to trash whatever they could get their hands on. The Palisades Parkway was still closed from ten miles above the George Washington Bridge. Fine—he would take the Tappen Zee Bridge instead. He had to assume that with respect to Ivan Tervakalio, no news was good news.

Chuck stopped at his office to check the mail. The first message

179

in his phone mail said simply this: "Why don't you come up and see me sometime?" but Chuck recognized the voice as belonging to Betty Blondell. The second message went like this: "Why not join us for a bite and some drinks? We'll be at the Other End at eight." The voice was Tony Felder's.

He hotfooted it over to the Other End and made it by eight thirty. He had not expected to see Betty Blondell sitting with Tony and Simone, the three of them laughing, drinks on the table, but no food.

"I see you're wearing your designer stubble," said Tony, signaling for the waitress.

"Your hair's all mussed," said Simone.

"A roughed-up macho jacket over a tee shirt, showing your neck muscles," said Betty. "If your intention was to turn me on, you're succeeding." Chuck, who since about his eleventh birthday had never wanted anything more than to be a sex object, was vaguely annoyed. "Bass ale on draft," he told the waitress.

"What's this?" said Betty, and she plucked a wood chip out of his hair, for he had taken the only open seat, the seat between Betty and Simone.

"I've been up north," said Chuck, and he removed the Reverend's jacket. The Reverend's black tee shirt, a size too small, was tight over his pumped-up muscles.

"Oooo," said Betty.

"Oh, yes, the Last of the Patriarchs," said Tony. "How is the old fraud?"

"He's dead," said Chuck, suddenly realizing that he was hungry, and man, that beer tasted good.

"How's Jane?" said Simone.

"I don't think it's hit her yet," said Chuck, for there are times when an evasive banality is best.

Tony looked at Chuck with a cocked eyebrow and an ironic grin.

"Please give her my sympathy," said Simone.

"Yeah, give her mine too," said Betty, "but let's talk about something else."

"Like what?" said Simone.

"Food," said Chuck.

"Sex," said Betty.

Chuck groaned.

"I've been reading this book that Tony loaned me," said Betty, "*All for Love,* it's called. It's by an evolutionary biologist named Lionel Lyons."

"Obviously a pseudonym," said Chuck.

"It's about sexual selection, rather than natural selection, about the peacock's tail, rather than the lion's tooth," Betty said, looking Chuck in the eye and poking him in the chest. "It's about adaptations that help us get on in our conspecific, rather than our extra-specific, environment—with other people, especially the opposite sex, rather than the weather. The important point is that these adaptations can be behavioral as well as physical, the bird's song, not just its bright feathers, not just tits and ass or lats and abs, but conversation, a sense of humor, art, music, *literature.* Everything you value most, like Jimmie Joyce or the blues, is the result of sexual selection. So there," and she giggled and blushed fetchingly.

The waitress arrived. They ordered, a salad for Betty, fish for Simone, chicken for Tony, and a twelve-ounce bacon cheeseburger with onion rings for Chuck. "And drinks all around," said Chuck.

"Betty has the fervor of the recent convert," said Tony.

"She's an enthusiast," said Simone.

"An extremist," said Chuck.

"A true believer," said Tony, "but in different things at different times."

"What's this business of talking about me as though I wasn't here?" said Betty. "So I've had a revelation. What's wrong with that? St. Thomas couldn't have explained why we're sitting around here talking, but Lionel Lyons can. We're showing off our wit and wisdom, our store of ideas, our skill with words—all of which are fitness indicators. We're trying to seduce each other," and she put her hand on Chuck's forearm.

Chuck's reaction was to think, and the thought did him little credit, that if Betty had come on like this a year ago, he never would have gotten involved with Claire. And then he thought, and this thought did him even less credit, that Jane's and Betty's sudden ardor was a sign of favor from the Gods for what he had done and an encouragement to keep on doing it.

"You've got to watch out for these evolutionary anthropologists," said Simone. "Tony's got a book by one of them who argues that murder is an adaptation, that we're genetically programmed to kill whoever has what we want or stands in our way—if we think we can get away with it. It's understood that we want what we want to entice the other sex and that what the enemy is standing in the way of is a piece of ass."

"Yes, let's talk about murder," said Chuck.

"The idea is that men kill each other ultimately over women, is that it?" said Betty.

"Ultimately...over whose genes get passed on," said Tony.

"Then how do you explain the Mafia hit man?" said Simone.

"The mafia hit man kills someone because his capo told him to," said Tony. "He does what he's told because he wants to maintain or improve his position within the family. The capo gave the order because he wants to improve or maintain his power, prestige, or property. All these, when abundant, are signals to women that he'll be a good provider, even that he has good genes. It goes without saying that neither the capo nor the women know what's motivating them."

"Wars?" said Simone.

"The Trojan War is the prototype of all wars," said Tony: "it was fought over Helen, that is, for the power, prestige, and property that attracts women."

"Drive-by shootings?" said Simone.

"Teenage gangs are descendents of the Yanomamo," said Tony; "in some Yanomamo tribes forty percent of all the men who die are killed by other men over women."

"There are also women murderers," said Simone.

"They kill rivals, or men who betray or forsake them, or children who get in the way of the men they want," said Tony.

"The creep who holds up a Seven-Eleven and shoots the teenage clerk?" said Simone. "The assholes who lynch a black in Texas? The redneck who beats a guy to death in a barroom brawl over an imagined slight?"

"The pipsqueak and the redneck were going after the loot or the rep that would allow them to swagger before the nymphs of their choice," said Tony; "assholes lynch blacks because blacks are reputed to have bigger pricks. Genocide is often justified by attribution of a depraved and inviting sexuality to the victims."

"If all that is true, why aren't there even more murders?" said Simone. "And how come there are different murder rates in different countries?"

"You never get your human instincts raw," said Tony. "Circumstances blanch, boil, and braise them."

"Or smother them in onions," said Chuck. The waitress arrived, distributed the food. "Let's have another round," said Chuck.

"We talking about sex or murder here?" said Betty.

"What's the diff?" said Chuck.

"That's what I've come to think," said Betty. "We may all want to kill someone, but we don't because of inhibitions built into us by education or because we fear the consequences—that is, we fear revenge from governmental surrogates of the clan. Some of us fear God. The question is not Why do some people kill? but Why don't we all do it all the time?"

"Because murder mysteries, crime shows on TV, shoot-'em-up movies and the like allow us to do in our imaginations what we don't dare do in the flesh," said Tony. "Murder and sex, that's what our entertainments are about."

"Damn right," said Chuck. "And a good thing, too."

"Now wait a minute," said Simone. "Now let's hang on a little minute. I don't want to kill anybody." She paused, as though to look within. "I just don't want to kill anybody. I really don't."

183

Tony put an arm around Simone's shoulders and pulled her to him until corners of their heads touched. "I can believe that of you, love, but not of anyone else I've ever met." Simone unstiffened, smiled, gave Tony a peck on the cheek. Tony beamed.

"Killing someone is the worst thing you can do," said Simone. "If you take away a person's life, you take away everything else. I mean, death is so . . . so irrevocable."

They ate and drank in silence for a while. Then Betty spoke, and her voice was conciliatory. "I can imagine people who would never kill, even to save the life of a child. But couldn't that be because of the strength of her inhibitions rather than the absence of a 'disposition' to kill? I mean, isn't that what the doctrine of original sin is all about?"

"Whether we are socially constructed or evolved or made by God in His image, we have a tropism toward murder, or most of us do," Tony said, looking at Simone. "That's all I'm saying."

"If you think about it, the fact is . . . that murder is banal," said Simone.

twenty two

I caused the widow's heart to sing for joy. [JOB] ❡ *It seems to me that true love is a discipline, and it needs so much wisdom that the love of Solomon and Sheba must have lasted, for all the silence of the Scriptures. Each divines the secret self of the other, and refusing to believe in the mere daily self creates a mirror where the lover or beloved sees an image to copy in daily life; for love also creates the mask.* [W. B. YEATS] ❡ *This appetite, which was implanted in our natures for the purpose of propagating our species, when excessive, becomes a disease both of the body and mind. When restrained, it produces tremors, a flushing of the face, sighing, nocturnal pollutions, hysteria, hypochondriasis, and in women the furor uterinus. When indulged in an undue or promiscuous intercourse with the female sex, or in onanism, it produces seminal weakness, impotence, dysury, tabes dorsalis, pulmonary consumption, dyspepsia, dimness of sight, vertigo, epilepsy, hypochondriasis, loss of memory, manalgia, fatuity, and death.* [BENJAMIN RUSH, Medical Inquiries and Observations, Upon the Diseases of the Mind]

CHUCK WAS AWAKENED by sunlight on his face. He realized that he was hung over. He became aware that he had to pee something awful. He saw that he was wearing only his briefs, rather than pajamas. On the nightstand was a handwritten note:

Chuck—

We had to pour you into bed. Simone
and Betty undressed you, you lucky devil.
　　　　　　　　　　　　　—Tony

Chuck remembered ordering brandies all around, but after that nothing. He started to take off his watch, which Simone and Betty had overlooked, getting ready for a shower, when he saw that he had better move it if he wanted to catch Claire at the gym. So he settled for a quick hair-comb and a toothbrushing. From the amount of sweat on her shoulders, Chuck gathered that Claire was near the end of her run. He fell in behind her, marveling once again at how nicely she moved. He loved her unformed, adolescent's legs, for starters, but those buns! that waist, her back, her shoulders, her red hair, tumbling down, the ends sticking to the sweat on her back and shoulders. He caught up with her, kept pace—"Hi there," she said—for a couple of laps until she had done her thirty. Then they walked off the tightness in their legs, side by side.

"You growing a beard?" she said.

"I can't believe I forgot to shave," he said.

"Looks good," she said.

"Has anyone yet today told you how beautiful you are?" he said.

"For God's sake, keep your voice down," she said. "No one tells me that but you"—and here Claire whispered—"but that's because right now you're the only one trying to get in my pants."

"Lunch?" he said.

"You're on," she said.

"The hideaway?" he said.

"Kelty's," she said. "I didn't get a chance to eat last night."

Kelty's was a survivor of the forties, when the Upper West Side had its Irish enclaves. It was a couple dozen blocks south of the campus; it was dark, its lunchtime clientele mainly people who work with their hands; and you could get a corned beef sandwich with two inches of meat. You could get Irish lamb stew, Claire's favorite. Chuck arrived early, claimed a booth in back, by the dartboard, ordered a beer, unfolded a copy of the *New York Times*.

The waiter who delivered the beer was one of those hostile black Irishmen with a courteous manner. "It's nice to see you again, sir," he said. "It's been a while."

"Too long," said Chuck, who so far as he knew had never seen this guy before.

"And I hope your tall friend with the red hair is well," said the waiter.

"You can see for yourself," said Chuck; "I'm expecting her any minute."

"Ah, sir, when I see her walk in the door I know that a benevolent deity directed me to this job," he said.

Chuck, now that he was a proven tough guy, just leaned back in the booth and looked the waiter over coolly. That's when Claire walked in, evidence of a benevolent deity. She nodded to the waiter, slid into the booth, and said hi to Chuck, for they had long ago agreed to eschew even the social peck, the chaste hug, in public.

"Ma'am," said the waiter to Claire, "the usual?"

"And what is that?" said Claire, for they had only been in this dump twice before, for Pat's sake.

"Michael O'Shea's on draft," said the waiter.

"Then what are you waiting for?" said Claire.

"All my life I've been waiting for you," said the waiter.

"Why don't you just pretend my ass is the Blarney Stone?" said Claire.

"A pleasure," said the waiter, but when he saw Chuck starting to slide out of the booth, he took off.

Now that they were no longer visible to anyone, Chuck took Claire's hand and kissed her knuckles. She disengaged and patted his cheek. "Whew," she said, "I'm beat. I'm going to cut my afternoon class and get into bed."

For the first time Chuck noticed that Claire indeed looked weary, shadows under her eyes, cheeks pale, her birthmark prominent, hair curling in a nimbus as it dried from the post-workout shower. "How'd things go at the festival?" he said.

"They went well," she said, her face brightening. "Some of us read in this student lounge on Saturday night and I didn't get the hook. The section I read them from 'On the Way' especially went over well. And I like workshops, talking shop with other poets—I always come away with something. And, you know, you make contacts. For example, this character asked me to read at his club in Newark. Another guy asked me to submit poems to his magazine."

The thought crossed Chuck's mind that the interest of these two guys in Claire was likely to be the same as that of the waiter, who just then came with Claire's beer and two menus. Claire ordered the lamb stew and Chuck ordered a brisket sandwich with horseradish on the side. The waiter went off. Claire and Chuck clinked glasses, drank.

"So when I get home last night at about eleven, I'm tired but upbeat," Claire said. "As I'm trudging up the stairs I'm thinking how nice it would be if you were waiting for me instead of Ivan. You'd pour me a glass of wine, massage my trapeziuses, let me babble on, sympathizing with everything," and she gave his hand a squeeze. "But Ivan was not even there for me. Not a sign of him. And he wasn't there to pick up the phone when I kept calling him Saturday night either."

"There's something I've got to tell you," Chuck said, looking around. That's when the waiter arrived with the food, in record time. He distributed the sandwich, stew, a steel bowl of pickles, a pot of hot mustard, a pot of horseradish, looked the table over, departed.

"So I called up this Greenspacer—Mavis is her name—who's always making goo-goo eyes at Ivan," said Claire. "No answer. So I call up Saul Green, founder and CEO. No answer. Finally—this is after midnight—a kid answers at the Greenspace office: Goo-Goo Eyes and Saul Green are in jail, but no one has seen Ivan since he walked off in a pet about something." She placed a spoonful of stew in her mouth, chewed, swallowed, said "Ummm."

Chuck salt-and-peppered his brisket of beef, spread hot mustard on one side of the sandwich, horseradish on the other, bit in, would have said "Ahhhh," but his mouth was too full.

"Understand, by now it's way after midnight," said Claire. "Still, I call Ivan's sister.

"About Ivan," said Chuck, "there's something—"

"Of course, that's what I called her about," said Claire. "About Ivan. Svetlana's voice is like a foghorn anyhow—I'm sure she's the result of some hormonal calamity—but when I woke her up, well, you know how a record sounds when you slow it down. Of course, soon as I asked her if she knew where Ivan was, she became her usual bossy self: she's coming right over, we'll call all the precincts and hospitals, she knows someone who knows someone in the New Jersey State Police, she knows a crackerjack private detective, she knows a lot of the Greenspacers, and whatall, and she'll bring some torte she bought just that afternoon in the German bakery."

"Is everything all right?" said the voice of the waiter, whom neither Claire nor Chuck had seen arrive.

"Go for another beer?" said Chuck to Claire.

"Let's," she said, "since I'm going to bed right after lunch anyhow." The waiter departed.

"Little by little I got her to slow down," Claire said. "She promised to hold off until tomorrow, and all the time I'm thinking she's the only person in the world who ever loved Ivan like that, maybe because no other man ever allowed her to love him, she's so ugly."

"And you?" said Chuck.

"Every now and then I feel a spasm of rueful affection, like when I think of some of the things we did together," she said. "If you stand back a little, he's not really a bad guy, you know. It's just he's an asshole."

"I've got to tell you something," Chuck said.

"Yes, I've been doing all the talking," Claire said.

189

The waiter came, exchanged full glasses of beer for the empties. He stood there, waiting for the other two to acknowledge him, but Claire and Chuck were looking at each other, as though half aware that something was about to happen. Finally, Claire looked up at him and nodded. He took off.

"What were you going to tell me?" said Claire.

"About Ivan, well, ahem"—and here he lost his courage and instead of the large revelation, gave her the small—"he was having an affair with Mavis Mills."

She slumped back in the booth. On her face was the kind of smile a little girl might use in an attempt to ward off a slap across the face by her father. "How—?" she said.

"I followed them to her apartment, saw them through the window with their shirts off, and he gave her a big production kiss goodbye, dry-humping her all the while," said Chuck.

She closed her eyes, turned her head to the side, hair swaying over her birthmark. When she turned back to Chuck and opened her eyes, they were teary. She started to wipe away the tears with her fingers until Chuck gave her his handkerchief. They both jumped as STIMP! a dart landed in the dartboard, which banged against the wall behind it, two yards from Claire's head. "I'm in no position to come on self-righteous," she said, "but it is a blow to one's self-esteem." STIMP! another dart hit the board.

"Don't be sad"—STIMP! a dart stuck in the board—"get mad," said Chuck. "That's what my mother used to say. She used to say that if my father had taken her advice he never would have died of cancer so young." STIMP!

"Let's get out of here," said Claire. STIMP!

Chuck took two twenties out of his pocket and placed them in Claire's hand. "Finish your stew while I walk to my apartment," he said. "Then take—"

"I couldn't," she said.

"All right, have a cup of coffee," he said. "Then take—" He

paused while a guy in dusty work shoes, overalls, and sweatshirt pulled out the darts. "Take a cab to my place, right to the door—you know the address?"

"444 West 110th," she said.

"O.K., take the elevator to the fifth floor, in case someone gets on with you, and then walk down a flight." STIMP! "My apartment is 4C; the door will be unlocked. O.K.?" He signaled to the waiter, who was leaning against the bar watching them.

"Is everything all right, ma'am?" the waiter said. "I couldn't help noticing—"

Chuck stood up, crowding the waiter, leaning over him, said, "I hear from Ms. Pigeous here that you said one word out of line and I'm coming after you," and he bumped the waiter, chest to chest, the two of them between the flying darts and the table.

"I wouldn't dream of committing an impertinence, sir," said the waiter.

Chuck turned to Claire, said "Later," turned to the waiter, nodded, and walked out, feeling good about himself. STIMP.

After Claire walked through the door into his apartment, Chuck lifted her into his arms, as you would lift a bride to carry her over the threshold, carried her into the living room, sat down, tipped over, so that he still had one foot on the floor, her legs were over his thighs, she on her back, he on his side, facing her. He tried to kiss her, but she moved her lips away. "I've been thinking about Ivan and Miss Big Tits there," Claire said, "and I'm doing what you said, getting mad. I could understand, maybe, if she were some kind of beauty or if she had a scintillating personality. But she's like mud on a fence. What can he get from her that he can't get better from me? In spite of our differences, I never held out on him sexually."

"Tony Felder would say that he's acting on the male disposition to disseminate his seed as widely as possible, so that his genes will prevail," said Chuck.

"'Disseminate his seed,' is it? Well, the times I've asked Ivan if he wanted to have a child, he'd say he didn't care one way or the other, so long as I took care of it," Claire said. " 'And where we gonna get the money?' he'd say. That's not the attitude of a man who cares much about whether his genes prevail. How about you—you want your genes to prevail?"

"Yes, before it's too late—little Claire running to kiss her Daddy when he comes home from work, little Chuck good at all sports from about age three," Chuck said.

"Would you be good to me when I was big-bellied and with a waddle and hors de combat?" she said.

"After my fashion," he said.

"Would you put up with me when I'm bitchy?" she said.

"I'd sop up your vitriol," he said.

"Would you be there for me when I'm down in the dumps?" she said.

"I'd go down on you to bring you up," he said.

"Would you support me in a style to which I am not yet accustomed?" she said.

"Yes, by God," he said, "even if I have to sink so low as to write a textbook."

"Would you cheat on me?" she said.

"That would be like blinding myself so I could wear dark glasses," he said.

"Would you kill my husband for me?" she said.

"I already have," he said. Oops.

"There are two theories about daydreams," she said. "One is that they are a substitute for action. The other is that—and I agree with old Willie Yeats about this—'in dreams begin responsibilities'—including daydreams. So watch what you daydream about."

"This is no daydream," he said. "I killed Ivan."

"Go on, he's off sulking somewhere," she said. "When it comes to the sulks, he's got a Ph.D."

"Claire, I followed him to the demonstration," he said. "I followed him when he went off to sulk. We got in a fight and I threw him off the Palisades, ten stories down to the Hudson."

She propped herself on an elbow, the better to look at him. "You're beginning to scare me," she said.

"Sometimes I scare myself," he said. "Not then, but now."

"Tell me you're kidding," she said.

He propped himself on an elbow, so that they were nose to nose. "This is no kidding," he said. "I killed Ivan. Ivan is no more."

"He means it," she said, looking skyward. She plopped down on her back, put her hands over her face. She didn't move. He didn't speak. After two very long minutes she moved her hands down far enough to expose her eyes. Claire's eyes were big to begin with, but right now they looked like two cups of black coffee. Through her fingers, not very distinctly, she said, "You did that for me?"

"For us," he said. Now he got the kiss he had been denied earlier. He disengaged, slid his hands under her, and rolled her over, so that he lay stretched out on his back and she lay stretched out on top of him. She wedged her face into the crook of his neck, sobbing lightly, quietly, gradually subsiding, until damn me, if she wasn't breathing the way you breathe when you're asleep, her tears drying on his cheek and neck.

For two hours Claire lay sleeping on top of Chuck, breathing softly on his neck, her belly against his, one of her legs between his, one of his between hers, and Chuck would have been hard put to call up another two hours when he had been so at home in the world. She twitched violently; he stroked her shoulder and said, "It's okay"; she gave him a squeeze, straightened her arms as though doing a push-up, got her feet on the floor, sat sideways on his lap. Because she was wearing black panty hose or leggings or whatever you call them under her shorty overalls it is unlikely that she felt him getting hard. "Got to go," she said and started down the hall to the john at the end of it.

By the time she came back from the john, hair combed, color in her cheeks from a scrubbing with cold water, so that her birthmark was faint as a memory, eyes clear, Chuck had coffee made. They sat on opposite sides of the kitchen table so that they could look each other in the face. "We can't let what I did to Ivan become meaningless," Chuck said. "We've got to make something come of it."

"Like what?" she said.

"He died so that we could be together," he said.

"Maybe it's about time you divorced your wife," she said.

"It's not so easy," he said.

"That's what they all say," she said.

"Jane just inherited something like a million dollars," he said. "If I sue for divorce she'll spend every cent to prevent it, if she has to, once she finds out I want to marry another woman."

"A million dollars . . . ," Claire said. "And now I'll have to see if those lawyers will take me on full time, so I can pay the rent. Ivan wasn't a great provider, but he did usually manage to scratch up half of what we needed to get by."

"I've got two, maybe three thousand dollars worth of rare books . . . ," he said.

Claire went over to the stove, fetched the coffeepot, poured them each a fresh cup, replaced the pot, sat down, swept the hair away from her left eye, said, "Now there's something I have to tell *you*."

"That you want to spend every minute of the rest of your life with me?" he said.

"Every other minute," she said. "What I have to tell you is that I'm pretty sure I'm pregnant."

Put that in your smipe and poke it. He gulped coffee, burning his mouth. "Somehow I'll find the money for an abortion," he said.

"I'll not have an abortion," she said.

"Claire . . . ," he said.

"You're the father," she said.

"How can you know that?" he said.

"I always wore a diaphragm when I did it with Ivan, *always*, seldom as that was," she said, "but these last two months I've been coming to you entirely unprotected."

Chuck did not pause to consider the ethics of Claire's subterfuge, though a more experienced man might have been flattered; instead, he focused on the consequences: "That means we can't put off figuring out how to kill Jane," he said.

"What happened to your finger?" she said.

twenty three

The human intellect itself is a product of sexual rather than natural selection. [MATT RIDLEY, The Red Queen: Sex and the Evolution of Human Nature] ❡ *When I'm good, I'm very, very good. When I'm bad, I'm better.* [MAE WEST] ❡ *A woman without a man is like a fish without a bicycle.* [IRINA DUNN, FLO KENNEDY, GLORIA STEINEM, AND ANON.] ❡ *At any time during the life of a female canary, she can be induced to sing simply by injecting a male-level dose of testosterone.* [DEBORAH BLUM, Sex on the Brain: The Biological Differences between Men and Women] ❡ *If you block testosterone in a baby finch, it doesn't matter if he hears a whole operatic suite from his fellow finches—he doesn't sing.* [DEBORAH BLUM, Sex on the Brain: The Biological Differences between Men and Women]

TWENTY MINUTES AFTER SHE LEFT, for Claire was in no mood to make love, Chuck, who was sitting at the kitchen table processing mail, was overcome with loneliness, the empty apartment around him become sinister. He could turn on the TV for company, as though he were already a widower, take out his dumbbells and get some exercise while he watched one of those shows about forensics, see what he was up against. He could go to the Other End, where there was sure to be some student or faculty member he knew well enough to sidle up to—sure, some suspicious jock, some painfully polite nerd, some coed thinking sexual harassment. He could call up Betty Blondell, play the gallant, three women on his string. And risk losing Claire? Not a chance. He was about to become a father, time to take his responsibilities seriously. Well then, he could go for a long walk down Broadway, another way of getting some exercise, fall into a rhythm conducive to thought, for he had nine months, more like eight, to figure out how to kill Jane and marry Claire, or his child would be born a bastard. It was still light out, the days getting longer, a promise of spring in the air, a promise of rebirth. So that's what he did, walk down Broadway, thinking.

It wasn't until about 96th Street that Chuck felt his body rhythms fall into tempo with his stride, to the beat of "Blue Monk." The ideal, of course, would be for Jane to blow herself up while doing something characteristically disagreeable, hoisted with her own petard. Once when they were eating at the College Inn, an upscale greasy spoon, and the menu read "Baked Lasagna and two vegetables, $7.00," Jane ordered mashed potatoes and rice as her two vegetables. Wouldn't it be nice if somewhere there were two starches that when eaten together formed a fatal poison without antidote? But why should her eating habits get him so mad? Come to think of it, what had Jane ever done that would justify his killing her? What crime of hers was equal to the impending punishment?

Well, she had blackmailed him, more or less, into marrying her. How about that? That's not nothing. Two: she had allowed herself to get physically repulsive, for Chuck would have minded far less if she had only become morally repulsive. Three: she stood between him and Claire. Did he not have the right to go after a little happiness before the lights went out? It's a constitutional guarantee, for Christ's sweet sake. Aside from all that, Tony Felder would say that in killing Ivan and preparing to kill Jane, Chuck was acting on a disposition programmed into the male genome by evolution. It followed that Chuck's motives would be not personal or, even less, social—the dimension Chuck valued least—but human.

Satisfied, he opened the door to the Banana Republic on 86th Street, for he no longer had a field jacket, and he was squeamish about wearing the Reverend Hartung's barn jacket, as though it carried some polluting residue of its prior owner, even though Betty Blondell said he looked good in it. He held the door open for a tall Asian woman with amazing legs and admirable posture, black boiled-wool jacket over a black dress. Her smile fell on his face with an instant sensation of warmth, as though someone had turned on a sunlamp. He followed her into the women's section, not because he intended to make a move on her, but because merely to be in the presence of female beauty acted on him like a tonic. On the tables were clothes that anticipated warmer weather; on shelves and hangers were wintry items at reduced prices. The Asian woman picked a top off a table; it was black, ribbed, surely cotton, sleeveless, turtle-necked. She draped it on her breast, held it up by one hand across her midriff, the other pressing it against her shoulder, looked in the mirror to see how she looked, making little dipping and turning movements, a small, bemused smile on her face.

Needless to say, Chuck fell in lust. He imagined himself coming up behind her, pressing his crotch against her heart-shaped derriere, cupping her breasts in his hands, kissing her on the neck (like Dracula?). Chuck performed the interesting internal maneuver of recoiling from himself. Here he was being unfaithful in thought to the woman he loved and for whom he had killed a man, for whom he was scheming to kill his own wife, and who was carrying his child. It is well known, of course, that a man can love one woman and lust after another, lust after many others, in fact. Oh, hell, he can love one woman and still love another, or three. But the crucial question is this: can you be held responsible for your thoughts, your fantasies? Jesus Christ, of New Testament renown, thought so. He said, "You have heard the old-timers say 'Do not fuck around.' I say, if you even think about it you're as bad as doing it. Dig?" In that little speech you can see the collapse of classical civilization and a move toward thought police and Big Brother. No, you have got to be allowed reprehensible thoughts, abysmal fantasies.

That's the liberal ideal. But let's consider Claire's theory of daydreaming: Does not a fantasy prepare you to do in fact what you've done in fantasy? Does not daydreaming about doing something ready you to do it? Can we not go a little further and say that a fantasy, a daydream, not only prepares you but *disposes* you, inclines you, even encourages you, to get off your ass and get it done? Is not a fantasy that disposes you to crime also criminal? We read, do we not, that serial killers of the organized type, in the particulars of their MO's, make fantasy flesh? Was there not that boy who, after reading a Superman comic, donned his mother's cape and jumped out of a second-story window, expecting to fly? Chuck had gotten this far in his thinking when by way of reparation he picked up one of the cotton, ribbed, turtle-necked, sleeveless tops, size extra-large, to buy for Claire, then headed for the men's section, and he forbade himself even a glance at the striking Asian woman.

In Chuck's unphilosophical view of things, for every plausible thesis there has got to be a credible antithesis, so they can prop each other up. Thesis: fantasy readies you for action. Antithesis: fantasy is a substitute for action. In that respect it is like literature, which, in Tony Felder's formulation, allows you to experience in your imagination what you can't or won't experience in the flesh. And that explained, Chuck thought as he paid for a barn jacket (dark olive, leather collar and trim), a photographer's vest (for during the summer months, when one wears only pants and a shirt, it is hard to find a place to put your wallet, your sunglasses, your little memo book, your pterodactyl, especially if there's no back pockets in your pants), and the black ribbed top, that explained why Chuck had become a literary man. Chuck had become a literary man because there was so much he was denied, or denied himself, in the flesh. Ahead of him, as he swung down Broadway, he saw the banal Synthesis looming: fantasy and action are both fueled by desire; if you can't get no satisfaction in the flesh, you settle for fantasy.

Which do we admire more, the heroic fantasizer or the hero of action? Well, a writer puts his (or her) fantasies into words so as to generate fantasies in others, for which they are grateful. A man of action embodies or lives his fantasies, so the story of his life can generate inspirational daydreams in his admirers. As he swung into Filene's Basement on 79th Street, Chuck was trying to remember if he had ever read of a great writer or a great actioner who had wound up contented. He concluded that great writers and great actioners can't get no satisfaction either.

From a plain pipe rack he removed a black, long-sleeved polo shirt, a Calvin Klein label, size extra-large, looked as though it would fit. Yep, as the mirror in the dressing room told him, it fit pretty well, though loose, of course, around the waist. He emptied the pockets of the Reverend Hartung's barn jacket, his wallet, his little memo book, his pterodactyl, and transferred them to the homologous pockets in his own new barn jacket from Banana Republic and put the jacket on over the black polo shirt and looked in the mirror, which said *It's you.* He folded the Reverend's jacket and his own blue Oxford button-down shirt into the big plastic shopping bag from Banana Republic, went out of the dressing room, paid for his new shirt, departed Filene's, heading downtown.

Well, Chuck was not looking to inspire daydreams in others. He just wanted to live with Claire. When he went to bed at night, she would be there. He could kiss and hug her—for starters. All night long, as he slept, he would inhale the perfume of her being. When he awoke in the morning, she would be next to him, her hair mussed, a crease in the cheek she had been sleeping on, willing to be touched. They would have breakfast together, plan the day together, come back to life together over coffee. During the next twenty-five years, for with just ordinary luck he could expect to live another twenty-five years, he would observe the softening of her features in response to his kindness and generosity, the poems she dedicated to him, the way as they got older they both became not fatter but leaner, like two strips of rawhide, indomitable in the face of a hostile world so long as they were together, her solicitude after his operation for prostate cancer, for he just knew he was fated to come down with prostate cancer.

In the window of Blue Lou's, right above 73rd Street, was a sign announcing that Levi's were for sale, $34.95, just the thing to go with his new barn jacket, for dark olive and light denim blue went together like oil and vinegar, say, or life and death even, or Lockhart and McCoy. The woman behind the raised counter (Mrs. Blue Lou?) looked as though she should be in a black shawl selling figs and cucumbers in some parched open-air market east of Aden.

"You want?" she said.

"Stonewashed 501 Levi's, size 32 waist, 36 length," Chuck said, for when it came to pants, more than anything else, he hated highwaters, for 501's had a button fly, a low rise, and a trim fit, to go with his rejuvenated condition. He also did not like looking up to this woman with her mustache, for the chair she sat on was on a platform behind the raised counter. Who did she think she was, a judge or something?

She gestured with her chin toward the back of the store, where Chuck could see Levi's folded in piles on shelves. He fetched himself a pair of stonewashed, etc. "Where can I try them on?" he said. With what he took to be a sneer, she gestured again with her chin toward something over his shoulder, a cubicle behind a curtain that was worn to near transparency. 501 Levi's are "regular fit," meaning straight legs, meaning tight around the ass, meaning they showed off Chuck's bulging calves and thighs. He nodded at himself in the mirror with satisfaction, ripped off the price tag, went out of the cubicle, gave the tag and a credit card to Mrs. Lou. She examined the card carefully, turning it over and over, checking the photo against Chuck's face, for his Citibank Visa card had a photo of his face look-

ing quizzical on it, finally zipping the card through some authenti-
cating machine. She gave him the sales slip to sign, said, "In my
country we like man with stomach." Her expression was stern.

He nodded, folded the chinos he had been wearing into the big
plastic shopping bag that held the old barn jacket, the old Oxford
shirt, and the new vest, walked out, turned downtown, thinking. To
kill Jane was to assert that *his* happiness was more valuable than *her*
life. Try arguing that to a jury. Wait a minute: to kill Jane was not to
assert that his happiness was more valuable than her life in general
or absolutely or in the eyes of God or by law or certainly not in the
eyes of Jane. That's the kind of mistake French philosophers always
make. No, to kill Jane was to assert that his happiness was more valuable than her life *to him.* And there was no doubt that to Jane her
happiness was more valuable than *his* life, which she had gone a long
way toward blighting. No again: he was still making a Frenchified
mistake. Who said that performing an action asserts *any* proposition, anyhow? The truth is that to kill Jane is to kill Jane. An action,
then, does not imply its own justification (except to the actor, and
not always to the actor, for it's possible to commit an act you can't justify and not give a fuck), and he turned into the Eddie Bauer's right
there next to Barnes and Noble on 66th Street, across from Tower
Records and the Pottery Barn, diagonally across from Lincoln Center and Juilliard, an epicenter of civilization.

At first he didn't see anything he wanted except two giggly high
school girls, and what were they doing out after dark, for the sun had
gone down, yes, the sun had gone down. But then in the store's
shoe section, in a corner and unattended, he saw them: Gore-Tex
boots, actually your typical construction worker's boots, light tan
Nubuck, yellow soles with lugs to grip the earth, man, saying don't
fuck with me, what the rest of his ensemble called out for. A pair of
size twelves fit him better than any shoes he had ever before owned:
snug and soft, supportive but not confining, firm but pliable, like a
good woman.

The cashier was sandy-haired and plump and messy, nails bitten down, shirttail hanging out, mustache in need of a trim; his name badge read "Sven." He gave Chuck a long, wary look, to the verge of rudeness. When he bent over to process the credit card, Chuck saw a bald spot spreading out from the crown of Sven's head. There wasn't a ponytail, was there? No. There was a jolt in his chest, a ringing in his ears, a warmth in his head, a dimming of his vision; he held onto the counter. What was this Sven was humming? Well, what do you know? This was not the sort of square you expected to be humming Miles Davis's "Doxy." He lifted his head, looked Chuck in the eye, said, "I believe we have met."

"Not likely," said Chuck.

"In the Hi, Sailor bar down there by the meatpacking plants?" said Sven.

"Never been," said Chuck, bending over to remove his loafers, which he placed on the counter. "Just throw these out," for then and there he resolved never to wear loafers again, especially not loafers with tassels. At least he had never sunk to the ignominy of wearing sandals. "I'll just wear these," and he picked up the Gore-Tex boots before Sven could wrap them.

"Ah yes, yes indeedy," said Sven: "that's more like it." He looked the loafers over critically. "Still, there's plenty of wear left in these."

"You can have them, if you want," said Chuck.

"I couldn't," said Sven. "I couldn't wear another man's shoes unless we were already good friends. Shoes are so intimate, don't you think? Besides, they're too big," and he held them up, turned them this way and that, looking them over, "but then a man's man doesn't have wimpy feet."

On his bare socks, silent as a pard, Chuck carried his Gore-Tex boots to the dressing rooms, put on the boots, regarded himself in a surround of mirrors. Did he always lean forward like that? He had never before thought of himself as simian. Well, if Claire didn't mind, the rest of the world could take gas.

He swung out the door of Eddie Bauer's, hung a left, heading downtown, whistling "Blue Monk," did an about-face without breaking stride, headed uptown, homeward, for some process had concluded itself. The question was not does he have a right to kill Jane, but does she deserve to die. The answer was Yes! Who said so? He did. Period. End of sentence.

He crossed Broadway, so he could walk up the other side, the west side, see something new. And there outside the Barnes and Noble a couple blocks north of Filene's bending over—ah me—bending over to look in a window was the striking Asian woman. She straightened, turned, saw Chuck looking at her, said, "Hi."

"Hi yourself," he said.

"I don't think you remember me," she said.

"You are not the sort of woman a man forgets," he said.

"Dorothea Chin?" she said. "Your seminar on 'Novels of Empire.' Remember?"

"I remember sneakers, jeans, sweatshirt, a white throwaway painter's cap, and a very smart paper on *The Plumed Serpent*. You're not the woman you used to be."

"You're not exactly the man you used to be either," she said. "But down deep I'm still the wide-eyed go-getter who had a crush on her big, buff professor."

"You did?"

"We all did," she said.

"Why did no one tell me?" he said.

"Well, we decided you were one of those faithful husbands," she said. What Chuck wanted to know was exactly how far had his head been up his ass. "You remember Millie Thorpe? She bet me a dinner in André's she could get you in bed before I could." Right then Chuck knew he was getting old. He should have been born thirty years later. He would be a different and better man if he had been taken up by someone like Dorothea Chin or Millie Thorpe during those dismal years in college or, better yet, during those dismaler years in high school, when so far as Chuck's experience went, such females did not exist. "But when we came to your office hours, you were all business; when we invited you to sorority dinners, you begged off; when we just happened to bump into you on campus or in the bookstore or in the Other End, you were merely polite." Well, regrets buttered no parsnips. Twenty-five years with Claire would make up for all past deprivations. Someone grabbed his arm from behind, squeezed his bicep, as though the Thought Police were onto him already.

"Gotcha," said the voice of Betty Blondell. "I've been looking for you."

"Dorothea Chin, meet Betty Blondell," said Chuck; "Professor Blondell, meet Ms. Chin," and Betty gave him a hug.

"Yeah, hi," said Ms. Chin.

"How do you do," said Professor Blondell.

"I'm on my way," said Dorothea. "Give me a call sometime. We'll have lunch," and she handed Chuck her business card, which he put into the outside chest pocket of his barn jacket. They shook hands and she nodded toward Betty and walked off, downtown.

"Trying to change your luck?" said Betty.

"You've already read too much," Chuck said, looking at the shopping bag of books with the Barnes and Noble logo.

"Here, you can carry them for me," Betty said, "counterbalance your own bag of tricks. What's in there?"

"Old clothes," he said. "What are you reading?"

"I'm reading books like *The Burden of the Flesh: Fasting and Sexuality in Early Christianity* and *Asceticism and the New Testament* and *Christianity and Sexuality in the Early Modern World: Regulating Desire, Reforming Practice* and *A New Song: Celibate Women in the First Three Christian Centuries* and stuff like that," said Betty. "You can't imagine the number of publications on such subjects— mostly written by women. Do you know why?"

"I can guess," said Chuck. They were walking along at a pretty good clip by now, in spite of Chuck's two shopping bags and in spite of Betty's high heels, for Betty never wore flats in public.

"No, you can't," she said. "I couldn't have myself. For women in the ancient world, celibacy was one of the few roads toward independence, then empowerment. Before anything else, you've got to get out from under men, so to speak, our bodies, ourselves. The female scholars who write all the books and articles on this subject see a relevance to their own situation."

"Sure, if no one wants to buy, it's a consolation to pretend you never wanted to sell," he said.

"Don't be such a Neanderthal," she said; "it's not like you. Suppose you're a woman and you chafe under the imposed powerlessness of the woman's condition. Suppose you're not submissive by nature? What do you do?"

"You marry a milquetoast," he said, "and browbeat him." It is not known if Chuck was thinking of himself.

"You could do that," she said, "hook up with some monster of resentment and passive aggression and nourish your contempt for him and your own self-hatred as they grow until there's no room for anything else."

"Whence this vehemence?" he said.

"I was talking about my parents," she said.

"O.K.," he said. "You use your sexual allure to manipulate him."

"A tried and true method," she said. "And we all use it, if we've got 'it.' But there are attendant dangers."

"Yes, and allure lacks staying power," Chuck said. "Nothing gold can stay."

"There's that," she said, and wasn't there mockery in her smile? Was she thinking of Jane? "But the real problem is that if you rely too much on allure, either you become a narcissist or you again fall into contempt for the man, for *all* men, and for yourself."

"The only way, then, is to acquire position, prestige, or possessions," he said. "Mae West, I understand, had bodybuilders to sleep with into her seventies, and she *never* had any allure."

"It's true that women in the ancient Roman world could marry into power, but it would always be derived, never truly their own," she said, "and never equal to their husbands'. Though you do hear of wealthy Christian women married to pagans who turned their homes into places of worship and prayer."

"Consciousness-raising sessions," he said.

"No, there was no other route save through celibacy," she said. "And there were contemporary traditions of various sorts that valorized celibacy: Gnostics, Stoics, Encratites, some Jewish sects, whoever wrote the Dead Sea scrolls, whoever wrote the apocryphal gospels. From these the women could get support—and even prestige."

"Yeah, well, sexual abstinence seems a lot easier for women than for men," he said, "or you wouldn't have all these priests with AIDS."

"It's not that abstinence is easier for women—it's that they have more good reasons for it. Anyway, the male bigwigs of the Church couldn't stop these groups of celibate women from growing in numbers and prestige. But the real models of women's liberation were all these celibate and itinerant prophetesses going around stirring things up."

"Charles Mansons in drag," said Chuck.

"The Church fogies thundered against them," said Betty. "Finally, the only thing to do was co-opt them. By the end of the third century Methodius wrote the first piece of orthodox Christian literature devoted to the proposition that virginity is the highest stage of human achievement. He claims that in heaven virgins would take precedence over all others except Christ himself. By and by, in the spirit of 'anything-you-can-do-I-can-do-better,' the priests imposed celibacy upon themselves."

"Like cutting your balls off so you can fit in your wife's panties," said Chuck.

"The recurrent outbreaks of female celibacy take different forms at different times and in different places—one form in second-century Egypt, another form in fourteenth-century Europe, still another in nineteenth-century America, but always with a religious vindication, as with all those itinerant mediums of the nineteenth century, and I see another emerging right here and now. If you like getting laid, you better get it while the getting's good."

"Why are you reading this stuff?" said Chuck.

"I'm still trying to figure how there came to be a correlation between celibacy and purity, between sex and sin," she said.

"What have you concluded?" he said.

"Sex is dirty," she said.

"If it's done right, says Woody Allen," said Chuck. "It is also unruly—which is why all totalitarian and would-be totalitarian organizations try to suppress it."

"My God," she said, "what did you do to your hand? I've never seen such colors. It's in itself a complete reason for turning away from the flesh."

"I nicked it against something nasty," he said.

"Here," she said, taking the bag of books out of his left hand, lifting the hand, touching it with her lips just behind the bandage. "Make it all better."

Out of the blue, or out of the black, big, fat drops of rain began to fall.

"Come on," said Betty, pulling him by the arm, "I know this nice tavern just a block over on Amsterdam." Amazing woman, this Betty: there she was, actually running in those high heels of hers. The tavern in question was Kelty's. Chuck pulled up, but Betty dragged him in. The presumptuous waiter was nowhere to be seen, thank God. They found an open booth away from the dartboard, though business was good. They sat facing each other and ordered brandy, as more warming than beer. Betty's hair had come undone a bit, was curling around her face. Betty seemed not to notice, but Chuck noticed, yes he did. He was not sure he was up to a Betty Blondell who had let her hair down.

"What I wanted to tell you is I've been having long conversations on the phone with Jane," Betty said.

"She can afford the tariff, now that she's an heiress," he said.

"That's not what I meant," she said. "We've been talking about women and Christianity, especially early Christianity."

Chuck groaned.

"We've been reading the same books," she said.

Chuck groaned.

"Jane's really charged up," said Betty. "She says she's always known in her bones about celibacy and freedom."

Chuck groaned.

"So we're going to air the questions surrounding Christianity, women, celibacy, and freedom in a series of radio shows," Betty said. "And before you make that awful noise again, how about this question to get the ball rolling: why is it that if you go into any Christian church in the world, you will see more women than men, whether we're talking Sicily or Iowa or Zimbabwe?"

"As Nietzsche said, Christianity is a slave religion, and, as the feminists always say, women have been treated like slaves," said Chuck.

"The Scriptures, never mind the Church Fathers, are full of passages telling women to honor and obey their husbands," Betty said.

"All right," said Chuck. "Christian piety gives you a sense of superiority. Everyone else is getting a soul kiss from Satan. Everyone else is deluded, in error, sinful, hell-bent. You can see how it would appeal to the powerless. It gives you a spiritual high to offset your physical low. Worse—"

"Slow down," said Betty. "What's the matter with you?"

"Worse, in your weakness is your strength," said Chuck. "In their bodily weakness and low libido women are in tendency pure; they naturally aspire to the condition of Mary."

"Bullshit," said Betty.

"Men in their lust aspire to the condition of pigs," said Chuck.

"Now you're talking," said Betty.

"Women embrace Christianity the way the ancient Jews embraced the doctrine that they were God's Chosen: 'You can beat me up and put me down, but God loves me better than you,'" said Chuck.

"You finished?" she said. "I thought we were having a friendly conversation here."

"Christianity is a religion for losers simmering with resentment," said Chuck. "It's the model for all true believers since."

"Whence this vehemence?" said Betty.

"I'm talking about my parents," said Chuck. "My father was also a milquetoast. My mother spent all her spare time doing things for her church." Chuck signaled to the waitress, ordered scotch on the rocks for two without asking Betty what she wanted.

Then, in a considerable non sequitur he said, "This two-thousand-year effort by women, especially Christian women, to suppress the male in men pisses me off."

"It's interesting to see that sensitive Charles Craig Lockhart, understanding C. C. Lockhart, kind and sympathetic Chucky, has a touch of misogyny in him," she said. "I like that in a man."

"The size of a man's misogyny is the distance between what a man wants, needs, from women and what he gets," he said. "In that respect it is parallel to a woman's misandry."

Betty fell back against the booth bench, then leaned forward, all the while looking Chuck in the eye, put her hand on his. "Why not let me try to make up the difference?" she said.

"Betty," he said, putting his other hand on top of hers, making a sandwich, "it's impossible."

"You're not going to get self-righteous on me, are you?" she said.

"Aren't you and Jane friends?" he said.

"So were Lancelot and King Arthur," she said.

"How about Christian celibacy?" he said.

"Christian celibacy gave me freedom *from* my college boyfriend, who got me pregnant and couldn't pay for the abortion and didn't want to get married and still wanted to get laid three times a week," she said. "I now see that he wasn't evil, just young and frightened and not too smart and the kind of lover who turns women against sex. I am now ready for freedom *to* . . . whatever. After fifteen years of penance for that abortion, I'm ready."

"Your timing is off," Chuck said. "If you had gone to Tony before he hooked up with Simone . . . As for me—" and here Chuck could have bit his tongue, but he didn't.

"Yes, as for you, you have Miss Pigeous, one-woman specific against misogyny," she said.

"Miss Who?" Chuck said.

"Don't bullshit me, Lockhart," she said. "That big redhead with the blotch on her face may be callipygous, but I'll have you know that my ass is pretty pulchritudinous, too."

Chuck signaled to the waitress to bring two more of the same.

"You trying to get me drunk?" said Betty.

He put his hand on hers and began to squeeze, real hard. "Betty, not a word, understand, *not one fucking word.*" When Chuck got truly mad, his neck bulged.

The waitress arrived with scotch on the rocks for two. As she left, Betty gave Chuck's hand a sharp rap with the back of the butter knife. He let go, shook his hand. She rubbed her red left hand with her white right. "We should be making love, not war," Betty said.

On the way back, in a taxicab, they kissed and felt each other up, but Chuck declined Betty's invitation to come up to her place for a nightcap.

twenty four

That love is all there is / Is all we know of love. [EMILY DICKINSON] ❡ *As for love, no man or woman can possibly love or be loved who lives other than a life of strict continence.* [DR. JOHN COWAN, The Science of a New Life] ❡ *If anyone says that it is not better and more godly to live in virginity or in the unmarried state than to marry, let him be anathema.* [THE COUNCIL OF TRENT, 1546–63]

ACROSS THE ROAD FROM THE Hartung place, three miles north, a quarter mile into the woods, on a two-hundred-acre lot owned by a paper company, was a one-room cabin. A machinist whose permanent residence had been in Sodus, New York, was allowed to use this cabin and the surrounding acre tax-free and for life in return for ceding his lot of twenty-five acres to the paper company. He had been using it as a hunting camp. It was now being used by Chuck and Claire as a staging area for their planned attack on the Hartung estate, inherited by Jane Lockhart upon the death of her father, the Reverend Luke Hartung, inherited by Charles Craig Lockhart upon the death of his wife, Jane, now illegally occupied by a certain redneck and his harem.

Though the cabin had not been ransacked, Chuck and Claire found little of value on the site, a bottle of propane outside (so with the help of a Franklin stove they had heat and light), two rolls of toi-

212

let paper in the outhouse, a bag of sprouted potatoes under the sink, salt, pepper, and, of all things, thyme. They agreed that the breakfast of stewed coydog and potatoes they had just finished was the best they had eaten in a long time. But the thought of all those Mason jars full of preserved food, of the root cellar full of potatoes, turnips, carrots, and apples, of those crocks of pickles and sauerkraut, those homemade condiments like pickled beets in apple vinegar being consumed by that hardcase redneck, who reminded him of Henny Kramer, put him in that state of unmitigated and implacable hatred he had only recently begun to allow himself. Claire argued that they should let the redneck off the hook, at least for now, and fix up the hunting cabin, or go house-hunting for something with a few amenities, for there were a lot more houses left than there were people alive, but the new Chuck Lockhart prevailed. That house was his: he would be irreparably damaged inside if he didn't fight for it.

In the chamber of his twelve-gauge shotgun was a round of oo shot; four more were in the magazine; four more were in a sleeve on the stock. Claire slapped the magazine into her Ruger semiautomatic .22. She was using Remington forty-grain high-velocity solid points, for Chuck had taught her to be more interested in penetration than expansion. From a seated position she could put five of these rounds into a one-inch circle fifty yards away. They looked at each other; he nodded; she turned down the wick on the kerosene lamp, blew out the flame. They stepped outside. It was cold, all right, but no colder outside than in, for they had not built a fire in the Franklin stove. The air felt fresh on their faces. Toward the east the sky was a lighter shade of black. They would walk along the west side of the road, the sunny side of the street, in effect, but ten or twenty yards into the woods, so they would be out of sight in the unlikely event of their coming upon a traveler.

They rock-hopped across the brook that formed the northern boundary of the Hartung estate. They circled around the pond that the Reverend had kept well stocked with fish, especially bullheads, also frogs, both good eating. They skulked through the softwood grove that ended not thirty yards from the house. Claire took a position at the house-side edge of the grove, behind a blown-over tree that had made the mistake of trying to grow on a shelf of rock. She rested the barrel of the Ruger on the bole and put the sights on the passage between the two stacks of firewood on the back porch. These stacks filled the whole porch, except for a central aisle running from the back door to the steps off the porch. And these stacks were neat, but precariously high, scary to walk between. Chuck leaned against the side of the shed, out of sight except for an eye he kept on the back door and, of course, the left side of his face.

By and by the back door opened and the redneck came out, wearing a flannel shirt under a leather vest, cowboy style, and carrying a canvas wood carrier, for the firewood stacked on the porch was reserved for bad weather. Chuck waited until the redneck was halfway to the woodpile before he stepped out and aimed his shotgun. "At this distance," said Chuck, "I could put a hole in you the size of a grapefruit."

The redneck raised his hands about shoulder high. "What do you want?" he said.

"My house," said Chuck.

"We been through this already," said the redneck. He let his hands sink to about breast high, as though they were too heavy to hold all the way up.

"You can take my visit here today as a formal notice of eviction," said Chuck. "*Effective immediately.*"

"Aw, come on, man, don't be that way," said the redneck with a shit-eating grin. But with a movement so quick and slick his hand was a blur, he reached inside his vest and drew a gun from a shoulder holster. Never having played a sport that made quick reaction time instinctive, Chuck simply froze as the redneck swung the pistol toward where it would point at Chuck's chest. There was a crack and the redneck's right eye disappeared, for Claire had shot him. He fell on his back, began to rotate his legs as though he was walking on an invisible treadmill, both hands on his right eye socket, throwing his head from side to side.

Chuck walked over, cupped his left hand—for it had healed—under the redneck's chin, pulled it up and away from the neck, put down his shotgun, pulled out his pterodactyl, put the redneck out of his misery. Chuck had never seen blood spurt like that before. He stood up and turned toward the house. Standing there on the porch, between the two stacks of firewood, was the woman who, as seen from either side, had the silhouette of a praying or preying mantis, the female of which species is known for its detestable habit of biting off its mate's head following copulation. She was holding the shotgun not braced against her shoulder, but out in front of her, as you would hold a basin of water.

When she shot at Chuck, but missed, recoil drove the stock into her watermelon-shaped belly so that she was thrown back into the stack of wood on her right. The first three feet of the stack, which was piled up to the porch ceiling, toppled over on her and propelled her at great velocity head first into the stack on her left, thus breaking her neck.

Three or four feet of this stack then also toppled over on her.

As for the other woman in the house, Chuck and Claire were not sure what . . .

Hours later he was awakened by the telephone.

"Mumph," he said into the receiver.

"It's Claire," said Claire. "Don't worry, I'm calling from a pay phone. Svetlana sent me out to buy brioche and confiture."

"Well, you don't really have to put up with her anymore," said Chuck.

"Now more than ever," she said. "After breakfast, we're going over to the Two Six precinct to report Ivan missing. You can't imagine how suspicious she is. 'Did you two have a fight? Are you seeing another man? Is he seeing another woman? It's impossible for me to imagine anyone hating Ivan enough to kill him, but maybe some crazy man? Has he been getting hate mail from fascists? Has he ever had fainting spells?' With her around I feel as though my head's in a vise."

"What line are you taking?" he said.

"I can't think of any reason for Ivan's disappearance," she said.

"That's best," he said.

"I want to be with you," she said.

"Lunch in our private grotto?" he said.

"Too dangerous," she said. "The less often we're seen together, the better."

"I can get to the Wanhope by four thirty," he said.

"You got a hundred dollars you don't need?" she said. "I'm broke."

"I'll have it," he said.

"You're on," she said.

When Chuck walked into room 1133 at the Wanhope Hotel, Claire was sitting on the bed reading the *Times.* She was dressed for business, in a black skirt suit with pin stripes. But he gave her a big kiss and a big hug anyway. "Ummm," she said.

He sat in the stuffed armchair and pulled Claire down onto his lap. She removed his hand from her breast. "I've got to unwind first," she said. "This day has been unreal."

"What have you been up to?" he said.

"First I had to call Saul Green and Mavis Mills—they're out on bail—and ask about Ivan," she said. "I've never done any acting, but my impersonation of a woman on the verge of hysteria was damn good, if I say so myself. But those two little shits were pissed off at Ivan for not getting arrested."

"What's their theory about Ivan's disappearance?" Chuck said, putting a hand on Claire's thigh.

"They think he's got the sulks, that he's off somewhere nursing a grievance," Claire said, giving him a peck. "Apparently Saul Green cut him off in mid-song."

"The poor guy," said Chuck, sliding up Claire's skirt so that he could put a hand on her naked thigh, but she was wearing those hateful panty hose. Claire's thighs were full and firm, the skin along their inside surfaces the most finely textured substance this side of stainless steel that Chuck had ever come across.

"He was thin-skinned about his music," Claire said. "What else did he have to prop up his sagging ego?" She bent over to remove her shoes.

"You," said Chuck.

She stood up to pull down her panty hose. "Anyhow, I implied to the cop who took our statement at the Two Six that Ivan was capable of suicide, though of the many things Ivan was incapable of, suicide would rank high. This cop was old and bored, big belly, lots of white hair, rum blossom nose." Chuck put his hands on Claire's beautiful bottom and turned her so that he could kiss her thighs, up and down, inside and out, front and back. "Don't give me a hickey," she said. "Svetlana has X-ray vision. But if she hadn't raised hell we would never have seen a real detective." Chuck removed Claire's panties so that he could put his mouth to the center of the universe.

"That's nice," she said, laying one hand on a shoulder and the other on the back of his head, to keep him where he was. "This detective, named Hector Suarez, didn't seem very interested either. When Svetlana broached my theory of suicidal depression, Suarez just smiled this really evil smile and said, 'Maybe he finally went to get himself some music lessons.'"

Unable to retract his head, Chuck laughed into Claire's plump and succulent pussy. "What are you doing?" said Claire, laughing, and she bucked upward with her pelvis, in effect punching Chuck in the mouth. He wrapped his arms around her knees and pushed with his head against her belly until she fell back onto the bed. He dove on top of her. Giggling like ten-year-olds, they wrestled, Chuck trying to pin Claire's arms behind her, but from the waist up Claire was a powerhouse. Finally, limp with laughter and out of breath, Claire said, "No more," and lay back, tangled in her business suit and blouse. Chuck, breathing heavily, rested his head where her thighs met her trunk, where it fit nicely. So *this* was happiness! (as distinct from mere pleasure), hitherto, so Chuck would have said, unknown to him. An emotion of some sort filled his chest; his ears rang; a warm black curtain came down in his head. ". . . stop fooling around and come up with a plan," Claire was saying. He rolled over and began to kiss her belly, the skin on which was nearly as finely textured as that along the inside of her thighs. "All right," she said with a sigh, "but afterward we've got to talk."

No, *this* was happiness, wrapped around Claire after lovemaking, Claire equally wrapped around him, no mistaking the aura of good feeling for each other they radiated, *ganz gemütlich.* Nothing was better than this, nothing, Chuck said to himself. Then he wondered whether it was unmanly to be this much in love. By and by, Claire extricated herself, went to the bathroom for a pee, came back with a towel, which she spread on the seat of the room's one easy chair, for she did not want to stain the fabric with their juices, sat. From his book bag Chuck removed a package: a triple layer of plastic shopping bags containing a freezer bottle, four bottles of beer held tight against it by a big rubber band. The blade of Chuck's pterodactyl begins with a conventional spear point, about halfway down becomes serrated, ends in a notch good for opening bottles. They clinked bottles, drank. Chuck stretched out on the bed, both pillows under his head. They each seem to have felt that to put on any clothes, even a pair of underpants, would have been subtly tactless, for one wears clothes to hide something, does one not? Besides, these two took pride in their bodies, as well they might. Besides, any attempt to refute the myth of the Garden of Eden was worth the effort, was it not?—even though you can't refute a myth.

"Ivan had a friend up there just north of the city in Valhalla," Claire said, "who runs a junkyard. He's an anarchist. He believes that it's your duty to break the law every way you can so long as you get away with it. That's his notion of praxis, and he acts on his beliefs, unlike these ivory-tower types such as you and me."

"Consistency is overrated," said Chuck. "I've developed an affection for people whose praxis is at odds with their theoria."

218

"The point is that he's got this serious crush on me—there's no mistaking the signs," said Claire. "I know he would fix up an inconspicuous junker for me, phony license plates and all, no questions asked. So one evening when you're at a meeting of PEN or at some publication party—and you schmooze with everybody so they'll remember you—I drive up to Hartungsville, knock on the door, and when Jane answers shoot her six times in the heart with that little .22 of yours. I leave the gun right there. I'm wearing cheap gloves and a long-sleeved shirt. I dump the gloves and shirt in three separate garbage cans at the first service area on the Thruway, wash my face (my hair's under a cap), so there's no question of powder residue. When I get back to Valhalla, I bury the license plates. Ivan's friend trashes the car and drives me back to New York in another car."

"You forgot to get rid of the cap," said Chuck.

"All right, wise guy, you got a better idea?" she said. "That's the way the Mafia would do it, and they never get caught, until someone squeals. The simpler, the better."

"Sooner or later we'd have to kill your junkyard amorist, just to feel safe, even if he's not the squealing type," he said. "No matter how we try to rationalize it away, we're going to feel guilt, you know —and guilt leads to paranoia."

"Well, I was just thinking of your remark that we've got to stay away from anything fancy, like the murders in those British whodunits written by high-toned old Christian women," she said, "curare in Lady Smythe-Bilkington's crumpet while she's having tea with the Vicar." She thought for a moment. "A hit person? How about your friend, the Guardian at the Gate?"

"You mean Hardcore?" he said. "He wouldn't do it. He thinks of himself as a good Christian. He's always bragging about the choir in his church. Besides, we've got to do this alone, no third party."

"No, *I* have to do this alone," Claire said.

Chuck was sitting on the bed opening another bottle of beer for Claire when there was a creepy electronic ring, made him drop the bottle. Luckily, no more than a mouthful splashed out. Claire sat up, reached for her pocketbook on the floor, withdrew a cell phone.

"Claire McCoy," she said. "Hi, Lana, any news?. . . I'm at work. . . . Well, I don't want to lose this job. Ivan and me, we didn't have any savings, you know. . . . He did? What did he have to say?. . . Yeah, all right, as soon as I can. . . . I don't have enough money with me. . . . Why don't we just grab something at the Other End?. . . Keeping busy is the best thing. Besides, I expect Ivan to slink in the door any minute, with his tail between his legs. . . . Yeah, see you soon.

"That was Svetlana," Claire said. "She wants me to bring home two salmon steaks, can you imagine? She thought I could make some asparagus and new potatoes in dill to go with. She's already got a Sacher torte for dessert. Also, that Detective Suarez called; he wants to talk to us—separately. That guy makes me nervous." She glunked some beer and stepped into her panty hose. "I've got to get moving."

"You've got time to finish your beer," he said.

She pulled the chair around so she could sit on it facing him where he was perched on the bed, placed her hand on his. She looked at him with an expression he would have described as understanding, but he could not have sworn there was no pity in it. There was enough of a smile for her lip to snag on her left eyetooth. When they were married he would pay for braces to push that tooth back in line, and aren't there procedures for removing birthmarks? Someone should make Claire's parents pay for their neglect, and Claire said, "I never meant to play the femme fatale. I've turned your comfortable existence upside down."

"If you can call suspended animation comfortable," he said. "Winter kept me warm, covering me with forgetful snow, feeding a little life with dried tubers. Then you brought me back to life, which is war, not, as I used to think, a balance of powers." You have to admit that was nicely said, well deserving of the powerhouse kiss, left him dizzy, she gave him before taking off.

Chuck watched the eleven o'clock news on Channel Four because of the anchorperson. She had tousled black hair, unusual for TV news types, a Mediterranean complexion, very full lips that bunched when she pronounced the vowel sound in words such as "glue." Kissing her would be like closing your mouth on two slices of a ripe plum. Just before the commercial break that precedes the weather report, she mentioned that the well-known folksinger Ivan Tervakalio had been reported missing.

> I'll sing you eight, O
> Red fly the banners, O
> What is your eight, O
> Eight for the Eighth Red Army
> Seven for the hours of the working day
> Six for the Tolpuddle Martyrs
> Five for the years of the Five-Year Plan
> Four for the years it took them
> Three, three, the rights of man
> Two, two, a man's own hands
> Working for his living, O
> One is workers' unity
> And ever more shall be so.

twenty five

"Welcome to my house! Enter freely and of your own will." *He made no motion of stepping to meet me, but stood like a statue, as though his gesture of welcome had fixed him into stone. The instant, however, that I stepped over the threshold, he moved impulsively forward, and holding out his hand grasped mine with a strength which made me wince, an effect which was not lessened by the fact that it seemed as cold as ice — more like the hand of a dead than a living man. Again he said: — "Welcome to my house. Come freely."* [BRAM STOKER, Dracula] ❡ *In the darkness spirit hands were felt to flutter and when prayers by tantras had been directed to the proper quarter a faint but increasing luminosity became gradually visible, the apparition of the etheric double being particularly visible owing to the discharge of jivic rays from the crown of the head and face. Communication was effected through the pituitary body and also by means of the orangefiery and scarlet rays emanating from the sacral region and solar plexus. Questioned by his earthname as to his whereabouts in the heaven-world he stated that he was now on the path of pralaya or return but was still submitted to trial at the hands of certain bloodthirsty entities on the lower astral level.* [JAMES JOYCE, Ulysses]

ECAUSE HE HAD NO CLASSES ON FRIDAYS, because Claire would be working, because he had already prepared next week's classes, Chuck went to bed on Thursday night thinking that he would sleep late, have himself a leisurely brunch at an outdoor table among the waitresses with tight black leather pants, drive the scenic route through the Catskills to Sacandaga, get there early enough for some outdoor exercise, splitting wood, raking up leaves that the Reverend had been unable to gather for his compost heap last fall, load up the hibachi to grill a couple of steaks, for if Jane didn't want hers he just might slice it up for his lunch on Saturday, but wouldn't you know that some fool had to wake him up with a telephone call at seven thirty.

"Mumph," he said.

"He's still alive," said Claire.

"Who, what?" said Chuck.

"*Ivan is still alive*," said Claire.

"He can't be," said Chuck.

"When I got up this morning I found his hat on the kitchen table, where he always leaves it, so he can put it on first thing with his coffee," she said.

"Calm down and think," he said. "Could he have had a spare?"

"I think I would have known," she said. "This place is so small..."

"Under the bed?" he said.

"And this is not a new hat," she said. "You can see the place where the lining came loose and I had to—" and here her voice broke, "sew it back."

"I'm telling you, Claire, no one could have survived that fall," he said, and a mechanical voice told Claire to put another quarter in the slot—which she did, cling.

"What you mean is I'm being haunted by his ghost," she said. "I knew it," and her voice was sepulchral.

"I mean no such thing," Chuck said. "Tell me everything that happened from the time you got home."

"Well, Svetlana and I had dinner together—" Claire said.

"Was the hat on the table?" he said.

"Course not," she said. "And then she went off. She's like Ivan in that she thinks helping with the dishes is beneath her. At least

223

she left the bottle of vodka, which I pretty much demolished before falling into bed." A voice asked for a quarter, which Claire dropped into the slot, cling.

"Could she have taken the hat out of her handbag and placed it on the table as she walked out, you know, while you were distracted?" he said.

"I would have seen it while I was cleaning up," she said. "I cleaned up the whole place, bedroom, living room, and kitchen, just to have something to do."

"Don't take this wrong, but could she have left it on a chair, say, and you picked it up and put it on the table out of habit, I mean, while you were thinking of something else?"

"Sooner or later I would have noticed it," she said. "I kept coming back to the kitchen to rinse the sponge and whatnot. I even went through everything in the one closet we have, in the bedroom. On the shelf there's this really strong cardboard box that came with oranges and grapefruit. My father sent it one Christmas. I put it on the kitchen table to see if there was anything I wanted, 'cause I've got my summer stuff on one side, the side the oranges came in, and Ivan has, *had*, his stuff on the grapefruit side, shorts, a bathing suit, tank tops, sandals—" and her voice broke.

"In our bedroom closet, on the shelf, is a box much like yours," he said. "It's where we store our Christmas decorations. On top of this box I keep my two hats, a hunting cap my father-in-law gave me and a floppy hat I wear in rainy weather. Now! Picture yourself standing on a chair to get your box down. You carry it into the kitchen, place it on the table. When you open the box, Ivan's hat, which you never consciously saw any more than you consciously see your hassock, 'cause it's always there, Ivan's hat I say, slid off the box and onto the table."

"How did you know we have a hassock?" she said.

"How much did you have to drink by this time?" he said.

"Too much," she said; "way too much. But I know Ivan had to be wearing his hat when he left that morning. He would never appear in public without it."

"He was wearing his new hat, which he bought just for the occasion," he said. "He kept the old one, out of the way, up in the closet, as a back-up, in case a seagull shat on the new one."

"Sometimes I think you see it as your life's work to turn all the world's poetry into prose," she said.

"I love the poetry in your poems," he said, "and above all I love you."

"I'm still creeped out," she said.

"I can under—" he said.

A voice asked for a quarter. Claire said, "Fuck you." Then she said, "I've got to get going. I can't afford to lose my job."

Well, Chuck was pretty creeped out himself, if the truth be known. It was not as though his conscious self had suddenly started to believe in the supernatural—he was not that far gone—but something in him had. And that something, an anxiety-begetter whatever else it was, was not compatible with the leisurely day he had dreamed up for himself. So he went to his office instead, no sitting at an outside table, reading the *Times*, admiring the curves inside leather pants, like a man who has it made. Before anything else he went into the departmental kitchenette for a cup of Simone's macho coffee. As though she had been waiting for him, Simone followed him in even before he had helped himself to a half teaspoonful of powdered ersatz cream.

"I've got something to tell you," she said. "Can we go into your office for a minute?"

"Sure," he said, with a premonition that he would not like what he was about to hear.

Simone shut the door to his office behind her as she entered. Chuck was surprised to see that she was blushing. Her shapely lips were fuller than usual, as was the white men's-style button-down-collar shirt she wore under a blue blazer, for Simone was putting on curves. "I want you to congratulate me. Twice," she said, and she held out her left hand, on the ring finger of which was a ring with a big blue-gray star sapphire on it. "I finally got Tony to propose last night. Then I accepted."

Chuck hugged her, kissed the air by her right ear. "Congratulations," he said.

"You're doubtful, I can tell," she said. "All you married men around here live through Tony. Well, I want you to know I've made him the happiest he's ever been in his whole life. He told me so himself. And the healthiest! Above all, I brought *order* to the confusion and waste in which he lived and moved and had his being. He's writing at least a page a day on his book, a kind of record for him. And people look at me as a kind of Grundy."

"Jesus, Simone," he said; "you don't have to tell me you've been good to and for Tony. Anybody can see it."

"Every night we have one drink, and one drink only, while we make supper together, Tony always horsing around, finding ways to touch me," she said. "After cleaning up, we go for a brisk walk, one mile out, one mile back exactly, by my pedometer. When we get home we each take a big mug of coffee, he to his study, me to what used to be a maid's room, which I fixed up into a study for myself. He writes on his book while I take care of business or write letters to my thousand close relatives. At eleven Tony fixes a cup of green tea and some cookies for me, a brandy for himself, and we watch the news together, holding hands. After Jay Leno's monologue, we shower together and go to bed, sometimes to sleep."

"Sounds idyllic," said Chuck.

"It is," said Simone. "And I've been readmitted to graduate English."

Chuck hugged her, kissed the air by her left ear. "All right!" he said. "Congratulations again. Welcome aboard," he said.

"I know that Tony pulled a few strings, called in favors," she said, "but he won't admit it. Once we're married I'll not have to work. I can make it my job to show that his advocacy wasn't misplaced," and she gave him a look.

"Of course it wasn't," he said, for Simone had been an A+ student, and he gave her another hug, for Simone had become an armful.

She pushed him away. "I'm going to get that Ph.D., and I'm going to get it with honors," she said.

"The department's about to lose its best secretary ever," he said, for Chuck was not an experienced flatterer. Simone's smile managed somehow both to grow and become shy. Her blush deepened. Who could have known she was so much in need of affirmation? Tony, apparently.

"Tony wants you to be best man," she said. "And I want you to sponsor my dissertation."

"On what?" he said.

"On Charlotte Brontë," she said.

"Why?" he said.

"Tell you later," she said.

Sitting in his office, mulling over Simone's news, Chuck doubted that either she or Tony knew what they were getting into, for Simone was clingy and Tony traveled light. Then the thought crossed his mind that he was being not only unkind but presumptuous. Tony, after all, was at least as smart as he was, and far more experienced. Then this thought generated another: what Tony did for Simone, he could do for Claire—pull a few strings, call in some favors, get Claire admitted to graduate English. Along with admission went a stipend of fifteen thousand a year. And anybody who thought that pulling strings was unethical might consider that there was not likely to be another student in the program anywhere as capable as Claire—unless it was Simone.

He was wondering whether he dared to call Claire at work, so he could tell her his idea, when she called him. "I just got a call from Svetlana, who got a call from that detective, Hector Suarez, with the evil smile, who got a call from the Two Four Precinct: they found Ivan's guitar," she said.

"Where?" he said.

"Washed up on the rocks on the New York side of the river at about 113th Street," she said.

"How do they know that it's his?" he said.

"On the bottom of the guitar is glued a piece of leather about the size of three postage stamps side by side," she said. "On this piece of leather the name 'Tervakalio' was burned by Ivan's friend up in Valhalla."

"When one year my parents sent me to camp, my mother had to sew name tags on the collars of all my shirts, tee shirts included," he said.

"Don't you see?" she said.

"See what?" he said.

"*It was found on the New York side of the river,*" she said. "*It was found just north of 113th.* That's where we live, I mean, where we lived, where Ivan lived, *just north of 113th Street.* That guitar was going home to him."

"Aw, Claire," said Chuck, helpless as the least inspired of men before the occult operations of female thought.

"Suppose what it really was doing was coming to haunt me?" Claire said.

"Now listen—" he said.

"I'm so spooked I can't think," she said. "My boss asked if I wanted to go home. But I need the money. Even more, I need to be around other people, and I don't mean Svetlana."

"Look, Claire—" he said.

"Instead of trying to argue me out of it, you could sympathize," she said.

"Suppose I come down to pick you up, and we go first to the Bronx Zoo, because the company of animals is therapeutic, then to the Botanical Gardens, because plants are exemplars of self-possession, making a day of it—then we'll eat down in the Village, listen to

some blues, because the blues turn pain into pleasure, then go back
to my place, where I'll make slow gentle love to you 'til your toes turn
cherry red. I'll even make up your lost day's pay."

Claire did not at first answer. Then she said, "You're on."

So that's what they did, and if Chuck had ever spent a better day,
he couldn't remember it.

Claire refused to spend the night. She wanted to be home in case
Svetlana called. So he poured himself a long drink, turned on the
TV, watched a show called *The New Detectives* with one eye while
with the other he read a whodunit written by a former pathologist.
At eleven o'clock he turned on the news, in the course of which the
anchorperson with the plummy lips informed her viewers that there
was bad news for fans of Ivan Tervakalio, Bard of the Movement—
his guitar, which he had named "Sweetlana," was found in the Hudson. And we were shown a picture of Hector Suarez, burly-plump,
balding from the front back, his smile not so much evil as knowing,
holding the guitar upside down and pointing to a strip of leather
glued to the bottom.

That night as he was drifting off to sleep, Chuck pictured himself
and Claire in a postapocalyptic paradise of pleasure there at the Hartung estate, now that spring was putting on a show. There was a nimbus of leaflings on trees. Early flowers, the names of which Chuck
did not know, were poking out their heads. The brook, replete with
melting snow, roared. Phoebes were building a nest on the front
porch. A black bear, expelled from his den by momma, so she could
better tend to her new cubs, was seen rummaging around in the
compost but made its getaway before Chuck could fetch his rifle.
Chuck was turning over the soil for a garden about the size of a tennis court for Claire to plant, for the Reverend Hartung, like every
serious gardener, come April bought more packets of seeds than he
had any hope of planting. Each morning they rose from bed and
stretched their arms like young gods.

But dammit, there seems to be something that can't stand per-
fection built into the very structure of things. Why does there always

have to be a flaw, a fault, a defect, why always a taint or stain, why a spot, a blot, a blotch, a blemish, why a warp, a crack, a crevice, why a fly in the ointment, a serpent in the garden, lint in her navel, a grain of sand in the condom, why? Always skulking around, could give you the creeps, a wraith in the early morning fog, a shadow in the pines, always at a distance, but not quite out of sight, was the redneck's second woman, holding a shotgun out in front of her as you would hold a hot cookie sheet covered with apple fritters. She must be a sister, maybe even a twin, of the woman who died under the woodpile, for in silhouette they looked very much alike. They looked like preying mantises. Claire and Chuck decided that they would have to set a trap, catch this specter, take away her gun, scare the bejesus . . . and Claire, enjoying herself at the zoo, threw her ice cream cone over the fence to the bear, which said, "Where's my hat?" and Simone opened her white men's-style button-down-collar shirt, pointed to her chest, and said, "See?"

twenty six

"Please let go. I don't like being mauled." / "This isn't mauling, this is hanging on." [JANE GREER AND ROBERT MITCHUM, The Big Steal] ❦ *"If I had any sense, I'd walk out on you." / "You haven't got any sense."* [JOAN BENNET AND DAN DURYEA, Scarlet Street] ❦ *Take me back, Baby / Try me one more time / Take me back, Baby / Try me one more time / If I don't suit you, Baby / Won't be no fault of mine.* [JIMMIE RUSHING]

WHEN, EARLY IN THE AFTERNOON of an overcast Saturday, Chuck arrived at the Hartung estate, the front door was closed but unlocked. He opened the door gingerly, as though afraid it was wired to a pipe bomb, and sang out, "Hellooooo."

Jane's voice answered with an "In here" but neglected to say where "here" was. Chuck headed for the kitchen. "No, in the den, dummy," said Jane's voice. In the "den"—the Reverend's name for a room with bookshelves, a library table, a lectern, stuffed chairs, a TV, a painting of Christ with a crown of thorns and a face like Rasputin's—Jane lay on the floor, her arms and legs spread, very like a starfish. Actually, she lay not on the floor but on a shiny new exercise mat. She was wearing a brand-new bright orange sweat suit, soaking up the world's light. Next to her on the mat was a volume the size of those books you used to see on coffee tables but no longer see. Its title was *The Book of the Abs*. Jane flexed her knees, clasped her hands behind her head, strained, and pulled her head and shoulders a good inch off the mat.

She rolled over, so that she could push herself up into a sitting position, and patted the floor next to her, meaning he should sit. "I expected you yesterday," she said.

He sat. "You know how I get these anxiety attacks," he said. "I needed a day of total irresponsibility and self-indulgence. So I spent the day at the Bronx Zoo, subwayed downtown for some fried pork with yellow rice and black beans at La Ultima Copa, then moved it crosstown to catch Sultan Le Souk" (born Willie Brown) "belt out some blues, better than thirty hours with your shrink or a week in the Bahamas."

She gave him a long look. "You're not fucking some hypersexed little undergraduate, are you?" she said. "I know what they're like, pagans with tattoos on their butts and itches in their twats."

"I wish," he said.

"If I find out, I'll leave you singing the blues quicker than you could say 'muff,'" she said.

"Promises, promises," he said, but he had a (fake) self-deprecating grin on his face.

She pushed him over on his back and dove onto him, nearly breaking his left leg off at the knee, for it was caught under him. She bit him on the nose, hard enough to leave dents. "Don't think I don't know what's going on," she said. "I may be stupid, but I'm not abstruse." She rolled off him and assumed a sitting position with her legs crossed underneath her, like a snake charmer.

"You tell me: what's going on?" he said, sitting up, rubbing his nose.

"All these years you've been the Big Cheese, the Big Professor," she said, "always a hundred adoring students in your lecture course, fifteen more in your seminars, people asking you to read a paper here, to serve on a panel there, to write an article for this rag, to write a review for that one, to attend this meeting, that cocktail party, you've even been on TV! And then there's all those committees where people have to listen to what you say, there's always people around you who have to listen to what you say, people have to *defer* to you, which is what I'm supposed to do because you make the money, and what do I do? I make your bed. And I have to lie in it, too. Well, I don't have to be downtrodden anymore, and that's what really bugs you."

"Downtrodden!" he said.

She pushed him over on his back, got on her hands and knees, and leaned over him like a predator at its kill. "I got more money than you'll ever have," she said, her breath smelling like prune juice, "not that I won't give you an allowance of walking-around money. I already pledged twenty-five thousand to KWAP and they damn well better give me my own show 'cause Betty Blondell, that's a fine Christian woman, she's going to help but that's only a start. You'll see, from now on people will have to defer to *me*, whether you like it or not."

"I like it, I like it," he said, propping himself up on his elbows.

She put her face real close to his and in a husky voice said, "You'll see, things will be better between us, once we're equals."

He collapsed backward, spread his arms out to either side in imitation of the Rasputin lookalike on the wall.

She reached a hand under his neck, grabbed his jacket by the back of the collar, and started to pull him to his feet. "Come on," she said, "I need you to do something for me. Two things. What's this? A new jacket? My father's wasn't good enough for you?"

"No more hand-me-downs now that my wife is a millionaire," he said.

"I want to submit a sample column to the *Speculator*," she said. "The editor is one of Betty Blondell's students, by the way. I need you to write me three letters in different styles asking me to solve moral problems. I'll quote the letters and solve the problems and that'll be the column."

"Jane, you can't—" he said.

"I'm not going to say the letters are real, but I'm not going to say they're fake, either," she said. She wrapped her arm around his and led him off the mat, and Chuck began to see how he could have some Nabokovian fun writing those letters. "Besides, that's probably what people who write those agony columns, Ann Whatsherface and the others, do when they run short of material," she said. She led him to the sofa, turned him around, and sat him down on it. Ow, dammit, what was this he was sitting on? It was a video, still in its box and entitled "Buns of Steel."

"I want you to be my personal trainer," Jane said. "I want to be built. Dr. Lena works out every day, and she's got a black belt in whatchamacallit."

"All I know how to do is lift weights and run," Chuck said.

"If you don't want to do it, I'll hire a professional," she said. "And while I'm at it, I may get some breast implants. You'd like that, I bet."

"The more, the merrier," he said.

She sat on his lap, snuggled her head under his chin. Then in a sex-kitten voice, she said, "Come on, Daddy, it'll be fun working out together." She wriggled her derriere in his lap. "I'll be teacher's pet again, like when we were first married. I know that every now and then you'll have to discipline me, like with a good spanking," and she began to rotate her bum in his lap.

Now wait a minute. Did Jane have a masochistic streak he had never noticed all these years, a missed opportunity?

She straddled his thigh and began to rock and roll. "Mmmm: I can feel that you still love me," she said, and she reached under his still-buttoned-up barn jacket for his crotch, but she immediately felt that the hard object she was trying to impale herself upon was above rather than below her hand. "What's this?" she said, and she slid her hand into the pocket of his jacket and withdrew her late father's Ruger Bearcat six-shooter. "What did you think you were going to do with this?" She rotated the cylinder, looking it over.

"Well, I thought I'd—" he said.

"Idiot!" she said. "You've got six rounds in here."

"Well, it *is* a six-shooter," he said.

"What you do is, you put a round in the first chamber," she said; "then you skip one, then you put four rounds into the next four chambers. That way the hammer rests on an empty chamber."

"I see," he said.

"You know what?" she said. "I think this gun would be safer with me. If you banged into something with this gun in your pocket you could shoot your balls off," she said.

"It would make life a lot simpler," he said.

"Not for me," she said, unzipping his fly, for Jane was feeling her way to the position that, rather than renunciation, the better way to dominance over a man was to become the sexual aggressor (for money was an aphrodisiac). Come to think of it, maybe all that's needed is the will to dominate.

The next day, Sunday, was pretty much a bummer: first the memorial service, then the funeral, then a reception. Jane spoke with restraint and with what you might call dignity at the service, though Chuck winced when she said the Reverend had been "manly and orientated toward life" or when she spoke about the "mahtoor love between he and I that never took a vacation." At the funeral Pastor Verplank spoke well of his colleague. At the reception, Chuck cast himself into the role of butler, greeting people at the door, seeing that they had a drink, passing out canapés, organizing the local help, Junie Kay, Terry Lynn, and Billie Barb, who did the cooking and cleaning up. Jane was always saying to him things like "Charles dear, this is Dr. Wickery" (who had pronounced the Reverend dead). "Will you see to it that he has a nice glass of that single-malt Scotch? There's a dear." Where did she get that voice anyhow? Margaret Dumont? And why was she trying to lord it over these hicks?

Billy Van, out of pity, it seemed, pulled Chuck into the kitchen, gave Junie Kay, who was burly plump, a friendly slap on the behind, produced the bottle of single-malt Scotch, poured them each a stiff one. The smooth, florid skin on his meaty face was stretched tight, as though ready to burst outward. Well, as long as he got Jane's business done before his heart attack. Apropos of nothing, he began to talk business. He advised Chuck not to sell the Hartung house yet, for real estate prices hereabouts were down, although they would go up soon, and Billy would gladly undertake to inform Chuck as to when they were as high as they would get. Did Chuck know that Billy also handled real estate? As for the hundred-acre woodlot—it hadn't been logged in thirty years. The smart thing for Chuck to do was log it before he sold it, and Billy just happened to know an honest logger, which is a rara avis, make no mistake. And Chuck, don't sell it before you have it surveyed! The redneck who owns the property on your north is a notorious land-grabber. By the way, the surveyor that Billy works with is a real scientist, not one of these itinerant redneck dowsers. Just let him (Billy) know when he (Chuck) was ready to make some decisions. Chuck assured Billy that he would pass on the advice to Jane.

So that evening, the guests all gone, sitting in the den sipping coffee, listening to the bang and clatter from the kitchen, where Terry Lynn and Co. were cleaning up, Chuck passed Billy Van's advice on to Jane. "Yeah," she said. "Ask him if he wants to pay the taxes while we hold on to the house and land. And you, do you want to mow that big lawn, do all the routine maintenance and paperwork, post a guard every night so the house doesn't get broken into by one of these local retards? Owning a house is a pain in the ass."

"I guess," Chuck said. "Just the same, I can see the appeal of a summer getaway," though it must be said that Chuck was not thinking of making his getaway with Jane.

"You know, that hand of yours is beginning to smell," Jane said. "I wish you'd get it looked at."

twenty seven

"Last time I looked, you had a wife." / "Maybe next time you look, I won't." / "That's what they all say." [BARBARA STANWYCK AND ROBERT RYAN, Clash by Night] ❡ *There is no peace, saith the Lord, unto the wicked.* [ISAIAH] ❡ *The goal for every female animal is to find a mate with sufficient genetic quality to make a good husband, a good father, or a good sire. The goal for every male animal is often to find as many wives as possible and sometimes to find good mothers and dams, only rarely to find good wives.* [MATT RIDLEY, The Red Queen: Sex and the Evolution of Human Nature]

THEY WERE ON THEIR WAY TO NEW YORK, Chuck driving, Jane lamenting that Billy Van would have custody of her father's estate for six months in case there were any claims against it, Chuck thinking how for two days he had been right near Lake Sacandaga, where you could rent boats and his wife did not know how to swim, another missed opportunity, but best not to psycho-analyze himself about his inability to act, maybe just as good he didn't risk bringing on another Dreiserish American Tragedy but in reverse, Lena Pitts on the radio denouncing in thunder a bill be-fore the Minnesota state legislature, a bill providing for a civil union

237

license that would give same-sex couples those legal benefits accorded man and wife, the car radio losing the signal from Schenectady but not close to finding the signal from New York, so that Dr. Lena's voice came and went amid static:

"... the same legal benefits for perverts as for men and women married as nature and God intended! ... What's next—equal rights for pedophilia and bestiality and sadomasochism and cross-dressing? *Awk kwissrississ* ... encourage perversity and immorality and lead to the demise of our youth and the family and destroy our civilization ... *sssssscriss* ... signs of apocalypse everywhere ... kids doing drive-by shootings, shooting each other in school, shooting their parents, shooting off their mouths instead of listening to their elders ... *sssssssssooo* ... kids having babies at eleven or twelve or thirteen and killing them, wrapping them in a towel and burying them or flushing them down the toilet or selling them to Arabs ... *kwak* ... kids on drugs or alcohol or Twinkies like never before ... *squizzisssis awk kwawk* ... kids in day care, no wonder they turn out evil ... *squisss* ... smut ... we've got people shacking up, making babies, moving on, shacking up, making babies, moving on, not seeing their kids, moving away, judges saying 'no problem' ... It's the revenge of the children brought up by a generation who invented a whole new and improved way of life ... *errrsssssuuu* ... abortion. You get pregnant, you don't want it, suck it into the sink. No problem ... chaos in the home, therefore chaos in society, no problem, lack of home, lack of parents, lack of family, lack of community, lack of stability, lack of religion, lack of God, and there's a big wind blowing, if you never prayed before, you better start now ... *sssz*. Period. End of sentence."

"... started on those letters for the *Speculator* column," said Jane. "Are you listening to me?"

In fact, Chuck had not been listening to Dr. Lena either. He had been thinking how he and Claire would fix up the Hartung property. They would have an outdoor hot tub—and a swimming pool too, for that matter, why not a sauna? maybe turn one of the outbuildings

238

into a gym. Above all, there would have to be a nice quiet study for Claire, with a whole bunch of up-to-date reference books, how about the *OED* for her birthday? at which point Jane asked whether he had been listening to her.

"I was daydreaming," he said.

"It's not normal to prefer the pictures in your head to what's going on around you," she said. "That way lies masturbation."

He could pull a Chappaquiddick, drive the car into a deep pond. "Want to go the rest of the way through the Catskills," he said, "take in some scenery? We could have a picnic by some scenic little lake."

"What I was saying was," Jane said, "that we ought to start planning my *Speculator* column. What would be some good moral dilemmas for me to solve?"

"You're thinking of students as the letter writers, right?" he said.

"Students, faculty, administrators, Building and Grounds, Security, Health Service shrinks, whatever they do, I don't care, whoever needs help," Jane said. "Moral problems don't depend on the surrounding circumstances, you know."

"Dear Dr. Jane," Chuck said in the voice of a schoolboy reciting a poem, "the chairman of my department is standing in the way of my tenure just because I'm screwing his wife. Is it all right to kill him? And how should I do it? I know one of the Ten Commandments is that you're not supposed to kill anybody, but the people in the Bible are always smiting each other anyhow. Signed 'Bothered and Bemildred.'"

"Very funny," said Jane. "All right—Dear Bothered, the Old Testament also tells us not to commit adultery. If you weren't screwing your chairman's wife, you wouldn't feel the need to kill him."

"Excellent!" said Chuck. "But you haven't solved his problem. He's madly in love with this woman, but every night she goes to bed with her dork of a husband."

"Let him love her at a distance, like those poets you told me about, the whatchamacallums," Jane said. "The troupers?"

"The troubadours," Chuck said. "He can't live without being near

239

her, touching her, holding her, sharing his life with her. He can't think about anything else. She's the same way."

Jane gave him a long look, and he could feel his neck and face reddening. "Let her get a divorce, then," she said.

"Her husband's a Catholic," he said.

"Why are you being such a pain in the ass?" she said. "You're supposed to be helping me."

"The woman's suffering something awful," Chuck said. "She too is madly in love, but she feels sorry for her husband—it's not his fault that she's in love with someone else."

"Let her go to a convent," said Jane.

"Bingo!" said Chuck. "But how about the man? He's showing all the symptoms of love mania. The only alternatives are murder or suicide."

"A real man has self-control," she said. "He doesn't give in to his emotions like some school girl."

"Right you are," he said. "O.K., here's another: Dear Dr. Jane, my girlfriend has real big boobies. They are a great source of comfort and satisfaction to me. But she wants to have one of those breast-reduction procedures. She says they're always getting in her way. How can I convince her that she should not trifle with what God in his generosity has wrought? Signed 'Oral Fixated.'"

"Dear Oral," said Jane, "your girlfriend's breasts are off-limits until you marry her. Then it will be her duty to honor and obey you. Next time you have a date, read the Bible with her instead of slobbering on her breasts and making her feel self-conscious about them. You are making her feel that a stigmatation attaches to breast size."

"Positively Solomonic!" said Chuck.

And that's how they passed the time until they reached dear old New York.

"Where are you off to?" said Jane, for Chuck was throwing books and papers into his book pack.

"To my office," he said.

"No, you're not," she said. "You're going with me to Health Services and you're going to get that hand taken care of. I don't care if they have to cut it off. I can't stand to look at it anymore. And the smell! How can you stand it?"

"It's like the way no one minds the smell of his own farts," Chuck said.

The doctor on duty, Dr. Courtney Levine, was young, thin, long-faced, and topped with lots of thick, black, unruly hair. She had the look of a smoker.

"What a mess," she said, putting on a pair of rubber gloves. Then she cut off the bandage that had been clean and dry when Chuck wrapped it around his hand just that morning. "Yuck," she said, "this is gross. You have your hand in a latrine lately? What's this?" and she put on her glasses, lifted Chuck's hand to where she could study it: "a fight bite!" She sat back, took off her glasses, looked Chuck over. "How's the other guy?" she said.

"Well, the truth is I tripped and put my hands out in front of me to break the fall and came down on my hand teeth first," said Chuck.

"Sure you did," she said, "but that's neither here nor there. What you need is hospitalization and an I.V. drip, if not surgery. But first we'll see what a course of antibiotics can do. Take these faithfully," and she handed him a prescription (for amoxicillin), "and come back in three days if this paw doesn't get a hell of a lot better," and she tapped the damned paw in a way that made him wince.

Jane took his arm as he walked out of the doctor's office. "Where to now?" she said.

"My office," he said.

"I'm going with you," she said. "I want to see what's such a turn-on about walking to your office through those grungy tunnels."

There was Hardcore, at the entrance. He opened the door for them.

"Jane," said Chuck, "this is Hardcore Psychopompus. Hardcore, this is my wife, Jane Lockhart," and he slipped the man a dollar.

"Pleased to meet you," Hardcore said, and he offered his hand to Jane, but she pretended not to see it.

"Yeah, hi," she said. When they had moved on a bit she said, "You know what your problem is? It's, you know, what the French say, whatchamacallit, nostalgia for the boo. Why do you always want to lower yourself?"

The sound of a wounded elephant trumpeting in the distance echoed down the corridor. Jane clutched Chuck's arm. "What's that?" she said.

"The spirit of place become audible," he said.

"What?" she said.

Chuck did not lead Jane down to the left, past sweating brick walls and the sound of sighs to RESTRICTED KEEP OUT. But the way to his office led inexorably through Graffiti Gallery:

DESTRUCTION COMETH;

AND THEY SHALL SEEK PEACE,

AND THERE SHALL BE NONE

"You said it," said Jane.

Sitting on the bench outside Chuck's office, nose in a book, only the right side of her face visible, was Claire McCoy. Jane paused in front of Claire and looked down at her, but Claire did not lift her head, so Jane followed Chuck into his office. "Isn't that your Ms. Pigeon out there?"

"Who?" said Chuck, and he poked his head out the door as though to check. He winked at Claire and mouthed the word "Wait." Claire nodded. He pulled his head back in.

"What does she want?" said Jane.

"Advice, I imagine," said Chuck: "I'm sponsoring her thesis for the M.F.A."

"So long as that's all she wants," she said.

"Don't be ridiculous," he said, and he dropped into his swivel chair with a sigh that was a touch too theatrical.

Jane walked around his office, studying how things were arranged. "I want you to help me turn the spare bedroom into a study," she said. "And I want you to find out about a computer course I can take. I'm going to need a computer to . . . well . . . because you've got to have one. Don't worry: it won't cost you a cent. But see if there's some way I can get one cheap through the university. Of course, what I really need is an office like this one. Well, one step at a—"

"How about we talk this over tonight," he said. "Right now I've got to—"

"Well, pardon me," she said with heavy scorn. "I'm just your wife. I wouldn't want to get between you and your entertainments," and she flounced out.

Claire sidled in. "I had to see you," she said in a whisper loud enough to carry over to Grant's tomb. She shut the door behind her, unaware perhaps that male professors have had an open-door policy since the crime of sexual harassment was invented. A succession of expressions twitched across her face without any one of them settling in, as though she didn't know which one she needed for what she wanted to say. Her poor face was pale and hollow-eyed, her birthmark a hot-looking scarlet. What did he exist for if not to kiss that face back into a complacent bloom? Finally from her repertoire of smiles she pulled out one that was wry and lopsided, the left corner of her mouth not quite rising to the occasion. "You look . . . well, crestfallen," she said, "a good word, that—I don't think I've ever used it before."

"I can't find the right note when I'm talking to Jane," he said. "Everything I say makes her sad or mad."

"That comes from insincerity," she said.

"Lockhart's Half-Baked Theorem number 37 has it that 'sincerity in a man is always a pose,'" Chuck said.

"And in a woman?" said Claire.

"According to theorem 38, when a woman plays a part she becomes the part she plays," said Chuck. "She is never more sincere."

Claire sighed at Chuck's playing the wiseass at a time like this and slumped back in her chair. "This morning when I got up, Ivan's hat was on the kitchen table," Claire said. "That's why I had to see you."

Someone noisily turned the doorknob, rattled the door, knocked, said, "It's me."

Chuck strode to the door and in a loud voice spouted some professorial double-talk about the metaphysics of the caesura. As he opened the door he was saying, "A caesura after the fourth foot in iambic pentameter usually expresses—" and there was Jane.

"I was talking to Simone Song—she's gaining weight, you know, someday she's going to be fat—when it occurred to me that since I'm on my way to the drugstore anyhow (to get some Citracal—Dr. Lena thinks it's the berries), I could have your prescription filled," and she smiled sweetly. "Oh, hi there," she said, as though she had just noticed Claire.

"Mrs. Lockhart, nice to see you again," said Claire, standing up out of respect for her elders.

"How do you get shoulders like that?" said Jane. "I want some."

"I was sort of born with them," Claire said, and she blushed.

"You may have been born with dem bones, dem bones, but not with that muscle," said Jane.

"There are these machines in the gym . . . ," said Claire.

"Could you show me how to use them?" said Jane.

"I guess so," said Claire.

"When?" said Jane.

"Well, I usually get to the gym about eleven on weekdays," said Claire.

"Good: I'll see you then," said Jane, and she bustled out, ostentatiously kissing Chuck on the cheek as she left, having forgotten, apparently, about the prescription.

"You've got to get me a gun," said Claire.

When they were seated facing each other across his desk, Chuck said, "Tell me about Ivan's hat."

"There it was, on the kitchen table," she said. "There's nothing more to say."

"Was it a third hat or—" he said.

Claire sighed again. "It was the same fucking hat that I put on top of the same fucking carton containing summer clothes and occupying the same fucking top shelf of the same fucking closet in my dismal fucking bedroom in my dingy fucking apartment and I can't take much more of this."

"Well, Claire, is it possible, you know, could it be, that you, what I mean is, could you have, you know, just inadvertent—?" he said.

"I am well aware of the alternatives," she said. "One: Ivan is not dead. Two: his ghost is haunting me. Three: I'm going crazy."

Finally Chuck did the right thing: he walked around the desk, bent over to embrace Claire, pulled her to her feet, and hugged her and hugged her. She was unbending at first, stiff as an ironing board, then she suddenly collapsed against him and began to cry. He held her even tighter and began to rock from side to side, saying, "Claire, oh Claire, poor Claire, dear Claire, dear sweet Claire, my own Claire, my only Claire."

She got her hands between them, pushed him back. "Yeah, I know, but what are we going to do?" she said.

"First of all, give the hat to the Salvation Army; better yet, throw it away; best of all, burn it," he said.

"I don't want to hear any more about that hat," she said, "not one fucking word."

"I'm going to take Jane for a ride," he said. "I'm going to drive her into a lake. She won't wear a seat belt because of her father's idea that the seat-belt law infringes upon your God-given right to be an asshole, so the chances are she'll bump her head on the steering wheel or dashboard or windshield or something when we hit the water. Then I'll swim to the surface, take a couple of good belts from the pint bottle of bourbon I put in the big side pocket of my barn jacket for just this purpose, to explain how it is I drove into the dumb lake. And I'll bump my forehead on something to explain why I didn't rescue Jane—'cause I was goofy from drink and a hit on the head as I floated out the car door (which opened on impact)."

"You forgot about air bags, dummy," Claire said. "Jane's not going to bump her head on anything. And if she's not tangled up in a seat belt, what's to stop her from opening her window, holding her breath until the cab is full of water, and pulling herself out the window and up to the surface? Don't tell me that when you see her splashing around wildly in a circle and begging for help you're going to be able to just stand there and watch her go under."

"That business about holding her breath—you can't imagine what a klutz she is," he said.

"Yeah, and even if everything went according to plan, some assistant district attorney out to pile up a record of convictions would prosecute you for manslaughter, seeing that you were driving while drunk. What you can't imagine is how vicious those bastards are," she said, speaking as her parents' daughter. But now she was wearing a rueful smile. "Oh, Chuck," she said, and reached across impulsively to clasp his hand, which was resting on the desk.

"Yeeouch," he said, for she had clasped the wrong hand.

"Sorry," she said. "What did you do to that hand, anyhow?"

"I cut it on Ivan's teeth," he said.

"We will never get rid of the son of a bitch," she said.

> I'll sing you nine, O
> Red fly the banners, O
> What is your nine, O
> Nine for the days of the General Strike
> Eight for the Eighth Red Army
> Seven for the hours of the working day
> Six for the Tolpuddle Martyrs
> Five for the years of the Five-Year Plan
> Four for the years it took them
> Three, three, the rights of man
> Two, two, a man's own hands
> Working for his living, O
> One is workers' unity
> And ever more shall be so.

twenty eight

How shall we tie down this wild beast? What shall we contrive? How shall we place a bridle on it? I know no way, save only the restraint of hell-fire. [JOHN CHRYSOSTOM, De Inani Gloria] ❡ *For when I had this work in hand, it was announced to us that an old man of eighty-three, who had lived with his wife in continence for twenty-five years, had just now purchased a lyre girl for his pleasure.* [ST. AUGUSTINE, Contra Julianum] ❡ *Related to this paradox of concealed ovulation is the paradox of concealed copulation. All other group-living animals have sex in public, whether they are promiscuous or monogamous.* [JARED DIAMOND, The Third Chimpanzee: The Evolution and Future of the Human Animal]

CHUCK WAS BOOGYING UPTOWN to the beat of Lee Morgan's "Rumproller." He swivel-hipped between an old man with a cane and a freckled blonde in a sari. He circled around two professors with short pointed beards of the kind he thought of as Machiavellian, heads together, speaking low. One watched Chuck pass and nudged the other, who glanced at Chuck; they tilted their heads still closer to each other, beards practically touching, resumed their mutter. Chuck nodded absentmindedly to the longtime graduate student who was well known in the neighborhood for walking his rubber plant around the block, once in the morning and once in the afternoon, "to give it an air bath." A guy bopping along behind his bass viol case, which had wheels on the bottom of it, nodded in

247

return. A student-aged woman in just shorts and a tank top on this coolish day jogged by, showing off her bod, bless her. She swerved in front of Chuck to avoid a frowsy woman passing out leaflets (they announced a talk by Rabbi Schwartzbaum entitled "How to Recognize the Messiah When He Comes"), thereby cutting him off, his toe meeting her heel, both stumbling, neither going down. She fell right back into her jog, looked back over her shoulder, and mouthed the word "Sorry," precipitating in Chuck that feeling of déjà vu, a trapdoor into the haunted house of his mind. Just what was it that had conjured up that ghost hovering and nebulous, always dissolving just as Chuck's gaze was about to light on it? Finally the nacreous glitter gathered itself into a figure bowed down on his hands and knees as though praying to Allah, a blond head, a balding crown aimed his way, a ponytail. Now really, could that really have been Ivan Tervakalio who bumped into him, nearly knocked him into the cellar of Poppa's Minimart, on that day when he first met Claire?

"Hi there, Professor," said Hardcore, "you look like you're pondering the relations between Being and Nothingness." Say what? Never before had Hardcore shown a penchant for *blague.* Chuck shook his head, not to deny Hardcore but to shake off a ghost.

"I was lost in the alternative," said Chuck.

"Now what might that be?" Hardcore said. "I thought Being and Nothingness was the whole shebang."

"Fantasy, the imagination," Chuck said.

"First your pal, Professor Felder, tries to fuck with my head, now you," said Hardcore.

"You've got to understand," said Chuck. "Tony doesn't believe in anything. He just likes to play with ideas. Ask him someday for his proof that the world is not flat, not round, but square." He put his hand on the knob of the door to Gwinnett Hall.

"You're not going to deny me?" said Hardcore. "Like it's not the place of a homeless nigger to think about such things."

"I can't imagine anybody better qualified," Chuck said.

"Let me tell you what he said," Hardcore said, holding Chuck by the arm, "and I mean exactly what he said. Ready?" Chuck nodded. " 'If to you something is this or that, it *is* this or that . . . to you.' You want to hear it one more time?"

"Well, it's either a truism or a solipsism," said Chuck, who, after all, was a professor.

"What's this 'solipsism'?" said Hardcore.

"The idea that you can't get out of yourself," said Chuck.

" 'Cept when you're inside your lady love," said Hardcore.

"Tony would say that if to you, you get outside yourself when you're inside your lady love, then you get outside yourself when you're inside your lady love . . . to you," Chuck said.

" 'A thing is what it appears to be to him to whom it appears' is what the good professor said," said Hardcore. "But he wasn't finished. He said, See that thing across the street the dog just pissed on? If to you that's the bottom half of an elephant's leg that it left behind on its travels, it *is* an elephant's leg, etcetera . . . to you. But wait. Then he says, If to me that thing across the street is a locust stump because my father used to use locust wood to make fence posts, lasts forever, then it *is* a locust stump . . . to me. And if to you that thing across the street—"

"Enough!" said Chuck. "Disagreements, after all, are common. What you do is you walk across the street, look at the thing closely, let loose with a kick. If it kicks back, it's an elephant's leg; if ants come charging out, it's a stump."

"Now Professor, you know as well as I do that what that thing's supposed to stand for you can't get close to," said Hardcore. "We're talking about Being here."

"Okay, you get a referee," said Chuck, "an expert in elephants or locust wood."

"He gonna say the thing is a hydrant," said Hardcore.

"In a case like this you got to go with the majority," said Chuck. "You don't want to wear yourself out being contrary."

"And what happens next? If the minority get uppity, the majority say God told them it was a hydrant," said Hardcore. "They invent a church with dogma to prove God put that hydrant there Himself. Then they go on a crusade to wipe out anybody who says different."

"Shit happens," said Chuck.

"So where we at?" said Hardcore.

"There are people in my profession who would say we have arrived at an aporia," said Chuck.

"Where's 'at?" said Hardcore.

"Falling from a plane without a parachute," Chuck said.

"That's what I like about hanging around a university," said Hardcore—"the enlightenment you get."

What's this? What the hell—some vandal had razed the Graffiti Gallery, slapped a coat of whitewash over everything. Chuck, to his surprise, felt a sense of loss. After all, a man needs a superego, if only to defy it.

Lounging on the bench outside Chuck's office, one arm thrown over the back, one leg crossed over the other, his hair combed straight back and held in place by some kind of goo, was Tony Felder. Chuck vaguely disapproved of Tony's attitude, perhaps because Claire had been sitting on that bench when Chuck first saw her. Freethinker though he was, Chuck felt that one should not sprawl on a shrine. Tony rose as Chuck unlocked the door and followed him into the office.

They sat facing each other across Chuck's desk, Tony wearing our old friend, the shit-eating grin. "Bless me, father, for I have sinned," he said.

"So I've noticed," said Chuck.

"We are born in sin, thank God," said Tony.

"Yes, thank God," said Chuck.

"But all my sins, except the last one, were venial," said Tony. "You are the only one I could come to. I need someone who has been there and given himself absolution."

"I'm all ears," Chuck said.

"The flesh is weak, mine more than most," said Tony. "Betty

Blondell conned me into going up to her place for 'a quick lunch,' some leftover braised short ribs and dumplings. Well, I hadn't had any meat with fat on it for months, so I went. Before I knew it I was boffing her on an antique couch no wider than an eel. Then I went down on her 'til she came. Seems there really are some women who yowl at the moment of truth."

"Well, you're wrong: I've never been *there* with Betty," said Chuck.

"I didn't mean Betty; I meant Big Red with the brand on her cheek," said Tony. "You're not going to deny you've been *there* with her?"

"Not a word," said Chuck.

"I'm waiting for absolution," said Tony.

"Sounds to me like you committed not so much a sin as an act of charity," said Chuck.

"The sin was not against Betty, even less against God, that fucker, but against Simone," said Tony.

Hit me with a stun gun, why don't you? Chuck realized the enormity of what Tony had done with a systemic and palpable shock. "Yes," he said after a pause, "she's invested heavily in your relationship."

"Chuck, she's reconstructing her self-esteem upon that shaky foundation, rebuilding her whole personality, in fact," said Tony. "Day by day I can see it taking shape. She's always had smarts, but now she's able to put them to work. She'll get that Ph.D., and she'll get it quick—unless I fuck up."

"Seems to me she's making you over at the same time," said Chuck.

"Should I confess to her?" said Tony.

"Absolutely not," said Chuck. "It's enough that you confessed to me—why cause needless misery?"

"You know her better than me—will Betty keep her mouth shut?" said Tony.

"Maybe not if she thinks Simone is as shameless as you are," said Chuck. "I'll talk to her."

"Shameless!" said Tony. "I haven't slept since I bit into Betty Blondell's apple."

"Your penance is to remain faithful to Simone for two years," said Chuck.

"Some penance," said Tony; "it's like pulling the plug on a man drowning in his bathtub."

"It's going to be harder than you think," said Chuck.

"I don't suppose I ever mentioned to you that Simone is working at becoming the best lover east of the Mississippi," Tony said, rising from his chair. "My survey of the field is so far incomplete, alas, but provisionally I'd have to say she's succeeding."

"And bring her a big bunch of flowers today, just because," Chuck said.

"Good idea," said Tony, heading for the door, "though I've never been able to understand what it is with women and flowers."

Someone had obviously been waiting for Tony to leave, for he was already standing in the doorway, and let's hope he didn't overhear any of the conversation. "Professor Lockhart," he said, striding boldly into the office, "I'm a detective working out of the Two Four," and he held up some kind of I.D. with a badge on it.

"I was just about to leave," said Chuck.

"Hector Suarez is my name," he said. "Me and your chairman, Wynn O'Leary, we go way back."

"Seems I heard—didn't you play football together?" Chuck said.

"Not so much together as against each other," Hector said. "Spanish and Irish gangs were seldom on the same side in those days."

"Not even in church?" said Chuck.

"We didn't go to the same church," said Hector, a serious chill in his voice. "He went to St. Gregory's; I went to Holy Name."

"Well, it's been nice chatting with you, but I've got to move on," said Chuck, rising.

Hector smiled in a way that involved no more than a withdrawal of the upper lip, so as to expose some teeth. "You're kind of fidgety, aren't you, Professor? Just relax for a minute," he said. "See, I'm looking into the disappearance of Ivan Terracotta."

"Never met the man," said Chuck.

"Well, now, you met his wife," said Hector.

"Who's that?" said Chuck.

"Claire McCoy," said Hector.

"Ah yes," said Chuck. "Wonderful student."

"That's why I'm here," said Hector. "Wynn was kind enough to let me look at the evaluation cards you all write for your seminar students. I don't mind telling you that everybody who wrote a card for her thinks Ms. McCoy is the berries. But *your* card! I haven't come across praise like that since the way Sister Mary Margaret McCabe used to go on about the Virgin Mary. You a Catholic?"

"You sound like a character in Graham Greene," said Chuck.

"Never met the man," said Hector.

"No, I'm not a Catholic," said Chuck.

"I'm a recovering Catholic myself," Hector said. "You get to know Ms. McCoy outside the classroom?"

"Well, I'm her advisor," Chuck said.

"There's that," said Hector. "What else?"

"Sometimes I bump into her in the gym," said Chuck. "Sometimes we exchange a word or two."

"Bump into her, do you?" Said Hector. "Come on, you know what I'm getting at."

"You got some *cojones*," Chuck said.

"Don't be so hostile," said Hector. "No one would blame you. That's a lot of woman there."

"She's married and I'm married, or she *was* married," said Chuck.

"Why do you say 'was'—you know something I don't know?" said Hector.

"Claire, uh, Ms. McCoy told me about the guitar you found," said Chuck.

"I thought you didn't know she was married to Ivan Terrapoppino," said Hector.

"Look, you called him 'Ivan Terracotta,'" said Chuck. "How the fuck was I to know you meant Tervakalio?"

"Terracotta, Tervecchio, what's the diff?" said Hector. "I got people who say they've seen you having beers with her in the Other End."

"An academic department is a gossip mill," said Chuck. "If I was having an affair with Ms. McCoy I would make sure not to be seen with her in public."

"Unless you wanted to show her off," Hector said.

"That's the kind of pipsqueak you think I am?" said Chuck.

"Jesus, you're touchy," said Hector. "Okay, let me ask you this: she ever say anything that could cast light on old Ivan's disappearance? Myself, I never liked folksingers."

"No," said Chuck. "Nothing I can think of. Poetry is what we talk about."

"Nothing surprises me anymore," said Hector. "You know, you ought to do something about that hand. Some of those colors I've never seen before." Suddenly he leaned forward. "You know a guy named Oreo Hunter?"

"No," Chuck said.

"You ever hear of *The West Side Whatsis*?" said Hector.

"No," said Chuck.

"You got a field jacket?" said Hector.

"No," Chuck said, and a muffled electronic chirrup made him jump, wimpy as it was. Hector pulled out a cell phone, pressed a couple of buttons, and clapped it to his ear. "Yeah?" he said. "You don't say . . . Go on . . . Go on . . . What do *you* think? . . . Maybe there's a God after all . . . Still, we got to have our own look-see . . . Yeah, I'm ten blocks away, interviewing a professor . . . I hope so, see you in fifteen minutes."

"Trouble?" said Chuck.

Hector gave Chuck a long look, clearly weighing whether or not to speak, and finally said, "That was my partner, just got a call from New Jersey. The state police over there say some guy confessed to doing in our Ivan, tall, long, thin face, field jacket, blue bandanna, not entirely sane. You know him?"

Chuck shook his head.

"For my sins, I've got to go over to New Jersey," said Hector, holstering his phone and walking out, "see if we can put closure to the case of Ivan the Terribillio."

> I'll sing you ten, O
> Red fly the banners, O
> What is your ten, O
> Ten for the days that shook the world
> Nine for the days of the General Strike
> Eight for the Eighth Red Army
> Seven for the hours of the working day
> Six for the Tolpuddle Martyrs
> Five for the years of the Five-Year Plan
> Four for the years it took them
> Three, three, the rights of man
> Two, two, a man's own hands
> Working for his living, O
> One is workers' unity
> And ever more shall be so.

twenty nine

Nothing is secret, that shall not be made manifest. [LUKE 8:17] ❡ *A soft answer turneth away wrath.* [PROVERBS 15:1] ❡ *If the female gets the chance, she will eat him, beginning by biting his head off, either as the male is approaching, or immediately after he mounts, or after they separate. It might seem more sensible for her to wait until copulation is over before she starts to eat him. But the loss of the head does not seem to throw the rest of the male's body off its sexual stride.* [RICHARD DAWKINS, The Selfish Gene]

CHUCK REGISTERED NONE OF THE SIGHTS on his way to the gym, he was in such a hurry to get there. He wanted to catch Claire before she left, just to be with her, of course, for there is nothing he wanted more than to be with Claire, to be with her always, but also to tell her that someone had confessed to "doing in" Ivan. The question was whether this was good news or bad. If this "confession" got the cops off the backs of Claire and Chuck, if it got Ivan declared dead, so that Claire could marry Chuck, once he got rid of Jane, the news was good. But if the confessor was some harmless nut, Chuck would not be able to let him take the rap...or would he?...Look at it this way: suppose the nut were to be put in an institution that gave him the treatment he needed?...and they soon found the medication that worked...they would have to release him. He would be better off than before he confessed. Hadn't Chuck read somewhere that people confessed to crimes, and even committed crimes, just to get back to jail? So Chuck noticed nothing and deceived himself on the way to the gym.

Once there, he hustled out of his teaching togs and into his gym-wear, shorts and a singlet, for Chuck had calves and biceps worth exposing to the world. Outside the men's locker room, he paused to survey the scene. Ah yes, across the basketball court, in the glassed-off area that housed the machines, was Claire, balm to his eyes. She was wearing a tee shirt and bib overalls that ended in short pants, so that her adolescent legs could break his heart. She was bent over and saying something to Jane, who was seated and pulling down on what looked like the handlebars of a bicycle; this was attached to a cable that ran through an overhead pulley and down to a rack of steel plates that went up as Jane pulled down. He threaded his way to the two women in his life through students running, stretching, jumping in place, making out, and was careful to say hi to Jane first. He merely nodded to Claire, for as evolutionary anthropologists tell us, an aptitude for deception is built into the human genome.

"Professor Lockhart," said Claire.

Jane struck a bodybuilder's pose. "Will you still love me when I'm built like Arnold Schwarzenegger?" she said. "Why did you never tell me that working out was so sexy?" She stood up and gave Chuck an ostentatious smerp on the cheek, taking possession, one eye on Claire. Jane was wearing the bright orange top to her new sweat suit (although Chuck in all their years of marriage had never seen so much as a drop of sweat on her) and a pair of tight black Spandex tights. In Chuck's uncharitable view she looked not like a praying mantis but like a tropical spider. He grunted.

"Don't be a wallflower," she said. "Come on and join the party," and sotto voce she said, "Which of these dumb machines will make a girl's titties grow big?" So Chuck fixed her up with an apparatus in which like a fledgling too big for its nest you flapped your arms against resistance, guaranteed to enlarge your pectorals and elevate your breasts, while Claire did about a thousand push-ups and Chuck fooled around with a hundred-and-fifty-pound barbell, and he helped Jane to position herself on the slant board for sit-ups ("Good as Ex-Lax, right?" she said), while Claire did too many sit-ups and Chuck fooled around with fifty-pound dumbbells, and then they all switched to machines that were supposed to strengthen your grip and mold your forearms, and then they switched to devices that were supposed to shape up your legs, Jane mounting the exercise bike next to Claire's and trying to goad her into a race, pedaling like mad, her whole body jerking from side to side on the down strokes, but getting nowhere, for Claire did not notice or did not let on that she noticed, her nonchalant skill and strength making the pedals blur and the wheels sing, and then Claire said she was going to run her laps, and Jane, staggering off her bicycle, said, "Enough narcissism for one day," and if he had let himself, Chuck would have felt at least a twinge of sympathy.

"See that," Jane said, pointing, "that's a symbol of what we've been doing today, a stationary bicycle: going around in circles to nowhere."

"The body's like any other temple," he said: "it requires maintenance, lest it sink back into the aboriginal shapelessness toward which all things aspire."

"'Aspire,' my asp!" she said. "I'll tell you what the body is. It's what my father said it is. It's a lure and a trap. To you and Ms. Kissy Face over there it's an idol is what it is, a fetish, it's, it's, it's a graven image. Period. End of sentence. Besides, I ache all over."

"Maybe you shouldn't have tried to do so much your first day," said Chuck.

"Why didn't you stop me, then? You're the expert," said Jane.

"You seemed to be having a good time," Chuck said.

"I've got to blow this hole," she said, and she stomped off unevenly on a boozer's legs. She did not acknowledge Claire's wave.

What Chuck wanted to do was catch up to Claire and run with

her side by side, even if it was only in a circle. But it wouldn't be smart to let Jane see them running together. On the other hand, it would take her at least twenty minutes, probably much longer, to shower and dress. So he moved out onto the track and sprinted after Claire until they were running in tempo side by side.

"Are you crazy?" Claire said.

"I've got to talk to you," Chuck said, "something Suarez told me. It seems that—"

"Go to your office after your class," she said. "I'll call you from a pay phone. Now beat it."

Just then Jane stepped out of the women's locker room, for she had simply thrown her new yellow warm-up jacket over her sweat-shirt. She put her hands on the rail around the track and watched the other two run, wearing a poker face. But when after one more go-around Chuck peeled off to greet her, she smiled sweetly and said, "Would you mind taking care of supper? I'm bushed."

"I'll bring home a barbecued chicken," he said.

"Go to Poppa's," she said. "And get a pound of that potato salad they make with marshmallows."

"Take a nice warm bath," he said, "relaxes the muscles."

"Maybe I'll finally get to use that bubble bath," she said, which bubble bath was a present from Chuck way back last Christmas, for Jane was not big on the sensuous indulgences.

They exchanged pecks and Chuck watched Jane limp out of the gym before rejoining Claire on the track. But when they came round again, Jane was standing by the rail again, holding on to it, poker-faced. And when after another go-around, Chuck peeled off again, Jane was gone. And when he turned to rejoin Claire, he could not at first find her anywhere, not until his eyes flicked toward the women's locker room, into which he watched her back disappear. There are times, you have to admit, when women can be so exasperating.

He had some free time before his class, so he reduced his sperm count by lounging in the sauna for half an hour. After his class he lounged in his office for half an hour, waiting for the phone to ring. Just the same, when it rang he visibly twitched in surprise. It was Claire, good as her word, as always. "What's so important you couldn't wait until Jane was gone to tell me?" she said.

"That sly-boots Suarez came by," said Chuck. "Our 'interview' was interrupted by a call on his cell phone. It seems that someone had confessed to murdering Ivan." The silence on the other end of the line was so lengthy that Chuck said, "Claire?"

"Sometimes I forget that we did it ourselves and find myself rooting for the police to catch the bugger who killed him," Claire said.

What suddenly possessed Chuck right then, like an evil spirit, was the paranoid delusion that someone had bugged his phone. He therefore tried to repair the damage. "I suppose it's possible his paranoid delusion that we were having an affair could have driven him to kill himself," he said. "And then, we don't really know that Ivan is dead."

"What?" Claire said.

"You know, along with other things, like not having a job, his music not getting anywhere, his feeling that they didn't value him enough at Greenspace, his whole sense of being an all-around failure," Chuck said.

"Are we talking about Ivan Tervakalio here?" Claire said.

"In any case, Suarez described this guy as not entirely sane," said Chuck.

"What did he look like?" said Claire.

"Me," said Chuck.

An electronic voice told Claire that more talk would cost more money.

"Shit," she said. "See you tomorrow."

"When?" he said, but the line went dead, yes, the line went dead.

Chuck, after too much bourbon, was eating barbecued chicken and a salad, while Jane, after too much red wine, was eating potato salad and a roll. Refilling her glass, Jane said, "Your friend there, Claire Whatsherface, is a show-off. And didn't you once tell me her name was Caledonia Pigeon?"

"What was she showing off?" Chuck said.

"All those sit-ups and push-ups, and before you came, chin-ups," Jane said. "Women aren't even supposed to be able to do chin-ups."

"Anybody can do chin-ups," said Chuck. "Getting strong is not like learning to play the violin: you don't need aptitude. Exercise a muscle and it grows strong. It's automatic. It can't not happen. If you want to do a lot of chin-ups you start by doing one a day three times a week, then two a day three times a week, then three—"

"She was showing you that she's a better woman than I am," said Jane.

"Now, Jane, doing one thing better than someone else doesn't mean you're all-around better," said Chuck. "I'll bet neither Christ nor Joan of Arc ever did a chin-up, yet I'm sure you consider them better men than Arnold Schwarzenegger."

"I won't put up with your condensating to me," Jane said. "You hear me?" and she stood up.

"I wasn't condensating," he said. "Come on, Jane, sit down."

"You were implying that I think I'm like Joan of Arc and that neither of us were much as women," said Jane.

"I was implying that someone who works out a lot can get a superiority complex," Chuck said. Maybe the Christians are right to say that one sin leads to all the others, viz., murder to lying. At least it would not be fair to say that Chuck had fallen into sloth.

Meanwhile Jane was giving him a long, sober look. Finally, as though she had arrived at a decision, she said, "I'm driving up to Sacandaga tomorrow."

"What's up?" Chuck said.

Jane shook her head. "Billy Van wants me to speak to this guy from Schenectady who specializes in auctioning off the stuff left in houses when the owner dies, sort of ghoulish," she said.

"Ahh," said Chuck.

"Seems in spite of all the stuff Daddy gave away, there's a lot of antiques left," she said. "Want to come along?"

Damn the woman, she knew he had a class tomorrow afternoon.

"Can't, but bring me back a memento . . . like, say, oh, your father's old bone-handled straight razor. Are you going to sell all the guns?"

"Maybe not all the guns," she said. "You wouldn't want to miss your session among the bodies beautiful, of course."

"Listen, Jane—" he said.

"Would you mind cleaning up?" she said. "There's not much to do. I want to curl up with the latest issue of Dr. Lena's newsletter. You ought to read it. There's this piece in there called 'Flesh and the Spirit: Are They Married or Just Shacking Up?' "

"Being and Nothingness," Chuck said, but not loud enough for Jane to hear. Well, he did the dishes, put away the leftover quarter of a chicken, and wiped up. He prepared his class. He then told Jane he was going out for a bottle of brandy, better than Sominex, for he had the antsy feeling that augured sleeplessness.

"Who's Dorothea Chin?" Jane said, looking up from Lena Pitts's winged words.

The world around him kept making Chuck jump with surprise lately. And he felt a short, sharp "guilt-pang," his own silent word for the phenomenon, as well as blood rushing to his head (or draining from it, who knows). "An ex-student—why?" he said.

"Her card fell from your new barn jacket when I was hanging it up," Jane said.

Chuck considered that unlikely. For one thing, there was a flap on the outside breast pocket of his barn jacket. For another, you don't hold a coat upside down to hang it up. So now she was searching his clothes. Where was that Ruger Bearcat, by the way? "Where's the card?" Chuck said.

"I threw it out," Jane said.

He did get the bottle of brandy, but he also called Claire on a pay phone.

"Can you talk?" he said.

"For the moment," she said. "Svetlana likes to soak in a hot tub with a drink, cigarettes, and a gothic romance. She's going to stay over for a few days to buck me up, she says."

"Poor Claire," Chuck said.

"I'm sleeping on the couch, which is too short," she said. "At least Ivan didn't snore."

"Poor Claire," he said.

"It could be worse," she said. "My father threatened to fly in from New Mexico to be with me in my hour of need, but when I told him Svetlana was already here, he said, 'That's all right, then.' I think I can safely say that his feeling for me is weaker than his hatred of Svetlana."

"Poor Claire," he said.

"Have you got enough money for us to get a room at the Wanhope?" she said. "I need to be hugged and coddled."

"I can get it," he said. Then, remembering, "Wait a minute, Jane—"

"Be there in a minute," Claire shouted, over her shoulder, apparently. Then in a low voice, into the receiver, she said, "Svetlana wants to know whether she can borrow Ivan's bathrobe, except Ivan never had a bathrobe. I've got to go. And, oh yeah, she got some news from Suarez."

"What did he say?" Chuck said, as an electronic voice told him that if he wanted to talk more he would have to pay more.

Chuck spoke quickly. "Jane's going to be out of town tomorrow," he said. "Can we meet at our hideaway? At eleven?"

"You're on," Claire said. Then the line went dead, oh yes, the line went dead.

The minute Chuck lay his brandy-sodden brain on the pillow that night, snapshots of his future life with Claire began to float before his inner eye: Claire in her bib-overall shorts, kneeling in the grass bordering her garden in Sacandaga, twisting around in triumph to hold up for him to see a bunch of just-picked radishes, her eyes bright with pride and pleasure; Chuck teaching Claire to shoot the Reverend's nifty Marlin lever-action .22; Claire and Chuck walking hand in hand along Lower Broadway, stopping in this little store or that so Claire could pick through the *schmatta*; Chuck and Claire cooking together, he making the gravy for the roast pork shoulder, she making the asparagus and mashed potatoes; Claire and Chuck stalking through the reeds, rushes, and cattails at the edge of a lake, his trusty Winchester Model 12 shotgun in hand, when the two of them simultaneously see a large animal crouched in the grasses before them. They can't make out . . . Could it be a giant sloth? . . . They can't see its face, which is nearly in the muck underfoot, but the balding crown of its head was pointed toward them, its blond hair pulled back into a ponytail.

I'll sing you eleven, O
Red fly the banners, O
What is your eleven, O
Eleven for the Moscow dynamos
Ten for the days that shook the world
Nine for the days of the General Strike
Eight for the Eighth Red Army
Seven for the hours of the working day
Six for the Tolpuddle Martyrs
Five for the years of the Five-Year Plan
Four for the years it took them
Three, three, the rights of man
Two, two, a man's own hands
Working for a living, O
One is workers' unity
And ever more shall be so.

thirty

Behold, I stand at the door and knock.
[REVELATIONS 3:20]

tHE NEW JANE'S SOLUTION to the problem of breakfast was a banana, get that prune Danish out of here. Her new breakfast beverage of choice was green tea, so that when Chuck made it to the table, hung over and grumpy, there was no coffee. Nor was there instant coffee in the house, for neither Chuck nor Jane was as depraved as that. He removed from the cupboard an unopened bag of coffee beans ("Colombian Supreme") that his sister had given him for Christmas. He poured too many beans into the little grinder his sister had given him with the coffee. As the grinder ground, he boiled water, two large mugsful. He dropped the grounds into the water, turned the water off, added too much ground chicory, stirred gently. While waiting for the solid stuff to settle, he noticed that Jane, unusually silent, was looking at him with an expression he did not like. It was the look of an appraiser who sees evidence of termites in the foundation.

"Sure you don't want to come along?" she said.

"This is the last week before the spring break," he said, "time for mid-term tests and papers. Students are freaking out . . ."

Jane nodded as though a suspicion had been confirmed. "I'm out of here," she said, standing, checking her pocketbook for something, picking up her gym bag, and walking toward the front door, but without the usual proprietary kiss, without warning him not to leave crumbs on the table. Chuck was well aware that he should run after Jane, find out what bug was up her ass, mollify her, but the first mouthful of coffee was running through him like a mild and slow and beneficent electric shock. "Have a nice ride," he shouted, to which she replied, "You bet," before slamming the door behind her.

Chuck, walking slowly along Broadway to RESTRICTED KEEP OUT, fell into one of those receptive moods during which the mind is empty except for what the eyes see. It pleased him that the low and unbroken layer of clouds overhead was dimpled like a mattress. He liked the spooky flickerings of silent lightning that played around the dimples. In this lurid light, the reds and oranges and yellows in the scene before him were abnormally bright, the rest falling back into a film noir. A man, hunched over, one shoulder unnaturally higher than the other, stood looking up at the traffic light reverently, his lips moving in prayer. When it changed to green, he dropped his head still further and crossed himself.

A tall young woman, black slacks, short black jacket, long black hair, like Vampira's, walked toward Chuck, a half-quenched wicked smile on her face, correlate of some evil thought, he assumed, and good for her. An ambulance screamed along Broadway, heading north. Smoke steamed out of a sewer cover. Though it was early in the day, a street vendor was closing shop, packing away the used novels of murder and horror displayed on a sheet of Masonite supported by milk crates. His sweatshirt and cap had on them the Raiders logo. Six yards uptown tendrils of smoke rose from a card table off which another vendor, this one in a black hooded cape with a red lining, was hawking incense. At the entrance to Gwinnett Hall, Hardcore was playing with a huge goofy rambunctious black dog.

This dog had long wavy black hair that fell over its eyes, impressive teeth, and paws the size of squash rackets. A little stuffed monkey, toy or transitional object or familiar, hung from its chops. Hardcore pried the monkey out of the dog's bear-trap jaws. Again and

266

again he would offer the monkey to the dog and then jerk it away as the dumb mutt tried to mouth it. Pretty soon the two of them were moving in circles, Hardcore spinning backwards, the dopey animal revolving around him, jumping a foot off the ground after the monkey à la Tantalus. Then Hardcore stopped, put one of the monkey's feet between his teeth, and bent over so that the dog could close on the monkey's head. Then they had a tug of war.

The dog won by jerking its head from side to side until the monkey was yanked out from between Hardcore's teeth. While this was going on, Chuck sidled by and put his hand on the knob on the door to Gwinnett Hall. That's when the dog jumped up on him, rested its forepaws on his chest about clavicle high, so that they were nose to nose, the monkey dangling from its maw. The dog looked into his face with one eye, for the other was covered with hair. Chuck looked back.

"Let him pass, Carlo—he's one of us," said Hardcore. The dog lifted its chin and pushed its face forward as though offering a tooth hold on the monkey to Chuck, who declined. Carlo pushed off and came down on all fours.

"Carlo?" said Chuck.

"That there's an Italian sheepdog," said Hardcore. "A Bergamasco is what they call them."

A tall, slim, stylish black woman came out of the Godiva Chocolate emporium next store and clipped a leash onto Carlo's collar. "Thanks, Core," she said. "You're a sweetheart." She hand-fed Hardcore a chocolate cordial, patted his cheek, strutted off with her dog and its monkey.

Hardcore, with a shrug, said, "One of my admirers," and ostentatiously chewed the cordial.

Chuck nodded, opened the door to Gwinnett Hall, and descended to his subterranean sanctuary.

Man, it was hot down here today—and damp too; as above, so below. Drops of condensation ran down the whitewashed walls of the Graffiti Gallery, the walls of which were no longer pristine. In large, shaky letters, written with a broad, black marker pen, were, once again, these words:

DESTRUCTION COMETH;
AND THEY SHALL SEEK PEACE,
AND THERE SHALL BE NONE.
—Ezekiel 7:25

Of course destruction cometh. It always cometh. How many cells of the body is it that die every day? What is it, two hundred thousand brain cells every time you take a stiff drink? Trees die and fall over. Grasses wither. Sudden rain rusts the summer corn. The salmon drops its load and floats away belly up. The old lion leaves his pride to the bumptious challenger, finds a grassy knoll with shade and a view, lies down and daydreams his way into the darkness that never ends. Birds fall to earth, worn down by flying. Now where was it that a four-story building just collapsed, was it Brooklyn? All over the earth there are places where a crumble of stones is all that survives of great cities. Everything that lives dies. As for peace, when has the world been at peace since across an African savanna two bipedal males holding clubs first saw each other? In spite of the heat, worthy of Louisiana, Chuck felt a chill. Oh, Claire, dear Claire! He needed Claire, Claire's body, to warm him back into life. He walked fast through the tunnels toward Claire.

The bar was off the door, a sign that she was not only on time, but early, and what had Chuck done in a past life to deserve a lover like Claire? He opened the door and stepped in, closed the door behind him, looked down for the two-by-four to prop under the doorknob, looked up—where the hell was Claire?

At the tone the time will be eleven-oh-five exactly, said the radio sitting there next to the kerosene lamp on the chair without a back.

Something poked him in the back, right under his rib cage.

"Stick it up, Big Boy," said Claire's voice. Chuck turned, pressed himself up against Claire; Claire pressed herself up against Chuck. He wrapped his big arms around her and slid his hands down to cup her ambrosial derriere, for Claire was steato- as well as callipygous.

And now back to Dr. Lena, Conscience of America, said the radio.

Claire's smile was at once impish, indulgent, and just plain happy, and Chuck could not resist kissing it, no reason why he should. The kiss, in my opinion, is insufficiently appreciated, not something to be taken for granted. It is of course always pleasurable if you are attracted to the person you are kissing, but there are times, times that cannot be predicted, when a kiss can make your hair stand on end. For Chuck and Claire, this was one of those times. They disengaged, Chuck looking dizzy, Claire looking dazed, both, well, let's admit it, panting. "Hoo boy," said Claire, and she bent over to place on the floor a bottle of champagne, the one she had used to poke Chuck in the back, right under his rib cage.

. . . begin the last hour of today's show with an e-mail from Max in Detroit, said Dr. Lena. **He wants to know whether America is in decline and heading for a fall. You bet. Let me count the ways.**

Chuck lifted Claire and hugged her, his cheek against hers, his mouth by her ear. "I love you," he whispered. There, he had said it, not something he could have managed had she been able to see his face. She pushed him back, hands on his biceps.

"What's this you say?" she said, for she had read as much as he had written of his essay on love among the modernists.

. . . signs of decadence and degeneration everywhere . . .

"It seems there's no other way to put it," he said. She bent over, picked up the bottle of champagne, led him by the hand down the steps into the well before the furnace, sat him down on the sleeping bag, popped the cork on the bottle, poured them each a stemmed plastic glassful, touched her glass to his, drank. "Ahh," they said. They drank again. Claire filled their glasses again. They touched glasses again.

For one thing, nobody has any respect, any decency, any restraint—they'll kill someone on impulse, and then blame "society," and then the victim's family only cares about getting on TV or suing someone...

"To love," said Claire. They drank. He kissed her.

"To togetherness," said Chuck. They drank. She kissed him.

"I've been thinking," she said.

"Always dangerous," he said.

... slovenly housewives sitting on the couch watching those obscene soap operas with queer leading men and eating bonbons, and at night their beer-bellied husbands watching cop shows with bad language and gratuitous nudity... everybody's fat except those narcissists that go to health clubs to work out and make out...

"You're not going to kill Jane," she said. "I'm not going to kill her either. We haven't got what it takes."

"I'm just waiting for the right scene to set itself," he said.

They drank. For maybe two minutes neither of them said anything. Then Claire said, "We've got to decide, are we just going to go on as we are, live for the moment, let tomorrow take care of itself? Or are you going to divorce Jane?"

... liposuction, nose jobs, hair transplants, vitamins and supplements, think they're going to live forever... tanning salons...

"She'll pauperize me," he said.

"What have you got that's worth more to you than getting rid of her?" Claire said, and in the air was the unspoken question as to whether his possessions were worth more to him than Claire. But what Chuck really shrank from was not so much the material loss as the inevitable ruction, the emotional storms, the way Jane would carry on.

... When the Romans made themselves strong by working their farms and training for war, they ruled the world; when they got pretty boys to massage them, they lost it... I

270

bet they no longer teach kids that story about the Spartan boy and the fox ...

"Nothing," he said.

"You've got tenure," she said. "She can't take that away from you. You've got a decent salary. How much of that can she grab? We'll manage. I learned how to be frugal the hard way."

Chuck leaned over and kissed Claire on the knee where it showed beneath her yellow slicker, for rain was predicted.

... all those ads for high-tech mattresses, medicines for allergies, for muscle aches, headaches, hay fever, flatulence, hemorrhoids ... a nation of hypochondriacs and self-pitying milksops, crybabies and whiners and hand-wringers ... ooo they're being mean to me ...

"Besides," Claire said, "I love the idea of us setting out together sans baggage to make a fresh start. The more we leave behind, the better." She poured them each another glass.

In the distance they heard the sound of an elephant, blood running from a spear in its side, trumpeting its fear and rage, whirling this way, then that to face a tormentor.

"If things got really desperate I suppose we could write a textbook together," he said.

... no one wants to do any menial work anymore, they'd rather be on welfare, so we let in these stone-age subtropical immigrants to do it, and that leads to tedious pieties about multiculturalism ...

"We're going to refurnish our lives is what we're going to do," she said.

Chuck's mind lit up with a picture of a bare apartment, wood floors gleaming. He then saw himself and Claire walking hand in hand through a flea market. "Fuck this meeching, caitiff cowering," he said. "Let's do it."

... it's the same as the way everybody's gotten so sentimental about animals. A healthy masculine society doesn't make a fuss about entertainments like bearbaiting, bullfighting,

271

cockfighting, dogfighting, never mind the treatment of circus elephants. But now we've got all these self-righteous vegetarians who can't get it into their heads that God put animals here on earth for our use . . .

"Whooee," said Claire, and she hurled her yellow rain cap up in the air like a graduating cadet. She glunked the rest of her champagne and jumped up onto the narrow strip of floor between the well and the bulging boards of the coal bin, all the while belting out "Night Train": "Ta-dum, ta-dum, ta-dum, te-dum. Ta-dum, ta-ta-ta-dum, ta-dum, te-dum. Ta-dum dum. Dum. Dum-dum."

. . . of course that's what's behind everything else: we've substituted consumerism and sex for God . . .

Chuck joined in, "Ta-dum, ta-dum, ta-dum, te-dum," while Claire strutted her stuff from left to right, from right to left, across her narrow stage, everything jiggling, as she'd flash open her slicker and then close it, making a moue. She stopped, center stage, and threw open her slicker to either side. Then she held her arms loosely by her sides, shook her shoulders and swayed her hips until the slicker slid to the floor. Maintaining the full frontal position of her upper torso, she rotated her hips to her audience's right, lifted her right leg and placed her right foot on her left knee, thus forming with the whole of her right leg and the thigh of her left leg an isosceles triangle. She raised her bare arms and smiled brilliantly. Somehow this corny pose against the bulging, white-flaking horizontal slats that held back the coal piled higher than Claire's head, somehow this pose let off a big emotion in Chuck, the pang in his chest, the warm blackness in his head, the weakness in his legs.

. . . no one has enough of anything, everyone wants more of everything, get some monstrous SUV so you can drive it to the shopping mall . . . What happened to "Use up, wear out, make do, do without"? . . .

Claire was wearing form-fitting, calf-length, high-heeled boots snug around the flesh on top and a denim skirt, but between these were visible, of each leg, half a calf, all of the knee, and much of the thigh, pure gold. Chuck watched carefully, standing front row, center, neither of them now ta-dumming "Night Train," though Claire was still moving in rhythm. She lowered her right leg, faced forward entirely, and began slowly, provocatively, to unbutton her blue cotton sleeveless sweater, from the top down. With her left hand she reached under the now unbuttoned sweater and into her bra, from which she pulled out her incomparable left breast, which from hands-on experience Chuck knew to be slightly the larger of the two.

America is gobbling up the universe. It's one big appetite, especially sexual appetite. Sex, sex, and more sex. Look at women's magazines. They all have cover stories about how a woman can make herself into one big erogenous zone, like a baboon's behind. Look at men's magazines. They all have cover stories about how a man can train himself to keep it up for an hour or go five times in one night, preferably with five different women...

Chuck was raising his hands to applaud when the door burst open behind him and slammed into the wall, as though someone had kicked it in. Chuck jumped. The police? Morlocks? He turned in a crouch. It was Jane.

Because of the strong light behind her, what Chuck and Claire saw was pretty much a silhouette. But the door, of its own weight, began to swing closed, and the less light shone in, the more you could see of Jane, whose eyes were abnormally large and whose lips were compressed into a wrinkled circle about the size of a marble between those wide jaws. Then a little smile played over her face that could make you believe in demonic possession.

Well, it's too late for us to go back to that old-time religion. We're besotted with tolerance, which is no virtue. You want to know about tolerance? Check out Deuteronomy 13. It says right there if some prophet or dreamer says, Let us go after other gods, that prophet or dreamer of dreams "shall be put to death." And "if thy brother, the son of thy mother, or thy son, or thy daughter, or the wife of thy bosom, or thy friend,

which is as thy own soul," says, Let us go and serve other gods, "Thou shalt surely kill him; thine hand shall be the first upon him to put him to death...and thou shalt stone him with stones, that he die." That's the kind of tolerance we need.

Chuck glanced toward Claire, who had already covered up. When he turned his eyes back to Jane she was rummaging around in her pocketbook among the eyeglasses (with holder string), lipstick, comb, hairpins, compact, compass, handkerchief, aspirin, Ex-Lax, Rolaids, allergy pills, bottled water, tape measure, balled-up receipts, loose rubber bands, loose change, keys, penknife, nail file, nail scissors, cell phone, wallet, appointment book, memo book, miniature New Testament, photo of her father in laminated plastic, six ballpoint pens, and the Ruger Bearcat .22 six-shooter, which she finally extracted. Her glasses were hanging by the holder string from the barrel. She advanced to the edge of the well, pointed the gun at Chuck, said, "Back off, asshole," and she gestured with the gun toward where she wanted him to retreat, her glasses sliding off the gun. Chuck backed up to the stairs leading out of the well. Jane jumped down into the well.

The only thing that can save us is WAR!—a holy war. A holy war on tolerance!

Jane turned her attention to Claire. "As for you," she said, "we could have been friends. You could have come to me for advice. But now it's too late for that." Claire said nothing, kept her eyes on the gun.

"Come on, Jane," said Chuck, "we didn't want to fall in love—it just happened to us, like getting caught in an avalanche."

War is the graduate school of virtues. It teaches stoicism, selflessness, sacrifice, yes, discipline, respect, obedience; it stifles dissent, puts down anarchy, quashes hedonism. You can't stray, go your own way during war—you have to march in step to patriotic music, onward God-filled soldiers marching on to war.

"Shut up, asshole," Jane said to Chuck. To Claire she said, "Men can't help themselves, but a woman can. Don't you know that the whore betrays all decent women, spreads disease, uses up money that should go to the wife, breaks up families, and thusly undermines civilization? A more is whore dangerous than a hordarian barbe." She kept the gun on Claire, who kept her eyes on the gun.

War on freethinkers! War on atheists! War on liberals!

"Put the gun down, Jane, so we can talk," said Chuck.

War on feminism. War on same-sex marriages. War on fornication.

Jane moved the pistol with a steady hand to the right, lowered the muzzle, and fired a shot between Chuck's legs. The slug ricocheted off the floor, off one of the walls on the corner of the well behind Chuck, off the other wall, and, just about spent, hit Chuck's leg, whence it dropped to the floor. "Keep your mouth shut, asshole, or I'll shut it for good. Right now my business is with your whore," and she turned her attention, and her gun, to Claire, who was in a half-crouch, ready to leap, well, somewhere.

War on death taxes.

"Unh-unh," said Jane. "Naughty-naughty." Claire straightened up, still eyeing the gun. "In more civilized times they stoned adulteresses to death," said Jane, and she moved into the two-handed combat stance, left hand cupping the right in support, "but now we have more efficient means."

War on the ACLU.

"Jane, no!" said Chuck, raising one hand like a traffic cop. Claire threw herself to the right, already in the air as the gun went off. She hit one of the upright posts that held back the horizontal slats that held back the coal, hit it as a blocking fullback blindsides a linebacker who is just standing there flat-footed, minding his own business, looking across the field under the impression that for him the play is over. **(War on Head Start.)** The post went down, for it was fairly rotten where its base was set into the concrete floor. **(On trial lawyers.)** There was a loud crack as one of the horizontal slats broke under the weight of the coal, then a louder crickrackarack as the other slats broke outward pretty much at once. (**Unions.**) The coal burst through in a mighty wave. It crashed into Claire, carried her in its crest, where when Chuck last saw her she was trying to right herself, roared into the well in a dense cloud of black dust, broke down on Jane like a tsunami on a sand castle. (**The minimum warwk**)

She managed to get off one more shot before the coal engulfed her entirely, her mouth as wide open as it could get, but whether in shock or to say something or to scream Chuck could not tell over the roar and rumble of the coal. The last thing Chuck saw of her was a hand holding the pistol and pointing toward the ceiling. He was himself backing up the steps out of the well when the coal hit him knee high and knocked him over.

Whether he passed out or not is unclear, but in any case, when he came back into his self-possession, all was quiet. He could not see anything, not because he was under coal, or because he had gone blind, or even because the air was thick with coal dust, but because the coal had buried the two battery lanterns and had knocked over the kerosene lamp that once stood next to the radio on the backless chair Claire and Chuck used as a table. "Claire," Chuck said in a quavery shout.

"Over here," Claire said.

It was only when he started to extract himself from the coal over his legs that he realized something was wrong with his right knee. The pain focused his attention. Across the well, by the furnace, there was a sudden flicker of flame on the coal above the spot where the kerosene lamp had stood. Chuck could see, dimly, that coal had filled the well and overflowed onto the floor around it. Claire was half buried, not perpendicular to the floor but at a slant, facedown, in the position of a swimmer who stops kicking and allows her legs slowly to sink, yes, stops kicking and allows her legs to sink. There was no sign of Jane. Chuck crawled to Claire, dragging his right leg.

"I could see her finger tightening on the trigger," she said. He scratched, scrabbled, and scooped coal away from Claire's lower body until he had cleared her thighs. He then kneeled by her head, put his hands under her armpits, and pulled. Claire screamed. "My back," she said. "My back, I've hurt my back."

Chuck sank back onto his heels. Trying to rub the coal grit out of his eyes just put more of it into them. The single tongue of smoky flame that fluttered up from between lumps of coal the size of Brazil nuts kept all the shadows in motion. Was Claire crying or laughing as the shadows at the corners of her mouth went up and down and a tear rolled from her eye, started down her cheek, ran across her nose, and left behind a streak that seemed to squirm? The moving shadows on the wall scared him in a way that nothing else had scared him since he was five years old.

"Where's Jane?" said Claire. "Find Jane, for Christ's sake, Chuck, find Jane. Oh God, what have we done?"

So far as he knew, they hadn't done anything, but anyhow he crawled toward the spot where he had last seen Jane's hand. There, its barrel pointing at the sky, was the Ruger Bearcat. He pulled it out of the coal and put it into the side pocket of his once dark olive sports jacket, now black, and he began to scoop out coal, his fingers laced together. The work went slowly, for coal kept sliding back into the hole almost as fast as Chuck could scrape it out. He was drawing out a double handful when something seemed to clutch his hands and then let go. There in the space he had just cleared were four fingers sticking up half curled over. Quickly he removed enough coal from around the hand for him to get at the wrist. He felt for the pulse: nothing, but that didn't mean much, for Chuck had never been able to find even his own pulse.

Chuck worked frantically to get the coal off Jane, even though there was no seeing to the bottom of his hole. The fire was lower but wider, more glow than flame, for the kerosene had burned off and the coal had caught. The cloud of coal dust was just as dense, but swirling in some draft. To Chuck's more or less deranged eyes, it seemed to form a black halo around the fire. As Chuck pulled arm-fuls of coal to the surface of the hole, the shiny surfaces of individual pieces caught light at all angles. But what's this? The door opened a crack, then halfway, then all the way, and the light poured in: Jane's arm, you could now see, was erect and it was unearthed almost as far down as the elbow. The silhouette of a man stood in the doorway. "Good God," said the voice of Tony Felder.

"For God's sake, come help," said Chuck: "Jane's under here." Although he was wearing an elegant suit in muted plaid, probably selected for him by Simone, he immediately came over through the cloud of dust, fell to his knees, helped Chuck scoop out coal. "I was walking to your office when I heard a tremendous crash," Tony said. "At first I couldn't tell where it came from. But then I saw coal dust seeping out from around the door." Finally, lying on their bellies, drawing up armfuls of coal, they uncovered Jane's face, shoulders, and arms. Then, each of them with a grip around one of Jane's wrists, they pulled her out of the hole. Tony started mouth-to-mouth resuscitation. The door, of its own weight, had closed again, but now it swung open. Once again a male figure was silhouetted in the doorway, the light shining in from behind him. "God-a-mighty," said the voice of Hardcore.

"Quick, go call for an ambulance," said Chuck. Hardcore propped open the door with the two-by-four and ran off.

"Chuck," said Claire, making Tony jump, for he had not known that Claire was anywhere near. He spit out a glob of black phlegm, went back to work on Jane. Chuck crawled over to Claire. She was lying with the right side of her face down, so that she could look toward where Chuck and Tony had been digging out Jane. She was obviously in great pain. "Listen," she said, her words punctuated by gasps. "Our story is that Jane wanted to write a pilot . . . for a radio serial about graduate students . . . living down here . . . They ran out of fellowship money . . . and had no place else to go . . . We were helping her . . . blocking out a scene . . . with ideas about how to furnish the place . . . trying things out . . . I was horsing around when the coal bin disintegrated."

Chuck took out his handkerchief and wiped away some of the coal dust around her mouth and eyes. While Chuck was having hysterics, Claire, good girl, was being practical, inventing that doozy of a cover story, in spite of her pain. He took off his jacket, folded it into a pillow of sorts, felt the weight of the Ruger, which he removed, slid the jacket under Claire's face, kissed her on the lips, crawled back to Tony and Jane.

"Anything?" he said to Tony, who shook his head, signifying "No." Chuck passed the Ruger to Tony and said, "Hold this for me—and not a word, not a word to anybody." He tipped forward to rest his forehead on the coal, for he suddenly felt dizzy, the ringing in his ears, the warm blackness in his head. Tony put the gun in a jacket pocket and put his face close to Jane's. He held her mouth open and looked inside. He inserted his pointer finger, pushed it in as far as it would go, worked it around down there, extracted a lump of coal. He pushed down on Jane's chest, released, sat back, leaned forward, pushed again, released, and so forth.

Hardcore rushed through the door, carrying a fire extinguisher. "They're on the way," he said. He rushed over to the fire and spritzed it. Tony again bent over to look down Jane's throat. Again he inserted a finger, worked it around, extracted a lump of coal.

"No wonder," he said. He gave mouth-to-mouth another try, but not for long. Hardcore came over, the fire extinguished, the smoke circling with the coal dust.

"That your wife?" he said to Chuck, who looked down on Jane, whose little mouth was open like that of a chick in a nest looking to score some eats from momma bird.

"Was," said Chuck, his voice choked up with emotion (to his own surprise).

While the EMS crew bustled around Jane, Chuck sat by Claire, holding her hand. "I didn't *intend* to knock that post over, Chuck," she said. "I was just trying to dodge the bu—" and she threw a significant look back to where Tony was picking the coals off Claire's legs, for as Chuck understood it, no normal male could resist acting upon an excuse to touch Claire's legs. The EMS guys very carefully slid Claire onto a stretcher, strapped her down, took her away.

Tony sat with Chuck, whose back was against the wall, legs spread out before him, as they waited for a second ambulance, for as one of the EMSers said, feeling Chuck's knee, "Looks like a gone anterior cruciate to me." Tony had too much class to congratulate Chuck on his deliverance, which in any case was not yet how Chuck saw it, so they sat for a while in silence. But as the silence began to feel charged with all that might have been said, Chuck said, "You were on your way to my office?"

"I was going to ask you to speak to Betty Blondell," said Tony.

"Weren't you the one who said that Betty was about to become interesting?" said Chuck.

"She says she's in the grips of a compulsion to confess," said Tony.

"I can't believe she'd want to do that much damage to Simone," said Chuck.

"She's got an exalted view of confession," Tony said. "It cleanses the soul, don't you know. She wants me to confess first."

"Well, it might in fact be easier for Simone to hear it from you," Chuck said.

"I don't want her to hear it from anybody," Tony said, "as per your advice—remember?"

"It just occurred to me for the first time," said Chuck: "Confessing is a disguised form of braggartry."

"It's that, too," said Tony. "That, too . . . for starters . . ."

thirty one

Amor vincit omnia.
[A CHARACTER IN CHAUCER]

aFTER HIS RIGHT KNEE had been probed by various hands and a number of devices, Chuck lay in a bed in a room he shared with an oldster who looked like he was heading for the last roundup. Chuck was about to get up and hop one-legged to the nurses' station in search of news about Claire and, of course, Jane when a head appeared at the edge of the curtain separating Chuck's space from that of the oldster next store, who periodically mumbled "momurdrum pushnik." Dr. Seward, as he introduced himself, looked too young to be that bald—and what do you have to do to get that kind of shine on your scalp?—though his mustache was a real bush. He explained that Dr. Harker, the distinguished knee expert, would do the "procedure" day after tomorrow. Meanwhile, Dr. Seward went on, Dr. Renfield, the hand expert, wanted to "go in" right away to see what was up with Chuck's hand, for he had seldom encountered a filthier hand than that, unless Chuck felt that hanging on to a left hand when you already had a right was redundant, if not profligate. Ms. McCoy's condition was "stable." Even if the doctors had known she was pregnant it is unlikely that they could have pre-

281

vented the miscarriage. Attempts to resuscitate Mrs. Lockhart were not successful.

The operation on Chuck's hand was done with a local anesthetic and something that did not put him out but just made him not give a shit. At one point he sang out

> She's got a face like a monkey
> Feet like a bear
> Mouth full of tobacco juice
> Ss-sis-squirting everywhere
> But I love her
> Love her to the day I die
> She's my loving baby
> Love her til the day I die.

Dr. Renfield came over, bloody scalpel in hand, and gave Chuck a long look, the expression on his face serious. It must be something about the way he used his sunlamp, because Dr. Renfield always looked as though someone was holding a flashlight under his chin. "If you want to know the truth, I don't think Ivan Tervakalio could have sung it any better," Chuck said. Dr. Renfield merely shook his head. In his doped-up condition Chuck slept very well that night, thank you.

Man, that pus squirted out six inches when he cut down to the fascia, said Dr. Renfield, the morning after, while Chuck was still working on his breakfast toast and coffee. "That *eichanella* is a bitch."

"*Eichanella?*" said Chuck.

"*Eichanella carodins,*" said a new voice, the voice of Hector Suarez, who walked over to the bedside. "Morning, Professor," he said, helping himself to a piece of toast. "It's a bacterium we sometimes find in the knuckles of a guy who punched out another guy, lives under your gums."

"Yes, the human mouth is a cesspool," said Dr. Harker, who had just come in the door. "By comparison, the human knee is as clean as Mary's twat." He pulled the covers back to expose Chuck's knee, squeezed it, said, "That hurt? Thought so. Well, we'll have you back on the treadmill in no time."

"I don't use a treadmill," said Chuck with dignity.

"Don't expect to do any one-armed chin-ups using that left hand," said Dr. Renfield, spreading strawberry jam on a slice of Chuck's toast. "You waited too long."

"Did you hear the one about the guy who took too long to come?" said Dr. Seward, who placed one hand on the back of Dr. Renfield, between the shoulder blades, and one hand on the back of Dr. Harker, between the shoulder blades, and herded them toward the door. "Well, it seems this premature ejaculator went to his doctor . . . ," and out they went.

Hector Suarez pulled over a chair and helped himself to another piece of toast, the last.

"That loony who confessed to killing Ivan Tervakalio? He couldn't have done it," he said. "He was already in the paddy wagon while old Ivan was still singing the blues."

"That so?" said Chuck.

"Being that you and Mrs. Tervakalio are such good friends, I thought you'd want to know," he said.

"Ms. McCoy," said Chuck.

"Whatever," said Hector.

"Have you seen her?" said Chuck in a voice that mimicked the indifferent tone of a man who has troubles of his own.

"We just now had a nice little chat," Hector said.

"How is she?" Chuck said.

Hector paused. "Well, she's a little concerned, you know, because she can't feel anything from the waist down."

Chuck didn't say anything, but we can imagine how he felt.

"It's not just that she can't *feel* anything from the waist down, you understand," said Hector. "It's a shame, a well-set-up woman like that."

Again Chuck did not say anything.

"You two going to get together, you know, now that you're both free?" said Hector.

"If she decides to go after a Ph.D. we'll probably work together," said Chuck.

"Of course, she's not the woman she used to be," said Hector.

Once again, Chuck did not say anything, though the temptation to pull out his I.V. and strangle Hector Suarez with the tubing was very great.

"You two gonna sue?" said Hector. "You could make a bundle. By rights that coal should have gone out with Prohibition."

"No," said Chuck, for who knew what the university lawyers would turn up in the process? Besides, Chuck had a kind of esthetic reluctance, a sense that it was bad form, to sue people for something that wasn't their fault.

The operation on Chuck's knee went well, although the damage was too great for mere arthroscopic surgery. Dr. Harker had to do some serious cutting. The resulting scar was not large, but Chuck liked it. He did not like the cumbersome apparatus, made of steel rods and a cuff around his ankle, a collar around his thigh, that kept him from bending his knee. Good boy that he was, Chuck, over the weeks that followed, carried out Dr. Harker's orders about physical therapy to the letter. But to Harker's prescription he added an hour's worth of routines of his own devising. A number of these concentrated on his left leg, for Chuck had read somewhere that exercising one leg or arm also developed the other, amazing if true. Once he was able to discard the brace, therapy became a daily and reliable source of pleasure. His daily visits to Claire in the hospital were something else.

Her skin seemed to get whiter by the day, except for her birthmark, which got redder. She wouldn't say much, not that she was apathetic or out of it. It was more as though some absorbing interior process was going on, a symposium among the various parts of her personality, that she did not want to interrupt. She ate very little, would have eaten less, if the nurses hadn't threatened to put her on an I.V. (She ate only one from the box of chocolate truffles Chuck brought her.) The result was she put on an intense, ascetic, wide-eyes, slightly fanatical look, as though she were St. Theresa or someone, lying there on her back, staring at the ceiling. But then from time to time, more often as the days went by, she would snap out of it, her features would soften, she would smile and reach up to Chuck, so she could pull him down and kiss him, and he would melt.

After his own discharge from the hospital, he would bring along with him, on his regular late afternoon visits to Claire, often his second visit of the day, a pint of Irish whiskey in a silver-plated flask he bought especially for the purpose. The two of them would sip the whiskey before and while Claire picked at her dinner and Chuck ate the (usually pastrami) sandwich he had brought along with him. And they sipped some more over their coffee, for the jolly hospital worker who brought around the food took to them, and therefore against the rules brought coffee for Chuck, and in violation of all rules she even from time to time had a drink with them, "just a taste." And Claire would become more like her old self and they would talk and talk as they did during the springtime of their relationship, about life, love, literature, and, believe it or not, current events, for during the day when she was not communing with herself, Claire watched political talk shows on television, and Claire saw the old American puritan-missionary spirit in our assumption that everybody else in the world should be made to be like us and in the activities of conservatives at home, their watchwords being "discipline, punish, censor, and convert," Chuck nodding agreement but not saying anything, for he felt that a strong interest in politics was another species of bad form. Well, by the time of the ten o'clock news the flask would be going on empty, and after some lingering hugs and some serious kissing, Chuck would walk the sixty-something blocks home and sleep well.

Her own surgery had been described by Dr. Morris as "exploratory," but the explorers had failed to discover the cause of her paralysis. Nor did any of the new hi-tech diagnostic tools and imaging mechanisms turn up any organic explanation. Ultimately, Dr. Morris wanted to "go in" again to look around some more. Claire was reluctant. "I'm being punished," she said to Chuck.

"By whom?" he said.

"By the structure of the universe," she said. "By my own psychology."

Chuck was relieved that Claire had not mentioned God, but he was unnerved by her implication that the universe had a moral structure. Still, if things are what they appear to be, and it appears to you that the universe has a moral structure, then the universe has a moral structure . . . to you. In a fit of pique, apparently, Dr. Morris had Claire removed to the Rusk Institute for Rehabilitation Medicine. While she was there learning how to use a wheelchair, Chuck saw to it that Jane was buried next to the Reverend Hartung. Billy Van, who was handling Jane's estate (soon to be Chuck's), remarked on how distinguished Chuck looked with his limp and cane. Chuck did not have anything to say at either the memorial or burial service, but the Reverend Verplank had plenty to say at both. Chuck did not pledge a large donation to the church in Jane's name; he did not tell Billy Van to have the woodlot surveyed.

He did walk through the house and outbuildings, now essentially his, though he had a hard time getting a handle on that fact. He tiptoed through the house, opening drawers and closets with the feeling that he was violating something. Chuck deduced that there was at least one squirrel holed up in the house. It had chewed out pieces of the Reverend's sweatshirts, probably for a nest. It had chewed up the cork stopper in the carafe that held olive oil on the kitchen table. It had chewed into a bag of Cheese Doodles. But Chuck felt good about all that cast-iron cookwear in the kitchen, the three-piece waffle iron, the cornbread griddle, all of it tempered and clearly in steady use, something hard and enduring in the loose flux of American life. And he handled with something like reverence the old tools, the drawknives, the leather punch, the wrenches and snips maybe seventy years old, a section of railroad track used as an anvil, a pair of pliers maybe a yard long probably used by blacksmiths to hold something in the fire, the peevee, the crosscut saws, the adze, the broadaxe, an ancient Stanley dowling jig kept in its original box, a wrench of the kind you used to get with your car when you bought a Ford. He looked over the pornography collection, in the spirit of nothing human being alien to him. He thought of burning the collection, along with the Reverend's socks and underwear. But he didn't do it, for Chuck would have found it uncomfortable to live with evidence that he too was tainted with puritanism.

The area in the back of the house, the chopping block, the face cord of wood, one by four by eight, the soft-wood grove with one tree fallen over, the porch with firewood piled on either side of the door, was haunted. Chuck mulled over what it meant for something to be haunted: an emotionally charged event, especially if it is an occasion for guilt, seeps into the surroundings in which it occurred . . . to you. Well, the event in question had only occurred in one of the fantasies Chuck used to slide down on into sleep—another instance of how fantasy makes something happen. To the south of the house was a piece of lawn a little bigger than a tennis court. That's where he would have a swimming pool put in. Speaking of fantasies, what Chuck saw in his mind's eye was Claire swimming the length of the pool, her strong legs kicking up water like an Evinrude.

He was gloomy as he drove home along the Thruway, which had always seemed to him like a covert experiment in sensory deprivation, tall trees on either side of the road packed so tight you couldn't see anything beyond them. He tried half-heartedly and half-consciously to cheer himself up with a fantasy of Jane, still alive, happily married to Pastor Verplank, inviting Charles and Claire Lockhart to a party to celebrate her recent acquisition of a radio talk show out of Schenectady. He rushed through the door into his apartment, already loosening his tie, anxious to get out of the black suit and into a tub of steaming water, so he could stretch out and sweat out his miseries, a snifter of brandy by his side, a whodunit in his hand. But the phone was ringing before he had closed the door behind him. A voice hoarse and breathless said, "This is Tony. Get over to my apartment. Quick. Don't ask why. Just do it."

Simone answered the door to Tony's apartment. She looked as stiff and brittle and colorless as an icicle. She nodded toward the living room, where Tony sat in a stuffed chair, naked from his navel to his knees, his shirt rolled up, his pants down, beads of sweat on his forehead. A drop of blood welled out of the little round hole in the skin above Tony's hip bone and ran along the crease between thigh and trunk and disappeared into his public hair. "I was playing with that damned pistol of yours when it went off—must be there was coal dust in the works," he said, and he blotted up a drop of blood with what looked like a dishtowel. "What I need to know before I go to the hospital is whether the thing can be traced back to you."

Chuck was shaking his head when Simone said, "What really happened was that I shot him. I was aiming for his prick, but I missed."

No one said anything while Chuck looked at Simone, his scalp prickling, and Tony looked down at his shrunken dangle and Simone looked, well, you'd have to say like Joan of Arc. "Betty Blondell, you see, felt the need to confess," Tony said. "She had the nerve to ask Simone's forgiveness."

Chuck finally spoke. "All right: Say you bought the gun on 116th and Morningside from a guy who used to live in a cardboard box on one of the rest areas overlooking the park. Say he was a little shorter than average and a little heavier than average, a light-skinned black guy, looked like Representative Bob Barr of Georgia. Say he wore a black hooded sweatshirt, jeans, and big sneakers. Say you chiseled him down to two hundred bucks. The ammunition came with the gun."

"I've never seen you take charge like this before," said Tony. "What's made you so masterful?"

"Get the details straight in your mind before the cops come," said Chuck: "how exactly you were holding the gun when it went off,

where Simone was and what she was doing when the accident occurred."

"Accident," said Simone.

"Pull your pants up," said Chuck; "I'll help you down to find
a cab."

"Can't stand up," said Tony. "My hip's ruined."

"Shit," said Chuck.

"Simone will call EMS as soon as you're out of here," said Tony.
"Do one last thing for me, then beat it."

"What's that?" said Chuck.

"Tell Simone," said Tony, "tell her that a man can love a woman
with all his heart and still go for a quickie with another woman."

Simone, who had been holding her head stiff and high, looking off toward something in the far distance invisible to other eyes,
dipped her head, looked down, and a round and fat tear rolled down
her cheek on either side. Chuck walked over to where she was sitting, pulled her out of her chair, and hugged her hard and close, until he felt her sob. Then he let go. The idea was to let her know that
she had not expelled herself from her community by shooting Tony.
(It's the isolates among us who are really dangerous.) "After this,
you're stuck with each other for good," said Chuck. "You know that,
don't you?"

"I know," Simone said, sniffled, hugged him lightly, and pushed
him out the door.

To celebrate Claire's release, Chuck bought her the Mercedes of
motorized wheelchairs. You could go down Grand Canyon or up
Mount Kilimanjaro in that thing. It had *two* cup holders. But on the
whole Claire preferred her old-fashioned secondhand self-propelled
prop from a horror movie. True enough, she could turn on a dime
and pop wheelies on it. The main thing, she said, was that she
needed the exercise. And indeed, her arms and shoulders, always
impressive, were now prodigious. Adolescent boys stopped dead in
their tracks, thunderstruck, to stare at them. Chuck, as you might

expect, loved to look at them, to stroke them, to feel Claire's arms around him, but if pressed he would have to admit that sometimes he missed their former softer surface, for Claire was also on a strict diet. She ate as little in the way of carbohydrates and fat as you could without making a complete pain in the ass out of yourself. The result of diet and her daily two-hour workouts was that from her irresistible neck to her scooped-out hipbones she was built like a gymnast in exceptionally good shape.

Below those hipbones, things were not so good. Claire was no longer callipygous. Her tush was becoming squishy. Her legs were losing definition, in spite of Chuck's daily massages, in spite of weekly electronic treatments meant to get things moving again on their own, for it was becoming clear that Claire's problem could not be strictly physical. For example, she had control of her sphincter and urinary apparatus, but her vagina was without feeling. Chuck's attempts of various kinds to stimulate at least a little lubrication were unsuccessful, nor was Claire's remark, meant to be consolatory, that the mouth was a more intelligent lover than the cunt, exactly to the point.

For propriety's sake, it was a year before Claire would move in with Chuck, while he paid her rent and utility bills, gave her some wheeling-around money, although by degrees and by calculation they allowed themselves to be seen together often enough to be taken for granted as an item. In nice weather you could see them at one of the Other End's outdoor tables having a late afternoon drink, joined sometimes by Simone and Tony, joined sometimes by Betty Blondell and her great new friend, the graduate student and ex-nun, Tina Venturi, long black hair, an athletic slouch, a derisive smile, thought nothing of bicycling a hundred miles north into the Catskills, south to the Pine Barrens, east toward the Hamptons. It was two years before Claire, in the face of Hector Suarez's suspicions and Svetlana Tervakalio's opposition, could get Ivan declared legally dead or irretrievably gone, so she could marry Chuck.

Everything considered, they decided, a small ceremony in the university chapel would least offend either the structure of the universe or Chuck's esthetic sensibilities. Simone was maid of honor, Tony best man. Momma and Poppa McCoy came for the ceremony, he with his child bride, now middle-aged but still with furry legs, she with a pleasant, slim young man whom Chuck took to be queer. Poppa had become stout; Momma's hair seemed not so much uncombed as uncombable from some electric disturbance barely contained by her skull. From him Claire and Chuck received as presents large handmade his-and-hers silver belt buckles, Western style, and from her they received a set of eight handmade coffee mugs with creamer and sugar bowl to match. On the whole they seemed philosophical about Claire's choice of a husband fifteen or twenty years older—at least she would be taken care of. But you could see that they were wondering what was in it for him, his wife being a crip and all. The other guests were Chuck's sister and brother-in-law, a few colleagues, and the members, all female, of the poetry workshop Claire had organized. At the, well, let's say "intimate," reception, held in a room in the Faculty Club, Momma McCoy took a piece of wedding cake in hand and slapped it into Poppa McCoy's face, like something out of the Three Stooges, whereupon the child bride let loose with some inspired bad language.

Gradually Claire became a creative money manager, a champion housekeeper, and a wizard cook. She would not let Chuck hire someone to help with the housework, out of pride and out of a refusal to be a boss, paying someone to do your dirty work, though as Chuck observed, there's more than one way of being a boss. She had, however, bullied and sweet-talked a carpenter, looking over his shoulder the whole time, to arrange things so that locked into her leg braces, a crutch under an armpit, she could reach sink, stove, chopping block, and refrigerator without moving more than a step or two in any direction (Chuck set the table and did much of the shopping, but Claire would not let him wash up, for he never put things back where they belonged). Invitations to her intimate dinners for six or eight guests were highly prized.

It pretty much looked as though in spite of Simone's encouragement she had given up on the idea of going after a Ph.D. What for? She didn't need to teach. Chuck had plenty of money, and she trusted him not to leave her. A poet has to read what feeds the poetry, not what a professor assigns.

When they did not have guests for dinner, summer or winter, sunny or snowing, they took a postprandial stroll, usually down Broadway, sometimes uptown among the Dominicans where you could buy neat root vegetables unknown to Anglo grocers or buy discounted "irregular" sportswear, sometimes east across 125th Street through first black then Spanish Harlem to the shrinking remnants of an old Italian 'hood, where you could still buy a spaghetti machine, Claire in her no-nonsense wheelchair, Chuck pushing it, people coming to recognize them, nodding or smiling, saying "Evening," or "Howyadoin'," even the young men standing on corners above 135th Street, Claire nodding in reply, as though they all lived in a village out of some misty fable.

Sometimes, while Simone's still very Korean mother (who had moved in with them) babysat with their pretty little son ("Charley" by name, after his godfather, Charles Craig Lockhart), Mr. and Mrs. Anthony Felder would join Mr. and Mrs. Charles Lockhart for the postprandial stroll, Tony still limping but sporting a hundred-and-fifty dollar cane (a present from Simone). In fact, the two couples spend a lot of time together, especially during the summer at the Lockharts' country escape in Sacandaga, New York. In the mornings they all write, Simone on her dissertation, Claire on her poetry, Chuck and Tony on a book they mean to call *Literature as Equipage*, for Chuck could never figure out how to end his essay on love among the modernists. In the afternoons they hang around the new pool, where Simone pesters Tony to exercise the muscles around his prosthetic hip joint, where Claire holds on to the side of the pool while Chuck moves her outstretched legs up and down as though she were kicking, or they go to the Saratoga racetrack, or to the Adirondack Museum, or to a casino run by Native Americans, or out on the lake to troll from a rented pontoon boat. Some afternoons, each simply goes his or her own way, Claire to garden, dragging her legs along between the rows, Chuck to chop wood, Simone to practice scales on her guitar, for she is taking lessons, Tony to the shop, for to his own surprise he has discovered in himself a real gift for woodworking. In the evenings they tend to just sit around and talk or watch a movie, sipping on drinks. Neither of the four seems to hanker after anything more exciting.

The publication of Claire's volume of poems, *On the Way*, had a good effect on her personality. She laughs more and looks worried less; she is now more likely to look outward and around than inward and down (although it is true that on some days, apropos of nothing, she gets bad-tempered and shrewish). She even accepted, and without getting mad, two of Chuck's suggested changes for the poem about the actor in a period extravaganza—"For careless girls with low ambitions" instead of "For chi-chi girls," etc., and "archaic slouch" for "antique slant." It helped that the reviews, such reviews as a first volume of poems gets, were enthusiastic. The poems about Claire's stay in the rehabilitation hospital, mostly about other patients, a hydrocephalic girl and an armless baby, oldsters with new parts, a few about the nightmarish paraphernalia of treatment, and certain apocalyptic poems in which the air is thick with black dust and someone or something out of sight is screaming especially were singled out for praise. When she performs these poems at readings, for locally she is in demand, people gasp, some cry. On these occasions she never fails to read a poem entitled "Bard of the Movement," which is dedicated "To Ivan."

The bard of the title was big, clumsy, gauche, but good with all kinds of tools and a first-class musician, his notes always right on pitch, whether played or sung, his phrasing impeccable. There was something both selfless and childishly greedy about him. He was susceptible to temper tantrums, but he was never petty. His impracticality, his total lack of avarice, his unconcern for the minimal comforts that even a small regular income could provide, were both

293

infuriating and endearing. That he always wore a Greek sailor's cap to hide his bald spot was both ridiculous and pitiable. The tone of the poem is wry, affectionate, and ambiguous: one experienced reader of poetry could decide that the bard is a saint, another that he is an asshole. The poem does not mention what a detective hired by Svetlana discovered, that the Bard of the Movement had been having an affair with Mavis Mills.

I'll sing you twelve, O
Red fly the banners, O
What is your twelve, O
Twelve for the chimes of the Kremlin clock
Eleven for the Moscow dynamos
Ten for the days that shook the world
Nine for the days of the General Strike
Eight for the Eighth Red Army
Seven for the hours of the working day
Six for the Tolpuddle Martyrs
Five for the years of the Five-Year Plan
Four for the years it took them
Three, three, the rights of man
Two, two, a man's own hands
Working for a living, O
One is workers' unity
And ever more shall be so.

Claire gets considerable satisfaction out of the poetry workshop she presides over on Thursday nights to a group of parishioners at Corpus Christi Cathedral there on 121th Street. She and another group of parishioners are working hard with Father Walsh to win control of a local vacant lot, so they can turn it into a garden, get the local kids involved taking care of it, for gardening is medicine for many ills. The university wants to turn it into a parking lot. It looks as though Claire will win a seat on the local school board come election time, even though Chuck continually warns her that she already has too much on her plate, what with her frequent participation in demonstrations on behalf of the environment and victims of anything everywhere, Chuck in tow. She writes letters to her congress-people.

If you asked her she would say that she is content. She has become a minor local celebrity. She doesn't have to worry about money. Her deep affection for Chuck has never been in question. Above all, she has as much time as she needs to write her poetry, which has become less about herself and more about the world. It is true that when in an ad on TV she sees a babe in arms, she will grow wistful, may have to wipe the water out of her eyes. She is sentimental about all young things, even tadpoles. But one part of her firmly believes that someday, someday *soon*, her paralysis will go away, even as she becomes more and more a kind of professional cripple. Another part of her believes that maybe her shrink is right, that she won't get better until she works through her free-floating guilt.

And Chuck? He's all right. As Claire has her poetry, he has Claire, although he well knows that no one ever truly "has" another person. It's enough that she clearly likes to be with him, that she depends on him for this and that, that she will "do" him (sexually speaking) once or twice a week, that with him at least she's a good listener and a straight talker, that she is there for him when things go wrong. It is enough that every night he gets into bed next to her, hugs and kisses her good night, that she is still there when he wakes up in the morning, enough that the left side of her lip sometimes snags on an eyetooth, that she gives him her wry but forgiving smile when he says or does something dumb, enough that he is a felt presence behind the words in her new poems, such is his faith. He can't believe Claire would mind that ever since Dorothea Chin stopped by his office to say hi (she had just been in the library looking for an annotated edition of Sun Tsu's *The Art of War*, big with her businessman coworkers) he has been having lunch with her maybe once every two weeks.

He also has the occasional lunch with Betty Blondell. "Maybe you heard," she said one time when they were eating in Kelty's, "that Tina Venturi has moved in with me."

"People talk about you less than you imagine," he said, but he didn't look surprised. The black Irish waiter brought their food, a chicken pot pie for Betty, a brisket sandwich for Chuck, gave Chuck a knowing look.

"She has no money and she doesn't know how to do those little things that need doing," Betty said, "domestic economy and so forth, buying toiletries, leaving a tip at Christmas for your super, dealing with panhandlers. I'm teaching her."

"Whatever I know about a nun's life comes from the Marquis de Sade," he said.

"I bet you think we're having a lesbian affair," she said.

He looked at her, the new short hair, severely pulled back, the minimal makeup, the black blouse buttoned up to the neck, the blazer. He made a gesture signifying it would be no skin off his nose.

"Well, we're not," she said.

"Why aren't you?" he said.

"The whole point of our relationship, from where I stand," Betty said, "is that I get from Tina everything you need from a spouse, without the miseries of sex."

"Without which life is not worth living," Chuck said.

"Without which you have leftover life to live," Betty said. "Sex saps your energy and crowds out thinking about anything else. I've written another book during the last two years while Tina and I have been close. You'll get a copy when it comes out."

Chuck came close to saying something about sublimation but at the last minute held back.

"Giving into sex...well, it's like a tropism toward sin, toward all the sins, and you know it," Betty said.

"In effect, you're saying that Mother Nature is a psychopath," Chuck said.

"She can be turned into a useful citizen with sedation and discipline," Betty said, but now she was laughing at herself.

"Leather goods and whips," said Chuck.

"Ooo, makes your bottom feel so warm," said Betty.

"By the way," Chuck said, "was that you who wrote those retrograde slogans on the tunnel wall?"

"I was a different person then," she said, "but I stopped after Tony asked that question about the relation between sex and sin. That was like the serpent and Eve, you know—I got all morally discombobulated."

"Then who took your place?" he said.

She put her hand on his, the one holding a pickle. "No one can take my place," she said. "In spite of all, someday I'm going to let you show me why you think sex is good for you. You like braised short ribs?"

The waiter was standing by their table. He was looking at Betty's hand on Chuck's. "Everything all right?" he said.

"It was," said Chuck.

"Please give my regards to your tall, redheaded friend," said the waiter.

"Beat it," said Chuck.

Betty, looking amused, said, "As for the graffiti artist, how about your doorkeeper friend?"

So Chuck, who had been avoiding tunnels of all sorts, even the subway, went to see Hardcore.

"Hi there, Professor, good to see you again," said Hardcore. "Where you been?"

"I've developed a phobia of all things chthonic," said Chuck.

"Catonic . . . ," said Hardcore. "Me too . . ."

"Say Core," said Chuck, "was it you?—"

"That was a terrible thing happened to your missus," said Hardcore.

"Terrible," said Chuck. "But what I wanted to ask was—"

"You seeing Big Red anymore?" said Hardcore.

"From time to time," said Chuck. "But tell me, are you the one?—"

"Let me tell you, boss, you won't catch me defacing no university property, no way," said Hardcore.

"Who, then?" said Chuck.

"Must be the Holy Ghost," said Hardcore.

"Him again?" said Chuck.

It is very seldom nowadays that there flashes before the screen of Chuck's mind a vision of a man on his hands and knees, looking down, a strand of bloody spittle hanging from his mouth, his balding crown prominent. After all, Chuck and Ivan were rivals for the same woman. They fought; Chuck won—nothing to feel guilty about there. That's the way it goes with human males, that's the way it has gone with human males since before humans became human. And after all, it's to the benefit of the species that males who know how to prevail mate with the most desirable women—so long as they have offspring. But from time to time, more often than Chuck would like—and always with a pang in his chest, a warm rush to his head and dizziness—a black-and-white vision out of nowhere will light up the screen of his mind: a face pale and dusty, sightless eyes looking upward, small mouth open like that of a chick in its nest. Those pangs and that dizziness, by the way, are side effects of Chuck's recently discovered coronary artery disease. Medication and exercise, however, are helping to keep his cholesterol down. As for restricting himself to eating red meat no more than once a week, there are limits to the willpower of the most conscientious of men. Claire, at least, insists that he eat fish every Friday.

On some subliminal level Chuck has transformed his pursuit and capture of Claire into a fabulous romance, with Claire, of course, as at once the grail maiden and the grail, with himself as the questing knight. Can you see the tunnels and the furnace room as the mazy forest and the Castle Perilous? How about Ivan as the dragon and Jane as the necromantic crone? By comparison, his current life is a descent into the quotidian. But when on rare occasions Claire wheels over to him, her face contorted by anguish, says "I'm losing it," and he lifts her out of the wheelchair, carries her over to the bed, stretches her out over him, chest to breast and all the rest, so she can cry herself to sleep, tears on his neck, and wakes up two hours later in the mood for love, then the quotidian seems enough, more than enough.

Yes, Chuck also yearns for children, and he wants them now, before he's too old to teach his son how to ride a bicycle, to swim, to roller skate, to do the Ali shuffle, to act like a man. But Chuck too believes that Claire will soon throw off her paralysis, even as he gets some kind of probably unhealthy satisfaction out of tending her, fussing over her, getting her things. For example, during the spring or fall, while they're taking a long weekend at Sacandaga, Chuck likes to carry Claire out to the front porch, which faces east, wrap her in a comforter-like affair closed on two sides and fleece-lined that he ordered especially from L. L. Bean, bring her coffee, juice, toast, and marmalade on the side, for Claire likes to spread her own marmalade, for Chuck has a heavy hand, and sit right next to her and watch the sun rise through the trees, his heavy hand on her calloused one. Usually Claire glows under these attentions.

But not always. Just the other day, for example, when Chuck came home from work, Claire was at the sink peeling potatoes, for, diet or not, Claire was Irish. Her back was to the kitchen. She did not hear Chuck come in, for Dr. Lena Pitts was on the radio telling a young listener who wanted to become a lawyer, and telling her in no uncertain terms, that it was her duty before God to become a prosecuting attorney rather than some shyster for the defense. Chuck tiptoed up to Claire, placed his crotch against her shapeless derriere, his arms around her arms, thus confining them, his hands on her breasts, which he squeezed, except for the two middle fingers of his left hand, which no longer bend. He then kissed her on the neck.

"God damn it!" she said, freeing herself by flapping her arms as a chicken flaps its wings, letting Chuck have an elbow in the ribs ("Woof," he said), turning in a tangle of crutches and braces and legs to face him. "What do you think you're doing?" she said. "That's what you think I am, a toy you can play with whenever you feel like it." Chuck's face fell. "Couldn't you see I was doing something?"

"I'm sorry, Claire, I—" Chuck said.

"How would you like it if I came up behind you while you were sharpening your phallic axe and grabbed you by the balls?" she said.

"Well, it depends on how—" he said.

"What the Big Professor does is important, what I do counts for nothing," she said. "Well, pardon me, I have to get back to my non-work," and she turned back to the sink.

"That's not fair," he said. "I never—"

"Let's not talk about it anymore," she said. "I want to listen to the radio. Period. End of sentence."